PRAISE FO.

"In this Southern Gothic love letter to the spookier side of New Orleans's storied past, Arden spins out a moody tale of magic and mystery . . . A thoroughly satisfying page-turner and a strong debut." —*Publishers Weekly*, Starred Review

"Debut author Arden offers readers a full plate of Southern Gothic atmospherics and sparkling teen romance in a patiently crafted tale that will best reward careful readers . . . Satisfying teen entertainment but also a cathartic, uncompromising tribute to New Orleans." —*Kirkus Reviews*

"A slow-burning novel in the tradition of Anne Rice." —*Rue Morgue Magazine*

"A smart story with a surprising amount of emotional depth . . . in the grand tradition of *Buffy* and *The Lost Boys*." —*IndieReader*

"Nothing short of a stunner." —*Examiner.com*

"Eerie, magical, and gritty, getting into the grimy seams of New Orleans in the tradition of Anne Rice or Poppy Z Brite." —*SP Reviews*

"Beautiful yet sinister." —*Gothic Beauty Magazine*

PRAISE FOR THE ROMEO CATCHERS

"Fans will be floored. *The Romeo Catchers* is an intense dream-scape of a read full of magic, menace, and mystery."
—Tonya Hurley, *The New York Times* bestselling author of the ghostgirl series and the Blessed trilogy

"A meticulous blend of witchery, New Orleans lore, and teen angst." —*Kirkus Reviews*

"Every bit as engrossing as the first book." —*School Library Journal*

"Adele's supernatural roller-coaster ride continues at breakneck speed, with shocking revelations along the bloodstained way. Readers will be enchanted and horrified in turn."
—*RT Book Reviews, Top Pick*

"A magnificent supernatural saga." —*Kirkus Reviews,* on *The Cities of Dead*

The Gates of Guinée

ALSO BY ALYS ARDEN

The Casquette Girls Series

The Casquette Girls

The Romeo Catchers

The Cities of Dead

The Gates of Guinée

ALYS ARDEN

Published by For the Art of It

www.alysarden.com

ISBN-13: 978-0-989757768

Cover illustration by Galen Dara

Cover lettering by Parajunkee

Map illustration by Mystic Blue Signs

Chapter heading illustrations by Christy Zolty

Printed in the United States of America

To my dad.

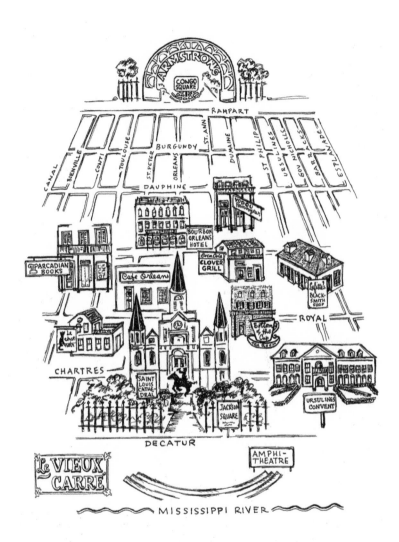

PART I
THE GATES

Legend does not contradict history. It preserves the fundamental matter but magnifies and embellishes it.

—*Adrien Rouquette*

CHAPTER 1

TRAITOR

April 30th

The metallic aftertaste of her blood still tugged at my senses.

The girl lay unconscious against the attic wall in Raúl's chains, her wet auburn hair even more vibrant now against her pallid skin. Dark circles had formed beneath her anemic eyelids, and her clothes were charred in spots, muddy in others, but the base notes of jasmine from her Dior eau de parfum still drenched her collar.

I set a glass of water on the floor next to her, offering none to Carina or Josif, and stretched out my arm, flexing and straightening my wrist, the newly formed skin taut. It had been at least a century since I'd needed to heal so completely, and despite the pain, or perhaps because of the pain, it was reinvigorating. Or perhaps it was the anxious words Adele had said to me on the Moonwalk: *"He knows about the grimoire."*

Callisto Salazar knows about our book of shadows.

Which also meant he must have figured out Adele's connection to León. What other concern would he still have with her?

In my human years, I might have felt panicked by this news—my family's gravest enemy, a witch now imbued with unprecedented power, going after my ancestral rites—but I wasn't panicked.

I wasn't human.

My teeth sank into my bottom lip, pricking blood. I'd spent the last four hundred years looking for that book, but this was the first time I'd felt on the precipice of discovering it. I'd shed my skin under the Flower Moon, and I was ready to devour every last Ghost Drinker if need be.

I tapped Callisto's ring against the floor, imagining it on Jakome Salazar's finger, imagining his coven slipping into the darkness, attacking us in our slumber all those years ago. I had been only a child but still remembered the distress echoing through the silent stone walls of the palazzo. How my mother had stashed the four of us in a hidden chamber. How Gabriel and Emilio had refused to stay hidden. How tightly Giovanna had wrapped her arms around me whilst we waited in the cold. It was a lifetime ago. Several. But now, mayhem gave monsters the freedom to stretch, and I was going to rip Callisto Salazar limb from limb.

I didn't know for certain if I could ever truly get my magic back, but I knew in my blood that if there was a chance, it lay in that book. In that spell, *l'elisir di vita*. If it could give León, a mortal witch, eternal life, who knew what it could do for a vampire?

I was ready to shed this skin a final time.

The witchling stirred, awakening. She might have borne the name of the Salazar coven, but a true Animarum Praedator she was not. She'd shown her Spektral magic to me twice now, and it had nothing to do with drinking spirits. Her sculpted brows, perfectly trimmed cuticles, and designer blouse revealed her privilege, and I wondered which of her insecurities Salazar had exploited so she'd do his bidding. Had her father not given her enough affection when she was a child, or had she been rebelling against her mother's fine Southern pedigree when she rode on the back of Callisto's bike, wind blowing her hair?

Being a witch hadn't been enough for her, and surely he'd promised her the magical universe.

Traditionally, vampires healed the wounds we inflicted so our victims could slip back into society none the wiser, our dark secrets remaining hidden in the obsidian of night, but the gashes in her neck were still raw. *She won't be slipping back with anyone.*

I grazed her silky blouse with my knuckle and then ripped the sleeve with a quick, loud tear.

Her eyes popped open. She looked away from my fangs as she discovered the morose nightmare she'd been having was reality.

"Don't fret. I'm not going to rip any more of your clothes away."

She returned her gaze and made a valiant attempt to spit in my face. I grabbed her jaws, pinching, and a sound gnarred from the back of her throat, the snarl of a wild little beast.

"But he might rip off your head," Carina jeered from her shadowy corner. Moonlight from the window spilled ghoulishly over her cheeks. She was still pale and gaunt from Lisette's feeding early in the evening. Such a loss of blood would have been life-threatening for anyone but a Ghost Drinker.

Josif grunted from the adjacent corner, but my attention didn't waver. As I'd suspected, beneath the torn silk, the girl bore a circular Maleficium. The mark of an Aether.

"Annabelle Lee Drake. The witchling who sold her coven down the River Styx. What silver did Callisto offer you?"

"Uncuff me now," she demanded, only hints of her Elemental persuasion tugging at me to follow her commands.

I smiled. "With my venom still coursing through your veins, you're going to have to try much harder than that to use your magic."

7

Her gaze drifted past me to Raúl's body across the room. It lay crumpled, his head tossed lazily atop his chest. She tried to preserve her stern expression, but the fantasy—whatever game of house she'd thought she'd been playing with Callisto's coven— eroded behind her eyes. "He's going to come for me," she whispered, gripping onto her increasingly slippery delusions. But then she tilted her chin up, mood shifting, or so she wanted it to appear, and looked at me with bitter virulence. "And you're going to regret this when he does."

I huffed a laugh. I could see how Callisto would have admired her spirit. It was unfair to call her naïve, to blame her youth; Carina and Josif had centuries of wisdom and were still taken in by Callisto's posturing. "I hope he tries," I said, standing.

And I truly meant it. Taking Callisto within the borders of the Vieux Carré would certainly be easier than infiltrating the plantation he'd turned into his magical fortress—I'd have the full strength of my family.

Thump-thump.

I was confident in my ability to kill Callisto, but I'd need every vampire with me if I was going to get Macalister LeMoyne back alive as well. My teeth gnashed. Surely Isaac would break the Trapping curse now that Mac's life was at stake?

I needed a new plan. Magic. A coven.

I needed Adele.

I wanted her here with me.

Thump-thump.

My spine stiffened, realizing the pulse was not only mine. I strained, listening, but all I heard was the night's maelstrom on the streets.

"What?" Annabelle sat up, suddenly interested. "See, I told you Callis was coming for me."

Screams, shatters, cracks of magic, all muted by the walls of the old house, but beneath it all, there was a little thump. *She's here.*

"Oh, that's not his worried face," Carina said. "That look means the witch is near."

"What witch?"

"The one he ripped Raúl's head off over—"

"Adeeeeeeele!" Annabelle screamed, thrashing.

I ripped off her sleeve, gagged her, and darted into the hallway. Lisette stood hidden in the shadows, staring back in at Annabelle with a mild indifference I didn't quite believe. There was something else. Disappointment maybe. I closed the door and twisted the key.

The creak of the front gate echoed in my ears. I tore down the stairs, paused at the foyer mirror—just a quick check for blood on my face, my clothes, my hands—sucked back my fangs, and whipped to the door, opening it just as she raised her fist to knock.

She stood before me in the haze of magic under the Flower Moon, her pulse charging. She was damp and disheveled, and she still smelled of river water. It took all my strength not to pull her inside, away from the nightmare swirling the city.

"We're going to get your father back, *bella.*" I knew it was the only thing she wanted to hear.

"And we're going to avenge yours," she said, her eyes dark with deadly determination. Something had changed.

Everything had changed.

She, too, had shed her skin.

I stepped aside so she could pass. Across the street, almost hidden by a fern on the balcony, Isaac's wings fluttered. Our gazes locked. I swung the door closed and twisted the lock.

I had been wrong before. She was safest here with me.

CHAPTER 2
BEDLAM

Observe. Adapt. Dominate.

I repeated the mantra as I soared down Royal Street, dodging people, cars, and spells, but it was like my synapses weren't firing. Pink memory powder clouded the humid air, and a sparkle of cyan twinkled in the sky above thanks to the Daures' protection spell.

My shoulders burned from flying, but I didn't care. I didn't feel anything other than the certainty of her last words: *"If you follow me, I'll scream for Nicco, and you better pray he doesn't hear me."*

I didn't want to observe or adapt. I wanted to turn back, swoop down to the Medici house, pound on the door, and beg Adele to come with me.

I'd only followed her to make sure she arrived safely.

Keeping her safe was all I'd ever been trying to do.

Remnant traces of the heightening elixir coursed through my bloodstream, catapulting the heartache into the stratosphere.

Nicco was probably telling her how I'd refused to help him. How I hadn't woken her up or told her his plan. Leaving out the part where I was just trying to protect her. *Like how I'd omitted that part after he threw her out the attic window.*

Would Adele tell Désirée and Codi about the spell I'd used on her? Codi was going to kill me.

"Whoop! I fuckin' love this city!" Down below, three bachelor-party loudmouth types staggered down from Bourbon so blitzed they didn't seem to notice the chaos around them. *"Dude, are those fireworks?" "I wanna blow some shit up."*

Before they could even strike a match, the Borges cousins stomped up behind them.

With a giant breath, Remi blew a puff of memory powder, and Manon closed in with a compact mirror. Non-possessed mundane were escorted out of the perimeter of the Quarter while the Possessed were rounded up like zombie-cattle and taken back to the Borges'. *I should go back there and help.* But I didn't turn around. I was paralyzed, gliding through the magic-drenched current in the solitude of the sky. Not that you ever really felt alone in New Orleans. The Royal Street ghosts were nowhere to be seen, even by my magical eye, but I could feel their nervous energy vibrating through the dormer windows of the attics they haunted and from the dark alleys where they lurked.

An otherworldly feeling nagged at me—something was wrong. But the first responder protocol pounded through my head louder, instructing me. The voice of my father, commanding me. *Adapt, Isaac. Drop to the ground and help. Dominate.*

I'd tried to dominate, and I'd failed. *Epically failed.* I'd pushed Adele into the lion's den, straight to her family's sworn enemy, who even Adeline Saint-Germain had warned her to stay away from.

The screams on the street below sounded distant as the memories chilled my bones, shivering my feathers. *The flowers releasing from the palm of my hand, the intention of the spell coursing through my veins, the lifelessness in her muscles when I lifted her into my arms.*

She'd been defenseless with me. Now she's defenseless with them.

Olsin's premonition played on repeat in my head. Over and over. A car alarm sang in the distance. Water gushed from a hydrant where an SUV had crunched into it.

I was just trying to protect her.

"Isaac!" a girl shrieked from a storefront below. "*Behind you!*" Codi's cousin Poppy dropped a giant burlap sack with a heavy clank and threw her arm into the air, pointing.

I looked back—a trio of souls were speeding down from the roof of Vieux Carré Silversmiths.

I jerked my wing in fright and knocked myself out of the Air current, cursing as I fell to the street and shredded across the pavement, landing at her feet. I whipped a gust to shield us, but I could barely slow them down. "Run!" I yelled as the bright orbs fought through the Air.

She dug something out of the bag. "Drop the shield," she said, cranking some kind of ballerina box.

"What?"

A jangling melody began to play.

"Drop the shield!"

I let go, and the orbs hurtled toward us. "Um?"

She flung the dancing ballerina through the open front door of the crashed SUV. It landed on the driver's seat.

"Nice aim, but unless that thing is an actual explosive device—"

"Shut up," she whispered, pulling me across the street into the gutter, her hand covering my mouth as we crouched.

I could barely hear the delicate music box over the gushing hydrant and the car alarm screeching in the distance. The orbs slowed, hovering in the middle of the street as if looking for us.

The water pooled closer, and the souls turned our way. Poppy's grip tightened.

But then the car alarm stopped, and the street went silent.

My pulse pounded as the tinkle of the mechanical music rose through the heavy stream of water.

Lulled by the twirling ballerina, an orb floated into the car, and the two others followed. But then, mid-phrase, the music stopped.

"Shit!" Poppy whispered as the souls started to speed back.

I jumped up, whipping a gust, and the car door snapped closed. "I don't think so."

The souls bounced off the dark glass window, trapped inside.

As we crept closer to the vehicle, she motioned to the pooling water, and it swirled up off the ground with a sparkle.

"What are you . . . ?" I asked as she glided the stream into the exhaust pipe.

"We can't leave them for the owner of the car." She pushed the gold wireframe glasses back up the bridge of her nose, concentrating, and I squinted through the tinted windows. As the Water poured through the air vents, she spun her hands, congealing it into a sphere, and then trapped each of the souls inside it.

Fully focused, she slowly opened the car door. "Hand me the teapot."

"Teapot?" A bunch of silver pieces had spilled from her sack into the gutter. I grabbed it, removed the lid, and held it out as she guided the bubble our way. I was fully invested in her Elemental magic, but my back stiffened with the souls so close. She poked her finger into the air, and the bubble burst, pouring the stream of magical Water along with the souls into the teapot. It was weirdly mesmerizing until I realized she was *pouring people into a teapot*. I looked away—it was too much of a headfuck.

"Lid!" she yelled.

Shit. I slapped it down. "It's cool. They're secure."

She peered up at me over the rims of her glasses, shoulders unclenching. Her dark hair had been bleached out, and now faded streaks of turquoise and emerald made her seem like some kind of water nymph. She eyed my torn shirt. "You're bleeding."

"Come on, let's get off the street," I said, shivering, hoping she was going to take the teapot. As she shoved the remaining silver pieces into the sack, I realized it had been a while since I'd seen her around. "Wait, didn't you go on that ghost-hunting trip upstate? Is Chatham back, too?"

"Yeah. Apparently, the whole event in Shreveport was an elaborate ruse to get Chatham out of town. Callis poisoned one of Ritha's relatives in Mississippi so she'd be MIA, too."

Spit flew from my mouth as I suppressed robust expletives.

But then a small beacon of hope shimmered through the disaster of a night. The Daures were a second family to Adele; she'd feel safe staying with them until we figured out how to get Mac back. I needed to talk to Chatham. He could get Adele out of the Medici house.

Poppy strained, lifting the sack. I traded it for the teapot of souls.

"What's in here?" I asked, adjusting it on my back. "I don't think you're planning a tea party."

"Hardly. We've run out of things to contain the souls in. We had to start doubling up."

Doubling up. The haunting feeling flooded back. The soul. Jamal. The two of them in the pickle jar. This time it was no longer a nagging feeling but an explosion of urgency. *Fuck.*

I set down the sack and leapt into the air.

Julie.

I soared back to the Tremé, ignoring the chaos below, hoping I wasn't too late.

By the time I glided through the broken second-story window of the assisted living facility, I was in a total panic. *I shouldn't have left Adele in the cemetery just to save those random souls. If I hadn't, Julie never would have followed me here.* The room was exactly how I'd left it: table, chairs, and the pieces of a BINGO game knocked around. The residents were crowded around Julie, who still lay on the floor.

She was curled up, brow taut, translucent muscles strained as if fighting the pain. Stormy popped up from her shoulder, and the grannies and grandpops parted ways for me.

"Julie!" I fell to her side. Stormy yelped.

"Did that bird just turn into a boy?" asked a skinny white woman with pink curlers. "And I thought I'd seen it all."

Julie looked my way, forcing a smile. "*Mon cher.*"

I pushed her raven hair from her face. Her chest glowed faintly with the invading soul. "You're going to be okay." I scooped her up, cradling her somberly, and headed back the way I came. She felt like buttery smoke, weighted with pending death. Only, death she'd already been through. Now, a finality waited for her that no one should have to experience.

I've gotta get her to the tearoom. Chatham will know how to help her.

"Excuse me, son." A gray-haired Black lady in a floral bathrobe stepped right in front of me. "Are you the new Jamal?"

"Oh. Um . . ."

They all took a step closer, each one more frightened than the next. With his last dying breath, Jamal had asked me to look after them. If I didn't protect them, who would? *Shit.* I needed a hexenspiegel.

Julie winced. She was the only one in imminent danger. *Dominate.* "I need to get Julie to someone who can help save her life, er, spirit. I'll be back. I swear."

The woman crooked an eyebrow like I was one of her kids who wasn't going to be back until Christmas.

"Promise me, if anyone comes around—I mean *anyone*—do not let yourselves be visible. Hide in the walls. Hide in the floor. Hide wherever you can. Do you understand?"

"I gotchu, sonny." She looked like she didn't take shit from anyone.

"And be on the lookout for any more glowing orbs. They are not to be messed with unless you want to end up like Jamal."

Gasps went around the room. The lady clutched her robe to her chest.

I started for the window, hoping they couldn't see the fear on my face.

A wisp of words floated up from Julie. "*N'oubliez pas . . . Jamal.*"

I strained to hear her voice. "English, please—"

Stormy barked, standing over the jar of pickled okra. Inside it, two orbs bobbed through the vinegary water, lighting up the glass with a greenish glow.

Shit, Jamal. I whipped a quick gust, and the jar slammed into my hand. *Rest in peace.*

Stormy bounded to my side, and I took a running start. The spirits yelled goodbyes to their friend as I jumped out of the window and rode the current down to the street like a wave at Rockaway Beach, not really caring who might see me. I needed to get her home.

Julie was silent all the way to the tearoom. By the time we arrived, my panic was explosive. "Chatham!" I yelled, nudging the door open with my foot.

Poppy was unloading her loot onto the zodiac tables while her two younger sisters poured bottles of Florida Water into crystal pitchers, lining up the empties. Chatham was behind the counter in a heated discussion with Fiona and Edgar. Little flames flickered on the glass shelves all around the tearoom, floor to ceiling—I stopped short in disbelief.

They weren't flames; the crystal balls and antique telescopes had been replaced with glowing orbs sloshing inside perfume bottles, wine bottles, and vials usually reserved for crystal essences. A shiver rocketed up my spine.

Julie softly groaned, but the witches just stared at me, none of them hurrying over to help. The two youngest girls still had their party dresses on. How were they not cold? The room was freezing.

"Where did you go?" Poppy asked.

"Where's Adele?" Dahlia chirped.

That's when I realized: *They can't see her.* To them, I was just standing with my arms out in the air.

Edgar noticed the glowing jar in my hand and hurried over.

"There's—there's two in there. One's Jamal," I stuttered. They couldn't see Julie, and I was going to have to tell them. They'd already suffered such a great loss tonight.

Edgar took the jar from my hand. "I'll make some shelf space for them."

I nodded, and he looked at me with concern.

"Isaac . . . What's wrong?"

"S-she needs help."

Chatham marched over to us. "Adele?"

"It's-it's Julie—"

Comprehension washed over his face. He rushed back to an old leather doctor's bag and pulled out a tin, mumbling words as he tossed its contents into a mortar. He strode over, already grinding the pestle. "How long has it been?"

"Um . . ." When had I left the assisted living home to go back to the cemetery? "A couple hours."

He scooped the powder out—it had a sweet scent like vanilla and grapefruit—and said the words:

> *"No dust, no ash, no soul in sight,*
> *May this magic bring your spirit into*
> *light."*

He blew the turmeric-colored mixture toward us. The girls ran over as the magic dusted her ghostly figure and an outline of her form sparkled gold.

"Julie!" Dahlia cried.

Fiona's hand flew to her mouth, and eyes widened all around the room. Poppy made a frightened choking sound. She'd seemed so tough on the street with the souls, but this was different. This was family.

"Ohhh, my baby," Chatham said, stroking Julie's face.

She softly smiled. "But it is I who remember when you were born."

"Let's get you somewhere more comfortable and take a look at that thing inside you." Chatham took her from my arms and passed her to Fiona. "I'll be up in a minute."

The girls fluttered around their mother as she rattled off instructions. Flowers to bring her. Crystals. Tonics.

Edgar asked, "Isaac, where is Adele?"

"Yes, is she at the Borges'?" Chatham said. "Can you get her? I want her here with us. Especially given the circumstances with Mac. When the boys get back from this soul-run, we'll convene with Ritha's coven. I'm still not exactly sure what's going on, but I can count on one hand the number of times the Quarter has gone on magical lockdown!"

My gaze dropped to the floor. I hadn't just failed Adele tonight. And Mac. I'd failed everyone. All the witches of New Orleans. The entire city that was just starting to feel like home. *I should have gone out to the swamp with Nicco. I should have come straight to Edgar and Olsin when he suspected Callis's coven was up to something for Beltane.*

"*Isaac,*" Edgar asked more sternly, "you did find her after the incident at the party, right? Codi told us you were together."

"What incident?" Chatham asked.

"With the . . . *Fire witch,*" he answered.

"He's not a witch," I snapped, and the room went silent. The

18

aggression in my voice felt like an unfamiliar beast. I hated it. I hated all of this. I looked up, checking my tone. "She's with him."

Chatham's chest puffed, and Edgar clutched a fistful of his kimono.

"I couldn't stop her. She's scared. She said it's the only place she feels safe." The thought killed a little piece of me.

Chatham adjusted the glasses on his nose as if he wasn't seeing the picture correctly. "Adele is with the Medici vampires?"

I nodded, and he made a beeline for the door.

"Darling!" Edgar yelled, kimono fluttering behind as they exited the tearoom.

I breathed a sigh of relief. *They'll bring her back.*

"Isaac, do you want to help me pick flowers for Julie?" Lilly, the littlest Daure girl asked, taking my hand and wagging it.

"Um . . ."

If I was here when Adele got back, she wouldn't want to stay. But where else would I go? I could go to the Voodoo shop, but Dee might have heard what I'd done . . . What if she didn't want me there anymore?

I pulled out my phone and sent a text to her and Codi: *SOS. HQ. ASAP.*

I turned back to the little girl. "Maybe later. I've got to go out there and help, but I'll be back to check on Julie. Take good care of her for me."

She nodded. I glanced at Poppy, who was giving me a look that said I was up to something.

But I wasn't. I was the opposite of being up to something.

I opened the door and soared down the street to the brothel.

I had to tell them everything.

CHAPTER 3
IL LATO OSCURO

Seven nights, seven moons, seven gates, seven tombs. Ren's words looped through my head as I ascended the stairs next to Nicco. I was scared that if I stopped repeating them, if I stopped focusing on my father, I'd mentally bleed out after the fight with Isaac. Each chant, each step forward, was a stitch in the freshly salted wounds.

I reached for my medallion, but it wasn't there. It had been too clunky for the delicate Beltane dress. My cheeks burned as I thought about the silk organza lying on the bedroom floor in the brothel. An invisible stitch popped. I clenched my fist tighter.

Breathe, Adele.

I took a shuddering inhale, Désirée's magic still slowly working on my bruised ribs.

The shadows darkened the deeper we went into the Medici house. The temperature dropped throughout the parlors, and the air dampened, and in the silence, Isaac's words, Adeline's warning, and Olsin's premonition echoed like taunting goblins, telling me to stay away from Nicco. "*He's a monster, Adele.*" "*Ne fais pas confiance à Nicco—!*" "*You're dead; your blood is on his lips.*"

My nails dug deeper into my palm. Maybe a monster was just what we needed to beat Callis.

I gazed at the flame in the wall sconce as we walked by, and an image rose from the back of my mind: the Fire witch. The sound of his bones crunching as I slammed the iron rod into his spine. His eyes closing. Maybe I am a monster.

I felt Nicco glance my way, and a magical chill swept up my spine.

Guilt pecked at my soul, but I refused to let it. *I don't want any eighteenth-century side-eye, Adeline. When Gabriel threatened you and your coven, you didn't run and hide, you got closer and closer to him. You would have stopped at nothing to save the Count and our family's legacy, and that's what I'm doing now.*

I imagined Cosette standing up to the pirate to protect her sister, and Morning Star storming through town looking for her brother. Would they all think I was a traitor for being here? Naïve? I remembered a ghostly version of myself sitting with Nicco at the Clover Grill less than a year ago—that girl had been a pawn, a rook; she hadn't even known she'd been thrown into the game. But now I knew exactly what I was walking into.

Emilio had killed my mother and left his own sister for dead. He was a psychopath. Gabriel might be the playboy-diplomat, but he'd stalked Adeline with deadly intent. And as for Nicco, he was the only vampire to ever kill his Maker, and whom León Saint-Germain—as close to a brother as one could be without sharing blood—considered so formidable, he'd hidden from for all these years. Rightly or wrongly.

They were vampires.

Predators.

Medici.

Sworn enemies of my family.

And despite all of that, each step I took next to Nicco felt more magnetic than the one before. This was where I belonged. They were the best chance I had of saving my father. Ironic, given that they'd spent centuries hunting Adeline's. I might have come to the dark side, but not with a blind eye. Ever since Callisto Salazar had come into my life, my guard was up—I couldn't imagine a day when I'd ever let it down.

As we crossed the final parlor, voices arose from the dining room ahead: Gabriel, Emilio, and Lisette and Martine, speaking aggressively in Italian and French.

Nicco paused and gave me a quizzical look.

"What?"

He inhaled deeply and took my clenched fist. Gently, he stroked my knuckles until I released my fingers to reveal the contents of my palm: the five burnt buds of chamomile. I hadn't even realized I was holding them.

His brow furled. "What are they from?"

The invisible stitches started popping faster than I was prepared for. "Nothing. They're nothing."

I let them drop to the floor.

My fingernails had dug bloody gashes in my palm. I pulled away, but he gripped me tighter. "It's noth—" I swallowed a gasp as he pulled my hand to his mouth, his tongue sweeping my palm.

Thump-thump.

His not-so-innocent smile pressed into my skin, and my heart galloped.

"No open wounds when entering a room full of vampires, okay?" His thumb glided over my palm as he examined the perfect new skin. "Even if they are my family."

The edge of my mouth twitched. "Okay." For the briefest moment, I almost forgot about everything that had happened tonight.

The paintings in the wallpaper whispered, warning me to stay clear of the monsters residing here, telling me of the horrors they'd witnessed in this house.

I ignored them and strode into the room.

My plan was too dangerous to involve any of my friends, but the Medici were immortal.

This was their feud, and I was certain they'd want to see it through to the end.

Nicco's hand drew to my shoulder as we approached his siblings standing around the dining room table. A gentle touch, but a strong signal to his family that he was trusting them with me. "Adele's here," he announced.

Unfazed by my presence, they barely looked up from their debate, almost as if they'd been expecting me.

It ignited a warmth from within.

The room was exactly how I remembered it from his dream. On the far end, an ornate buffet displayed crystal decanters, long velvet curtains draped the windows, and an exquisite Venetian chandelier hung overhead, its colored glass casting fairy-tale-like shadows on the occupants beneath. Only now, instead of Callis's roaring-twenties-clad coven bound in the fourteen seats, the chairs had been pushed away and Nicco's family of vampires were poring over stacks of maps and old engineering drawings, shifting chess pieces around on them as if staking out battle-grounds.

Despite the swirling doom of the city, there was no sense of panic, no injuries being tended to. They were all practically glowing. Hair shinier, skin dewier, lips wettened, pursing into devilish smiles. Lisette's forehead pinched with concentration as the boys furiously pointed, speaking in rushed Italian, and Martine yelled at them in French. While the witches panicked, the vampires were enlivened by the attack.

I looked straight at Emilio, and my voice rose, steady as the river on a scorching summer afternoon. "I wish you'd killed them all in 1930."

Their conversation halted. The delicate Ingénue was gone forever. I wasn't sure yet who the girl was in her place, but I knew she was going to save her father, and her city, and stop a centuries-old bloodbath.

Emilio tossed down a black bishop and looked up. "If you know any Astral witches with a proclivity for the past, I'm up for causing a ripple in the time continuum."

"I'll be on the lookout."

Gabriel's mouth pursed deviantly. "*Benvenuta, bellissima.*"

As we took our places at the table, Nicco didn't insert himself between me and his brother, just stood steadfast at my other side. I set my bag down, scouring an architectural drawing. Gabriel turned it toward me. It was the plantation across the river. "Where did you get this?"

"*Société historique de la Nouvelle Orleans.*" His French was more fluid than his English. I could only imagine how eloquent he was in Italian. "The one advantage to Callisto's coven occupying a château protected for its historical significance."

"Two whole centuries," Nicco snickered. "I have hats that are older."

A laugh slipped from Martine.

Emilio exchanged a look with Gabe. "Niccolò making jokes? The end really is nigh."

"We're dangerously outnumbered," Nicco told me *en français* with his usual seriousness, as I fought a smile, "so we're determining the best way to infiltrate undetected." He nodded to a stack of engineering drawings, unrolled and weighed down by heavy candlesticks. The top one showed a grid of tunnels—a sewerage map, if I was reading the title correctly. "With a hostage involved, there is only one shot."

Hostage.

My father is a prisoner of magical war.

Emilio pointed to a single road that led to a Storm desolate area. "We use the river to our advantage and create a choke point here. As they leave the property to ghost-hunt, we can pick them off until they're weak enough to overpower."

"You saw how many ghosts they drank at D-MORT." Nicco gripped the edge of the table. "We don't have time to starve them out. We have to be more aggressive."

The Medici glint brightened in Emilio's eyes, like he'd been waiting the last hundred years for this part of his brother to reawaken.

"Plus," I said. "Callis can fly now."

"Callisto Salazar cannot fly," Emilio balked.

"He *flew over the river* with my father."

Gabriel crossed his arms. "Whatever we do, we need to do it now. If the Salazar magic allows Callisto to steal other witches' Spektral magic, the longer we wait, the more powerful he'll become."

"We can't let that happen," I said. "If their headquarters are too fortified, and we're too outnumbered, and Callis has too much power, there's only one other option."

They all turned to me.

"We have to take away his power." Nervousness engulfed me as the reality of leaving this world came just a little bit closer.

"Unbind his coven?" Gabriel asked. "He will have their grimoire even more guarded than your father."

Lisette's eyes pulsed. I assumed Gabriel still didn't know about her connection to the Monvoisin book of magic. "Maybe Adele should take back her Fire! Isn't that how they became so powerful in the first place?"

Nicco hissed.

"Is such a thing even possible?" Emilio's tone dripped with doubt.

"There's another way," I said, the anxiety morphing into a thrill. "We can take away Callisto's power—all of the Salazars' power—without ever stepping foot on the property."

Lisette's hair fell across her shoulders as she crossed her arms. "Pray tell."

"We break their magical line. If Callisto is impenetrable,

then we go up one branch of the family tree. If we take out Jakome, they'll all lose their magic. I get my father back. You get your family's mortal—well, immortal—enemy."

All three sets of Medici brows tightened, and my confidence eroded. The plan, now spoken aloud, did sound ludicrous.

"Jakome Salazar was a brilliant witch," Emilio said. "One of the most powerful of our time. He's not some simpleton to be summoned by a witchling."

"Or even a high priestess," Gabriel added, trying to soften the blow.

"Who said anything about summoning him? The last thing we need in New Orleans is more Salazars."

Nicco leaned closer. "Are you suggesting—?"

"*Sì.* We go to him. We go to the Afterworld."

CHAPTER 4
RECOIL

White light flashed behind my eyelids just as it always did right before I went down. I braced myself on the wall of the dark hallway, trying to be casual, trying to fight through it and ignore the incessant energy of the witches buzzing all throughout the house. Ritha had warned me not to heal the Lafayette Water witch, but she was one of Codi's relatives who'd gone head to head with a Ghost Drinker looting Palermo's. I couldn't say no. She'd nearly lost an eye.

Ritha proceeded to yell at me in front of everyone like I was a child, incapable of managing my own magic. "*It's not life-threatening, Désirée! Go take a rest before you deplete yourself completely!*" But even if they'd saved her eye, without my help she'd have been left with a disfiguring scar.

My mouth went dry as I slid along the wall, the gold shimmery makeup on my shoulders smearing against the burgundy paint, and for the briefest of delusional seconds I wished Codi was here in case I lost time—or any of my coven members, I mentally corrected.

My knees wobbled.

No recoil. I need to check on Sébastien.

I launched myself off the wall and sauntered into Ritha's library in a way that might have simply looked like I'd had a Zaka night buzz, but there'd been nothing typical about this year's feeding of the spirits. Tonight, Ritha's orange-colored library looked more like a supernatural ER. We'd run out of cots, so people were laid out on the floor tucked beneath blankets like caterpillars. I recognized a Pink Power Ranger sleeping bag—a Christmas present from my aunt when I was six—now wrapped around a blonde woman with a head bandage. I glanced at her arm. Mundane.

Sébastien was on the blue leather sofa on the other side of the room. *Why is it so far?* I could barely hear my own thoughts as I meandered through the caterpillar maze. A combination of injured witches and mundane folks. The latter, of course, didn't understand why they were here, magically tied to beds and chairs, and they thought we were mental for holding mirrors up to their faces, searching for the souls of others. Dizziness netted my consciousness, a dark, wet blanket dragging me down.

A billow of nausea made me jolt up. *Dammit.* The nausea always came after the light.

My mother turned away from the drunk, sash-wearing bride-to-be she was helping and caught my eye.

This is bullshit. Isaac's Spektral doesn't kick his ass like this.

"Isaac's so scared of his Spektral magic, he's hardly scratched the surface of his abilities," she said.

"Mom!" We had rules about my mother's telepathy. *And so what if Isaac never uses his Spektral magic? Adele and Codi don't have recoil!*

"You're far ahead of those two in your practice. Who knows if they'll have growing pains?"

"Mom! Get out of my head!"

The injured looked at us, dazed and confused, all heavily sedated with Ritha's magic.

"Shield yourself properly if you want privacy." My gran's voice filled the room as she entered with a swift stride, Remi and Manon at her heels like her little pets.

Oh, okay, sorry I couldn't shield from my mother's Spektral while also trying not to pass out after bringing Sébastien back from the edge of his grave, not to mention healing the three moronic frat boys who kept touching my hair, the manager from Tropical Isle whose breath smelled like salami and cigars, and Suga and Pixie, two of Bourbon's finest burlesque dancers!

My head swirled again, and I stumbled the last few feet to Sébastien, who was now sprawled beneath a mauve-colored afghan crocheted by my great-grandmother way before either of us were born. He shivered beneath the turquoise tassels. It was a miracle he was still alive. As long as I lived, I'd never forget the smell of his burnt flesh.

Actually, it wasn't a miracle he was still alive; it was magical.

His current wardrobe added to the surrealness of the night. We'd had to strip off his chemical-soaked clothes, so now he wore my uncle's old Reggie Bush jersey and some cut-off sweats. Very *un*-Sébastien. His broken glasses rested atop a jacket that could only be Nicco Medici's.

The room tilted, and I quickly knelt beside him, sure his internal organs wouldn't appreciate it if I crashed on top of him. His superficial wounds had healed, and I think I'd gotten all of the broken bones, but he still hadn't really woken up. Maybe it was better that way. It was one thing using the memory powder on a stranger but totally weird to blow it at a friend.

Okay, he wasn't exactly a friend, but I'd known him my entire life. French Quarter rats and all.

Pixie groaned from her pallet on the floor as Ritha tended to her back. She'd been trampled by partygoers chased out of a trance club by a cluster of souls. She was lucky to have escaped with only a back injury. I cringed at the thought of lying face down on a club floor and pulled the small bottle of homemade antiseptic from the pocket of my party dress and spritzed my hands with it until they glistened. The scent of juniper brought an instant calm.

"What did you find?" Ritha asked her pets.

"Charity Hospital looks like a war zone," Remi reported, arms behind his back like a soldier. "If we set up there, folks would die of dysentery before we found a way to exorcise them. Plus, it's outside of the lockdown spell."

"But the Ursuline convent would be perfect," Manon said. Her braids were swept up into two jumbo plaits, and her skin glistened like she'd been running.

"Lots of small rooms," Remi added.

"How big is the kitchen?" my mother asked, putting up a magical shield between her and the douche-canoe SigEp frat boy she'd just finished examining. If he tried to touch her hair, Goddess help him.

Remi cracked his neck. "Big but not industrial."

"But the property is a nexus for magic," Manon said, and they both shot me *stupid-little-cousin* looks.

Whatever. How was I supposed to know about the Casquette Girls Coven's antique sleeping spell?

"If the kitchen isn't industrial-sized, it won't work," my mother said.

"Planning on hosting a dinner party in the middle of a supernatural siege?" I asked. The sarcasm was unnecessary, but I figured they'd ignore me the way they always did when discussing their "private coven business."

Ritha and her minions did ignore me, but Sébastien stirred. I placed the back of my hand on his forehead—still warm.

My mom came over with a cool rag soaked in a holy basil tonic for his head. "We need to move people. We can't handle the volume here. The Possessed are now five to a room; they need to be separated ASAP before they become a danger to one another."

"Not to mention the wounded," Ritha said. "We don't have room for them all here, but they need to be monitored and powdered before they're released out of the Quarter to the mundane hospitals."

"Hospital," I corrected. "Singular." Only one had reopened since the Storm—an immensely sore subject with my father and one of his opponent's favorite media talking points.

"Orleans," Sébastien muttered.

Everyone turned his way.

"He's awake!" I touched his shoulder. "Sébastien?"

"Orleans," he muttered, again.

Manon crossed her arms. "I don't think the fridge at Café Orléans is remotely suitable for our needs."

Sébastien's eyeballs rolled beneath his lids. I always knew I liked him. "Orleeeeeeeeeans," he mumbled, extra emphasis on the American vowels. Sébastien Michel spoke perfect French.

"The Bourbon Orleans!" I said. "Across the street from the café."

"It's been closed since the Storm," my mother said. "But I don't think it sustained any major damage, it's close, and it's got at least a hundred rooms and a restaurant. The kitchen must be large."

Ritha rubbed her temples. "We can use the refrigeration at the bars along Bourbon for any overflow."

I now realized why they kept bringing up refrigeration. My stomach wrenched. They needed a morgue. "We can't let all these people die! We have to figure out how to get these souls out!" The outburst depleted my remaining energy.

Manon turned to me. "We're going to war, Désirée. There will be casualties."

That's a little dramatic. Again, the light flashed behind my eyelids. *No. Not in front of Ritha. Not in front of Thing One and Thing Two. I refuse.*

"What the hell?" yelled the SigEp guy, aggressively ripping

away his splint and smacking his frat brother with it, diverting everyone's attention. *Thank Goddess.*

"I thought you mirrored them!" Ritha snapped at Manon.

"We did! They're not possessed; they're just idiots."

Ritha strode over to them, blew a fistful of chamomile in their faces, and they went down like sacks of oysters. She turned back to my cousins. "Go to the Bourbon Orleans. Check the power and water. If they've been cut, have your Uncle Morgan get them running. I want *every* room secured before sunrise. Bring every witch we can spare. The most sickly will remain here; the rest get transported. Ana Marie, cleanse the kitchen and bring the dead over with your sister. I know you'll handle them with grace." She paused, glancing at the corner altar she'd built for Ghede-Linto. "There's too much death in this house."

I made a mental note to *never* eat at the Bourbon Orleans when this was all over.

My mom kissed my cheek. "You looked beautiful tonight, baby." I glanced down at my Hexennacht dress as she shuffled Remi and Manon out of the room. It was a cute dress.

Ritha came over to me and Sébastien, removing a tin from her apron pocket.

"What should I do?" I asked, aggressively suppressing a yawn.

She smeared a greasy salve over the still-open-but-not-nearly-as-deep-as-when-he-arrived burn on Sébastien's face.

"You, my dear, go sweep the altars and refresh the offerings."

"I'm tired of being the Cinderella stepchild!" What would she have me doing if I'd joined the family coven?

"Désirée, I'm *gifting* you the responsibility of tending to our ancestors while your cousins were sent off to turn a hotel into a magical asylum."

I gulped.

"If I have to explain to you the hierarchy of tasks here, then perhaps I was wrong when doling them out."

"I'm sor—!"

"Cinderella? Child, please."

"I'll make fresh coffee for great-gran—I know she liked it with condensed milk!"

"That's more like it." She gave me only a slightly more approving look and then went on her way out the room. "Heavy on the chicory!" As her voice faded down the hallway, I wondered what my ancestors thought about this mess. Goddess only knew what would have happened if Ritha and Chatham hadn't had the foresight to protect the cemeteries.

"Are you Isis?" Sébastien asked, and I nearly jumped out of my skin. He was gazing up at me with droopy eyelids.

"The Egyptian Sun goddess?"

"Technically, yes, I suppose." He patted his face for his glasses. "But I was referring to *Shazam!* DC Comics, 1976, issue twenty-five." He squinted up at me. "Désirée Borges?" I almost reached for his glasses, or what was left of them, but then I realized foggy vision might work in our favor given what was going on in the room. "What happened?"

"There was an accident in the lab."

"What? No, there wasn't. There was a motorcycle gang. We were attacked. Someone—that guy always hanging around Adele with the hair . . ."

"There was an explosion at D-MORT. You barely got out alive."

"What's that smell?" He sniffed his arm. "It's . . . embalming fluid."

Gross. "See. Mortuary explosion."

"Why are you here? Is this a FEMA tent? Is Isaac here? Where's my sister?"

I wanted to grill him on what happened. I wanted to know every single detail about how Callisto Salazar's coven did it. What magic they used. How they invoked the power of the Flower Moon. But I knew I should be trying to help him forget everything about the night rather than helping him access his memories.

"Yeah, we're with FEMA. Isaac's around here somewhere." Instead of reaching for a scoop of memory powder from my apron, I squirted an eyedropper of my sleepytime potion into a cup of tea and helped him take a sip.

His face curdled. "Tastes like feet."

"It's the valerian root. Try to get some sleep."

"Your arms are shimmery," he said, eyelids heavy again. "Most people think Isis didn't come around until DC's New 52, but they are wroooong." His words began to slur. "Did you know she traveled the Middle East freeing enslaved children?"

"Is that so?"

"And she could manipulate natural . . . elements." His eyes sagged closed.

If he only knew how much this Isis and I had in common.

The blistering burn on his shoulder hadn't healed properly. Ritha would kill me if she found out I was still using my magic. *But it's Sébastien.* French Quarter rats for life. I placed one hand over the wound and waited for the ethereal tingling of my Spektral.

Instead, I got an electric shock and fell over, clutching the back of the couch. I bit my fist, swallowing a scream. *Magic is pain. Growth is pain. I accept this challenge with grace.*

Panting, I opened my eyes and was relieved to find the blisters had gone down.

Success.

I made it halfway across the room before I felt like I was going to pass out. *No. Do not* let Ritha down. I wanted to work with our ancestors.

Fingers grazed my hair across my back, and I snapped upright.

"How's your hair so straight?"

My nostrils flared at the frat boy's uninvited touch. "Magic,"

I said through clenched teeth. *Do not lose your cool.* But then his hand slithered up my leg. I bolted forward.

"Where ya going?"

Don't let him see you rattled. I spun back to him.

"Aren't we going to play doctor?" He waved his finger in the air.

I am *not* in the mood for this shit. "Yeah, it's time to play."

I murmured words I wasn't supposed to use, pulling the last bit of magic from the depths of my soul.

A look of horror corrupted his *J. Crew* catalogue face as his finger elongated, blackening and growing scales. It slithered through the air, splitting open at the end to reveal a flickering tongue.

I hissed, baring my teeth, and the snake mirrored the sound and plunged its fangs into his chiseled jaw. He shrieked like a little boy. Douche-canoes number two and three yelled as it struck again.

"Hope it's not venomous," I said, and walked out of the room, hiding the snicker.

The snake charm would wear off in a few minutes, and he'd be dosed with memory powder, but I hoped he dreamt about it for the rest of his life. I hoped he heard the hiss in his ear if he ever thought about touching a Black woman's hair again. But the adrenaline plummeted as quickly as it had risen, and I fell against the hallway wall.

I nearly sank to the floor, breaking into a feverish sweat. I shouldn't have done that, especially after healing Sébastien.

Worth the recoil. Totally worth the recoil.

I teetered to the kitchen, brewed a fresh pot of coffee—extra chicory—drank a cup before pouring it into the carafe, and then put on another pot for the rest of the fam. It was going to be a long night. I wolfed down a handful of granola and filled the tray with some orange-blossom cookies, my great-grandad's fav.

As I entered Ritha's spiritual room with the tray, the hairs on the back of my neck rose, just like they had when I wandered in for the first time at four years old and every time since. That first time had been with Remi and Manon, who were both older but had run screaming at the sight of the wingspread owl affixed at the top of our ancestral altar. But I was enamored with it. When I'd discovered Ritha standing in the door, I thought for sure I was dead meat. But she picked me up to get a better view. I touched its talons and beak and feathers, and Ritha told me that its eyes were always open, watching over our family both dead and alive, seeing things for us that we might not be privy to in the present. Of course, I didn't know what that meant and just thought we had an owl as a guard, the way the bars on Bourbon had big fat men standing in front of them.

She went on to explain who each of the people were in the photos: generations of Earth witches. When I went to kindergarten the following year, I'd wanted to know what animals guarded each of my classmates' families and had been stunned to find out that none of them had altar rooms in their houses. I'd felt sorry for them.

I brushed the ashes from the seashells, swept the altar clean, and replaced the cloth with a fresh scarf. A bright red silk for the aggression pounding through the magical streets of the city. After replenishing the vases with fresh cuttings, I plated the cookies, poured the coffee, and spiked it with spiced rum. I said a devotion to my great-gran and gramps, and to Marassa and Makandal, and to all the generations in between. The exhaustion crept up on me, and I was yawning hard and trying not to fall asleep when a coconut bowl filled with fish bones rattled. I blinked, staring at the dozens of tiny bones shaking inside the bowl, sure I was hallucinating.

Heat crept up my arms, and the bowl shook more violently. I reached out to calm it, but the coconut tumbled to the floor, spilling the fish bones. *"Shit!"* Now they had to be cleansed.

They were oracle bones, kind of like runes, used to communicate with the dead. Ritha always promised she'd teach me to use them. I picked them up, placed them into a bowl of Florida Water, gave it a few swirls, focusing my intention, and then put them back into the coconut shell to dry.

Warmth snaked up my spine, and I slowly turned my head, ready to flatten that guy if he had followed me into this sacred space. I'd have to cleanse the whole room again. But no one was there.

Tap. Tap. Tap.

When I looked back, the coconut bowl was knocking against the altar. The bones rattling. "Not again!" I reached out for it, but white flashed across my eyes. *Shit.* All I could do was brace myself as I hit the floor. Cheek resting against the rug, I saw the bones gliding over its leaf pattern.

I blinked, trying to focus. I couldn't sit up. All I could read was . . .

HEL
MISS
SPI

"Gran," I moaned, torn between alerting her and not wanting her to know that I'd ignored her warnings. I tried to call out again, but it didn't matter. Darkness took me.

I woke up to my phone vibrating against the wooden floor.

I sat up quickly, my arm accidentally sliding over the fish bones, scattering them everywhere as I slid open a text message from Isaac: ***SOS. HQ. ASAP.***

It was just to me and Codi. *Weird.* Adele must be with him already.

I gathered the bones back up and swirled them with the smoke of dried lemon balm, more concerned about Isaac's SOS. *That'll do for now.*

I texted Ritha that our ancestors were well taken care of and snuck out of the house for HQ.

CHAPTER 5
INTERVENTION

"The *Afterworld?*" Gabriel gave me a patronizing glare, and the room fell silent, kicking my confidence into a downward spiral.

Even Nicco didn't say anything. Not exactly the reaction I was hoping for after divulging my plan.

"I mean, *I'm* going to the Afterworld. I'd never ask anyone else to do something so unpredictable."

Nicco's brows pressed even tighter.

The doorbell rang, and Emilio turned to me. "Who is that?"

"How would I know?"

"*We* don't get visitors."

Nicco bolted out of the room and down the stairs while the rest of us hurried to the landing, squinting down as he opened the door. Could Callisto have sent a messenger?

He turned back to look up at me, and my stomach lurched: I knew it was Isaac.

I swept down the stairs, the anger from our fight boiling back up, but then Nicco opened the door wider. "Oh," I said, simmering down.

"Addie!" It was Chatham, with Edgar in tow.

Shit. Did they already find my IOU? Does Chatham know I took the ghoststick?

"There you are!" He reached out but hesitated to cross the threshold.

Nicco wasn't exactly moving to give him passage.

Knuckles cracked, and I glanced back up at the landing. Everyone was gone except Gabriel, who was now perched on the top step, eyeing the Daures like a protective older brother. After the way the Hexennacht party had gone down, I understood his position, but he didn't have anything to worry about.

I passed in front of Nicco to the front steps. "Chatham, you're back!"

He pulled me into his arms. "Darling, you had me for a scare. All of us."

He squeezed my ribs, and I tried not to cringe. I didn't want to freak him out with the bruises. "I'm sorry. I'm glad you're safe and sound."

His hand slipped into mine. "No, I'm sorry. Don't get me started on that fool's errand." And without further discussion, he turned to leave, pulling me with him. I sensed Nicco's pulse.

"No!" I let go of his hand. Codi's two brothers waited out on the street. Were they supposed to be backup? This suddenly felt like an intervention.

"What's wrong?" Chatham asked. "Did you forget something inside?"

"I understand your concern, but I'm fine here, *merci*."

Chatham leaned closer. "*Adele*," he said in a hushed voice, "you can*not* stay here."

"*Yes*, I can."

His eyes grew with surprise. "But there's no need to impose when we already have everything you need at home."

"It's no imposition," Nicco said flatly from the door.

"It's safest at the tearoom behind the coven's protection

wards." Chatham's expression pleaded with Nicco for help. He got none.

"Then Nicco and his family should be there too," I said.

"Oh, I don't think that's . . ." Edgar started to say.

Nicco glared at him. "You don't think that's what?"

"We can't endanger our family or the rest of our coven," Chatham said, resolute. "Adele, you do realize that a member of this household *killed your mother*. Your father would—"

"My father would want me to stay where I felt safest!" I snapped. Chatham had good intentions, but I was over men telling me what to do or think.

"You might *feel* safe," Edgar said, almost begging, "but you're in shock—"

"I'm not going anywhere without Nicco! I'm not leaving."

Thump-thump.

They felt like the most defiant words I'd ever said.

I wasn't sure if it was his pulse or mine.

Chatham sucked in a breath. He couldn't make me leave, not with Nicco standing there. Not that he would have regardless. "Do you have everything you need?" he asked.

I nodded. I had the ghoststick and the map. That was all I needed.

"Do you have your phone?" Edgar's eyes welled, like he'd already lost me. "And your charger?"

"*Oui.*" I stepped back into the house, also getting teary. "And I'm fine."

"She's safe here," Nicco said.

"She'd better be, or I can promise that your family will not live to terrorize another member of this community."

My lungs pinched, waiting for Nicco's reaction.

"I'm sorry for your loss," he said, and swung the door shut.

I hated this. Papa Olsin, may he rest in peace, was wrong: Nicco would never hurt me.

But Papa hadn't been wrong about me opening the attic.

Papa was dead.

I started for the stairs, throat burning. I didn't want Nicco to see that all of the stitches holding me together were threatening to pop.

"Adele." When I turned back around, his eyes were filled with worry. "He's not wrong . . . about Brigitte . . ."

Defensiveness flooded my veins as the same old fight brewed. "I'm not going to let you push me away!"

He stepped closer and brushed the hair from my face. "Please, don't." His voice was soft. "But do you really feel safe here?"

"*Sì*. You're here." A clatter came from outside, and a chorus of muffled voices hummed. "Is that . . . ?"

"Chanting?" he finished.

"*Against thy enemies, you shall protect.*"

A chill pricked my spine, the words registering with eerie familiarity.

Gabriel whipped down the stairs and opened the door. "What do you think you're—?"

"*No harm will come under your mighty shield.*"

His fangs snapped out, but before he could pounce, Nicco smacked a hand on his shoulder. "It's a protection ward."

Protection ward?

I pushed him aside to see for myself. Edgar, Chatham, and the boys were standing on the street, facing the house, hands linked, chins up to the moon. Purple sparkles poured down from the wrought iron balcony above, lighting up the estate as their voices sang: "*To the people, to the witches, of this house. Reflect. Protect. Reflect. Protect.*" A hexenspiegel floated over the house.

Gabriel and Chatham exchanged a nod, and the tension diffused as quickly as it arose. Nonetheless, my pulse continued to rise, the chant echoing in my head. I backed away from the door, eyes watering as other words punched out of my memory.

His words. *"This secluded enough for you?"* The memory of his breath fogging against my neck.

"Reflect. Protect. Reflect. Protect."

"I'm going to smash you into the Underworld." I spun away from Nicco, cheeks burning, as if the Brute was right here, taunting me. *"You'll know what a real Fire witch feels like."* A hand brushed my waist, and I lurched forward, stumbling over my feet, but Nicco scooped me up just before I bit the black and white marble floor. "Got you!"

Panic erupted inside me. I clung to him, refusing to turn around.

"Adele, what's wrong?"

"Nothing."

"You think Niccolò will still want you after this?"

"Adele, you can go back with them if you want. You don't have to stay here."

"What?" I turned to face him, trying to act normal. "I don't want to go anywhere. Nothing's wrong." My lungs pinched. "I want to be here. I don't want to be separated." I blinked so the tears would stay locked inside. I couldn't look at him. *Breathe, Adele.*

His arms circled around me, and the weight of his shoulders was grounding.

Breaths passed. And so did the memory. The panic subsided.

"I'm okay," I said. "Sorry."

"Don't be." He pulled me down to sit on the steps next to him.

I had to say something or it would be weird. Weirder than it already was. "Callis told me that if I didn't bring him your grimoire, he would kill my dad." It was true. And it *was* distressing, even if it hadn't been the thing that caused the near-panic attack. "I would never betray you . . . but—"

"Adele, don't worry about me or my grimoire. I would never make you choose me over your father. We're in this together."

His hand slid over my hip, and he pulled me closer. "In this world or any other."

"Any other?" A smile peeked out.

"It is a pretty brilliant plan. I'm embarrassed to say I didn't think of it myself. I guess I don't think like a witch anymore."

I slid my hand up his sweater sleeve to the mark he kept so well hidden. "Maybe you should."

As my fingers grazed his skin, he shuddered, and it made me swell with power.

No Ghost Drinker could ever take that away from me. From us.

A crash came from above, rattling the chandelier, and I jolted back. "What was *that?*"

He gazed up at the ceiling, annoyed. "Remember those two witches from the swamp?"

"*Mm-hmm.*"

"I told you, we didn't kill them."

"Oh. I'd always been too afraid to ask what happened to them."

He squeezed my leg. "You can ask me anything."

"Do you still want to kill León?"

"*Sí.*"

"Will you come to Guinée to help save my father?"

"*Sí.*" A quizzical expression formed. "That's how you want to get to the Afterworld? The Gates to Guinée?"

"*Mm-hmm.*"

He was unable to hide the surprise in his voice. "You know the way to Guinée?"

"*Mm-hmm.*"

The way he looked at me, I swore I could feel my Fire. *We are going to do this. We are going to Guinée.*

I hoped one day the Daures would understand. I couldn't do it on my own, but I couldn't risk any of their lives. I needed the Medici to help me defeat Jakome.

Nicco I trusted implicitly. The others I trusted for now. We had a common goal that superseded the centuries-long feud between our families. The Salazars were the tie that bound us into a singular sinister tapestry. Time would tell what the final threads would reveal, but only one side would end up with the Medici grimoire.

L'elisir di vita.

CHAPTER 6
UNFORGIVEABLE

"The Gates of Guinée are *a fable*," Emilio scoffed.

Adele didn't waver.

"*Où sont les portes vers la Guinée?*" Martine's question sang through the air, the operatic training of her human years ever-present in her voice.

Adele turned to her. "They're gates to the Afterworld. Where the ancestors of the magical rest."

"Is my husband there?"

Gabriel sneered. "She said *the magical.*" It was rare to see my eldest brother jealous.

"Supposedly." Emilio smirked. "According to Voodooists."

"Not *supposedly*," Adele shot back. "The gates are real. Guarded by the Ghede."

I indulged her idea, letting my mind wander to a ghostly scene, to caverns so vast and deep they made our Florentine catacombs seem piteous . . .

Pools of water luminous as drenching moonbeams surrounded a prodigious castle of midnight-dark stone, with towers that spindled high into the aether. The eternal figures of my mother, father, sister, and grandfather Cosimo greeted us along with all the other Medici

*witches who'd been immortalized in oil paint in the grand hallway
of the palazzo where I was raised.*

"What makes you so sure the gates are real?" Emilio asked,
leaning over the table toward Adele. "The strata of magical myth
this city is built upon rival those of Crete and Sicily."

"Exactly," she said. "A city where the dead walk with the
living. Where the mundane go to mass and then have their tarot
cards read. Where people dance at funerals, and paint their
porch ceilings sky-blue to keep spirits away, and eat cabbage and
black-eyed peas for health and wealth. Folks come here to find
themselves and lose themselves and be themselves."

*"So," my father said, his cheeks flushed from the pomegranate
wine, "you've finally found someone who could occupy your mind
more than magic can, Niccolò?"*

*"Only took four hundred years," Giovanna taunted, taking
Adele's hand, pulling her along as if to show her something divine.*

"It was worth it," I said, and Adele glanced back to me.

"People see only what they want to see and believe only what
they want to believe. What *we* want them to believe," she
continued. "We keep things hidden with masks and glitter and
songs that steal your soul and drinks that steal your memories.
We sing in the streets, cry in the streets, and bleed in the streets.
New Orleans will be your muse. She'll fuel your dreams and
your vices and your kinks. She'll tie you up and make you beg
for more, all while you search for the je ne sais quoi giving you
that joie de vivre, never knowing that the magic flows freely and
the dead thrive and the witches rule, so you buy a fucking boa,
slurp another Hurricane, and start telling your friends back
home how they'll never believe about this one time in Nola . . .
Why wouldn't the gates to the Afterworld be here? Hidden in
plain sight amongst the living, guarded by the dead, covered up
by stories of the magical?"

She loved her city the way the Medici loved Florence.

I realized what I'd said to Giovanna was true. It was worth it.

Every vein I'd ever pierced, every drop of blood I'd ever stolen, the decades of Séraphine's torture, the pain of León's betrayal, and every subsequent century I'd spent scouring the Earth for him . . . it had all led me to a witch with whom I could share my secrets and family and dreams.

"For weeks now," she said, "we've been trying to figure out the instructions, to separate the myth from the magical."

Wait, weeks? While I was scouring the swamps for Callisto, she was trying to convene with the dead? Not just convene, but cross over? *You did practically shove her back into her coven's arms.* My pulse rose, and Adele's gaze flicked my way. *Calm the hell down, Niccolò.*

"Ritha Borges has taken extreme measures to keep us from finding the gates," Adele said. "And Ritha *never* stops Désirée from pursuing magic. The opposite, in fact."

"*Pourquoi?*" Lisette asked. "Before tonight, why were you all trying to cross into the other side?"

Yes, bella, why? And who were you trying to convene with?

"A couple of Ghede told the rest of my coven that there's a place in the Afterworld where the spiritless souls can rest if they just deliver them."

She wasn't trying to reach Adeline, Nicco; they were just trying to solve the city's soul-crisis. My nerves settled, but a noxious wave of jealousy crept through me—they evoked the lwa? The witchlings were further into their magical upbringing than I'd realized.

Perhaps I shouldn't have been so surprised. The Borges most certainly descended from one of the Great African magical bloodlines and, whether I liked it or not, Isaac was clearly a descendant of *the* Norwoods of the British Isles. As for Codi Daure, before merging with the magical natives of this land, at least part of his family of psychics came from the Black Forest of Germany, and I'd put money on the Guldenmanns. Even Annabelle hailed from the Great French witches. Adele was the only one in her coven who hadn't descended from one of the Great magical families.

Yet the pull of her magic was so *powerful* . . .

León was a puissant witch, but not like her, and Adele had barely scratched the surface of her magic. Then again, what did I know about Le Comte Saint-Germain? Maybe I was blinded by my love for him. Maybe I didn't know anything about him at all.

"The gates are for the dead," Gabriel said. "It's been centuries since I've participated in any kind of African-rooted rites, but you can't just sashay up expecting to take tea with dear old Granny in Guinée. That's what the crossroads are for."

"We're not meeting Jakome at the crossroads. We have to catch him off guard."

"I sincerely doubt that even Ritha Borges knows the way to Guinée. Not even the most elite of *les sociétés secrètes* do."

Despite the night's perils, warmth spread from the pit of my stomach listening to Adele and my brothers discuss various aspects of the witching world.

Adele shrugged. "I don't know what Ritha knows, but I know the way."

Emilio scoffed again. "Baron Samedi only imparts that information to the dying—"

"Then I'll consider it a special invitation. If the Baron was so intent on me not knowing the way, he wouldn't have given the route to a dear friend whose mind is being slowly eaten by a two-hundred-year-old Italian teenage ghost, especially when said person is the biggest blabbermouth in New Orleans!" She pulled a scroll from her bag and quickly unwound it.

Each of us held down a corner as her fingers slid across the city map, from one starburst symbol to the next.

"Lafayette, Valence, St. Patrick, Cypress Grove, Holt, St. Roch, and of course, St. Louis No. 1. These are the gates." She looked straight at Gabriel. *Smart. She knows he's the one to convince and the others will fall into place.* She uncapped a marker and began joining the symbols together with straight lines, until shapes began to form: two upright coffins flanking . . . a mausoleum.

Lisette brushed her hair from her face. "*C'est le vèvè de Baron Samedi.*"

Adele threw the marker down.

Gabriel crossed his arms in contemplation.

"Those are the gates, and these are the instructions to serve the Ghede at the gates." She procured a scrap of paper from the pocket of her denim shorts and smoothed it out between her fingers. "*Seven nights, seven moons, seven gates, seven tombs.*" She gazed at me, anxious, as if speaking the words alone might summon the lwa.

I nodded for her to continue.

> "*Seven keys will let you enter,*
> *Nibo's axe, Plumaj's feather.*
> *Scent of night blossoms for Masaka,*
> *Sip of piman, dance the Banda.*"

I mentally recorded which of Samedi and Brijit's children she listed, cross-referencing them with every tale of Guinée I could recall from our centuries of visits to New Orleans. Every Fète Gede celebration I'd ever attended, every fetish market I'd browsed in Lomé, and every *mange-les-morts* ceremony I'd been invited to in Port-au-Prince.

> "*Silken rings for Zaranye,*
> *Oussou's pipe will get you high.*
> *Leave your ego in a jar,*
> *The family Ghede will take you far.*
>
> *Through waves of chaos, rocky cliffs of*
> *Abysmal waters,*

*Where for a mirror, Doubye will steer you
  through,
Truths, reflections, the bare depths of the
  real you."*

When León and I had gone on our sojourn all those centuries ago, we spent many weeks in Sicilia. We camped at the ancient necropolis in Cozzo Martice, swam naked in il lago di Pergusa, and made sacrifices at Demeter's ancient temple, for it was said that there, Hades kidnapped Persephone and took her back to the Underworld. In my wildest dreams, I'd never have believed that one day I'd be escorting León's descendant to the land of the dead.

*"Fields of poppies, whirls of pleasure,
Will satisfy your every urge.
And only when you're on the verge of erotic
  doom,
Will Ghede-L'Oraille set you free so you can
  bloom.*

*The sanctimonious need not cross,
Your lies will only get you tossed.
Twisted words and veils of secrets
turn to ash by licks from flaming tongues.
Only those who seek the truth will have any
  fun."*

The warnings did not escape me. You didn't have to be a high priestess in the Voodoo tradition to know that the Ghede were flagrant tricksters who loathed the hypocritical culture of their former Natural World. They encouraged the indulging of whims and the exposing of secrets. I steadied my accelerating pulse. I hadn't considered the Ghede when agreeing to this plan. The Ghede were going to be trouble.

"Follow the past, listen to lè mò,
And the secrets of the dead you will know.
Turn thrice and say the name of one who
* haunts you,*
And find the Gates to Guinée beyond you."

Adele sucked in a breath and waited.

In theory, her plan was brilliant, but in practice . . . too risky. The Ghede toying with the hedonic pleasures of a human, or even a witch, were one thing, but of a vampire? *What was I thinking?* It was a nightmare I'd never expose her to. "There are too many unknowns," I said.

She whipped my way.

"I'm sorry, *bella,* I shouldn't have made promises so quickly."

"I don't know," Emilio said. "What was that part about erotic doom?"

"We'll find another way. The Ghede unleashing the primal immoderation of a clan of vampires is not what we need right now."

"Or maybe it's exactly what we need right now," she snapped.

Emilio's tongue slid over his bottom lip as he gazed upon her with newfound admiration.

"Niccolò's right," Gabriel said. "The fantastical Ghede encouraging us to fulfill every urge, every desire? What if we became trapped in Ghede-induced blood-lust for eternity?" His eyes narrowed. "Or maybe that's exactly what you want? Use us to break the Salazar family magic while trapping us in the Afterworld?" His fangs snapped out. "Is that where you think we really belong, with the dead?"

She leaned in, unafraid. "*C'est ridicule, Gabriel.*"

"You really are the descendent of Adeline Saint-Germain!"

I inched closer in case Gabriel lost control.

"*Je t'accompagne chez Guinée!*" Lisette blurted.

Gabriel flipped back to her. "No, you will not!"

"*J'y vais!*"

As they began to bicker, I tried to take Adele's hand, but she pulled away. "*Bella*, it's too dangerous for me to be there with you." I lowered my voice. "In our world, I trust myself. I can control the thirst. But in the Afterworld, where the Ghede rule . . ."

"I trust you, Niccolò. In this world. In every world."

"I would never risk your safety."

"I'm not scared of you!"

"You need to be!"

"No, I don't. Not if it means saving my dad." Her breath shook in her lungs. "What if . . . what if you turned me? Then could we go?"

"*What?*"

"Then you wouldn't have to worry about hurting me. Maybe that's what Papa Olsin saw in his premonition! You weren't killing me, just making me into a vampire?"

"That *would* be killing you!" I shouted, louder than I'd intended. "This plan is unsound. We need—"

"I think it's sounding sexier than ever," Emilio taunted, fangs bulging.

"Stop looking at her like that," I hissed.

"Or what? You'll rip off my head?"

Adele trembled. "I don't care if I die."

"*I* care if you die." My fingernails dug into the table. Suddenly, I didn't know if I was saying it for her sake or mine or all of the other vampires in the room.

"Leave it to a Saint-Germain to cause dissonance amongst the Medici," Emilio said.

She looked up at me. "So much for us being in this

together."

"We *are*."

"No, we're not. We haven't been ever since you went after Callis without me. We promised each other we wouldn't go after him alone."

What? She doesn't know? Wasn't that why she was here, and why Isaac was spying from a fern across the street—because she'd found out everything?

"Adele, I tri—"

Tears welled in her eyes.

I couldn't bear to cause her any more pain. "It was too dangerous. I thought Emilio and I could stop him in the swamp and they'd never even make it back into the city. We arrived moments too late. I'm so deeply sorry that we did."

"You thought you could take down a coven of Ghost Drinkers with *just* Emilio? The good ole Carter Brothers . . ."

"*Basta, fratellino,*" Gabriel said, with disappointment, "*o le dirò la verità*—"

I shot him a look. "It's fine. She's right."

Adele's eyes lit with fire. "I know the Medici ego is legendary, but this is absurd, Niccolò. It's Floralia! You saw the dozens of witches who could have helped!"

"I know. It was a plan wrought with arrogance. In hindsight—"

"If we'd worked together, we'd have had a chance. You didn't even warn anyone! We were taken totally off guard, and now the whole city is screwed—all because you wanted to be the hero! Papa Olsin died!"

"*Cazzate!*" Emilio boomed.

The room fell silent.

"*Non farlo,* Emilio," I said. "*Fermati.*"

Adele whipped his way. "What? Tell me."

"*Fratello, per favore non farlo,*" I pleaded.

"*Pssss,*" he said, brushing me off. "It's one thing watching you act like a lovesick puppy, but another entirely to let you take the fall for that moronic witchling."

Adele's gaze shot back to me. "What is he talking about?"

I should have known he followed me to Jackson Square.

"You're correct, *bella*," Emilio said. "The city is in turmoil because of someone's ego, but it's not my brother's; it's your petulant little boyfriend's."

"What?"

"Much to my chagrin, Niccolò called you, even though it was *ridicolo* to bring a magicless witch with us out to the swamp. You didn't pick up."

"You could have found me—"

"Ohh, he tried."

I considered knocking him out cold, but a childish, devilish part of me wanted her to know the truth, even if it caused her pain. Especially if it did. That part of me wanted her to forget about the Air witch permanently.

"We arrived at the moon ritual too late to stop it," Emilio said, "because Niccolò met up with Isaac, who refused to give up your location, even after my brother, my own flesh and blood, resorted to *groveling*."

Bastardo. I did not grovel.

"Niccolò even asked him to join us to defeat Callisto. A request he denied, sending the *good ole Carter Brothers* off to break up the Animarum Praedators on our own. Niccolò thoroughly warned your side. If your own coven member didn't relay the message—"

She spurted a laugh. "You're lying. I was with Isaac all night."

When no one said anything, she looked at me.

"He . . . said you were sleeping."

The fire in her eyes was replaced with a hollow look.

And a cloak of shame fell upon me.

"*Bella*, I'm sorry."

CHAPTER 7
TELL ALL

The floorboards creaked as I paced in front of the fireplace. The brothel was always drafty, but something felt off about the blue room tonight. I stared up at the pineapple carving above the pocket doors. Adele had once told me that back in the day, hosts would leave a pineapple for guests upon their arrival, and if the guest ever returned to find a second one, it meant the invitation had expired. Of all the places in the city, HQ was where I'd felt most at home. Now, I felt like I'd come home to a second pineapple.

The front door pushed open, and someone rustled through the hallway. My pace quickened.

"Isaac?" Désirée yelled.

My palms broke out in sweat. *In here*, I meant to say, but the words didn't form. *I have to tell her. I have to tell her everything.*

Heavier footsteps followed Dee's. "Isaac?" Codi yelled.

"Blue room!" I forced the words out.

I hoped by some miracle that Adele would be with them.

When they entered the parlor, the hope snuffed out. *She's probably back at the tearoom with Chatham and just didn't want to see me.*

"What's wrong, man?" Codi asked. "Why's Adele at—?"

"I gave the ring to Nicco," I blurted, scared I would chicken out. "I know it wasn't mine to give, but after Olsin's premoni— I wanted Nicco to stay the hell away from her. I didn't think they'd actually be able to—! Désirée, how the hell did vampires do a location spell?"

They stared at me blankly.

"The Medici used magic?" Dee asked.

"That's how they found Callis."

"No way," Codi said. "Adele must have been with them."

I shook my head. "She was with me."

"But she knew you gave them the ring?"

I shook my head again and told them how we'd fallen asleep, and how Nicco wouldn't stop calling, how scared I was that he was going to kill her, and how I subsequently rendezvoused with him in Jackson Square and told him to fuck off.

"Isaac!" Codi yelped, "what were you thinking?"

"I don't know . . ." But the truth was, I did. "I was thinking Adele would want to go, and about the night at the convent when we got separated—how she almost died, how *you* almost died—and I just wanted to keep her safe. I didn't know how big Callis's coven was or that they had a magical fortress. Jesus Christ, I didn't think they'd take Mac! Or that they'd be able to suck down so many spirits and basically become invincible!" The more I rambled, the harder Désirée's iron-clad stare became until I couldn't take it any longer. "Dee—"

"Don't. Even. Talk to me."

"I'm sorry. I know I screwed up—"

"*Screwed up?* Screwing up is forgetting your girlfriend's birthday, or accidentally turning a transmorphic witch into a cat, or summoning the wrong lwa—screwing up is not *putting the entire city at risk of magical warfare!*"

Horror coated Codi's usual apple-pie gaze. "My grandfather

died protecting Adele from those succubi. If we had known, we could have—"

"I know! It's my fault." My voice cracked. "Now I don't know what to do. I just wanted to protect her."

"And what about us?" Désirée asked, seething. "Do none of us matter as long as Adele is safe?"

"No, I didn't think anyone else was in danger! I thought Nicco and Emilio would take care of Callis—they've been hunting him all along—this whole thing is because of a stupid feud between their families. Why did we need to be involved?"

"Sébastien almost died," Codi said. "His sister had a melt-down over the things he was saying. We had to use memory powder on her."

"If I'd known they were going to D-MORT, if I'd known Sébastien was there, I would have gone with them!"

"And that's the problem, Isaac!" Désirée's voice went shrill. "With both you *and* Adele. If you'd known, you would have just gone. Headfirst into danger. Just like her. We're stronger *together*. But you can't get that through your thick skull. You don't care about this coven. Nor does she."

"That's not true!" I didn't mean to yell. "I care about this coven more than anything. This coven is all I have!" I paced away as the pain threatened to swallow me whole. "I love you so much, Désirée. You're my best friend. I'd *never* want anything to happen to you, or to Codi, or to anyone in your families." I pinched my eyes tight. My chest felt like it had been scorched with dragon fire.

As the tears came out, a comforting weight pressed around me. "It's okay, man." Codi's arms clamped over my shoulders. "We love you, too." I couldn't ever remember being hugged by a man, not in any real way. He felt so . . . strong. "And we're going to get these bastards." My anxiety quelled, almost like magic. "We're going to get Adele back. We're not going to let anything happen to her. No matter what Olsin said."

I blushed when I caught Désirée looking at me. "Yeah." I quickly wiped my eyes. "Your dads are getting her now."

"Um. About that. They said she wouldn't leave, but they put a hexenspiegel over their house, so at least they have a little extra protection if Callis has something else planned tonight."

"So now we're protecting vampires?"

"We are when your girlfriend's with them."

She's not my girlfriend anymore—not after this.

Désirée's hands went to her hips. "Why the hell did Adele go to the vampires? If she was mad at you, she could have just come to me."

"Or me," Codi echoed.

I shrugged. "Gabe offered to help get Mac back, but Ritha slammed the door in his face. Adele freaked out . . ." I wanted to tell them the next part, how I'd used the magic to calm her down, but I was too ashamed to admit it. "She wants her dad back, so she went over there."

Concern flooded Désirée's voice. "She can't go after Mac. Has she lost it?"

"That's what I told her! But like you said, headfirst into danger."

Now Désirée was the one pacing. "Well, what's her plan?"

"I-I don't know."

"Think, Isaac! She wouldn't have just stormed over there for no reason. Her plan must be dangerous if she went to the dark side for help—"

"Oh, now you're really making me feel better," Codi said.

"I'm not trying to make you feel better; I'm trying to keep Adele from some kind of suicide mission! It's Halloween night all over again. Remember, she diverged from the coven's plan because she felt responsible and didn't want to endanger us, even if that meant locking herself in the attic with the vampires! Think!"

"*What* did she do?" Codi yelled.

I broke into a feverish sweat. "Sh-she came here first. This is where we got into the fight."

"Why did she stop here?"

"I don't know . . . to change?"

"Did she have on different clothes?"

I wasn't paying attention to what she was fucking wearing! I wracked my brain, forcing myself to relive the moment. She'd still been wearing the black button-down shirt and cut-off shorts. "She didn't change. She didn't have shoes on either."

"She was barefoot at the tearoom," Codi said.

"So she was walking through the freaking Quarter barefoot instead of going home for shoes," Dee said. "She must have come here for something important." She began flipping through bottles of potions and elixirs on the coffee table. "What did she take? Why did she go to the tearoom?"

"I-I don't know. She was behind the counter. I was in shock over my grandpa. She made us all tea. I didn't even know she'd left."

When I'd seen her, she'd been standing near the fireplace, doing something. *Rolling something up.* I stared at the blank space on the wall.

Désirée followed my gaze. "The map is gone. She took it."

"But why?" I asked.

"Oh, hell *no!* That is *my* map. That is *my* plan. She is *not* going to Guinée without me!" Désirée grabbed a bottle of piman from the fireplace mantel and shoved it in her bag.

"What does Guinée have to do with Mac?" Codi asked. "He's still *alive,* right?"

Désirée stormed across the room. "I don't know, but if she left already, I'm going to kill her myself, and she can stay in Guinée!"

"Where are you going?" Codi yelled.

"To find out!"

We hurried after her. I don't know which brought on more

fear: the thought of Adele being locked in a house with a bunch of revenge-seeking vampires or that she might have *gone to the Afterworld* by herself.

Then a more horrifying thought occurred. What if she'd gone to the Afterworld *with them*?

CHAPTER 8
SETTE LUNE

It already felt like a year ago when Isaac and I were talking to my father at the bar, escaping to his bedroom, visiting the statue of my mother in the garden—that whirlwind kiss of swirling flowers and magical Air. Had it all just been a distraction to keep me from Nicco? *Isaac couldn't have met up with Nicco. I remember him in bed with me as I slept. His scent. His warmth. His body curled up with mine under the invisible blanket.* I furiously blinked back tears as the wound I'd been so desperately trying to keep from splitting hemorrhaged, leaving my insides exposed for all of the Medici.

They all just stared at me as I fumbled.

Even after everything, I couldn't fathom Isaac lying to me like that. Sneaking away. He knew I'd been looking for Nicco. The humiliation settled deep in my bones. I pulled up the map, ready to leave, but Nicco put his hand on the paper, stopping me. Only then did I notice the ring on his finger. The Salazar triangular flame. *Did he steal it from the tearoom after Codi got his Mark, when he was being so affectionate with me? Is that why he came to the party? Had he just been pretending to woo me like he'd done with Séraphine?*

The chandelier overhead rattled.

Nicco took the ring off and placed it in my hand. "It's how we found Callis. Isaac gave it to us."

"More like threw it at you," Lisette corrected.

Nicco shot her a silencing look.

Isaac gave it to him? What did Isaac think Nicco would do with it without magic? *When did Isaac turn into such a child?* When *exactly* had Isaac met up with him? After we'd . . . ? My head swirled. I'd known something was wrong when our dreams connected. I'd wanted to leave, but Isaac had convinced me that Nicco was okay. Had he *known* Nicco was in trouble at D-MORT and kept me from helping him? *He hates Nicco, but he wouldn't do that. Right? Isaac would help anyone. It's his nature. Isn't it?*

I pocketed the ring. "I'm sorry if Isaac put you in danger, and I'm sorry if I caused any trouble here tonight—"

"You're not causing trouble."

"I'm leaving." I began rolling up the map, but again, Nicco's hand slid over mine.

"You don't have to go, but if you insist, you aren't going anywhere without me."

"I'm going to Guinée."

"Then so am I."

"Niccolò—" Gabriel's expression hardened.

"No more discussion, *fratello.*" Nicco's gaze stayed locked with mine. "I'm going to the Afterworld, and I'll return once we've obliterated all Salazar magic from the universe. Jakome started this war, and I'm going to end it."

Thump-thump.

He leaned closer, lowering his voice. "Adele, there's not a corner of Earth that I couldn't guide you, but the Afterworld is uncharted territory even for me."

"Then we'll chart it together," I whispered.

"We're going to get through this. *Te lo prometto.*"

"I'm going too!" Lisette said.

Gabriel pounded the table, shaking the floor. "You're not going anywhere near Jakome Salazar! Dead or alive or anything in between."

"Since when do you control where she goes?" Martine shouted in a high-pitched huff.

As their argument stirred up again, Nicco turned to Emilio. "I guess it's just the Carter Brothers plus one?"

"As much as I'd usually be in for this kind of romp—a seven-night ritual with you and a witchling?—count me the hell out. I'll go after Callis the old-fashioned way." He flashed me a glint of his fangs.

"Seven nights?" I asked. "We're going tonight. Now."

"Did you not hear your own instructions, or were you already too swept up by the poetic pull of the Ghede? The ritual takes seven nights. *Sette notti, sette lune, sette porte, sette tombe.* That's one gate per night. Seven moons for seven tombs."

Shit.

Emilio rolled his eyes like I was the biggest amateur in the witching world. "If this is the depth of the planning that's gone into this mission, nice knowing you."

Shit. This can't be right. *Shit. Shit. Shit.* This plan *has* to work. It's all I've got.

"Who exactly is this Jakome Salazar?" Martine asked, her French accent punctuating the syllables of his name. "And why is he so important?"

I started to explain how a witch's magic was connected to the spirits of our ancestors, but she cut me off with a wave of her hand. "*Non.* I did not ask why you want him dead. Why do they worship him like a god?"

Nicco and Emilio both looked to Gabriel, puzzled.

He turned to her. "Not that you are incorrect, *mon amour*, but how did you know Jakome's family idolized him as if he were divine?"

"Because of the shrine."

"What shrine?" I asked.

"In the cathedral. I saw it when I was draining one of the witches."

"In the cathedral?"

She shrugged. "I like my privacy when I feed."

"What makes you think this shrine is for Jakome Salazar?" Nicco asked.

"Because his name was carved into it with blood."

The boys looked at each other, and we all bolted out the door.

The St. Louis Cathedral was only a couple blocks away, but I was panting by the time we reached Pirate's Alley, trying to keep up. With just a few nods, Emilio, Gabriel, and Lisette peeled off in different directions. Emilio scaled the building so quickly, he was on the roof in seconds.

"They're going to clear the building," Nicco said.

"Didn't Callis call back all of his coven members?"

"Maybe. Or maybe that's what he wants us to think. Maybe this shrine is his Trojan Horse."

"*Allons-y*," Martine said, her hair whirling as she went through a door with a broken chain.

I hoped my encounters with Ghost Drinkers were done for the night. In the Natural World, anyway. I took one last look at the sparkle of the Vieux Carré protection spell before I followed them in.

"Stay close," Nicco whispered as we crept through the dark. My pulse accelerated, and his hand touched the small of my back, guiding me along. We followed Martine past the bell tower stairs and through a dressing chamber where hanging vestments had collected dust since the Storm. Their steps were completely silent, and I hardly breathed out of terror that I might give us away to some succubus witch hidden behind an invisibility spell —unlike Martine, who began a gentle hum, almost taunting whoever might be here to come and get her. She sailed through an entrance that led out to the altar, her hum growing to a song. So much for quiet.

"Don't stand too close to Gabriel in case he bursts into flames," came a voice close to my ear, and I nearly screamed, leaping away only to crash into someone else.

"Watch your mouth, Emilio," Gabriel said, holding me up, "or I'll douse you with holy water."

I stepped away from him, but my feet tripped over a mound on the floor, and I fell directly on top of something soft. Cold. As I pushed myself up, I realized I was touching someone's fingers. I was on top of *a body*. I shrieked, scrambling away.

Nicco pulled me close as I fumbled with my phone and shone the screen light down onto the corpse. A man's dead stare was gazing back at me. He had short hair twists and a Maleficium like Codi's.

"Your supper, sister?" Lisette asked, reappearing from the dark. She reached out with her foot and tilted his head to the side, exposing his neck. Bloody fangmarks.

"*Oui!*" Martine sang, voice echoing up to the ceiling frescos.

They all stepped over the body like it was a sack of potatoes, and I followed them out into the church. We emerged beneath the crucifix of Jesus. Despite the cathedral not having reopened since the Storm, a single candle was lit aside the holy table. In the darkness, the stained glass windows glowed, backlit by the moon, and the white eyes of the statues seemed to follow over my shoulders as we crept down the altar—Saints Peter and Paul on either side, and three angelic blonde women gazing down from above.

"Faith, Hope, and Charity, the three virtues," Gabriel said, catching my gaze.

I couldn't decide if they were comforting or creepy. Martine's

French hymn filled the domed ceiling, and the dramatic mezzanine archways that ran the length of the church suddenly felt more like the second tier of an opera house.

We paused at the edge of the altar steps, gazing out into the cavernous space. Nicco nodded to a shadowy object at least ten feet tall in the center of the room; it seemed to be growing out of the black and white marble floor like an invasive tree. It glowed with candles, and the wide center aisle was dotted with a path of tiny flames. His brothers peeled off to opposite side aisles, as if we needed to surround it as we approached. Even as they dunked their fingers into the basins of holy water and blessed themselves with the sign of the cross—I guess some habits die hard—their focus never left the structure.

Lisette and I hopped down the steps, following Nicco down the center aisle, the creepy-factor multiplying tenfold in the flickering shadows. The looming structure felt like some kind of evil Jack-in-the-box that Jakome himself might pop out of.

The supernatural sensation was dizzying, just like the first time I'd met Callis.

As we passed the rows of pews, I realized the flickering lights on the floor came not from candles but tiny, hovering flames, just like the ones the Brute had used to light the cemetery path. My stomach churned. *My flames.*

I commanded one to rise, trying to pull it from the floor, to no avail. Nicco turned my way as if he could sense my strain, but I stared straight ahead. The Ghost Drinkers might have taken my Fire, but my hatred for the Salazars burned brighter than ever. I was going to get my Fire back, whether Emilio thought it was possible or not.

As we came into the light, Nicco held out his hand, stopping us. "Don't break the circle."

On the floor, a ring of black salt encircled the structure. We edged around it to the other side, where Gabriel and Emilio were gazing up.

"*Très bien,* Martine," Nicco said. "*Très bien.*"

The shrine stood directly under a beam of moonlight shining through a large stained glass window above the choir loft. It looked holy, but definitely not of the Catholic variety. The shrine was centered around a tall tree stump, from whom a man had been carved in exquisite detail. He had a likeness to Callisto, but with longer hair, a thicker jaw, and a pointed beard. It was piled high with foliage and golden chalices overflowing with offerings: coins, chains, and bottles of perfume. Bread and cakes and wine. A coat of arms was carved into a piece of driftwood, featuring the pillar of a fortress. The burning candles immortalized the monstrosity in drips of wax.

"Martine?" Emilio's voice echoed in the vast empty space. "You didn't think to bring this up sooner?"

She ignored him, twirling, singing louder to the ghosts in the mezzanine.

"How was she supposed to know?" Lisette said. "She's not a witch."

"That little bastard," Gabriel muttered.

"I guess the Illargui ritual wasn't the only spell they were harnessing the Flower Moon for," Nicco answered.

"Who's Illargui?" I asked.

"The Basque lunar goddess," Gabriel answered.

"Why would he need more power tonight?" I twirled a lock of hair around my finger. "They caught us totally off guard with the swarm of souls."

"This shrine isn't about tonight," Emilio said. "Tonight was a mere battle."

Nicco nodded. "And they are already planning the next."

I stared down at a scroll of paper with **JAKOME SALAZAR** inscribed across the top. Next to it rested an athame. The words were written in an unfamiliar language.

"It's Old Basque," Gabriel explained. "A devotion."

Emilio squatted, getting as close as he could without

touching it. "Written in blood."

"Not just blood," Nicco said. "Blood magic."

"What does that mean?" I asked, feeling like the only one who didn't know.

"It could mean a variety of things." Lisette folded her arms. "None of them good. All of them dark."

"The spirits of our ancestors are only as powerful as we are. And we, they." Nicco circled the shrine, examining the detail. "Through the bloodline, our ancestors fuel our magic; and through our devotion to them and our practice, we keep them and the magicline strong. It's a symbiotic relationship. If I know Callisto and Celestina Salazar, this is no simple devotion. They've been honoring their dead since the moment they had enough magic to do so—when they stole Adele's Fire and bound their coven."

So not only did I give Callisto power, but I gave it to the spirits of all of his asshole ancestors too?

"It seems risky, so close to you and to the other witches," I said. "Why would they do this here? Why not on their territory?"

Emilio cracked his knuckles in a way that made me think he might go after them right this second. "The energy is stronger here. The Vieux Carré is built upon a city of dead."

"In the case of the Salazars," Nicco said, "I can guarantee that their Blood magic means one thing."

All three brothers spoke simultaneously: "Necromancy."

A shiver crept up my spine.

"This is the oldest cathedral in the country." Nicco's gaze traveled up to the crucifix high above the altar. "Callisto built the shrine here because he wants to be seen as divine. Worshipped. Idolized. They are obsessed with immortality—and with bringing back the dead."

"The Salazars have always wanted to play gods, and now they think they will be ones," Emilio said.

Again, Nicco nodded with his brother. It was so strange seeing them in such agreement. "They're not just trying to give strength to their ancestors. Callisto is going to try to resurrect Jakome."

"The very thing they were excommunicated from the witching world for all those centuries ago," Gabriel finished.

A candle flame popped, and we all turned toward Jakome's face. "You can't be serious," I said. "Bringing back the dead? Isn't that just some seventeenth-century we-don't-know-enough-about-the-world-yet-so-we-think-anything's-still-possible kind of thinking?"

"It's magic, Adele, not science," Gabriel said.

Emilio stroked his chin. "Why stop at Jakome? The Basque Salazars are one of the oldest witching families in the history of the magical world. They can trace their power back even further than we can—"

"Don't let Father hear you say that," Gabriel said.

"Who is to stop them from going even further up their ancestral tree?" Emilio asked. "All the way back to the first Salazars? They could take over the entire witching world."

Rage crackled inside me like burning tinder. The brass chandeliers overhead began to tremble. "Callis Salazar is not going to use *my* magic to destroy the magical world." The fixtures creaked, swinging back and forth. I envisioned the Quarter engulfed in flames and whipped my hand, ripping a chandelier from the ceiling, hurtling it toward the shrine.

Nicco leapt out, arms extended, catching it just before his toes crunched the salt circle.

I snapped back to reality, and the anger released.

He set the chandelier gently on the marble floor. "As satisfying as it would be to smash the pretty little Salazar shrine to bits, let's not give Callis the satisfaction of knowing that we are on to him." His eyes were shining rather than scolding. He turned to his family. "We've seen enough here."

I snapped a photo of the shrine, suppressing the overwhelming urge to send it to Dee and Codi so they could show it to their parents. They needed to know, but I couldn't tell them where I was, what I was doing. They couldn't come to Guinée. I'd send the message right before we crossed over.

"We should burn down the building," Emilio said as we headed back up the aisle toward Jesus.

"We are not burning down the oldest cathedral in the country," I said.

"It's really not *that* old."

"No," I said emphatically as I stepped over the dead Ghost Drinker lying in the dark.

"He still has a pulse," Nicco said in a way that implied instruction.

Emilio stooped to gather up the body, slung him over his shoulder, and zoomed off.

As we approached the house, Gabriel paused to stare up at the barely visible cloak of magic emitting from the hexenspiegel.

"What?" I asked, catching the slight curl of his lip.

"Something's wrong with that spell. The magic is weak."

"It's the gesture that matters," Nicco said.

I felt the Brute's arm pressing into my back as he unhooked his belt, and I snapped. "There is nothing weak about that spell."

They both turned to me.

"I didn't mean any offense," Gabriel said. "Just calling it like I see it."

"And I am telling you, there is *nothing* weak about the Daures' magic."

"I'm sure they're a fine family." He held the door open for me and the girls.

Nicco took one last look back at the hexenspiegel and followed us in.

We settled back in the dining room. Nicco leaned over the table, arms spread wide, deep in thought.

"We're running out of time," I said. "We need to figure out how to speed up the spell and get to Guinée."

Emilio rejoined us sans Ghost Drinker. "So, do you think we'll be invited to Jakome's welcome home party?" he asked.

"They're not going to resurrect Jakome, because we're going to kill him," Nicco answered. Then, as if still in a daze, he picked up one of the marble chess pieces and placed it at Holt Cemetery. "Maybe we don't need seven nights to get to Guinée . . ." He slid two more over to St. Patrick's and Cypress Grove. "Seven gates. Seven tombs. Seven *witches*. We split up and each open one gate at the same time, under the same moon."

"The Flower Moon." I swore I could feel the crackle of magic in my palms.

"Seven witches," Emilio said, turning to me. "Guess you'd better call your boyfriend."

"He's not my boyfriend," I practically spat.

He tickled my shoulder. "Something tells me you could still get him to come."

"Your coven—" Lisette started to say.

"*No.* My friends can't come with us. It's too dangerous." Another bang came from overhead, shaking the Venetian chandelier, and everyone looked up. "We'll take the two swamp witches," I said, "That's five of us and two of them. That is how you did the location spell, right?"

"That was different," Emilio said. "They cooperated only under duress."

"Well, I guess you'll have to conjure up some duress."

He raised an eyebrow to me. "I'm in," he said beneath the cool stare.

"You have four of us," Gabriel said. "I just spent three centuries locked in an attic. I am *not* risking getting stuck in the Afterworld." He turned and left the room at vampiric speed.

"Gabriel!" Before I could go after him, Nicco came up behind, arms circling me.

He rested his face on my head. "Let me work on him. Figure out anything else we need for the trip. We have to leave soon."

"*D'accord.*"

I couldn't help but lean back into his arms for a moment, breathing in his leather and soap scent.

"You know this would be a lot safer with your coven, right?" he asked.

My spine tightened.

"I know you don't want to put them in danger, but if something goes wrong on this trip and Callisto is tipped off, it's going to be that much harder to save your father. Everyone will be in more jeopardy, including your friends."

The harsh reality plowed over me.

A chime sounded, followed by a pounding from the front door. Emilio looked at me, and once again, I shrugged.

This time it was Lisette who opened the door as the rest of us waited on the balcony.

Before she could announce the visitor, Désirée barged past her. I ran down the steps as she yelled up to me. "I know what you're up to!"

I stopped right in front of her, energy reeling through my limbs.

She was furious. But beneath the anger in her eyes I could see the concern. The love. I also knew that if the situation were reversed and Ritha was in trouble, I'd never let her go without me. It was a split-second decision. I had to save my dad. Dee knew more about the lwa than all of us combined—this was definitely her territory. "We're going to Guinée to break the Salazar magical line."

Her eyes lit up. Whether it was with shock or excitement, I wasn't quite sure, but I knew she didn't need me to sugarcoat things. Before I could elaborate on the plan, the door opened wider, and Codi gazed upon me with a look of confusion, and right behind him . . . Isaac.

CHAPTER 9
SEI STREGHE

What does she mean, break the Salazar magical line? My nerves crackled like live wires as we stepped into the Medici foyer. They were all here. And all eyes were on me except for Adele's.

Gabe and Martine were gazing down from the mezzanine. Emilio—who I hadn't seen since that night in the park—was sitting near the bottom of the staircase with an expression that said he hoped some shit was about to go down. *That lunatic almost killed me.* And Nicco stood a couple steps behind him, hands casually in his pockets. Like there was anything fucking casual about Nicco Medici.

Aside from now wearing shoes, Adele looked exactly the same as when we'd parted, which was comforting. I'd half expected to see her wrapped in Nicco's clothes, sporting shiny new fangs.

As Codi and I walked by, Lisette whispered, "*Isaac*, this probably isn't the best time—"

Nicco, still watching me approach, pulled his hands from his pockets and moved to Adele's side. He stood shoulder to shoulder with her, as if they were some kind of unified force. It was a power move. "We're going to Guinée," he told us.

I took a deep breath, waiting for him to hold her hand and tell us this was also a surprise destination wedding, and they were getting married there in an ancient witch tradition.

"To kill Jakome Salazar."

What the fuck?

"Whoa," Codi said. Even Désirée seemed a little taken back.

Nicco looked straight at me, waiting for a reaction, and my heart pounded so hard I swear I could feel every spirit who'd ever passed through the Quarter. *What does this have to do with saving Mac?*

"Why do I know that name?" Codi asked. "Jakome."

"From the flashbacks." Adele held up the ring. "Callis's father is the tie that binds him to his magic. If we break it, the Ghost Drinkers will be weak enough to overpower—"

"And get Mac back," Nicco finished.

Désirée looked strangely conflicted. "That's . . . kind of genius, and kind of terrifying."

It's fucking insane is what it is. Of course, now that Adele came to him, Nicco has a plan to save Mac. "Should have known this was your idea," I muttered at him.

Adele whipped my way. "It was my idea! Nicco is graciously helping me, despite the potential perils."

"It was your idea to *kill* someone?"

"A ghost. The spirit of one of the most dangerous witches who ever lived. Whose son *has my father*." Something in her eyes had changed, and it scared me. The Adele I knew could never be so brazen about killing even a mouse.

Emilio hopped down the stairs. "Since when are you so sensitive to killing?" he asked me.

I glanced at Adele. How could he bring up this shit in front of her? In a flash of memories, I saw the blood everywhere, and her body, limp in Brigitte's arms.

"Is a vampire not more alive to you than a ghost?" Emilio continued, fangs visible.

"Ghosts aren't predators by nature, last time I checked." My Air rippled around the room.

Lisette brushed up to my side as he came toward me. One more step, and I was pulling the stake from my boot, but Nicco slapped his brother's shoulder with a firm grip, holding him in place.

Codi stepped up to my other side, trying to be casual. "Destroying a magical bloodline . . . that's intense. Like, against all witch codes forever and always."

The tension in the room de-escalated, but Adele's gaze remained fixed on me. "Nothing's forever." The tone in her voice was chilling.

I felt like I'd broken her. Broken us. Broken the coven.

The surge of emotion welled up again. I wanted to wrap my arms around her so badly. To comfort her. To tell her how sorry I was.

"We also have reason to believe," Nicco said, quickly regaining control of the room, "that Callisto has reignited his passion for necromancy. So, it's really just a matter of who gets to his father first: him or us."

"Whoa, whoa, *whoa*," Codi said.

Adele pulled out her phone.

"The Salazars are necromancers?" Dee asked in disbelief.

"Not successfully. But then again, they never had this much power before."

All three of our phones buzzed. Adele had sent us something.

Lisette leaned closer as I opened the photo. "It's an ancestral shrine, anointed with Blood magic."

"Has it ever even been done before?" Dee's eyes bugged as she zoomed in on the image. "Destroying a magical bloodline, not necromancy."

"Not that I'm aware of. It's unthinkable. For a witch to so

permanently obliterate another family's legacy." Nicco turned to Adele. "It's why they'll never see it coming."

Why do they keep looking at each other like that?

"I got the rest of the directions to Guinée from Ren," she said to us.

The insane scribblings of a madman. That was who we were relying on for instructions on how to not accidentally rip a tear between the worlds or some crazy shit like that.

"If we each take a gate, we might be able to get to Guinée tonight," she continued.

"Tonight's a powerful night in the cemeteries," Désirée said.

Wait, is she fucking serious? She can't actually be considering this.

"*Mangé-les-morts,*" Nicco said.

Codi turned to Dee, confused. "What's that?"

"In Voodoo tradition, on April 31, we go to the cemeteries with a feast for the dead. It's a whole thing. My family went out earlier."

"Why didn't you go?"

She quickly looked at him. "I, um, your parents were going to so much trouble for Hexennacht, I wanted to check it out." *Right, that's all it was.* She turned back to Nicco. "It's hard to believe it's a coincidence that Callis chose tonight to strike."

"Indeed."

She stepped up to Adele. "Seven gates, so seven witches?"

Adele smiled just a tiny bit. "Some might even think a coven."

No, covens are for witches.

"I'm in."

What? Who's running headfirst into danger, now?

Hope flickered behind Adele's eyes. "Really?" She pulled Désirée into a hug. "*Merci beaucoup.*"

Jakome Salazar was the Medici's enemy. How did they con Adele into thinking this murder-trip was about Mac?

"You can thank the Ghede," Dee said, regaining her preferred full arm's length distance. "I bet the members of the original Casquette Girls Coven can help us when we get there."

Nicco's back stiffened at the mention of the original coven, and I had a hunch it had something to do with Adeline Saint-Germain. A part of me wanted to flat-out ask him, but the rest of me didn't want to piss off Adele.

"So, who else is going?" Dee asked.

Lisette and Emilio both showed their hands. Five out of seven.

I ran my sweaty palms through my hair. The *one* thing I hadn't worried about tonight was this insane plan. *I am not going to the goddamn Afterworld.*

Suddenly all eyes were on Codi. Especially Dee's.

Come on, man, she already likes you—you don't have to go to the Afterworld. "I mean . . . we're still going to take the souls, right? There are hundreds of them in the tearoom. If just one escapes, it could mean—"

"*Oui, oui,*" Adele said. "It's way too dangerous to hold them at the tearoom. And they deserve a proper place to rest. We save the souls. We save the city from the Ghost Drinkers. And we save my dad." Her gaze landed straight on me, the last word a bullet to my chest.

"Okay," Codi said. "I'll do it. We have to get those orbs away from my family. There are kids there, for God's sake."

Adele turned to Nicco. "Well, now we don't have to bring the succubi."

What does that mean?

He leaned closer. "I know you're worried about them, but it's for the best." His hand lingered on her hip for just a moment longer than casual.

"We still need one more," Lisette said.

"No, we don't," Adele snipped. "Gabe is seven."

Wait, she isn't even going to ask me? I tried to convince myself that it was because she knew I didn't want to. Because she cared.

"*Non, je n'y vais pas.*" Gabriel leaned over the rails. "What language do you need me to say it in?"

The only person here with a brain.

Adele's jaws locked. *She really hates me that much?* Codi nudged at me like I should say something, but for once in my life I didn't have anything to say. I couldn't believe she didn't want me to go.

"Wait a second," Dee said. "I don't want to go anywhere without Isaac. This is going to be dangerous; we're stronger together. We're bound together."

Adele didn't flinch, but I knew what she was thinking: *We're bound together in perfect love and perfect trust.* I'd broken her trust. I deserved this. But I wished she knew how much I loved her.

Nicco leaned closer to her with a whisper. "Think about your dad."

She looked straight at me, her expression back to ice. "Well? Are you coming?"

My heart walloped so hard, I saw double. "Yeah . . . of course."

There was nothing I wouldn't do for her. Or for Mac.

"*Benvenuti.*" Nicco clapped his hands together. "We're set up in the dining room."

He and Adele led the way, and the rest of us followed them up to the second floor. It was the deepest I'd ever been in the Medici residence.

How the hell did we get here? As I passed a gilded mirror over the parlor fireplace, I caught my reflection and got my answer. We were here because of me. If I'd just woken Adele up, she wouldn't be in this desperate situation.

I fucked up, and now we all had to pay the price.

One thing was clear—before we left on this trip, I had to tell her everything I'd done. I couldn't let her find out from someone else. That is, if she hadn't heard already. But getting her alone was going to be tough, considering she wouldn't even look at me.

In the dining room, I took the spot at the far end of the table, hoping to warm up from the fireplace and be as far away from Emilio as possible. The elegant dining room looked like a war room. While we'd been dealing with the ramifications of the Ghost Drinkers, the Medici hadn't been slacking.

"We don't have a lot of time," Adele said, standing alongside Nicco. "We need to make a plan and go."

"Agreed," Désirée said, retrieving highlighters and a pad of sticky notes from her bag. "But we need to be meticulous. We don't want to take a wrong turn or not seal the portal, leaving our ancestors unprotected or our *ti bon ange* vulnerable."

"Our what?" I asked.

"Remember, the little clay pot I had in St. Roch, for my little soul?"

"Uh, kind of."

"In Voodoo tradition, every person has two parts to the soul. *Gros bon ange*, the big angel, and *ti bon ange*, the little angel. The little angel is kind of like your self-consciousness. When working with the lwa, part of your *ti bon ange* has to leave for a little while to make room for the lwa. Hence the little jar. We need to make sure they are kept safe."

"Wait, what are you saying? We all have to be a cheval to a Ghede to cross over?"

"I've never been to the Afterworld. I don't know how it works."

"But we have to leave part of our soul behind in a little jar? In a cemetery, the place where our enemies look for dinner?"

"Which is why I am saying we need to be *careful*."

"So, when we're on the other side, we'll only be part of ourselves?"

"I don't know, Isaac! When the Ghede come to the Natural World, they need the body of a witch as a vessel."

Lisette twirled her hair. "So they'll be our cheval once we're there?"

"I thought the Ghede were just opening the gates?" Codi said.

"Maybe." Désirée inhaled deeply through her nose. "I don't know."

My voice rose. "Does anyone know anything about this trip?"

Gabriel ran his hands down his face.

"Look," Nicco said calmly, "there are more unknowns than anyone would like, so we'll take all possible precautions, magical and otherwise. But if you don't want to go, speak now."

Everyone looked at me.

"What?" I mumbled. "I was just asking questions."

"A reasonable man," Gabriel said.

"The seven cemeteries are all protected," Adele said. "No one will be able to get to our souls."

How can she be so blasé, learning her soul is going to be split!

When she got no further complaint, she turned the map sideways so the three of us had a better view. "Here are the gates, the Ghede, and the keys."

"I still can't believe I missed the Baron's vèvè," Désirée said.

I wished I had.

"The eye of an artist," Adele said without glancing my way, leaving me trying to comprehend how I wasn't standing next to her and she wasn't looking up lovingly at me while she said it.

"So it looks like we need a mirror and a poppy for Doubye and L'Oraille?" Désirée opened up her grimoire. "I'll make a list."

"You can probably find opium in the house, if you look hard enough," Gabriel said.

"*Jesus,*" Codi said.

He shrugged. "It was the 1720s."

"Actually." Dee uncapped a pen. "That sounds right up the Ghede's alley."

I looked at her. "Do I have to remind you that you smoked a cigarette the last time we called on the Ghede?"

She snapped her fingers. "No opium."

"My Aunt Fiona uses poppies in her 'special' tonics. We can probably get some fresh cuttings from the garden."

"Great," Adele said as Désirée furiously scribbled Ren's directions into her grimoire. Suddenly I was struck with panic. *Susannah's grimoire.* But then the book appeared before my face. I guess Adele and I had had the same thought.

"Sorry," she said. "I forgot it was in my bag, or I would have given it back to you at HQ."

"Thanks." But what had she meant by that? Like she'd have given it back because it was mine or because she was giving all of my stuff back? She wasn't wearing the feather. She hadn't been wearing her usual jewelry all night. Other than the little constellation necklace. I'd taken it off when we'd—

"So, what do you know about these Ghede?" Nicco asked Désirée.

"Glad you asked." She laid her grimoire flat on the table. "We need to be thoughtful about who calls on which Ghede. They are the gatekeepers, after all, and we don't need any wild personality clashes." She looked at Emilio.

"You don't think diplomacy is my strong suit?" he asked.

"*No*, I don't."

The title ***The Gates of Guinée*** sprawled across the top of the double-page spread, and Baron Samedi and Maman Brigit's skeletal figures in Victorian funeral clothes had been drawn down the sides of each page. A massive list of Ghede, compiled by generations of witches, was inscribed between them. She'd highlighted a few. "There are hundreds of Ghede, but the seven we need to focus on are Plumaj, Masaka, Oussou, Zaranye,

Nibo, Doubye, and L'Oraille. Two of whom we've had personal experience with."

Codi leaned my way. "I'm not sure if that's a good thing or a bad thing."

"I guess that depends on how you feel about dry-humping me."

Désirée cleared her throat. "Let me know if a certain Ghede calls to you. After everyone is matched, study your Ghede so you have some idea on how to best serve them." She flipped through the pages searching for our seven. "Nibo comes as the spirit of a beautiful young man who was killed violently, so he's a special patron to those who die young. He's the Baron's right hand, like his first-born child. Caretaker of the graves. Effeminate. When he inhabits humans . . . *hmm.*"

"What?" Codi asked.

"He's inspired to lascivious sexuality of all kinds."

Gabriel's arms circled Lisette's waist as he kissed the crook of her neck. "Maybe I need to reconsider this voyage."

Ugh. As her Maker, does he force her to . . . be with him?

She blushed a little but didn't push him away.

"His key is an axe," Adele added.

Jesus Christ. I can't believe we're playing Ghede matchmaker.

I went to grab the pencil from behind my ear, but nothing was there. I felt like a dipshit and awkwardly messed with my hair instead.

Désirée moved on to Masaka, and I imagined Nicco kissing the crook of Adele's neck, his arms circling tighter around her, his teeth sinking into her flesh. I didn't even realize I'd gotten up until I was pacing.

"Masaka's an androgynous grave digger. Carries a shovel. Sometimes depicted as Nibo's assistant. Sometimes his lover."

"Night blossoms are his key." Adele turned to Codi. Her voice felt a million miles away. "Doesn't Edgar have a whole night-garden in the tearoom courtyard?"

"Yup, we've got oils, spritzes, tonics, you name it."

I paced faster. I still couldn't believe this was really happening.

Adele asked Nicco something in French, and I regretted the eight years of Spanish I'd taken in school. He nodded, giving her a curious look, then darted out of the room.

Why couldn't she just ask it in English? I continued pacing.

"Oussou's name means 'tipsy' due to his love of white rum and tobacco."

"Guess that explains why his key is a pipe," Adele said, fishing through her bag until she procured a pencil.

Nicco came back and handed her a notebook. She'd used French to ask him for office supplies?

I strode past the fireplace again, and when I turned back, she was standing right in front of me. I stumbled to a stop. "Hey."

Without a word, she held out the notebook and the pencil. Her expression was somewhere between empathy and aggravation, but either way, it read, *Please calm the fuck down.*

I sat at the table, my foot tapping mercilessly against the floor.

Are they my parents now? I opened the leather-bound book. It had the thickest, most luxurious paper I'd ever felt. Of course it did. It was Niccolò Medici's. Only the best of the best of the best.

I tried to tell myself that it was an act of kindness, that she knew how anxious the Afterworld made me . . . but I just wanted to stab the pencil into the sketchbook and rip it apart.

Even with the rage building inside, my fingers pushed the pencil around the page. I absentmindedly sketched out a pair of eyes as Désirée went on about Ghede-L'Oraille being a badass storm bringer. The keeper of the dead at sea.

"She has a sweet lightning bolt," Codi said, reading over her shoulder.

At first, I didn't have any intention with the sketch, but soon her face began to emerge from the page. The more detailed the sketch became, the more my blood pressure dropped. Adele had been spot-on about how to get me to calm down, and it made my heart ache.

I shaded the ringlets of her hair, listening to them talk about Ghede-Doubye, who collected keys and could give her cheval the gift of clairvoyance; and about Ghede-Zaranye, whose name meant spider and who represented the spirit of the first human soul to became a Ghede lwa. I shaded the folds of her dress, trying to suppress the growing tremors induced by all the talk of the Afterworld.

A shadow cast over the page as someone loomed over my shoulder. "The resemblance is absolutely uncanny," Gabriel said.

"*Sensationnel.*" Lisette leaned over my other shoulder. "*Elle est parfaite.*" She pulled the sketchbook out of my hand and passed it down the table.

Codi and Dee were engrossed in Dee's grimoire and passed it on to Martine without looking. She gasped. "My little muffin!"

Emilio took it from her. "I wouldn't say she tasted like a muffin. More like *un croque-en-bouche*, deceivingly sweet on the outside, rich and creamy on the inside." I flinched as a candlestick flew across the table, which he caught with the snap of his hand. "She locked you away for three hundred years, but you're still testy about my little bite, brother?"

All heads turned to Gabe.

"*Tu es un porc,*" Adele spat.

Emilio smiled, leaning back in his chair, and put his feet up on the table. "I've been called worse, even by you."

Nicco slid the sketchbook over with curiosity. Adele hardly gave it a glance, maybe because she wanted to forget Adeline's warnings, but Nicco's gaze lingered on the drawing, and before he caught himself, I saw the flicker in his eyes . . . fear.

Why does the portrait of a sixteen-year-old girl, dead for so many centuries, make you so jumpy, Nicco? For the first time, I wanted to go to Guinée. I needed to talk to Adeline Saint-Germain. I needed to know why she so desperately wanted Adele to stay away from Nicco. My witch's intuition told me it had nothing to do with him being a vampire, and everything to do with him being a Medici.

"And those are the seven Ghede," Désirée said, finally looking up from her grimoire. No one responded. "Did I miss something?"

"No." Adele slammed the sketchbook closed and slid it back to me without a glance.

Shit. I didn't mean to piss her off with the portrait. I wasn't even the one who'd passed it around!

She stood. "Moving on. Anyone have any preferences?"

Codi stretched his arms long. "I feel like me and Oussou are already tight, even though he did make me . . . dance a lot."

"Is that what you call that?" I asked.

Dee struggled not to laugh. "The Ghede don't make you do anything. They just bring out desires you already have."

"Codi's got some pretty big desires," I said, unable to help myself.

Dee bit her lip.

Adele grabbed a rook and placed it at one of the Northern-most gates. "Codi at St. Patrick's with a pipe for Ghede-Oussou."

"Isaac, you should take St. Roch since you're so intimately familiar with it," Désirée said.

"More like so scarred for life by it. Whatever. Just not Plumaj. We all know how that worked out last time."

Adele picked up the white knight and moved it across the map. "Isaac at St. Roch with a mirror for Ghede-Doubye."

I reached for Dee's grimoire and flipped the pages to get a look at Doubye. Her long lavender-colored hair flowed from under a tiara of skeleton keys, and she wore a necklace of . . . "Are those teeth?"

"Human teeth," Désirée confirmed.

I shuddered, scanning the map for the closest cemetery to St. Roch and found St. Louis No 1. "Adele, your family's tomb is at St. Louis, so your magic will be stronger there."

She glanced toward the cemetery, and her face paled. *Shit. What happened there?*

"Actually, since I *can't leave* the French Quarter," Lisette said, "I should take St. Louis."

I turned to her. "What do you mean you can't le—?"

Adele kicked me under the table *hard*.

Shit, what was that for?

"You should take St. Louis, Lisette." She moved a bishop to the French Quarter cemetery. "Are you scared of spiders?"

"I'm a vampire."

"Lisette at St. Louis with rings for Ghede-Zaranye."

"I'll take Valence," Nicco said, studying the map. "It's the furthest away from the French Quarter's protection shields, and I can get to it quickly."

Good. Valence was on the far opposite end from me.

Adele moved the black knight across the map. He looked at her playfully. *"Pourquoi est-ce que dois toujours être le chevalier noir?"*

Lisette and Codi both snorted. *Ugh. Codi speaks French, too?*

"Nicco at Valence," Adele said, suppressing a smile.

"With poppies for the storm-bringer," he finished.

"I suppose you've always had a thing for lightning." Her eyes flicked to his. Gabriel and Emilio also exchanged looks. "I'll take Lafayette and bring the axe for Ghede-Nibo." She grabbed the nearest pawn and put it on the board. Of course it was the closest cemetery to his. He removed the pawn and replaced it with a queen. She blushed.

For Christ's sake. It was like they'd done a hundred years of bonding in a couple of hours.

"Dee, maybe you could take Holt?" Codi suggested.

She gave him a look. "Oh, I get the pauper's cemetery cause I'm the only Black witch here?"

"*What? No.* I didn't even know that— It's the closest to St. Patrick's, and I thought we could drive together."

"I'm just messing with you. Glad to take Holt; it's near Bayou St. John, so you know the juju is strong."

"Yeah, that's totally what I was thinking too."

Adele moved the black queen to Holt. "Dee at Holt with?"

"Night blossoms for Masaka. We've already established a deep connection; I'm going to lean into it."

"That puts Emilio at Cypress Grove with a feather for Plumaj."

"Otherwise known as The Soul Catcher," Dee said.

Emilio smirked. "I'd like to see her try to catch my soul."

You have a soul?

Désirée closed her grimoire. "I wouldn't challenge a lwa, but you do you, boo."

Adele pulled her bag from the chair, the urgency coming back to her voice. "All right, let's split up to collect the keys and anything else we might need. We'll meet back here in an hour and head out."

Emilio cleared his throat. "Aren't you forgetting a very important part of this plan?"

"*Cosa?*" she asked.

"You do realize you can't just kill Jakome Salazar with an incantation? And forging a weapon that could kill the ghost of one of the Greatest witches who ever lived is a little above your magical grade."

"Will this do?" She placed a giant stick on the table. Huge rose quartz crystals had been adhered to each end like a double-sided spear. I'd never seen anything like it. It was beautiful.

Nicco picked it up. "A Schattengeist. The craftsmanship is remarkable."

Emilio looked at her again. "I guess you have thought of everything, little lamb."

"Adele!" Codi gawked at the stick. "Is that . . . ?"

"I know! I'm sorry!"

"That's why you were at the tearoom!"

"I left an I.O.U."

"My dad's gonna kill me."

"We'll bring it back in one piece, I swear."

He folded his arms over his head. "I guess this isn't entirely different than one of his ghost-hunting trips."

"Yeah," I said, "except that it requires leaving the Natural World."

"Details." Dee zipped her bag shut.

Adele looked at Codi meekly. "*Merci beaucoup.*"

CHAPTER 10
CRÈME LAVANDE

As I packed up the ghoststick, Nicco hooked his arm around Gabriel's neck and they walked out the door, speaking in Italian. I felt like a loser not wanting him to leave the room without me, but I could tell Isaac wanted to talk, and I knew he wouldn't approach me if Nicco was still here. Actually, he probably would.

I quickly rolled up the map as he inched his way over from Lisette.

Dee strapped on her bag. "Isaac, let's walk Codi home and then go back to the shop for supplies."

"Uh, I'll catch up." He pushed his hair behind his ears like he always did when he was nervous. Dee and Codi both gave him looks telling him what he was trying wasn't a good idea, but Isaac didn't heed their advice. Could this be any more awkward?

Codi sighed as he walked out the door with Dee. "Hey, Lisette, what kind of rings do you want for Zaranye?"

Codi!

"Definitely silver," she said, following them out, leaving just the two of us.

"Can I talk to you for a minute?"

Do I have any choice? I couldn't even look at him.

"I need to tell you something. Some things." He squeezed his hands as they began to shake.

"Tell me what?" A surge of rage expelled from my body. "How you gave Callis's ring to the Medici?" His face fell. "How you lied to me about knowing where Nicco was? How you *left me* when I was sleeping, and then gave me a statue of my dead mother to distract me from Nicco!" My eyes welled.

"That's not why—!"

"You lied to me." I gasped. "And you kissed me. And we . . ."

"I'm so sorry."

"My dad." I gasped again.

"Adele, breathe."

"Don't tell me to breathe. Don't tell me anything ever again!" I barged past him.

"Adele, I'm sorry!"

He rushed after me through the parlors. I had to stop at the mezzanine to catch my breath. I couldn't go downstairs; I didn't want the others to see me like this.

"Adele, I never meant to hurt you. Or anyone." His hand grazed my waist. Fractals of light exploded behind my eyes. The Brute's voice in my head: *"I thought you wanted to play rough?"* I jolted forward, slamming into the railing. *"See, she knows how to behave."*

Isaac pulled back in shock. "I-I'm sorry. I shouldn't have touched you." His voice cracked. "How could I already repulse you this much? I love you."

I flipped around "Maybe it isn't about you, Isaac! Maybe everything isn't—!" I froze in horror. Gabe and Nicco were standing in the corner, both staring at my waist where Isaac had touched me, brows pinched in concern.

Isaac's eyes grew big as he turned around.

Gabe shook his head at him.

"I didn't mean—" I started to say.

But he dove into the air and swooped away.

Neither of the Medici brothers took their eyes off me, and I twisted back around, clutching the rail. I stuffed the memory down, entombing it in one of the dark, dank mausoleums in the cemetery. I covered it with floral wreaths and candles, locked the little iron gate around it, but no matter how deep I mentally buried it, I could still feel the Brute's hands on my body.

Nicco slid down next to me on the banister. My eyes slipped shut. *I don't want to talk about it.* I didn't owe him or anyone else a fucking explanation.

"Do you want to go to your house and get the axe?" he asked.

The banal question made my pulse stop racing. I looked at him. "*Sì.*"

"You could clean up if you'd like." He very cautiously brushed a matted lock of hair from my face. "Not that there's anything wrong with the mud-caked look. If we were in London or Los Angeles, I'm sure all the girls would copy you."

I cracked a smile.

"Come on," he said, taking my hand. "Let's go."

The moon was still full and bright, shining down on the silent city, but fog was starting to roll in from the river. The air felt even heavier than usual, drenched with scents of magic and the shadows of spells: salt for protection, cinnamon for shielding, and valerian root to ward off enemies. We walked briskly; there wasn't time to dawdle.

When we arrived at the house, I twisted the key into the lock, not wanting to attempt magic in front of Nicco and fail. "Come on in, *s'il vous plaît.*"

He crossed the threshold into the dark house, and I shut the door.

The moon shone through the transom, highlighting his face, and it occurred to me that in all this time, I'd never really invited him over.

"I can wait—" he said.

"For me upstairs." I pulled him along. "I'm sure Mac would make an exception tonight, given the circumstances."

"An exception for what?"

"No guys in my bedroom when he's not home."

"Oh." He laughed, and I swear I saw color in his cheeks.

"Am I making you blush, Niccolò Giovanni Battista Medici?"

"Absolutely not." He chased me the rest of the way up.

My door creaked as I pushed it open, and the reality of bringing Nicco to my bedroom did actually make me a bit lightheaded.

I snapped on the lamp beside my bed and the one in the corner near my vanity. I'd forgotten my room looked like a tornado-wrecked atelier. "I'm— It's not usually this messy." I did a few swoops around the room, scooping up scraps of fabric, ribbon, and interfacing. "I was in a frenzy earlier trying to make a Hexennacht dress for the party."

"You should have seen our place earlier. It looked like a meadow of wildflowers trampled by a stampede."

I shoved it all in a pile in the corner. I almost didn't believe him; he was always so meticulous. But it was fun to imagine him in a panic over sugar cookies.

He meandered to my vanity. The original bodice I'd detached from the dress hung on the mirror. He brushed the sheer gossamer with his knuckle. "I'm sure you look just like a forest nymph in this version."

A wave of heat traipsed up my spine. "Maybe next Floralia."

I was wholly unsure where the words came from, but I held his gaze in the mirror as I said them. I wanted to believe that one day I would be bold enough to wear it, just like the actress who'd played Titania.

Like Maddalena Morosini.

"I'll weave you a flower crown fit for a fairy queen." He gazed at me so unabashedly that I nearly stepped over and wrapped my arms around him. But guilt crept over me like a dark, shadowy monster. Mere hours ago, I'd been lying in Isaac's arms, staring at the stars.

I never should have stopped looking for Nicco. Everything about tonight had been wrong.

He stepped to the wall near the little closet room, perusing the family photos, and I wondered if Adeline was disowning me right now, allowing a Medici so close to her magical hiding spot. I grabbed some clean lingerie from my dresser drawer, hiding the silky fabric in my fists. "Well, make yourself at home. I'll just be a minute."

"Don't worry about me," he said, sitting down on my bed. *At least I'd had the decency to make it this morning.* He lay back, hands cradling his head. "I can occupy myself."

"Undoubtedly," I whispered and escaped into the bathroom.

I leaned against the door. *Niccolò Medici is lying on my bed.* My heart rate went wild. I was hyper-aware that he could hear it. And hyper-aware that he knew he'd caused the spike. I reached for the doorknob and coughed as I clicked the lock. I didn't think he'd come in while I was in the shower, but there was a part of me that wanted him to. And another part of me that was scared I might somehow will it to happen.

I stripped off the denim shorts as the bathroom filled with steam, and any thoughts I was or wasn't having about Nicco quickly dissipated—if I'd had my Fire, I'd have set the shorts ablaze. Every time I looked at them, I saw that asshole's monstrous fingers pushing beneath the frayed edges. I quickly unbuttoned the black shirt, remembering how Mac had insisted I wear it; and just like that, I nearly burst into tears. *Dad, please just hang on.* I kicked the shirt to the corner with the rest of the dirty clothes, catching myself in the mirror. *Jesus.* I looked like someone crawling out of a Bourbon Street gutter at six a.m.

I wiped the glass with the side of my fist like it was the steam distorting my usual reflection. My eyes were bloodshot and— Nicco hadn't been kidding: there was literal mud in my hair. Deep reddish-purple blotches peppered the left side of my torso and arm, although they'd mostly cleared up near my hand where Dee had focused her Spektral. How much pain would I be in once Désirée's magic wore off completely? The steam plumed over the glass, once again obstructing my view. Good. I didn't want to see this battered version of myself.

I cowered as the water pelted the bumps and bruises, but I scrubbed myself nonetheless. I wanted to wash this entire night away, to make it disappear down the drain forever, and to start over beneath the Flower Moon. The scent of my strawberry shampoo filled the air, and I started to feel like myself again. As the hot water soothed my scalp, I didn't think about the atrocities of the night. For a few precious moments, I didn't think about anything at all.

But after I toweled off, wrung out my hair, and put on the fresh undergarments, panic set in. In my rush to discreetly grab lingerie, I'd forgotten something very important. *Clothes.*

I slathered lotion onto my legs, blotted creams onto my face, and blow-dried my hair, putting off exiting the bathroom. Walking out in a towel just seemed so *suggestive.* Butterfly wings beat wildly under my skin.

Jesus, Adele, it's Nicco! He's not going to think— I tightened the towel around my chest. Just as I'd convinced myself to suck it up, I saw the glorious hint of floral-printed satin peeking from beneath the used towels on the back of the door. I ripped it off the hook and slipped it on.

The robe had belonged to my mother. I remembered finding it in the trunk of her things, and how the silky fabric had made me feel sexy when I tried it on. I didn't want to feel sexy now; I just wanted to . . . *Shut up, Adele. Diane Von Furstenberg has made a million wrap dresses that look exactly like this. Nicco probably wouldn't even know the difference.*

I opened the door and walked out. He'd taken off his boots, lain back on the pillows, and was reading the copy of *Beloved* from my nightstand. I'd tied the sash so tightly, I had to suck in so it didn't pinch the bruises on my torso. *Act normal, Adele.* Cool, calm, collected. *I meant to do this, because I am fine parading across the room in front of Nicco in a silk robe. I'm so fine with it, in fact, that I'm going to grab my socks first.* I strode to the dresser, chose a black pair with gold fleur-de-lis, and put them on.

I felt his gaze follow me to the closet. The bed creaked. He shifted onto his side and pushed himself over as if making room for me. The butterfly wings suddenly felt pterodactyl, but I walked over. There was *no way* Nicco would make a move. It was not the time.

He set the book down as I sat on the bed. "Do you feel any better?"

I nodded. "Hopefully I smell better."

"You will always smell like lavender to me."

You'll always smell like leather and soap to me.

"That's how I found you at the river. I followed the scent from the bar."

Note to self: Never *run out of Brigitte's crème lavande.*

He tugged me closer, and I lay down on my side, head on the pillow next to his. The makeshift DvF slid off my leg, and I hurriedly pulled it back into place, but he wasn't looking at my leg. He was looking at . . . my waist. Worriedly. *The place where Isaac touched me. Where . . .*

"What?" I asked.

He replied in French, as if it offered more privacy. "You still haven't told me what happened tonight."

Thump.

"*Que voulez-vous dire?*" I asked back, despite knowing exactly what he meant.

Anxiety built in his brow.

"You already know . . ." I did my best not to let the words catch in my throat. "Callis had my dad tied up when I got to the bar. He would only free him if I walked down to the river with him." I paused. "I'm so stupid. I should have made him let my dad go first."

His arm slid around me. "Adele, your father never would have left your side no matter what bargain you struck." He was right. And Callis would never have agreed to it. Mac had become collateral the moment he'd stepped into the bar. "What else?"

"He tried to get me to join his coven again. He knew about Adeline, and the Count, and how your grimoire went missing when your family was murdered."

He stroked my back through the silk, and I couldn't look at him anymore—these things weren't what he was asking me about. "*Bella,* your bones weren't just broken. They were shattered. Savagely."

My pulse raced. The prod felt very unNiccolike.

"*Bella. Isn't that what he calls you when he wants something?*" How did Callis know so much? Had I really been that predictable? Naïve?

Nicco's gaze fell to my injured hand, and a darkness washed over his face. "I want . . . to know . . . who hurt you."

My eyes pricked, the memory writhing in my head as he

tried to exhume it. I banged it down with the shovel. I heard the witch's spine *crack*, again. And again.

"Why are you protecting your assailant?"

I slid my hand beneath the pillow. "I'm not protecting him," I nearly choked. "I killed him."

Surprise lit his stare. "*Oh*. Adele, I'm sorry."

Tremors quaked through my body, burning my lungs as I tried to hold the emotion in, but his hand grazed my face and the tears shook out.

He scooped me closer. "Adele, I'm so sorry I wasn't there for you." The tears came harder, and he wrapped around me, a strong, unbreakable cocoon. I gripped onto him tighter as I cried. I didn't want to think about it. He spoke gentle Italian I couldn't understand. Eventually, the tremors stopped, and the Brute's voice left my head, and all I heard were the soothing words. I released the vise-grip clutch, but I still couldn't look at him.

He stroked my cheek. "You know, the life of a Ghost Drinker is very, very difficult to take because of their temporary state of immortality."

"I saw it . . . I saw the light go out in his eyes." A latent tear rolled down my face.

He slid it away with his thumb. "If he met death at your hand, then death is what he deserved."

He was so sure. So steady. Just like always.

A wave of serenity washed over me.

He kissed my cheek, soft and lingering, and once again, I shuddered from his touch. *Nicco is a real Fire witch.* As real as I was.

I looked back over my shoulder at him as I buttoned up a pair of fresh black jeans. I no longer cared that he was watching me when I let the robe slink to the floor. The energy in the room had shifted so dramatically, I now found comfort in his watchful eye. Not that it mattered. I could have been stripping naked instead of dressing. His gaze might have been on me, but his mind seemed to be somewhere far away.

I stretched a navy-blue tank over my head and then a long-sleeved black tee. Who knew what the weather would be like in the Afterworld? Layers were probably best. *Layers.*

I scurried to my closet, pushing through the hangers to the very back: Nicco's green and black flannel and his leather jacket. I slipped them both on, taking a second to admire the tailoring of the jacket. I can't believe I'd hurled this thing off the balcony toward the bonfire. *Thank God I have a terrible arm.*

I tied my shit-kickers tightly and crossed the room to my vanity. A little SPF. Tinted ChapStick for protection from the elements. And a little mascara for . . . no reason whatsoever but to make me feel prettier. I pocketed a small pot of purple glitter from last Mardi Gras. Ghede-Nibo likes purple, right? I reached for a spritz of perfume, but then left it alone, breathing in the scent of Brigitte's lavender lotion. I tucked the gris-gris beneath my shirt and, out of habit, picked up my chain. The sight of the silver feather made my blood pressure rise. I unclipped it, tucked it into my jewelry box, and put the necklace on. The sun charm and Adeline's medallion hung loosely down my chest, the constellation at my throat.

I threw some toiletries into a bag along with an extra set of clothes and sat on the bed next to him. "Ready?"

He touched the shirt collar and smiled, coming out of the daze. "It still looks better on you."

"I know," I joked.

He yanked me atop his chest with that not-so-innocent smile. "You know it took me two decades to break this jacket in?"

"My fashion sensibilities thank you for it."

In a swirl, he had us on our feet, and we were out the door.

"One day, I'll take you to the finest leather tailors in Milano," he said as we bounced down the stairs. "You'll never find anything like them elsewhere in the world."

I paused on the last step.

He turned back. "Forget something?"

I lost all impulse control and wrapped my arms around him. "*Grazie*."

"For what?"

"I don't know. For being you." It was the truth. There wasn't a single thing about him that I'd ever change. He held me tight for another breath.

"*Shit*," I said. "The keys for Nibo and Doubye. Wait here." I ran back up to my room. *I can't believe we almost forgot them.* I grabbed the antique hand mirror from my vanity and stuffed it in my bag. As I crossed back to the door a final time, I stopped at my bed and dropped down to the floor, feeling beneath it for the leather diary. I didn't know why—it's not like it was my grimoire—but it made me feel closer to Adeline. It made me feel magical. *You're coming with me too.*

On the way out, we grabbed the axe from my dad's studio, and we were off.

When we got back to the grand foyer at *casa dei Medici*, I didn't know if it was all the lights being on, or that it now smelled like baked goods, or that someone was playing an old phonograph, but it felt lively. A stark contrast from my dark, quiet home. *What if I never hear the screeching of my dad's work tools again? Or him singing David Bowie full volume?*

I pushed the thought aside. I would not let that happen.

Nicco set the axe down next to the umbrella bucket. "There's something I need to do before we go. Are you okay here?"

I bit my lip. "Niccolò Medici, you're letting me stay at your house? With your family. *Without you?*"

He groaned, pulling me closer. "I'm clearly losing my grip on reality. Maybe one of those souls got me tonight."

"Don't say that."

"Don't worry about me, *bella*."

That is never going to be possible.

"All good here." I picked up the axe, swung it over my shoulder, and started for the stairs. "I'll go check on Gabe. Maybe he's not a total lost cause for the mission."

He laughed a little, hand resting on the door. "*Madonna mia,* help him."

CHAPTER 11
BASKET OF SOULS

"Rings, poppies, scent of night blossoms, and a pipe," Désirée listed out as we tiptoed around the frigid tearoom. The lights were off, but the room glowed like an underwater cavern, an ethereal sheen emitting from all the little bottles as if they were filled with billowing jellyfish.

Codi headed behind the counter, and Dee went straight to a cabinet near the front window, where incense was sorted by the lunar calendar.

I paused at the glass shelves, gazing at the glowing orbs. My soul might as well have been bottled up with them. I felt dead inside after the fight with Adele. I'd never be able to forget the feeling of her bolting away. I shuddered, trying not to let the souls' icy energy flood me, but their supernatural pulse quaked through my bloodstream. The floor no longer felt flat, and I toppled, dizzy with the sensation. My arm knocked the shelf, and a bottle clanked to the floor. "*Shit!*" The cork popped, and water sprayed in an arc. The soul plunked out.

"Dude, you're gonna wake up my parents!"

"Codi, soul!" Dee yelled.

I scrambled back as it charged at me like a little demon.

Onyx sprang over the counter, and Codi stood back up by the fountain in the window. He waved his hand, and a splash of Water rippled in front of me. The orb plunged into the magical shield, splashing the Water in my face. It hovered right in front of my nose.

"Thanks," I panted, trying not to have a heart attack. That was way too fucking close.

He spun the Water into a glowing bubble and sent it sailing back into the bottle, and with a snap of her fingers, Dee corked the top.

She looked down at me, a forceful edge to her voice: "Can you please be careful?"

Codi gave me an *oh shit* look.

"You know there is *nothing* I can do for you if you get Possessed?" Emotion built in her throat. "You're gonna end up like Ren!" She tightly crossed her arms and turned back to the incense.

"I'm sorry! I'm not gonna end up like Ren, don't worry!"

She sucked in a deep inhale through her nose.

Codi slapped his hand in mine and pulled me up. "Sorry," I repeated to him.

"No worries. Just be careful. Grab one of my grandpa's pipes off the mantel while I get the rings."

I turned to the fireplace, my thoughts still on Ren. How much longer was he going to be able to hold on? If we reached Guinée, I had to find the miracle man that Masaka and Oussou had told us about. The Ghede were great healers, right? Ren needed a miracle right about now, and I wasn't going to leave the Afterworld until I had one for him. Beneath a dreamcatcher, four hand-whittled wooden animals stared back at me: a rabbit, an owl, a bear, and one that resembled the whittler himself, a panther with its mouth stretched open, forming a bowl to hold the tobacco leaves.

Was Olsin already in Guinée? Did spirits cross over immediately or post-funeral? And which ones stayed behind like Julie?

As I picked up the panther, I closed my eyes and let my Spektral magic release from the depths of my spine. The cold flooded in as my magic wandered through the house. I sensed that Julie was upstairs somewhere. I winced from the cold. *She's in pain.* I shouldn't have left her for so long. The festering rage toward Callis threatened to boil over. *All of this was Callis's fault.* Nicco and his family would still be locked in the attic if he hadn't come to New Orleans.

"Raw or polished stones for Zaranye?" Codi asked, leaning over a tray of jewelry he'd removed from the glass case. "Should I bring eight of the same? Mix it up?" He looked at me, but I had zero input on what kind of jewelry a Ghede lwa would prefer.

"Whatever's shiniest." Désirée plucked several sticks of incense and moved on to the essential oils, which were stacked on a rotating pyramid display. "Moonflower, for sure," she murmured to herself and pulled a small brown bottle. "And I'm thinking evening primrose, gardenia, and wisteria." There was a hint of question in her tone, like she might actually want input.

"Grab the midnight candy too, the jasmine, and the four o'clock." Codi went into more details about their specific magical properties, like a human Wikipedia page.

Midnight candy? I'd never even heard of most of these plants. "Must be nice to be raised under the roof of witches."

"Yeah, that and I'm a botany major."

"You are?" I asked, meeting him at the counter. Désirée echoed the question, and I didn't feel quite so bad. "How did I not know this?"

He laughed and untwisted the cap from a small blue glass bottle. "When do we ever talk about anything normal?" He set a funnel in the neck.

"Truth."

Désirée carried over the oils, set them down on the counter

between them, and began unscrewing the dropper caps. "So you're studying plants?"

He pulled bottles out of a cabinet. "Yeah. Astronomy minor so my parents aren't totally devastated. They really want me to be the first witch in space, but astrophysics is not gonna happen. I have a fear of heights. And a fear of being close to enormous balls of burning gas." It seemed like Désirée wanted to ask something else. When she didn't, he smiled coyly, adding little drops of each essence into the blue bottle. "What did you expect? Oceanography? Nautical engineering? Marine biology?"

Her lips pressed together. "I don't know . . . I guess. Water witch and all."

"I told you that Water and Earth go together."

Her gaze fell to the counter. Was that a blush? Désirée Borges blushed.

Smooth. Very smooth. I had to hand it to him. If she leaned any further over the counter, they'd be touching.

I set the wooden panther down next to them. "Pipe."

"Perfect." His gaze lingered on her as he uncorked a large brown bottle whose handwritten label said *Moonwater.* "You know both of my brothers are Earth witches, right?"

"Wait, what?"

"Yeah, it's a thing in mixed-magical families. An Elemental magic reveal. I used to haaate that I was different from them. But I started spending more time with my grandpa, and then Poppy went Water, and once I found out about Morning Star joining the Casquette Girls Coven, Water just felt like my destiny." He filled the bottle three-quarters with the Moonwater, topped it off with something that smelled more of booze than celestial runoff, and then shook it up like a witchy mixologist. A potent scent wafted from the second bottle.

"What's—?" Désirée started to ask.

"*Kirschwasser.* Homemade. Won't kill you like the piman, but it will keep you warm on even the coldest Brocken mountaintop. It will act as a preservative for the nightshade essence plus give it a hint of cherry—much tastier if Masaka ends up throwing back the bottle instead of spritzing you with it."

She gave it a sniff, and her eyelids fluttered.

The constant chill of the room rippled up and down my spine like a taunting song. Codi passed me the bottle, and I took a swig. My face pinched as fire flooded my chest. "That's some cherry juice," I coughed, but the tingle traveled through my system, pushing out the cold.

He screwed a spritz pump onto the little blue bottle, handed it to Dee, and pushed a pile of silver jewelry toward her. "Scent of night blossoms for Masaka, eight amethyst rings for Zaranye, a pipe for Oussou, plus some bonus onyx and pyrite for our Ghede altars."

She checked the items off her list. "Perfect. Now we just need poppies for L'Oraille."

"We'll clip them from the garden on the way out." Codi packaged everything into a velvet drawstring bag embroidered with a moon, along with some tobacco and packs of matches. "So now, the fun part?"

"The ritual." Dee's eyes sparkled with excitement. "Let's go."

I pushed myself off the counter. "You guys have a warped idea of fun."

"Slow your roll," Codi said. "Hello, I meant the souls."

"Oh, right." Dee gave him an apologetic face, and we all looked out to the glowing room.

"How the hell do we get a thousand souls out of the house without waking up my parents, much less get them to the cemetery?"

Désirée picked up one of the glowing bottles and gazed into it. "Someone wise once told me that a magical dilemma should be solved with *magic*."

I was starting to regret every word that had ever come out of my mouth.

She put the bottle down. "Get out your grimoires, kids. We need to find a spell. And fast."

Upstairs in the Daure family room, twinges of magic crackled in the air from the witches who'd been coming and going all night long. A fire kindled in the hearth, but its warmth was dominated by the cold invading the house. The chill was even stronger here on the third floor and felt like it had taken up permanent residence in my bones.

Three podiums had been pulled to the center of the room, surrounding a basin. The podium across from Morning Star's ceremonial hide-skin dress held the Guldenmann grimoire, and on the wall behind it, a wind chime hung from a tree branch that seemed to grow from the house. Like most things at the Daures', it was unlike any wind chime I'd ever seen—more like a set of bells of varying lengths.

Codi went to the German grimoire, and we fell into place at his sides with our own books of magic. I opened Susannah's sketchbook to a random double-page spread: a magnificent scene of a ship on an emerald-green ocean, heading off into the distance. In the bottom left corner, on a jut of rocks, two mermaids were singing into the wind. The spell was called *A Siren's Song to Call back the Captain from Sea.* I wondered how Susannah ended up on that pirate's ship in the first place? Would I soon be able to ask her myself?

Focus, Isaac. "So, what are we looking for? Assuming we aren't going to find a spell on how to move a thousand bottles of parasitic souls to Guinée."

"I don't know exactly," Désirée said. "Anything on souls. The Afterworld. Crossing over."

"Maybe it doesn't even have to be soul-specific." Codi scanned through an index with his finger, much of which appeared to be in the original German. "Maybe something that would help the physics of it."

"Yeah," Dee said, "if the jars were all dollhouse size, we could put them in my bag."

Codi looked up at Morning Star's dress, his forehead tightening with thought. "I'm looking in the wrong place." He walked over to the dress and thumbed the long fringe that hung from the sleeves. "We can't fit them in your bag, but we could fit them in a bottomless kishi."

"What's a kishi?" I asked.

He gestured to a row of baskets sitting at the baseboards beneath the dress. Some were several feet tall with tightly woven lids; others were smaller. Each had unique patterns and colors. "Kishi were a way of life for all native tribes."

"Same in Africa," Dee said, attempting to balance a round one on her head.

"The women in Morning Star's family passed down an enchantment through the generations for the kishi they wove."

I closed Susannah's grimoire. "What does it do?"

"All kinds of things. Protect and preserve the basket's contents from weather, animals, insects. Make the contents lighter for the carrier."

"A bottomless basket," Désirée said, thinking it through.

"Totally. Works for clay pots too."

"Cool," Dee said. "Grab a basket, and let's get the souls."

"We can't use these; it's all about the intention the witch weaves into the kishi."

"We don't have time to make a basket, Codi!"

He locked his fingers together and stretched out his arms. "You underestimate my talents in traditional crafts."

We followed him to an armoire near the fireplace, and he threw open the doors, revealing large wooden spools of . . . thread? Yarn? Hemp? Adele would know. "This is all *chahta nan tvnna*. Bison fibers, dogbane. Choctaw textiles are all deeply linked to the land and spun by the fingers of witches." He grabbed an armload of tall, dried ribbon-like stalks and spread them on the rug in front of the fire. "River cane and palmetto. Already prepped, dyed, and ready to go."

We knelt beside him.

"Did your grandfather teach you how to basket weave?" Dee asked.

"*Pssh*. No. Ten years of getting shipped away to Choctaw summer camp. Adele used to get soooo upset every summer when we all left and she had to stay behind. She cried when Mac told her she wasn't part-Native. She always made me teach her everything when I got back. She's probably the only white girl who knows how to tan hide for moccasins and bead an *isht Vskufvchi* with a proper Choctaw *nish-tu wa-ki* pattern."

"What's an *isht Vs* . . ."—my tongue twisted up trying to pronounce the second word, but I pushed it out—"*kufvchi?*"

"A sash. With an alligator entrails pattern."

Right.

As he threaded the first couple pieces of cane, I pictured a mini-Adele begging for an alligator-guts sewing lesson. His fingers worked swiftly as he sang the chant.

Désirée's foot tapped anxiously against the floor. Five minutes later, the bottom layer was barely finished. She looked at her phone for the thirtieth time, and then shoved it into her back pocket. "Step aside."

"I'm going as fast as I can!"

"You chant. I'll weave." She raised her left hand, and the strips of river cane stood up.

Codi continued the magical words, and she swirled her hands, the cane threading together. Almost instantly, the basket was three feet tall.

"Damn." Codi wiped his brow.

Désirée smirked.

"You def would've won the prize at summer camp."

Her smirk slipped into a hidden smile. A few stalks later, and the basket had two tightly woven back straps and a lid that could latch closed. She held the basket up to me. "Turn around."

"Oh, hell, hell, hell, hell no. I will carry you to the end of the Earth, but I am not carrying a basket of souls—"

"It's enchanted! They won't be able to hurt you!"

"My Spektral magic already feels like it's turning to ice inside my body just being in this house with all of them!"

"Fine, I'll do it," she said.

"No, I'll do it. It's Morning Star's enchantment, and it's my honor to wear the magic of the matriarchs who came before me."

I don't know if Dee was more impressed with his magic or his feminism, but she looked like she was about to jump him as he picked up the kishi.

"Only one way to see if it works, right?" he said. "On to the library."

As I followed them out of the room, the temperature dropped so drastically it was dizzying. The library was up ahead, the craft room to the right. A tea set sat untouched on a tray outside the fourth door in the hallway. Just like last time we were here, something compelled me to try the handle. The door creaked open.

Inside the dark parlor, a lone candle burned on the mantel. My teeth chattered. Their footsteps came up from behind me, and Codi sucked back a giant breath.

A bright beam of moonlight illuminated a mound of Hexennacht flowers on a table in the middle of the room. Julie was strewn over it, weeping. Stormy lay on the floor beside her, alert and protective. As I approached, I saw the face peeking through the petals. Two coins hid his eyes. Olsin.

It wasn't the souls emitting the cold; it was Olsin. It was death. "Why-why is he here?" I asked. *Where else would he be,*

Isaac? The city's under supernatural siege. "I'm sorry, I didn't mean it like that."

Codi wiped away the tears, a somber expression on his face. "Tonight, we honor my grandfather with German funerary magic. But he was a Water witch, so in Choctaw tradition, his body will be placed outside on wooden scaffolding. Probably on our property across the lake. Once the sun has taken most of him back into the natural universe, his brother, the coven Bone Picker, will scrape off his remaining skin and whatever's left until he's nothing but bone, and he'll be interred in our bone house."

"Uh-h," I stuttered, utterly unable to wrap my head around flesh-scraping fingernails, much less articulate a response.

"Dude," he said, hooking his arm around my neck. "I'm kidding. This isn't the eighteenth century. He'll go in St. Roch with the rest of the Daures after the funeral."

"You should see your face right now," Désirée said.

A chill rattled my insides, and I spun around. I swore I heard, from the corner near the window, the chuckles of the old man.

"What?" Codi asked.

"Nothing." I shook my head. "Come on, and close the door tight. God forbid a soul gets loose. We don't want them anywhere near Olsin's spirit. For his sake, and for the sake of your family's magic."

The severity of the thought registered on Codi's face, and he produced a long skeleton key. "Julie . . ." He looked around the room, not quite sure where she was. "Sorry, but visiting hours are over."

She looked up, struck with sorrow, and disappeared through the wall. I was glad he couldn't see the glowing parasite inside her.

In the library, all of the books sat on the floor in stacks, and the shelves glowed just like the ones in the shop downstairs, although not quite as brightly. A few of the jars were dark. Fuck.

"So how the hell do we get the souls into the kishi?" Codi eyed the jars along the wall, growing more nervous by the second. A fountain gurgled near the window on the other side of the room. "We can't let a bunch of souls loose."

The jars rattled at the sound of our voices, and the noise gave me an idea. "No, we do it safely, or we don't do it at all." I heard my father's tone in my voice, and it weirded me out. It had been souls who'd forced me and Adele into the cemetery. No matter how many twists and turns we'd taken, the slaps of her sandals had given away our route. I thought about Poppy's music box. "Noise. Noise will lure them in."

"Pied Piper style." Codi opened the kishi.

"Dee, put your phone at the bottom of the basket and play that Beyoncé track you're obsessed with."

"You put your phone in!"

"I'm not the one who wants to go to Guinée. Wait. I'll be right back."

I took off to the family room and grabbed the branch the wind chime hung from. It didn't have the lure of Beyoncé, but what did? I held it tightly against my chest and crept back as silently as possible.

"The *windspiel*! My German side," Codi said as I balanced it over the top of the basket.

We all crouched behind the piano.

Codi leaned back toward the fountain and the Water came to him. He spun a Waterball for each hand, and crouched over in a defensive position. "Just in case." Now, it made sense why there were so many fountains in this place.

"You're up, Earth magic." I pretended not to notice Dee shaking.

She slowly raised her hands. "*Laissez les bon temps rouler.*"

The corks trembled. There were hundreds of souls in the room—this was either going to be one of the best ideas I'd ever had, or the worst. Her face strained. She started to stand, and so did we. The corks rose from the bottles and showered to the floor. The jars rattled, glass clanking against the wooden shelves, water sloshing. We ducked back down as the neon spheres blinked, slamming against the bottles, trying to squeeze out, lighting up the room like a roller-rink.

This is going to be fine. Totally fine.

One by one, the souls found freedom. They floated around the room until there were dozens. I stirred the Air, and the chimes strummed. Dee squeezed my arm, fingernails digging into my skin. Stacks of books flew open, pages rustling, and I worried the sounds would distract the souls. It was dizzying trying to keep an eye on the closest ones, pushing them away with gentle gusts like playing a deadly game of Pong. The more nervous I got, the harder it was to control the breeze. I strummed the bells harder. Books spun up into the whirlwind along with some of the weaker souls. The bells clanked and clamored, and a bright blue orb gravitated toward the music.

I held my breath and tickled the bells.

It dove toward the basket. Others spun out of the Air to join their brethren, until just a few lingered in the twister. Every muscle in my back clenched as I guided the whirlwind into the magical trap, and the last few spun in along with the books.

In the wake of the chiming, a single leaf of paper floated down to the floor.

We crept over, still afraid to speak, and peered into the kishi —now a jingling, glowing discotheque for souls.

"That was cool, dude," Codi said.

"*Très* cool," Dee echoed.

A knot tightened in my stomach—we were one *major* step closer to actually going to the Afterworld.

CHAPTER 12
MIXED MAGIC

Codi carried the kishi tightly in his arms, pruning shears in hand, as we followed him out to the courtyard. Even with all the decorative evidence before my eyes, it was still hard to believe that just hours ago we'd been here celebrating Hexennacht, dancing under the Flower Moon. If Gran had been in town tonight, there was no way I'd have been able to skip out on the Zaka night cemetery feast.

Codi handed Isaac the kishi and knelt down near a flowerbed, but before he cut the poppies for L'Oraille, he held out his palm and let out an exhale. *An offering of breath.* Ritha would love him if she just got to know him—he's so respectful to all living things. He clipped a handful of pink, white, and red flowers, and handed them to me. "What?" he asked, and my spine stiffened.

"Nothing," I said, wrapping them up in a galaxy scarf. "That's the last key, let's bounce."

A small voice came from the house: "Codi?" Fiona's youngest daughter, who looked to be about eight, was standing in the door with tears in her eyes. "Where are you going?" she asked in creepy little psychic-kid fashion.

A twinge of pain formed in his eyes as he tried to make something up. "We're just taking the nightshift while everyone else rests. We made a magical kishi to catch souls. Didn't you make one in summer camp last year?"

Her face tensed. "You're lying. You're going somewhere else. Somewhere dark."

Isaac's brow creased.

Great. After all that trouble, a psychic-child was going to blow it.

I considered intervening so we could get the hell out of there. Codi couldn't lie to save his life—not that I thought it was a terrible quality in a man. But if his parents woke up and they called Ritha, we'd be screwed.

"Dee, I need the pipe for a sec."

"Okaaaaaay."

"Lilly . . ." He grabbed a peach from one of the exquisite party tables, took a big bite, and handed it to her. "Help me with this." He took her other hand and led her to the flowerbed near the fountain. She took a bite, juice running down her arm, as they both knelt down on the earth.

We followed them over as he dug a small depression with his hands.

I handed him the pipe.

"Thanks, I need the tobacco too."

I was intrigued. Presumably he wasn't going to bury his little cousin in the flower garden so she couldn't rat us out, which is definitely how us Borges kids would have rolled.

He hurriedly took a few more bites of peach until just the pit was left and then dropped it into the soil. Lily covered it back up as he packed the pipe, and I hunched down beside them, getting a better look. As he lit the pipe, I rummaged my memory for spells that used tobacco smoke.

Lilly watched intensely as he blew the smoke over the patch of dirt, whispering German words. He stirred the smoke with his fingers. "*Oka*," he said to her, and she ran off to the fountain and came back with her cupped hands filled with water to sprinkle over the patch.

The coil of smoke dove into the Water-soaked earth, emitting a trail of green sparkles. *Cool.* It seemed to be some kind of mash-up of German and Choctaw magic. The smoke seeped back out of the soil, and with it came a tiny green bud.

"Whoa," Isaac said as the little plant burst through the soil, rising six inches high.

Codi turned to his cousin. "Does this plant look healthy and strong?"

She nodded.

"It's because it's made from my breath, and I'm healthy and strong."

She nodded again.

"I am going somewhere, but I'll be with my coven, so we'll all be safe. Whenever you get scared that I'm not back, you can come check on this plant, and if it's healthy, you'll know I'm okay."

"But where are you going?"

"We're going to bring the souls back to the other side so they can rest in peace and the French Quarter can be safe again."

She wrapped her arms around him. "I don't want you to go there."

"I feel ya, kid," Isaac said.

"Why not?" Codi asked her.

"Because it's dark, and there's a scary mermaid."

He laughed. "Well, I'm not scared of the dark. Or of mermaids. And I have it on good authority that mermaids like Water witches." He pulled her pigtail. "We'll be so quick, you won't even know we're gone. Go back to bed. In the morning, you can tell everyone I took the souls, okay?"

"I love you." She gave him a tight hug.

"I love you too," he said, and she ran back into the house.

Some strange emotional sensation plucked inside my chest.

Codi quickly wiped his eyes. "Let's go before I change my mind."

Isaac lifted the basket onto Codi's shoulders, and we were finally off. Three witches with four keys to the Afterworld and a magical basket with a thousand souls. I wondered if the little girl was running straight to Chatham and Edgar.

As we walked down the alley out to the street, I leaned closer to Codi than I usually liked to be to people. "It's true, what you told her. We are going to make the French Quarter safe again, for her, and for everyone."

"I know. I just hate sneaking around."

"I know." Without thinking, I brushed his fingers with mine. He looked at me, surprised, and I jerked my hand back.

He pinched a smile.

Goddess.

When we got to the street, another girl's voice called out, one that was neither frail nor small. "This is the *stupidest* thing you've ever done." Poppy Daure stepped out from the shadows in front of the tearoom. It was like she'd been waiting for us.

"*Fuck,*" Codi said. I hadn't heard him use language like that since his leg nearly got cut off. "You don't even know what we're doing, Poppy."

Maybe she was the scary mermaid her sister had dreamed about us finding in the dark. Her hair needed a serious touch up. Even so, she had that natural-beauty quality.

"Yes, I do. Papa Olsin told me."

His attitude shifted. "You saw Papa?" And his gaze dropped to the two picnic baskets in her hands. "Poppy, you can't come with us."

"She'd be better than Emilio," Isaac said.

"She's not coming," he snapped. "We're doing this to protect our families. I'm not risking mine!"

"Chill out. I'm not going anywhere with those jerk-off-witches right across the river. I'm just here to give you a message."

Codi's eyes narrowed.

"Papa said to make sure you get these." She shoved the baskets at me and Isaac. "And to give you this message: Don't eat the food of the dead."

I peeked beneath the lid, and delicious scents wafted out. It was packed full of food from tonight's feast.

"I hope it's bottomless," Isaac said, practically drooling.

She didn't laugh, just shook her head at us and opened the front door. "Codi, there's a letter in one of them for you. I found it at the bottom of the basket when I started packing them. He must have written it before . . ."

"Poppy! Did you have a premonition? Is that where you saw Olsin?"

She nodded.

"What did you see?"

"A ritual. Gates." She shrugged. "Then nothing. Good luck, cousin. May your magic be as fierce as the mighty Mississippi."

He turned back to us, perplexed. And then a scream curdled into the night.

"Lilly!" Poppy called out, darting into the alley.

I barely caught the kishi as Codi transformed into Onyx and darted after her, and Isaac swooped ahead. By the time I made it to the courtyard, they were already hunched over the little girl, who was kneeling at the magical plant, crying.

It had shriveled and blackened like a smoker's lungs in the old PSAs.

Poppy shook her head.

"Lilly, I'm fine!" He thumped his chest. "I'm totally fine!"

"But you said—"

"What did you do to her, Codi?" Poppy asked.

"The same old spell my dad used to do when we were little

and he was going away on ghost-hunting trips. So she wouldn't be scared!"

Poppy crouched down next to her sister. "Lilly, he's fine. He's clearly just inept and did the spell wrong."

Harsh. And totally something I'd say to my cousins.

"I did *not* do the spell wrong."

A light flicked on in the house.

Shit.

"What's going on out there?" Fiona called out the window.

"Nothing, Mom! I'm just locking up!" Poppy yelled, giving us a look that said get out of there.

She picked up her sister. "Let's go to bed. You can sleep in my room."

While everyone was distracted, I whipped a finger toward the plant, breathing it back to life. "Lilly," I whispered.

When she turned to look, I nodded back to the plant. She gasped in relief.

And that magic, I could promise, would not be shriveling.

"See!" Codi said, "I didn't do the spell wrong."

"Whatever," Poppy said. "Don't forget your food."

As soon as we got off Royal Street, Codi paused. "What did Poppy mean about a letter?"

Isaac opened up his picnic basket and shook his head. "Just food."

In mine, an envelope rested on top of loaves of sweet bread that Codi called *stollen*. His name was written on the envelope in old-fashioned handwriting. I handed it to him, and he ripped it open.

The streetlamp shone through the single sheet of paper as he read it. "It's from my grandpa. He must have written it before . . ." He handed it to me, eyes welling, unable to read it out loud.

I cleared my throat:

Codi,

You've grown into a fine man and a fine witch. Shed no tears for me, for I am overwhelmed with joy to finally reunite with my beautiful Philomena. Philly needs me. And soon she will need you too.

Love,

Olsin

Isaac teared up. "I'm so sorry, man."

"He knew . . ." Codi said. "Why didn't he tell me goodbye? Why did he go down to the river?"

"He saved Adele's life," I said, suppressing an unfamiliar desire to hug him.

"I know. I mean, I'm glad he was there. It just sucks." He folded the letter back up. We walked the next block in silence, but then he asked, "What do you think he meant? About my grandma?"

Isaac draped an arm around him. "I don't know . . . but maybe you'll be able to ask her soon?"

For the rest of the walk, I couldn't help but think about my own ancestors. The slave market where people who'd been torn away from their families on the African coast were sold was mere blocks from where we were walking—Guinée was supposed to be the place where all the families were reunited in the Afterworld.

If they weren't, the universe was crueler than I could fathom.

And what was the point of all of this magic?

CHAPTER 13
BURDEN OF PROOF

I took a running leap and thrust myself over the cemetery wall. Shells crunched beneath my boots as I hit the ground in St. Louis No. 1. Adele thinks she killed a witch, but I needed to see the dead body for myself, the *onus probandi*. The lives of Ghost Drinkers are notoriously difficult to take, and I wouldn't let her live with the burden of being a killer unnecessarily.

That, of course, wasn't the only reason I was here.

If Adele had delivered a life-threatening blow to another witch, I was unequivocally sure he had threatened hers; and if this witch was still alive, like I suspected he was, he would soon wish he had died at her hand. That I could promise.

The fog thickened as I walked down a row of watermarked mausoleums, deeper into the city of dead. Earlier in the night, Isaac had babbled on about leaving Adele in a cemetery, and about there being blood when he'd returned and couldn't find her. If Adele had been frightened, she might have sought solace with her mother. I'd start at Brigitte's tomb.

I walked past decaying bricks, sagging fronds of ginger bulb, and concrete tears of weeping angels, thinking about the Ghede —it was impossible not to in a New Orleans cemetery. I imagined still being a witch, performing a ritual with borrowed bones, and asking the Baron to show me what had happened earlier this eve. But I wasn't a witch anymore.

Even so, I felt a tickle. A tug. *Magic through the billowing fog.* Not the Ghede's magic. *Some kind of protection spell.* I closed my eyes and opened my senses, letting the enchantment run through me. It was of the European variety. Similar to the one just placed on our home. A Daure spell—but not entirely. It also had undertones of Air magic, and the inexplicable taste of New Orleans Voodoo. A mixed-magic gumbo. *Adele's coven.* With the Animarum Praedators lurking, the French Quarter witches had been wise to ward the cemeteries.

The wings of a looming angel atop the **LE MOYNE** tomb rose out of the fog, her hand shielding her eyes as if watching out for predators, guarding those beneath her stone feet. Magic flowed through her marble veins cast by the eighteenth-century witches of La Nouvelle-Orléans—spells that would terrorize anyone who dared tamper with Adeline's bones. I wondered if she was still interred here or if León had ever managed to collect her. Tonight, nothing seemed out of place, though it was hard to tell with the dilapidated state of the cemetery.

"Allez, Brigitte, donnez-moi un indice."

I held out my hands and closed my eyes once again, letting the river breeze run over me. They'd used lavender in the protection spell, so it was impossible to differentiate Adele's scent. I inhaled deeper, and my fangs nearly jutted. *The undeniable aroma of blood.*

I zipped back up to the center aisle and then, at the obelisk, dove back into a row, the scent filling my senses. *Calm down, Niccolò; it's not her blood. You know the scent of her blood. You know the taste.* I skidded to a stop.

The sight was something any vampire would have seen, or more likely caused, dozens of times in their early years, but it was not what I'd expected to find, based on Isaac's mention of blood. The tombs appeared to have come straight from a Lucio Fulci film, having been stained with an enormous spray of crimson. I took another deep breath, trying to catch the scent of the dead—a somewhat futile exercise in a cemetery.

I changed tactics and lit the path with my phone. Three different sets of footprints marked the path: two were of boots. *Men's boots.* The third were smaller bare feet. In spots, the balls of the feet had left bloody marks as if someone had been chased across the jagged rocks.

I picked up a shell smeared with red. The scent was enough to confirm that it was Adele's blood, but I dragged it across my tongue to be sure. My fangs snapped. I whipped around the tombs like one of Fulci's beasts, looking for clues: *Smashed statue of the Holy Mother. Loose bars of a rusty mausoleum gate.* And there it was—a spot of rocky earth where a boot had smashed down so hard, it left the imprint of the pounded hand beneath.

Adele's hand had been ghastly when I'd found her by the river. Tripled in size, black in color, bones crooked.

I spun around. There was more blood.

More footprints.

No bodies.

Either they had both lived, or one had survived and taken the body of his dead friend. I crouched low to the ground, shining my phone over their tracks. Bits of the white shells were scorched where a Fire witch had lit his way. The lone set of bare footprints crossed them, presumably when Adele got away. I treaded lightly, scouring for more. And then a smashed banana leaf gave them away. It revealed not the single set of footprints of one man burdened by the deadweight of another, but two clear sets. One was distinctly the boot that had crushed her hand. The other was *enormous.*

I locked the scent of the blood spatter into my memory and paced down the row of mausoleums. Was it best to tell Adele, so she could rest easier knowing she hadn't ended someone's life, or would it frighten her more to know the assailants were still alive? Unless I ripped open the neck of every Ghost Drinker, which I'd gladly do, the scent of blood and shape of boot print likely wouldn't be enough to find the culprits.

Without my magic, I couldn't call on the Baron to show me what had happened. Unluckily for these Ghost Drinkers, there was another way.

But I couldn't do it alone. I needed a witch. A witch with a very specific Spektral power.

I whipped back through the Quarter, gaining speed with each passing block. All the lights at the tearoom were out.

Please let them still be at the Voodoo shop, I begged the gods as I hurried along.

Warm light filled the cracks in the curtains of the Borges' shop, and I felt pulses from the front room. I reached for my phone. Isaac's was the only number I had.

I watched his silhouette answer.

"Ask Codi to meet me on the street outside."

"Outside where?"

"*Vodou Pourvoyeur.*"

"What?"

"*Grazie.*" I hung up.

His face peeked from behind the curtain, and he scowled through the windowpane. The door opened, and the youngest Daure walked out to the curb. The other two witches watched from the door.

He nodded to me. "What's up?"

"I need your assistance."

"Uh, okay."

"Earlier tonight, Adele was attacked in the cemetery—"

"What? *Who?*"

"With your magic, we can figure that out. Will you help me?"

His eyebrows pressed tightly together. "Is that even a question?"

"Good. Let's go."

"Let me just tell—" He started to turn back.

I grabbed his arm. "This is probably best left between the two of us. If we are able to discover more information . . . it's not our story to tell."

He nodded and quickly turned back to the others. "Gonna run a quick errand with Nicco. Will meet you at HQ."

I gestured toward Basin Street. "Can you run faster in cat-form?"

"Hell yeah."

We arrived back at the cemetery in no time and both scaled the wall. Inside, I slowed to a speed he, a furry black shadow at my feet, could keep up with.

At the tombs, he darted from one bloody spot to the next, sniffing, licking, screeching. Then he rose tall. "What the hell happened here? Is this Adele's blood?"

"Other than her feet getting cut up running from these cretins, I don't think so."

"Why the hell was she running through a cemetery barefoot in the first place?"

"The question to answer is, who was chasing her?" I nodded to the largest pattern of blood spatter—a spray of crimson arching across four mausoleums, coating a pair of cherubs and a Madonna. "One of them lost an appendage, so he shouldn't be hard to identify." I crouched down at the second set of boot prints. "I've already searched for it. Don't bother."

"Wasn't gonna."

"But this gargantuan one didn't leave too many clues. I want to see his face."

I picked up a rusty metal bar, tossed it up with a flip and caught it. Slender enough to fit in Adele's hand. Whether it had been used as a weapon or not, maybe it contained the memory of the scene.

"There are bloody handprints on that mausoleum," he stuttered.

"Which might be useful if we were cops trying to bring the perpetrators in." I looked him straight in the eyes so he was perfectly clear on my intention. "I'm not a cop. And if these witches still walk this planet, I have no intention of handing them over to the authorities."

He nodded understanding, and I handed him the rusty bar. "Show me what happened here, like you showed Adele the memories locked inside the Salazar ring."

"So, uh, this would probably be a good time to tell you that I don't really know how to use my Spektral magic. I know I'm supposed to be a badass, youngest witch of one of the most powerful covens in New Orleans, but I just got my Mark—well, you were there."

"I can think of no better reason for you to figure it out."

"Yeah," he said, pumping himself up. "Okay. I got this." He bounced up on his toes.

"Are you ready?"

"Ready."

"I'm going to touch you to form a connection to the object. You don't have to be frightened of me."

"I'm not."

"I can hear your heart racing."

"Right. Okay." He planted his feet on the ground.

I took hold of his free hand and picked up the other end of the pole. "Close your eyes and concentrate on the metal. It's cool to the touch because of the elements. Rusty in your palm because it's been outside for centuries. It's old."

"Not as old as you." He laughed.

"*Concentrate.* Back in the tearoom, connecting with another witch flared your magic."

"It's so weird that you're a wi . . ." His words slurred.

The earth spun.

It was darker, but the night was clearer—before the fog had set in and the air had become so saturated with magic.

An obsidian outline of a man stomped toward us. I nearly pulled Codi off the path before remembering he couldn't see us. Flames sprang up from the ground, lighting the predatory look on his Basque face. I recognized him from D-MORT. From Halloween night. From my dining room table in 1930. And I regretted not slicing off that piece-of-shit Salazar's head and feeding his spirit to the rest of his family.

He paused in front of a grotto. Is Adele in there? I stepped closer as he reached in. The statue toppled onto him, and he heaved it back.

"Adele!" I shouted.

A small, shadowy figure sprang out. He caught hold of her leg, but his hand slipped, and she blasted toward us.

"Adele!" Codi cried, leaping toward her, but she ran straight past us, seething determination beneath the fear as the Fire witch went after her. I sped down the strip. Noises crackled from the adjacent row of tombs. The other witch? Show me your face.

"Adele! Behind you!" Codi screamed.

Footsteps came crashing up, and I skidded to a halt as the witch brought her to the ground.

"This secluded enough for you?" he grunted, crawling on top of her. My heart stopped dead. "Or do you want me to chase you around some more?"

"Get the hell away from me!" she screamed, flailing beneath his weight.

"Get off her!" Codi launched himself onto the giant's back, but he slipped right through him.

My fangs threatened to rip out of my gums, the desire to kill pulsing through my veins like an oncoming freight train. This is a memory, Niccolò; there's nothing you can do.

"Cemetery was a good idea," the second witch said, appearing next to me on the path. I memorized his features. Younger, blond beard. Aria magia. And judging by the filth coming off his tongue, Irish. "We can grab a snack after."

"Fuck you!" she screamed, and his boot came stomping down on her bones.

"That's the plan." The Fire witch's heavy hand slid around her waist.

Just where Isaac had touched her.

She kicked up like a feral fox trapped in the jaws of a grizzly, but he slammed her back down. Two feet taller than her, two hundred pounds heavier, and with her stolen Fire. The image burned permanently into my mind. I would never forget the sounds of her shrieks as long as I lived, be it another century or ten.

With a shove, her face hit the shells. My eyes welled, the feeling of helplessness surging as his arm dug into her back. A breeze of voices swept over us. I spun around, hoping help was arriving, but saw no one.

"You'll know what a real Fire witch feels like," he grunted. "Not some pathetic magicless Medici!"

At the sound of my name, phantom magic erupted through my palms, and the sky lit up as I cast the world's darkest curses on him. She twisted and writhed as he tried to unclothe her.

I am going to kill him. I'm going to fucking kill him.

"What was it you said that night at the convent? How you'd never betray Nicco?" The rusty mausoleum gate creaked open, and the spiked bars slipped apart and clanked to the ground. I grabbed one to crack his skull, to no avail.

"You think Nicco will still want you after this?"

The question echoed in my chest.

128

Metal scraped metal.

I felt the iron bar in my hand. Rusty. Cool to the touch. She's the one who suffered, but I couldn't bear to watch anymore. *I let go just as the Air witch's blood splattered across my eyes.*

We both fell back, the rusty gate piece clanking against the shells. *This was all because of me.* Panic rushed my veins as I stood. *He went after her to get back at me.* I saw Codi's fist coming, but I didn't move—my face cracked, and I spun back to the ground where she had lain. Blood spurted over the shells, this time mine.

"*Dannazione!*" I spat, clutching my nose.

"Stay away from her!" Codi's cheeks were wet with tears. "Stay away from her!" He grabbed my shoulders, and I allowed him to drag me up. "Stop walking her home from work and bringing her flower crowns. I don't care if you are a vampire, or a witch, or the goddamn Messiah! Trouble follows you, and now it's following her. Stay . . ."—he released me, stumbling back—"away from her." He twisted to the ground into the little black shadow and darted off.

I thought about how humiliated Adele would be if she knew what we'd done. What I'd done.

"Codi!" I yelled.

The black cat stopped and looked back.

"It's not our story to tell."

His yellow eyes glowed blankly, but he gave me a nod and disappeared into the night.

The modicum of joy I'd felt the last few hours with Adele in my house, with my family, with me, shriveled up like crackling frost. She hadn't been protecting her assailant. She hadn't even been protecting herself. She was protecting me.

That was why she didn't want to tell me.

I rose. I walked in her footsteps, imagining her suffering. Imagining the pain I would inflict on those witches now that I had seen their faces. I said a devotion to the sun, and the moon, and the stars, to the old Etruscan gods, and to the Holy Mother above that the two Animarum Praedators had both made it back to the plantation alive.

My mission was clear before, but now it glistened brighter than the Mediterranean: if I didn't find the Elixir, I would always be a monster.

Undeserving of her love. Or her protection.

CHAPTER 14
OPEN SECRET

"What the hell does Nicco Medici want with Codi?" I asked, sinking into the velvet beanbag chair on Désirée's bedroom floor and staring into the beady eyes of her pet tarantula, which chilled on my hand like it wasn't the apocalypse.

"I don't know. Psychic emergency?" She walked out of the bathroom in a plume of steam, her hair tucked beneath a plastic cap with bright orange flowers. No more shimmery makeup, gold bangles, or Hexennacht dress. She looked straight out of Gotham City in tight dark purple pants, shiny as latex, and a black vest. Adele was right about Dee always looking like a badass.

"I guess we'll find out soon enough." She pulled the cap off, and her long hair fell out, pin straight. She slicked it back into a ponytail, snapped on a pair of fingerless leather gloves, and zipped up a dark gray hoodie. "Boots or sneakers?"

"Huh?"

She held up the two pairs of shoes as if I didn't know the difference. "Like, should I be more prepared to run or for rugged terrain?"

I stared at the shoes. *Rugged terrain?*

She set down the boots, opting for the sneakers. "I don't want to be weighed down."

"I can't believe we're doing this," I groaned, letting my free arm fold over my face.

She grabbed a bag identical to her usual mini-backpack, just slightly bigger, and threw in a change of clothes, toiletries, two bottles of her homemade antiseptic, and three gris-gris necklaces.

"Who are those for?"

"Lisette, Emilio, and Nicco."

My eyes rolled back into my skull.

She wrapped seven Palo Santo sticks into a silk scarf and placed it into the bag, followed by seven cigars, seven packs of matches, a box of chalk, a bag of coffee, several boxes of candles, a flashlight, and batteries. It was like part-camping pack, part-Ghede ritual care package.

I tore into a lemon-poppyseed muffin I'd ganked from one of the picnic baskets.

"How can you eat at a time like this?"

"How can you not eat at a time like this?" I offered a bite to Spinderella, who remained uninterested.

"Make sure her terrarium is closed when you put her back."

She'd already taped color-coded instructions and a feeding schedule complete with menu on the spider's enclosure for her mother. How long did she think we'd be gone? She tightened the drawstrings of her bag. "Let's hit it."

I made sure Spinderella was snug as a bug and started for the door, but Désirée quickly opened her bag back up, hesitating. "What's up?"

She removed her grimoire, set it on her perfectly made bed, and re-strapped the bag on her back.

"Uh, what are you doing that for?"

"I just—" She straightened the corner of the book. "If something happens, I don't want to be the witch who lost our grimoire too."

My insides curdled.

"Not that anything's going to happen to us," she added. "I just don't want to risk it."

I followed her to the door. "Désirée, do you really think there is no better way to do all of this than going to Guinée?"

She stopped short and turned around in my face. "No. I don't. I want to go to Guinée."

There was a neediness to her voice that I wasn't expecting. I knew she wanted to prove herself to Ritha, but this was different. "Okay."

"I need to grab a few more things for the ritual from the shop. Be quiet in the hallway. The last thing we need to do is wake Ritha."

"Meet you down there. I'm going to check on Ren before we leave."

We split off in the hallway, and I took flight, not wanting to disturb anyone's much-deserved slumber. Borges family and coven members were crashed in every room, on every piece of furniture.

I cruised across the courtyard and straight down the dark hall of the guesthouse, doing my best to ignore the rattles of the doorknobs, fingernails raking against the walls, and moans of the Possessed.

I stopped outside Ren's door. He was sitting on his bed, jacket and top hat on. His walking stick was planted firmly on the floor, the crystal skull handle staring out at me along with his one-eyed gaze. A single purple sunglass lens was still intact; the other was MIA. It was hard to believe that the figure before me was even Ren. He'd aged two decades since I'd met him, just like my mom had before she died. These souls were a cancer, sucking out everything good in a person. I wanted to believe that Ren's soul was threaded so deeply into the heart of the city, it was indestructible. But he needed to be free to roam the streets to be himself. Ren needed New

Orleans, and New Orleans needed Ren. I couldn't let him die.

"What's all the ruckus about, Yankee?" His voice was deep and scratchy.

"Ren, you're there!" I'd have hugged him if he hadn't seemed so frail.

Shame suddenly struck me. Did he know I used the serenity magic on Adele? Did he think I was a horrible person? Had he told Ritha?

He rattled off something in Italian. *Alessandro.* And then he was singing what sounded like a children's song in French. It was getting difficult to discern real life from the dreams I'd had about him. If the Baron had shown him the road to Guinée, how much time did he have left? My nerves lit up, realizing how close we were to crossing over. "Why did you tell Adele the way?" I whispered.

"She's strong. I've watched her grow up into a marvelous young woman."

I imagined a younger, healthier Ren vivaciously telling an eight-year-old Adele stories about vampires as she sipped Shirley Temples on a barstool.

He looked back up at me. "You have to save her."

"What?" My mouth went dry. "Did the Baron tell you something about Adele? Did Olsin? What danger is she in?"

"She survived the fires. She survived the storms. And she'll survive this, as long as people fight for her. She needs you, Isaac." Hearing him say my actual name sent chills down my spine.

I nodded, realizing now what he meant.

"New Orleans needs you."

Was this what my pop felt every time he got *the call*? Fear of the uncertainty, the danger when Mother Nature was threatening to wipe a spot off the map. What would he think about this mission? Souls. Spirits. Succubus witches. There was one thing I knew for sure: He wouldn't hesitate. My grandpop wouldn't have. Neither would Susannah or any of the Casquette Girls Coven. *Dominate.* "Ren, I swear to God I'm going to find a way to save you. You just have to promise me that you're going to hang on until I get back."

He raised his cane. "That's the spirit, son!"

"I'm going to find that miracle man and get a gad, or do whatever I need to do."

And those souls needed a final resting place, otherwise why did I bother saving them from the cemetery protection ward? Julie got infected. And I'd lost Adele because of it. I lost her the second I closed those cemetery gates between us.

Ren jumped on the bed. "You have to fight for those you love!" Luckily, people were used to the sound of his voice at all hours.

"I'm gonna fight for you, and Alessandro, and Mac, and all of New Orleans. And I'm going to fight for Adele too."

I have to. I love her more than anything.

This was her plan, and I believed in her. I needed to show her, even if I thought going to Guinée was insane. I'm sure people thought that Neil Armstrong was insane for wanting to go to the moon. Was the Afterworld really that much weirder than outer space?

I swooped out of the guesthouse, back into the shop, and veered as I tried to stop suddenly, nearly smashing into an African mask. Désirée was standing in the middle of the apothecary, clutching a handful of silk scarves, and across the room, blocking the door, was . . . Ritha. She was hugging Marassa's grimoire.

Shiiiiiiit. My wings fluttered as I struggled to perch myself atop the mask.

"How did you kn—?" Désirée asked.

"Do you think you're the only one around here who talks to the spirits, child? They ratted out your ass quicker than you could throw a handful of bones."

"I'm going."

"I know that you're young and you think you're invincible. You have the power to heal and you are a great, *great*, witch. And one day you will be a magnificent high priestess of New Orleans. The greatest in the history of this city. But you are not a vampire. You are not immortal. I cannot bring you back from the dead. These are not spirits. These are not lwa. They are the Ghede!" Her nostrils flared. "*You are not ready for this.*"

Désirée's eyes glistened, but the lines in her forehead grew more intense, like she was commanding the tears away. "I am ready for whatever the challenges the Baron and Maman see me fit to serve—"

Ritha sighed. "I also know that if you are hell-bent on this path, there's nothing I can do to stop you. I could curse you inside a great live oak, and ask Gran Bwa himself to guard it, but you'd find a way out. You'd become his cheval and charge on headfirst to Guinée, all of the flora and fauna of the forest following you." She took a calming breath. "And that's not your fault. You get your hard head from me. The more someone tells you not to play with fire, the more gasoline you're going to pour on it."

I couldn't be sure, but I think Dee was *crying*.

"I don't know how you did it, but if you've been able to get this far with this lunacy, a part of me, at least, has to think it's your destiny, Désirée Nanette Borges, my youngest grandchild."

Désirée's back unstiffened. "I didn't get this far on my own . . . I had you as a teacher. And I did everything with my coven. I wouldn't be able to continue without any of you."

"Just promise me that you will practice patience, child. Look. Think. And ask your ancestors for guidance before you leap."

"*I promise.*"

"And if you are really going to Guinée before your time, you aren't leaving without this." She held out the grimoire.

Désirée's eyes lit bright. "But what if . . . ?"

"Then so be it. It's just magic. You are *my life*, Désirée. My blood. And I need you to have every protection I can give you."

Désirée hurried over and threw her arms around her grandmother.

"And that includes *you* too," Ritha said.

My tail puffed.

"You better protect my granddaughter. Don't let her courage get bigger than her brain. Or her magic."

I sheepishly hopped to the ground and turned back into my human form, embarrassed to have interrupted the family moment.

Désirée wiped her eyes as I walked over. "Don't you mean I need to protect him?"

"You'll protect each other." Ritha removed something attached to a leather cord from her apron pocket, placed it around my neck, and kissed my head. "I don't care if you're a New Yorker, dress warm. Those with our types of Spektral magic, once the chill gets in our bones, it's hard to think about anything else." She took Désirée's hands and squeezed a small pouch into it. "Gunpowder."

Désirée nodded.

Gunpowder? What the hell would we need gunpowder for?

But without another look, Ritha walked toward the back. "Send Marassa my love." She waited until she was engulfed in the shadows before blotting her eyes. I definitely knew where Dee got her badassness from. Before she stepped through the curtain, Ritha turned to the counter, her gaze resting on a potted orchid that didn't appear to be in great shape—kinda strange for an Earth witch. Especially Ritha. "They need you," she said.

"Who does?" Dee asked.

"The spirits." Her voice trailed as she stepped behind the curtain. "Something dark is coming."

A chill curled up my spine, and I found myself twisting the

leather cord between my fingers. A single long tooth was tied to its center.

Désirée's gaze lingered on the half-dead orchid.

"What's with the flower?" I asked. "Ritha has the greenest thumb around."

"It was a gift . . . for Hexennacht. From Fiona Daure."

"I hope she's a Water witch," I said.

"Me too." She turned back to me. "It's a wolf's fang," she said, of the necklace I was twisting between my fingers. "Extra protection from the spirits."

"Gotcha." I blew out a breath. "Did Ritha just give us her blessing? We're really doing this?"

She nodded. "I'll get the picnic baskets. You get the kishi."

I knew I'd be the one who ended up carrying the souls. But I didn't say anything. I barely even breathed as I strapped Morning Star's enchanted basket on my back.

Or as I carried it to HQ.

Once we were there, I hurriedly ditched my party clothes. If I was going to leave this world, I wanted my most comfortable pair of jeans, and then, bag packed, hair dripping, I stepped back into the blue room, ready to go. Dee had transferred piman into seven Mason jars, and was now cleansing the Ghede keys with river water. Codi was on the couch, hunched over his knees, fist in his palm, an intense look on his face.

"Good, you're back," I said, shaking out my wet hair. "You're on soul duty."

Dee licked a drizzle of clear liquid from her hand. *"Yup, that's piman,"* she choked.

Codi didn't respond. He didn't even look up.

"So what did the Medici want?" I asked him.

"Nothing." His gaze stayed locked on the floor.

Dee gave me a concerned shrug.

"It doesn't seem like nothing."

He squeezed his fist even tighter, and then he sprang up. His palms slammed into my chest, shoving me back so hard I fell.

"Whoa!" Désirée yelled.

"What the hell?" I jumped up. "Half an hour with Nicco Medici, and he's turned you against me?"

He came at me again, but Désirée got in between us. "Codi!"

I knew he wasn't going to hit me again, but I was concerned about the fire in his eyes, reflecting a part of him that had been scorched.

"Why did you leave Adele at the cemetery?"

"What?" The vague question landed harder than a punch.

"Why did you leave her alone?" His voice cracked.

"What are you talking about? I was trying to get the souls away from the protection ward. Away from her!" I remembered the blood. "Codi, what happened at the cemetery?"

"Nothing." He backed away, clutching fistfuls of his hair. "I'm sorry. I know you'd never do anything to hurt her. Let's go."

An image of Adele floated into my mind—when we found her down by the river—so broken and discolored and wet and cold, she'd looked more like one of the Storm-corpses I'd discovered than my girlfriend. She'd looked *dead.*

It wasn't just that, Isaac.

She'd been erratic at the shop. Irrational. I was so used to being around traumatized people amidst disaster, I'd gone into first responder mode instead of boyfriend mode. She was in shock, but now I realized I didn't even know what had happened tonight. Mac was taken, Olsin was killed, but what had happened to *her?*

Fuck.

"Codi," I stepped close, grabbing the shoulder of his shirt. "What happened?"

He jerked away without looking at me. "It's not my story to tell."

The chill in his voice made a wave of nausea wash over me.

Désirée froze in place, her nostrils flared with anger. I picked up my bag, but rage pummeled so hard through me, I nearly turned and threw it out the window.

Instead, I slung it onto my back, picked up the two picnic baskets, and headed for the door. "Are we going?"

I'd never seen Codi mad like that. Not even close.

What did he know? What the hell did Nicco know?

CHAPTER 15
CLOSED SECRET

It was a peculiar feeling, walking through the Medici halls without a paranoid vampire at my side.

Also strange was the inexplicable sense of liveliness in the house. Fires crackled in each of the parlors. Wall sconces, usually dormant, flickered with bright flames to accommodate human guests who didn't share the residents' super-senses. And perhaps most peculiar of all, I swore I smelled food. *Is someone baking?* I followed the scent with longing, even though the aroma of fresh-baked goods seemed so at odds with the planning of murder. It reminded me of how funeral homes hid toaster ovens so their parlors always smelled like warm chocolate chip cookies instead of formaldehyde and roses.

Thinking of death brought the phantom crack of vertebrae loudly to my ears, the sensation of the witch's bones snapping . . . splintering. The pain that had shot up my own arm when the pole made impact. What would it take to kill the spirit of Jakome Salazar? Adeline had once pondered whether she could kill a man to save the lives of many more; I was about to have to prove that I could. Kill his spirit, anyway.

A couple of turns led me to a large, open kitchen that looked like it hadn't been updated since the advent of indoor plumbing. A brass chandelier hung over Gabriel, who stood behind an island, an apron folded over his waist as he transferred sugar cookies from a pan to a butcher block.

I was acutely aware that he'd threatened my life on at least one occasion, not to mention the lives of my ancestors on several, but I still preferred him to join our group over his brother.

I set my things down against the wall. "Just the man I wanted to see."

He saw me savagely eyeing the tray. "We had some leftover dough, so I figured, why not?" He slid the cookies in my direction. "You must be hungry."

"A little." I bounded forward ungracefully, snatched one, and gobbled it up like a gremlin.

But when the sugary treat hit my stomach, the joy squelched, and the night's anxiety kneaded my organs into knots. I ate the second one slower.

He passed me a big bowl of fruit. Strawberries, blackberries, and little golden berries still in their blossomed husks. A variety of leftovers from the night's festivities. I chose a strawberry.

He poured me a glass of water.

"*Grazie.*" I drank it back without taking a breath.

"Apologies, we don't have anything else. Unless you want something harder." He tilted his head toward the counter.

I was soothed to see a bottle of Bourbon and not a carafe of blood.

"*Madonna mia!*" He went back to the old fridge and returned with a jug of a pink frothy concoction. "I nearly forgot. I didn't send all of the bubbly with Niccolò." He poured two glasses.

"To finding Jakome Salazar." He held his glass up.

I was in no mood to celebrate, but that toast changed my

mind. I clinked his glass and took a sip. *Oh, God.* It wasn't just champagne. *Bourbon. It's definitely also Bourbon.*

Gabriel added an extra shot to his, but I declined; the second sip of the cotton-candy cocktail was already spreading warmth through my limbs. "How many of those before I can convince you to come to Guinée with us?"

He slid down to his elbows. "A barrel of Bourbon would not get me to leave the Natural World. Unless you're going to enchant it like you did with the moonshine Halloween night."

A sly smile spread over my face. "Might I remind you, *you* threatened me first."

"It's not that I don't want to help, *bella*, but no amount of booze, eyelash-batting, or queenly speeches will change my mind." He rolled up his left sleeve. "My arm might bear this mark, but I'm a vampire, and who knows how our type would acclimate to the Afterworld? What if our senses are dulled? What if our vestigial heartbeats confuse the veil and we aren't allowed re-entry home?"

"Do you think that's a real possibility?" *Could Nicco be trapped in the Afterworld?*

"Probably not. But am I willing to risk it for you?" He refilled my empty glass. "No. And as much as I'd love to see my mother's beautiful face and hear my father's hearty laugh, I'd rather not take a trip down memory lane when it comes to the dead. I'm not of this time, Adele. Many have died by both my hand and my fangs. While this doesn't keep me up at night, like it does some, I'm not looking for a reunion with those I've slain."

I glugged back more pink drink. "Well, it's a wonder Emilio wants to go."

"Emilio sleeps fine. Always has."

I'm bringing a vampire without a conscience and trusting him around my friends. Not comforting.

"I don't think Nicco sleeps as well as he wants everyone to believe," I said, almost in shock that I said it out loud.

"Even after all these centuries, Niccolò blames himself for our deaths, and for the destruction of the entire Medici dynasty, both in the mundane world and the Magical. He would risk anything for a crack at Jakome. Or León, for that matter." He smiled at me over the top of his glass. "I'm beginning to believe there isn't anything he wouldn't risk for you."

I guzzled the rest of the drink, and warmth bloomed from my insides to the top of my head. He stared, analyzing my every reaction to the comment about his brother.

I'd never fought so hard to suppress the smile.

He leaned closer and spoke in soft French. "Adele, you're taking my baby brother and my baby vampire from me. If this ghastly quest is a ploy by you or your coven to hurt my family, I will not hesitate to kill your father myself."

I slowly raised my gaze to his. "Gabriel, I was under the impression you thought more fondly of me?" The seduction in my voice matched his, which I could only attribute to the booze.

"I also used to be very fond of Adeline."

I stirred a lone blackberry in my empty glass. "*Je n'aurais jamais. Never.*" I didn't want to play games with him. "I would never hurt Nicco, no matter what Callis wanted, or León, or Adeline."

"*Très bien, ma chère.*"

"I would never hurt Nicco, but . . . Gabriel, if you ever threaten my father again, you will see my Saint-Germain side re-emerge."

"Ruthless." He backed away, smiling that devilish Medici smile. "You're more like her every day."

"Don't forget, you were the one threatening to kill her father when she locked you up. Her only family. *Her* magical legacy."

He sighed. "I know. If I had broken out of that damned attic in her lifetime, we would have made a formidable match."

"From the little I know about her, I might have to agree."

He smiled, but then turned serious again. "In my stead, you must keep my brother safe. He's too smart for his own good. He's been alive for so long, he forgets that immortality is not synonymous with invincibility. *Protégez mon frère.*"

"I promise."

"And, Adele, if you see my sister on the other side, send her my love, *s'il vous plaît.*"

"*Je promets.*" I bit into the blackberry, and it melted on my tongue, both bitter and sweet.

"*Buona Floralia, bella.*"

"Ditto."

A racket came from upstairs, shaking the brass chandelier overhead and causing us to both look up.

"*Scusami.*"

Before I could comment, he'd sped off in a blur.

I poured a tiny bit more of the fruity drink and devoured most of the berries and another cookie. The booze eased my anxiety just enough for me to get the food down, all the while remembering Nicco's warning to *never trust a vampire.* Gabriel was a bit like the drink: beautiful and delicious, melting your guard away, but then before you knew it, you were teetering and passing out on a settee. Deceptively dangerous.

I stepped back into the hallway, on the lookout for Lisette.

The night Gabriel had showed me Giovanna's sword, he'd gone off like a Roman candle when I'd brought up Séraphine. She'd triggered something within him, and a different person had emerged. Someone more monstrous. Would he have attacked me that night, if I hadn't broken his nose? If Nicco hadn't intervened? Maybe Gabriel not coming to the Afterworld was a good thing after all. What if he decided to take a detour and go after Adeline's spirit? Broke my family's magical line like they think León did to his?

Note to self: Never bring up Séraphine to any of the Medici boys.

An arm slipped around my neck, another around my waist, and my feet lifted off the floor. I wriggled, but his hold was tight. "Okay, Gabriel, I got it. Always be on guard."

He gripped me tighter.

Goddammit. I'm still sore. But I dropped my weight like he'd shown me, like I'd done with that stupid Air witch, but this time, to no effect. I struggled to breathe. "Gabriel, you're hurting me," I stuttered. Dizziness encroached. *Never trust a vampire.* I tried to suppress the arising panic, but I began to flail. "*Sto—!*"

"*Shhhh.*" He shook me hard, in a way that said if I screamed for help, I'd regret it.

I stopped resisting, and he loosened his grip on my throat. "What's your problem?" I snapped.

I cringed as his breath dusted my ear. "If you see my sister on the other side, and she tells you anything at all about her death, you'd better remember the promise you made to me."

Emilio. My pulse raced.

"If you expose me, I will destroy you."

"Get in line," I spat, and started to yell for Gabe.

He grabbed a fistful of my hair and yanked it back, tearing at my scalp. "I dare you to scream."

"Do you know how many people have threatened me tonight?" My voice shook, though out of fear or delirium, I was unsure.

He rubbed his nose into my exposed neck. "I'm not them."

"She's going to tell him herself!" I jolted, feeling his tongue glide across my skin.

"No, she's not." The touch of his lips made my spine go limp.

"*Stop.*" A tear slipped out, and I hated myself for it.

"If you expose my role in Giovanna's death, I will take you

from Niccolò the way I took your mother from your father."

The tips of his fangs pierced.

"Emilio, stop!" I shrieked, bucking up against him; but he wasn't like the Air witch, he was like a steel clamp. "I won't tell!"

"What's wrong, *bella*? I thought you wanted to be a vampire?"

"I don't! Stop, *please*."

He licked the wound and tossed me to the floor. "See you in Guinée."

He watched as I scrambled up and ran down the hallway, sucking in a ragged breath, my dignity left on the floor at his feet. I wanted the rusty pole back in my hand. I wanted to impale his heart. Instead, I barged into Nicco's bedroom like a bull and slammed the door behind me. The metal lock snapped closed, and I threw my weight against it. As if Emilio couldn't push through with minimal effort.

All the momentum I'd built up over the last few hours deflated like a wilting balloon. If I couldn't even handle Emilio, how would I kill Jakome Salazar? I couldn't even handle the witches in the cemetery—I wouldn't have gotten away if it hadn't been for the coven's magic.

My lungs tightened thinking about what would have happened.

And I felt it again: *the witch's hands all over me.*

I looked around the room for any kind of weapon. I shuffled around the large oak bed frame and yanked open the nightstand drawer. *Why would Nicco have a weapon, Adele? He's a vampire.* I dug through headphones, passports, keys, and cash until I felt a heavy, slender object in a leather sheath. A dagger. I slammed the drawer and fell down to the floor against the nightstand.

I slipped the blade from its sheath, breaths getting shorter, and drew my knees into my chest, clutching the hilt. I couldn't stop shaking. All the threats of the night piled atop my chest at once, and the familiar old burn squeezed my lungs. *My inhaler.*

It was in my bag in the kitchen. The realization made me panic more, and I hugged my legs tighter, trying to convince myself I didn't need it. But I wanted the medicine. I wanted my dad. For a dizzying moment, I even wished that Isaac was here. His cool, soothing Air. He could always calm me down. *Why doesn't he know that? Why did he throw those flowers at me?* I wanted to scream, but instead I gasped for air.

Nicco's voice echoed in my head: "*You don't need to be calmed down. You're a Fire witch!*"

Tears streamed down my face. I angrily wiped them away.

I lifted my hands, dagger and all, and pictured myself as a tiny child, Mac instructing me to breathe. Then I heard her delicate voice over my shoulder, telling me to let it go. "*Allez, mon amour. Respire.*" My mother hadn't even been around when I'd started getting panic attacks. In fact, I was pretty sure her leaving is what had triggered them. "*Respire, mon amour.*"

But I listened to her anyway.

My lungs unlocked, and I released the breath, and the fire in my chest subsided just enough to take in new air.

Thump-thump.

I hated him.

For the first time, I realized how strong my mother must have been to put up with Emilio Medici for twelve years.

But I didn't have to put up with him. I refused to.

He isn't coming with us.

Emilio had bitten Adeline once, and I wasn't letting that psycho around her again. He would not get the chance to break our magical line or hurt the Saint-Germains.

Why had he been so confident that Giovanna wouldn't tell Nicco his big secret?

And then it hit me: because he was going to silence her. Would Emilio really harm his sister's spirit?

I had to protect Adeline, but now I felt like I needed to protect Giovanna too.

CHAPTER 16
SETTE STREGHE

The Ghost Drinker's threats ricocheted through my head as I drifted back to the house. *"What was it you said about never betraying Nicco? You think he'll still want you after this?"*

Thump-thump.

My pace quickened. She'd been so strong at the house. So confident. Focused on her plans, determined to save Mac. But she was pushing through this the whole time? *"Prima o poi lo ucciderò, cazzo."*

Something pricked my neck. I smacked it away, spinning around. I'd have sworn someone had jabbed me with a needle.

Thump-thump. Thump-thump. Thump-thump.

I gazed into the empty streets, listening, watching the shadows. *They aren't my heartbeats; they're hers.* I sped off in a burst of panic.

I should never have trusted them with Adele.

I blew in through the front door, looking around for signs of anything amiss. Nothing. Lisette shouted for me as I whipped past the library, but I refused to let go of the thinning pulse. I rushed through the parlors, hallways, to the door of my bedroom. Why was it locked? I twisted the handle so hard, it broke off in my hand.

Thump-thump.

I pushed it open. "Adele?"

The room was dark save for the moonlight from a single open curtain. I edged around the bed. She was huddled on the floor, gripping my Barbagio dagger as if ready to pound it into someone's chest.

"Adele . . ."

Was she hurt? Or in shock, the traumas of the night finally settling in? I crouched down slowly, careful not to startle her, and her gaze finally found me. Her eyes were freshly swollen from crying. "What happened?" I asked, controlling every inflection.

"Nothing."

I slowly wedged myself between her and the bed. I pushed away her hair, checking her neck. No wounds. She stayed silent as I checked the other side. The skin was perfectly smooth, no redness, no sign of recent healing. I mentally exhaled. My kill list was growing long enough tonight without having to add a member of my household to it.

Tears repainted the stains on her face. "Don't look at me."

"Why not?"

She turned to the wall, trying to blink the tears away. "I don't want you to think I'm weak."

"Weak?" I suppressed the image of her in the cemetery, and I was glad she was looking away. I knew the anger would be all over my face—it was hard enough keeping the rage from spilling into my voice. "Do you think me a fool?"

Her brow scrunched. "No."

"Only a fool could think you are weak." I resisted pulling her nearer while she was so closed off. "Tears don't make a person weak, *bella*, cowardice does."

"Nicco, what I said earlier . . . I don't want to be a vampire—"

"Of course you don't! And you never will be." Her words had jolted me. Did she now feel unsafe with me? "I would *never*. Not to you. Or to anyone!"

"I know. I don't know why I said it. I didn't mean to upset you."

"You're not upsetting me. You can tell me anything, Adele. *Anything*."

"Earlier . . ." More silent tears flowed. "I knew something was wrong when our dreams connected." She blushed deeply, eyes averted. "It was the one you didn't want me to see."

Panic plucked my nerves. When I was unconscious . . . I'd forgotten she'd seen— It wasn't the one I *really* didn't want her to see. "It was just a fevered dream, *bella*, a chemically induced fantasy." *My lips sliding over the curve of her throat, fangs pushing into her neck as she begged me to take her.* "There was an explosion in the lab, and I blacked out!"

"That's the point! I knew something was wrong. I should have known you were hurt and come to find you! I should have trusted my intuition instead of listening to Isaac . . . I tried to find you after the party— I shouldn't have gone off with him— If I'd listened to my magic, maybe I would have gotten to Mac before . . ."

My mind breezed over the mention of her and Isaac, remembering that she'd come after me, and I'd shut her out. *Again.* "I was here," I confessed, ashamed of how I'd cowered behind the door like a wounded pup.

"Emilio told me—!"

"What I wanted him to. My ego was bruised. If I'd just acted like a man instead of . . ." I saw the Fire witch crushing her. "You never would have ended up at the—" The word almost slipped out. "I wouldn't have taken my eyes off of you all night if I'd just let you through the door."

She turned inward to me. "It's not your fault."

"It's not yours either."

She came closer, and my palm slid over her cheek. *I want her.* Our faces brushed. *I want her more than anything.* Her lips parted mine—*I just bring trouble into her life*—and I jolted back, keeping her at bay.

Her eyes grew wide. "I'm sorry! I'm so sorry. I know you don't want me like that!"

"*You think Nicco will still want you after this?*"

"I don't know what's wrong with me!" She turned away, but I pulled her back even closer, holding her face to mine. "Adele, I will always want you. *Always.*" My voice shook. I wanted her warmth, and her humanity, and her beauty, but she deserved more than this. More than a monster.

Her eyes sparkled, and in the silence, her pulse finally steadied.

A sweet note hit my senses, and I sniffed the air between us. "Is that Bourbon? Are you drunk? Is that why you're coming on to me, *signorina*?"

She finally cracked a smile.

She climbed into my lap and hugged my neck tightly. "And I will always want you too, Niccolò Medici."

My arms snaked around her. I relished her words, and the thumps of her heart against mine.

"And I might have drunk some of the pink stuff with Gabriel."

I laughed. "Well, that explains everything."

I knew we had critical things to do, that we were losing time, the pull of the moon, but when she lay against my chest, my rational thoughts slipped away, rendering me unable to protest. I stroked her hair and absorbed her embrace, never wanting to leave this room. The words I'd written to her on the eve of Halloween floated into my head. '*Sometimes at night, the dark-ness and silence weigh upon me.*'

And I found myself reciting them aloud. "*Dovremmo vivere in uno stato di animazione sospesa, come per un'opera d'arte . . .*"

"*In quell'ordine d'incanto,*" she finished in nearly perfect Italian.

My fingers traipsed beneath the hem of her shirt, just enough to feel her skin. "You watched the film?"

"I might have watched it a couple . . . dozen . . . times. I thought it would be a good way to learn Italian."

"Oh, was that it?" I sat her up, staying wrapped around her.

"*Sì.*" Her smile was achingly sexy as she picked up my dagger from the floor and examined it.

It had been made with the finest Venetian steel, by the finest Venetian witches. It was the weapon I'd stabbed Séraphine with when she killed me, and the one I'd later plunged into her heart. "A parrying dagger." I moved it to her left hand. "Florentines are partial to fighting with a blade in each hand."

"Emilio gave it to you for your fifteenth birthday."

I'd never told her that, and it made my heart throb in a way she could never understand. She must have sensed my surprise.

"I saw it in your dream. Right before Gabriel and Emilio took you to the bordello for deflowering."

I laughed. "Well, you do know my brothers." I curled the fingers of her free hand around mine. "But you only saw half of the picture: the sword's mundane purpose. The real reason Emilio gave me this dagger, and why the Medici were so formidable, was that while one hand wielded a lethal blade, the dominant hand was free to wield magic."

She traced the gimmel rings carved on the hilt. "I saw these symbols all over the palazzo in your dreams. All over Florence."

"And one day you will see them with your own eyes." I wrapped her hand tightly around the hilt. "Would you be scared to use it?"

"No," she said without hesitation.

"*Bene, è tuo.*"

"No way." She turned to me. "I could never take it. You've kept it all these years. Decades. Centuries."

"You can, and you will. I'll teach you to use it, and you can rummage in my head at night for innumerable banal lessons from Gabriel."

"Did you just give me permission to be in your head, Niccolò?"

"*Bella*, I don't think you could ever understand how deeply you already are in my head." I got lost in her gaze. The same deep blue eyes as León.

"*Grazie, Niccolò. Lo ado . . . ro?*"

I nodded, though I was utterly unconcerned with her conjugation. I wanted to hear her speak Italian for the rest of my life. I wanted to take her to Firenze. To a real Floralia. I wanted to introduce her to my *famiglia* in the Afterworld. "You just have to promise me one thing."

"*Cosa?*"

"That you will drive it into the heart of any man—any witch —who ever tries to harm you."

"*Sì, lo prometto.*" She looked me squarely in the eye. "Or any witch who tries to hurt you."

My restraint had not been tested so severely since I was under Séraphine's control.

"We should go," I said.

She nodded, and in a whirl, I pulled us both up.

"Lift up your shirt."

She blushed.

"Just a little, I meant." I pulled the sheath from the floor and sat on the edge of the bed.

"Oh." She blushed again, this time at herself, and lifted the layers of clothing.

I tied the leather cord around her bare waist, the image of that heathen touching her raging inside me, and slid the sheath to the dip of her back. "Can you reach it easily?" I guided her hand with the weapon to the leather casing, and she slid the dagger inside.

"*Sì.*" She turned around as I stood. "*Grazie.*" She kissed my jaw, and I didn't think; I just let my face tilt into hers.

"We're going to get through this," I whispered.

"I know." She tugged my shirt, holding me in place. "There's one more thing."

"*Sì?*"

"Your brother's not coming with us. I don't trust him."

"Adele, we're out of time. I don't know if I can convince Gab—"

"I don't want Gabe to come either. I don't trust him around Adeline after what she did to him. And Emilio has already tried to kill her once. I hope you understand, but I have to protect my family too."

Thump-thump.

"You trust me, though, around Adeline?"

"Of course. You want León dead, not her. And he isn't in Guinée. If he were, you wouldn't be coming either." She paused, looking up at me. "I don't care if we have to bring one of the swamp witches. I don't care if I have to beg Poppy Daure. Codi will hate me forever, but I have to save my dad. And I have to do it without risking the Saint-Germain magical line."

There wasn't room to argue—Emilio had killed her mother. But bringing either of the elder Ghost Drinkers was out of the question. They were never leaving the attic. "There might be one more option, but you're not going to like it."

Her brow furrowed.

"A Ghost Drinker of sorts." I was already regretting this. "One you might be a little more familiar with."

Her eyes grew wider.

"I think she'd be easier to control than the more experienced witches."

"Annabelle? You're talking about Annabelle? What, you

think I can just text her and be like, hey, wanna switch sides and go to the Afterworld to kill Callisto's father?"

"Something like that. Only you don't have to call her. She's locked upstairs with the others. And I think I'd be the better one to flip her, per se."

"Annabelle Lee Drake is *here?* In this house? Right now?"

"*Sì.*"

She darted for the door, but I caught her and lifted her into the air.

"I want to see her!"

"*Bella*, I don't think that's a good idea. Let me talk to her." I set her down, and she whipped around. "Unless you have someone else in mind?"

She sucked in a hard breath.

"Emilio or Annabelle?" I asked. "I'm fully aware that neither choice is ideal. Emilio is unpredictable, and Annabelle is . . . Annabelle."

I heard the front door open downstairs.

"Your friends are here."

Her head fell back as she groaned. "I'll go break the news."

Lisette's chiffon skirt fluttered as she hurried to keep up. "What are we doing, Niccolò?"

"Slight change of plans. Emilio's out. Annabelle's in. And we're recruiting her."

Fear flicked in her eyes. "Why me?" she asked in French.

"Because she's your bloodline."

She bolted away, but I was faster and blocked her.

"So you *were* one of Adeline's coven members?"

Her fangs snapped out.

I let the fear fester for a moment before I spoke. "Don't worry, your secret's safe with me."

"Adele told you," she hissed.

"Adele knows? So that's what she met with you about those times . . ."

"How did you?"

"When Gabriel first brought you home, I was aghast. Your white hair and your golden eyes, radiant as the sun's rays. It was like Cosette Monvoisin, the great Madam, had stepped out of my dreams. Just cold and wild and lost."

Her brow pinched.

"But you couldn't be Cosette, because Cosette . . . would have tried to kill me."

"You knew my sister?"

"Not really." I stepped closer. "You saved Annabelle that night at the convent, didn't you? Helped her escape?"

She remained silent.

"I can see that you care for her. That you're ashamed of her recent choices."

Her gazed dropped to the floor.

"The only thing I don't know for certain is whether she descended directly from Cosette or you, if you had a child before you met human death?"

Tears dripped down her cheeks. "*I've never had a baby.*" She looked straight at me. "And now I never will."

"I'm sorry." It was a pain I understood too well. "I didn't mean to upset you."

"Why does it matter to you?"

"In case I have to kill her."

"You can't! She's carrying the Monvoisin magicline."

"Which she didn't hesitate to turn over to Callisto Salazar."

"I will get our grimoire back, even if I can never cast a spell again. I'd rather burn it than see it fuel his necromancy!"

"If you don't want to see Annabelle dead, then help me keep her in line."

"*D'accord.*"

"And when this is all over, I'll do everything I can to help you get your grimoire back." I unlocked the door and motioned her in.

The three witches all looked up with more rigor than usual. Tonight was their coven's big hurrah. Carina and Josif would surely have thought that they'd only need to make it until tonight. The fourth, our new Ghost Drinker from the Cathedral, was still unconscious next to Raúl's body.

I grabbed the wooden chair, placed it backwards in front of Annabelle, and straddled it.

"I'm hungry," she said.

"I'm here to offer you a proposition, Miss Drake."

"Whatever it is, the answer is no."

"I wouldn't think a girl as strategically minded as you would be so hasty." I turned to Carina. "Tonight, Callisto and his entourage were a mere four blocks away at Le Chat Noir. Did anyone even attempt to come for you, Carina?"

"Callis doesn't know they're here," Annabelle snapped.

"He knows exactly where they are."

"I don't care that he didn't come for them; he's coming for me."

"Because you're his special one, right?"

Carina laughed.

"Callisto is not coming, but I am here to offer you a way out of those chains, despite you being the last person who deserves it."

Her stare hardened, like I was about to make her do something ungodly.

"We're going on a little trip to the Afterworld."

"The *Afterworld?* Are you on some kind of vampire drugs?"

"The ritual requires seven witches to open the gates. We have six."

"I'll go," Josif barked.

Carina erupted in Norwegian about far worse consequences

than dying in an attic if he turned his back on the coven. He shot her a knowing look, as if to say, "Shut up, idiot," that if he got picked, he could escape and then free them both. Which was precisely why neither of them were coming. Annabelle was the only option.

"And why the hell would you all be leaving the Natural World in the middle of the biggest magical battle New Orleans has ever seen?" Annabelle leaned in. "Are you already giving up? Joining your ancestors for final death? You're just as pathetic as Callis says."

"Adele thinks we're going to kill the spirit of Jakome—"

"Breaking a witch's magical blood line?" Josif said with revulsion. "I wouldn't think even a Medici would stoop so low."

Carina slapped the floor with her foot. "Don't listen to him, Annabelle. It's a ruse. Mortals can't go to the Afterworld. Not even witches."

"Maybe yours can't," Lisette said, "but we're not just any witches. We're not mortal."

She was catching on quick.

"You're not witches at all!" Josif yelled.

Lisette's fangs snapped out.

"Who's Jakome?" Annabelle faux-yawned.

"Jakome *Salazar*?" Carina scoffed. "Only the greatest witch who ever lived. And Callisto's father."

Annabelle sat up and brushed her hair from her fiery eyes. I finally had her attention. "You said, Adele *thinks* that's why you're going, but why would a vampire really venture to the Afterworld? Certainly not to save a bartender."

"I've been returning to New Orleans for centuries, waiting to find the right magic to open the gates so I can get to Guinée to retrieve my grimoire."

Lisette glanced my way.

"I'm sure you've heard of the infamous Medici book of shadows? It's the whole reason Callisto took *that bartender* hostage."

"It's the holy grail of magic," Annabelle said. "Why would your grimoire be in the Afterworld? I thought Adele's ancestor—Saint-Germain, or whoever—had it."

"Saint-Germain did have it, until his lover stole it from him." As I stood, I hoped that my sister was watching from the other side and could get a good chuckle, *benedici la sua anima.* "In the early 1700s, I made a plan with my three siblings to reclaim our magical rites. Giovanna was to reunite with León, steal the book back, and bring it home to us. León was never able to resist my sister, and this time was no exception. She stole the book, but Giovanna had always been an orthodox witch. She was the only person who hated being a vampire more than I. She sanctimoniously claimed that vampires had no business with magic, that it would upset the balance of the supernatural world—"

"It would!" Josif yelled.

"She lied to us and told us that León threw her to the gutter after their tryst. She pretended to be devastated. It fueled our hatred even more. Giovanna always knew how to get her way with us. In secret, she had a Romani witch crone bind the book to her spirit. This way, when she met final death, she could take it with her to the other side, and the Medici book of magic would be safe from vampires forever, even if said vampires bore the name of its magicline." I shoved the chair off to the side, and it slammed into the wall.

Annabelle didn't flinch. She rose in her chains and came to us, crossing her shackled arms. "What the hell am *I* getting out of this besides out of your attic?"

"Is your freedom not enough?"

"Free for Callis to kill me for betraying him?"

I smiled coyly. "I know you only joined him and gave him your Great family's grimoire because he promised that you'd rule the most powerful coven in the world at his side."

Lisette's jaw nearly snapped.

"What do you mean, Great family?"

"Did he not tell you the history of your magical legacy? Of the Great Monvoisins? One of the most powerful witchlines to come out of France?"

She looked to Lisette.

A confidence exuded from her that I'd never seen before, and she truly did remind me of Cosette. "If you come with us, *ma fifille*, I can show you who you really are. Who you are meant to be."

"*Pfft.* You don't even have magic."

"But we will." I gazed at Lisette like she was the most beautiful woman in the world, which to be fair, wasn't that difficult, and she came closer. "In my grimoire, there's an old Egyptian spell to wake the latent magic of witches who have"— I brushed Lisette's arm with my knuckle, and she blushed—"our particular affliction. Once we have that spell, I will re-bind our circle. The new Medici coven will be the most powerful ever known to mankind, with the magic of the Medici witches, and the immortality and supersenses of the Medici vampires."

Lisette's arms slid around my waist. "I think you meant the Medici-Monvoisin coven, right darling?" she said sultrily into my neck. She bit my earlobe, and my resulting smile was genuine. I think I was actually starting to like her.

"My silly mistake." I focused back on Annabelle. "And as a descendant of the Great *La Voisin*, Catherine Deshayes, I am offering you a chance to be a founding member. Of course, to reach your full potential, you'll have to become a vampire. But that's your choice."

"I'm not a weakling like Adele," she spat. "I would *never* let you or one of your vamp-brothers have power over me like that."

"I can be your Maker," Lisette said. "I can teach you of your birthright, and how to be a better witch. How being an Aether is the greatest form of magic, a privilege not to be squandered with cheap manipulations and glamours."

Annabelle rolled her eyes. "Spare me the self-righteous crap. What's the catch?"

"No catch," I said. "Just a couple of ground rules."

She crossed her arms.

"You try to use your Aether magic on me or the others, and I will drain you quicker than you can blink. Use your Spektral magic for anything other than to aid the group, I drain you. Try to escape before we get the grimoire, your days in the Natural World are over. Am I clear?"

"You really are no fun at all." Her thin lips pursed into a pouty smile. "I can see why Adele is sweet on you. You're both *bores.*"

"Annabelle," Carina hissed. "You took a vow! If you betray Callisto, he will end you!"

"Let him try. I will be a true immortal." Her hand touched my chest, and she slid closer, peering up at me. "I don't believe, Nicco Medici, that you're as big of a bore as you let on to be."

"Aether whore," Carina muttered scathingly, but Annabelle's gaze never broke from mine.

"I guess you'll have to play if you want to find out. You have ninety seconds to decide." I turned and walked out, Lisette following.

"I'm coming! Let me out!"

When we were halfway down the stairs, Lisette grabbed my hand. "Niccolò," she whispered in French. "That spell you spoke of. Your grimoire. Was any of it true?"

"Mademoiselle Monvoisin, no one loved being a vampire more than Giovanna Medici. It freed her of the shackles worn by women of the time. Namely, her rat-faced husband."

Her brow only partially unfurled, but I offered no further explanation. She may have grown on me, but if she had been one of Adeline's coven members, one who had entrapped my family and was presently lying to my brother about it, I didn't trust her entirely.

"You can release her. Get her cleaned up and give her some food. She's in your hands. Don't let her out of your sight. She doesn't take a shit without your supervision."

She nodded. "Do you think . . . Do you think she could ever change? She's so young."

"I think she'll flip again as soon as a better offer presents itself." I turned to leave.

"Nicco?" Sorrow infiltrated her expression as she absent-mindedly covered the mark on her arm. "Do you think it's going to work? That you and I really count in the seven? We're not real witches anymore."

"We have our marks. Not even death—or vampirism—could take those away." I truly wished I could offer her a guarantee, but I knew no more than she did. "Hopefully they're enough for the Ghede."

I hurried back through the house, searching for Emilio. I found him on the mezzanine, gazing down at Adele's coven, contemplative. I knew he was thinking of Brigitte.

"You're out," I said. "We're taking the Aether witch. Adele doesn't trust you."

"*Psst*. Tell her to get over herself."

"You killed her fucking mother."

"I gave her mother life."

I shook my head. "Someone needs to keep an eye on Callisto anyway." I leaned on the rail next to him and hushed my voice. "And I need a favor."

He turned to me with curiosity.

"Do you remember Gorka Salazar? He's been with Callisto and Celestina since they first rose from their graves."

"The big bastard?"

"*Sì*. I have a warehouse down by the Esplanade pier. Find him. Secure him there for my return. Do what you need to, but do *not* kill him."

He raised an eyebrow. "Is that it?"

"No. There's another one. An Irish Air witch. Blond beard, early twenties. If he's still alive, he'll be missing an appendage. Most likely his right hand."

"And what am I to do with him?"

"Whatever you want."

He hooked an arm around my neck. "I was wrong, *fratellino*."

"About what?"

"When I said that she makes you weak."

I pulled away. Emilio's compliments were unnerving. His unpredictability was the only thing that had remained unchanged about him in all these centuries.

"I love her, Emilio," I said, somewhat sternly.

"I know, little brother. I also know you'll never allow yourself to have her."

"*Ho bisogno dell'elisir.*" I leaned back down on the banister.

"*Oh yes*, the Elixir. I'm sure one day you'll have it. And then you'll have her, and everything will be perfect. Just one question, Niccolò. It's easy enough to keep it from Gabriel, but how do you plan to keep your secret from Adele *in the Afterworld?* Besides the Ghede and their love for exposing the clandestine, don't you think you'll probably . . . run into her?"

My pulse sputtered.

"Oh, you didn't think I knew about your little eighteenth-century bloodbath?"

"I was just trying to save Gabriel and Giovanna."

"I'm not judging you, *fratellino*. I applaud you. But tell me." His arm hooked me closer, and he whispered in my ear. "Do you really love her? Or is this whole ruse just another one of your cloak-and-dagger strategies to get to *l'elisir di vita?*"

My jaw clenched.

"Don't forget that you told us you loved Séraphine too."

"I did love Séraphine. *Unwillingly.*"

Blood rushed between my temples like waves crashing upon

a rocky shore. I stared out at the chandelier. He was right. Adele and I would never be together. Even if I defeated Callisto, saved her father, got my magic back, and shed myself of this monstrous fate.

She was never going to speak to me after this trip.

A part of me wanted to sabotage the mission so my secrets stayed buried, as they had been for two centuries.

But another part of me believed enigmatically in her.

In us.

CHAPTER 17
SPELLBROKEN

Adele hurried down the stairs to the foyer with her bag and the axe on her shoulder. I tried not to stare at her shirt—Nicco's shirt, rather—or wonder why she was wearing it, or his jacket, or what they had been doing since we'd last parted ways.

"Didn't your dad ever tell you not to run with an axe?" Désirée said.

"Ha." She walked past us, into a library, nodding for us to follow.

"Can I set up in here?" Désirée asked, moving to an antique couch.

"Yeah." She shut the door behind us.

I lingered near the crackling fireplace. Adele twirled a coil of her hair; she seemed nervous. What happened to her at the cemetery? Was it related to why she wouldn't even look at me now? *No, she won't look at you because you practically paralyzed her with magic, you fucking asshole.*

"Where's everyone else?" Désirée asked.

"They're coming." She sat on the sofa and peeked in one of the baskets. "Is that . . ." She took a deep inhale. "Roast beef? Oh my God. Are there—? Can I have?"

Codi dropped down next to her. "Yeah, of course. I-I can go get more if you're hungry."

She quickly unwrapped a sandwich and took a bite. "There are, like, sixteen sandwiches in here."

"I just mean . . . if you need anything." His voice cracked. "I'm here for you."

"Oh, no." Désirée shot him a death stare.

Adele wrapped her arms around his neck. "I'm so sorry about Papa. I hope we see him in Guinée."

What the fuck does he know?

Codi nodded, and she let him go.

Adele took another bite of the sandwich and slowly chewed. "So, um. There's been a tiny change of plans."

I straightened. "We're not going to Guinée?"

"No, we're still going. Well, most of us are still going." She swallowed. "I made an executive decision. I hope it's okay. I just don't trust Emilio enough to come with us."

"No shit," I said. The words just slipped out.

She looked at me angrily. "I obviously don't have to explain why."

"Okay, so what, Gabriel's coming?" Désirée asked.

"Not exactly." She set the sandwich down. "Someone a little more familiar."

"Adele, *please* tell me you did not ask one of my brothers," Codi said, looking severe. "They need to be here to protect my family."

"No, I know that. Please don't hate me, y'all. It's An—"

"I'm back, bitches!" someone yelled.

We all sprang up.

"Was that?" Désirée asked.

"Annabelle," Adele finished.

We all flooded back into the foyer. I wasn't sure whose jaw hit the floor first, seeing Annabelle Lee Drake standing on the mezzanine, peering down on us like we were her peasant subjects. Lisette was standing next to her looking less than thrilled.

"Oh, *hell* no." Désirée started storming toward the stairs.

"No, no, no, no, no." Adele pulled her back. "I realize this isn't ideal, but desperate times and all that."

"I'm not that desperate!" Dee tried to jerk away from her grip, but Adele held onto her.

Annabelle didn't flinch.

I couldn't get over how completely normal she looked, better than normal, even. Had they given her a dose of vampire blood? Her hair fell across her face in waves. Her skin was dewy, lips glossy. Back on the river, I hadn't even been sure she was alive or if Nicco was sucking on a corpse. Now she wore shiny boots that laced all the way up to her knees, clean shorts, and a slinky top that revealed a lot of boob.

Adele hung on to Dee and scooped my elbow, pulling us into a huddle. "Unless one of you wants to invite Remi or Manon or Poppy," she whispered, "there aren't any other options!"

"I can't believe you called her!" Dee shrieked.

"I didn't. Not exactly. She was already—"

"Nicco kidnapped her when we went over there," I said.

"*What?*" Codi asked.

"Sorry, I forgot!"

"How could you for—?"

"I've had bigger things on my mind than Annabelle!"

"Look, it doesn't matter how she got here," Adele said.

Would it matter if she knew Nicco drank half her blood?

"She's here. She's willing to go. And I personally think she's a better option than Emilio. But if the group thinks otherwise, I'm open. It's just going to be a lot more complicated. Lisette and Nicco can control Annabelle; *no one* can control Emilio." She looked at me first.

"Considering Emilio still wants to *kill* me, I think I'm going to have to vote Annabelle."

"When you put it that way," Codi said. "I vote Drake too."

Désirée crossed her arms. "For the record, this is a very bad idea."

"We'll make it work," Adele said.

"And I'm not going to be nice to her," Dee mumbled under her breath.

We all peered back up to the mezzanine.

Annabelle smirked. "Are we doing this or not?"

Adele stalked over to the bottom of the staircase. "You do realize why we're going, right?"

"Sure. Do you?" Annabelle shuffled down.

"*Annabelle!*" Lisette hissed.

"To take down your coven once and for all," Adele said.

"But *you're* my coven, Addie." Annabelle touched the collar of the leather jacket. "I thought you threw this in the bonfire right after you confessed all your darkest desires?"

Adele's demeanor shifted. She stepped up to her face, and for a second, I felt like I was back in Brooklyn on the street. "You will *never* be bound to us."

Annabelle leaned closer. "You know, being bound to Callisto, I can kind of feel your Fire. Too bad you can't."

A loud slap startled us all.

Oh *shit*.

"You bitch," Annabelle hissed in the still of the room, holding her cheek.

A chuckle came from the mezzanine. Emilio was leaning over the balcony rail with Gabe and Martine. "You should be thanking your lucky stars she doesn't have her Fire. She nearly took out my eye with that slap."

Adele looked like she was going to maul Annabelle, but Nicco whizzed down the stairs, walking her away. This was going to be a fucking disaster.

Lisette leaned into Annabelle's ear. "If you continue to disgrace our family name, I will muzzle you, *ma fifille.*" And for the first time ever, I gave Lisette Monvoisin, Medici vampiress, props.

Gabe hustled down the stairs. "While I still have you all here, I have a proposition."

Adele looked to Nicco. He shrugged.

"In your absence, Emilio, Martine, and I will continue to watch the Animarum Praedators. Monitor all of their activity. Learn their movements. If any opportunity presents itself, we'll go in for Macalister." Adele's back stiffened. "And, of course, we'll aid the French Quarter witches in any way we can, defending the Vieux Carré if necessary."

"At what price?" I asked.

"You break the remainder of Adeline's coven's curse. We won't be of much use if we can't leave the Vieux Carré."

The color drained from Lisette's face, and she better resembled Julie. Adele's eyes widened—she looked at Lisette, and then up to Emilio who was staring down at her.

What the hell?

"Emilio's not trapped," I said. I didn't see how breaking the curse and promptly leaving the city was a good idea.

Gabriel turned my way. "Yes, and while I have tremendous faith in my brother's abilities, three is better than one against one of the most powerful covens to have walked the Earth!"

Adele's gaze flicked back to Lisette. *What is going on with those two?*

Then it dawned on me: the Memory Spell. Cosette Monvoisin had come up with that strand of the curse to protect all involved in case the vampires ever got loose and sought revenge. Would Gabe turn on Lisette? Was that what Adele was worried about? Not that I was generally in the mode of protecting vampires, but Lisette had been a member of Susannah's coven. And technically she had saved my life. Maybe Gabe would be over it by now, but he'd killed her once. Who was to say he wouldn't kill her again?

"We're not breaking the curse," I said.

His fangs snapped out. "Well, then I can't guarantee I won't start killing witches as soon as you cross over to the other side."

"Gabriel, calm down," Nicco said.

"I've been calm long enough, *fratellino*." He approached Codi. "I think I'll start with one of your brothers. Cameron will put up the best fight, don't you think?" He stroked Codi's chin with his forefinger. "Oh, what about both of them at the same time? That would be more fun."

Codi looked like he was going to blow a gasket.

Adele nudged between them and pressed Gabriel back. "Do not make me regret defending you."

"Do not make me break this curse myself by killing the witches who hold the remaining casts." He took a couple of steps back, eyes still fixed on Codi, then he glanced at me. "It's the two of you, isn't it?"

Lisette whipped to his side, saying something in French, but he ignored her.

Adele looked like she was going to throw up. "We, um . . ." The pitch of her voice rose. "It's just that . . ." *Shit.* Adele was the worst liar.

Fuck it. Our leverage was gone. We could never leave with such a threat to the French Quarter witching families. "We'll break the trapping spell," I said.

Everyone turned to me.

"But we can't give you back your memories. We don't know how to do it."

In a blink, he rounded on me, his breath on my face. "You're breaking the whole curse!"

I stared him down. "Final. Offer."

Adele squeezed her trembling hands. I'd never seen her visibly scared. *This is all so fucked.*

Lisette stepped up behind Gabe, her arms snaking around his broad shoulders. "Who cares, *mon amour*? Our freedom is the important part."

He turned around to her. "They've stolen one of my most precious memories—one of the most precious a vampire will have in all of eternity. I want to remember the moment you woke up mine." He cradled her face.

Oh, vomit.

"It wasn't them. And it doesn't matter; we have each other now." She smiled sweetly. "We can finally go to France like we always talk about."

For the second time tonight, I gave Lisette props. If I didn't know better, I'd have sworn she still had her Aether magic.

He said something in French and gently kissed her lips.

Martine zipped down the stairs and threw her arms around the both of them, ecstatic. "We'll all go to France upon your return, sister!"

Just your everyday beautiful, blonde, bloodsucking throuple.

Nice job, Codi mouthed. He clasped my shoulder, pulling me over to the rest of the coven.

Adele glanced at me. "*Merci.*"

And for the first time tonight, I felt like I'd done something right.

"Good thing you're such a practiced liar," she said, and walked back to Nicco.

For a second, I couldn't breathe. Something about being called a liar felt like the worst thing in the world.

An arm slinked around my neck. "Hello, lover. Miss me?" Annabelle asked.

I pushed her arm away. "As much as I'd miss the clap."

She saw me watching Adele and Nicco and leaned closer. "You know he's just playing her, right?"

"What?"

She walked away with a sly smile.

What the hell was that supposed to mean? How the fuck would Annabelle know anything about Nicco?"

Désirée looked up from her bag. "Do you guys have any candles? I only brought—"

Lisette blasted upstairs and returned in just a few seconds with an industrial-size sack of salt and an armful of candles.

"Goddess only knows whose magic has been on these," Dee muttered, and began burning some sage over them.

I poured the salt circle, trying to make myself useful.

Once we were ready, Gabriel, Martine, and Lisette—who I think was only pretending to be affected by this curse—stood beneath the chandelier. Nicco and Emilio went up to the mezzanine to watch from above.

It should have been Emilio and Giovanna that day, not Lisette and Minette. Bastards.

The five of us locked hands around the trio.

"I can't believe we're doing magic with a traitor," Dee said under her breath.

"What the hell do you think we're about to do in the cemetery?" Annabelle asked. "Play hopscotch to open the gates to the Afterworld?"

"In perfect love and perfect trust," I said, nihilistically.

The room went dark.

Adele's voice rose, strong and certain. "As curses come, curses go . . ."

The candles lit up all around us, and for the first time ever, the complete Descendants coven practiced magic together. In the shadows, excitement lurked on Gabriel's face. I wondered if he'd keep his word, if they would really stay and help defend the city or just peace out the moment we left. Gabe seemed genuinely concerned for Nicco and Lisette, but I didn't trust him as far as I could throw him.

Adele looked at me. It was now or never.

I felt around the room for the spark—when I concentrated, I

could feel the crackle of static—the magic that bound us to Gabriel and Martine and Emilio. That bound two of them to the Quarter. It felt old and deep-rooted, having passed down through so many generations. I had to force the intention out with my words:

"As curses come, curses go,
The time has ceased to trap a foe.
Once cast to stop a bloody spree,
We break the spell and set you free.

Everyone joined in the chant, and the energy brought me to my toes.

"No borders bind you, magic entwines you,
the spell will desist and unconfine you."

We all glanced at each other. The magic was undeniably stronger with Annabelle here. The Monvoisin magic completed our coven, whether we liked it or not. The lights flickered, the crystals in the chandelier shook, and the wind howled, swirling our voices around us. And just when the trembling floor seemed like it was going to swallow us up whole, the flames snuffed out, and we were left in the pitch black with a room full of freed vamps.

I pulled Désirée toward me in the darkness. She didn't even protest when my arms wrapped around her, because this was crazy, and stupid, and we just gave our only bit of power back to the vampires.

The overhead light turned back on, and I let go. Everyone was breathing heavily.

Adele stepped up to Gabriel. "Stay safe."

"Likewise, *sei un angelo.*" He kissed the top of her head.

I didn't get it. I didn't get anything anymore.

"There isn't much time before moonfall," Nicco said from the mezzanine.

And with that, we shouldered our bags. I'd always imagined the coven going on a camping trip together, but it had never involved vampires, a Native American basket of souls, or . . .

The Afterworld.

CHAPTER 18
SEVEN GATES

As Codi and I divvied the picnic baskets between the five of us, I felt Isaac staring at me, and I almost regretted wearing Nicco's flannel. It had felt powerful at the time, but now it was giving him so much anxiety that it gave me anxiety.

Gabriel slipped us some cookies and then leaned in to Lisette. "Did you feed?"

"*Jesus,*" Isaac scoffed. Codi and Dee squirmed uncomfortably.

"You do realize that once you cross over to the Afterworld, the only food for my family will be your coven, right?"

"Lisette, did you feed?" Dee asked.

"Thanks to the Ghost Drinkers, I've never drunk so heavily in a single night."

Serpentine smiles spread across each of the vampires' faces.

Gabriel looked to Nicco with the same question. "Brother?"

"I'm fine." He adjusted a satchel on his back. It looked like it had been stitched pre-war. "Extra fine," he added before Gabe could ask again.

"Is he extra-fine?" Annabelle whispered into my ear, sneaking up behind me.

I remained as stoic as possible. I refused to play into her bullshit any longer.

"Adele, this one's you." Désirée handed me a sheet of paper on which she'd copied the map, Ghede-Nibo's vèvè, and corresponding color-coded notes for Lafayette Cemetery. She gave Nicco, Lisette, and even Annabelle a gris-gris each, and we each went down the line collecting ritualistic items into our bags: salt, matches, silver scarves, black and purple candles, along with an assortment of Ghede lwa-specific items, and of course, a Mason jar of piman each.

"What about salt?" Isaac asked, studying his supplies.

"No salt since we're going full-tilt Voodoo tradition, tonight," Dee said. "Salt drives away spirits, *especially* the Ghede." Her mouth pinched into a frown. "I think that's where we might have gone wrong at St. Roch."

"*No* salt then," Isaac said.

"And FYI, I gave you each a pinch of gunpowder."

"Gunpowder?" Codi asked.

"In case you need to appease Ogun. It's said that he's the only one who can calm the Ghede when they are out of control."

What did I get us into?

Nicco turned to the group. "Get to your gates quickly, set up, and send a message to the group when you're ready. We'll start the ritual at roughly five minutes to the hour."

Annabelle turned to Lisette. "Do you know how to text?"

Martine hissed a response.

"It's a legitimate question!"

Désirée rolled her eyes. "The incantation is written on the back of your map. Memorize it. Take a photo of it. Whatever you do, don't lose it. Keep watch on the sky and wait for my signal to start the spell."

"And stay alert," Gabriel said, getting all big brotherly. "Souls are still rampant, and who knows if the Ghost Drinkers have all turned in for the night. Signorina Borges, I'll escort the two of you for extra protection. Martine, you go with Isaac."

Codi held up his hand to slap Gabriel's, which only caused him confusion.

"I'm going in the same direction," Lisette said. "I can take Isaac to St. Roch and get back to the Vieux Carré in time." She was blushing as soon as she got the words out.

Gabriel tugged her closer. "It's been a long time since you've performed a spell. Use the extra time to set up for the ritual."

"I can fly," Isaac said. "I don't need—"

"*Oui*, so can the souls." Martine ran tickling fingers up Isaac's arm. He curled away.

"Let Martine go with you," I said. "If something happens to you, we won't be able to do the ritual."

A laugh spurted from Emilio, and everyone else looked away, as if biting their tongues.

Isaac's gaze dropped to the floor.

"I-I didn't mean it like that."

"I get it." He pulled his army duffle tight.

Nicco brushed the inside of my palm. "I'll escort you to Lafayette and then keep going on to Valence."

"Perfect," Annabelle said. "I'll be fine on my—"

Emilio jumped down from the balcony with catlike grace. "I'll be escorting you, *amore mio*. If you try to fuck up the ritual, I will pull apart your bones and sacrifice you to the Ghede to open the gate."

Désirée leaned into my other side. "Is it bad that he's growing on me? Don't answer that. It's bad."

Out of the corner of my eye, I saw Nicco's lips pinch.

Codi slapped his hands together. "All right, let's do this." He strapped his bag to his chest, and Isaac helped secure the kishi on his back. I was still amazed that all of those souls were confined by a few strips of swamp grass. "See you on the flip-side." He kissed my cheek.

Emotion flooded me. "Watch your back, okay?" *If anything happens to Codi, I won't be able to forgive myself.*

"Chill," Désirée said. "Remember that we started planning this mission when you weren't even around. We're all *choosing* to do this."

I nodded, slipping on my backpack. "Don't do anything I wouldn't do."

"That I can't promise." And without any further affectionate goodbyes, Désirée ran her hands over her sleek ponytail, let it fall perfectly back in place, and joined Codi and Gabriel at the door. As usual, I envied her confidence.

My gaze briefly met Isaac's, and heat pulsed from my chest. I refused to let him edge in for an emotional moment. I didn't want to see the sadness in his golden eyes or feel how much he loved me in a goodbye hug. I couldn't. And in that quick glance, I saw that he knew what I was doing, and it hurt my heart.

He stepped out the door.

"Isaac!" I yelped, and he turned back, just as startled as I was. "Be careful."

"I will." He dangled the cord hanging from around his neck. "Don't worry about me. Ritha gave me a tooth."

I nodded nervously. I had no idea what that meant, but just like that, he was gone.

"Ready?" Nicco asked, picking up the axe.

"As I'm ever going to be."

He handed me the bunch of poppies, and we walked out with Annabelle and Emilio.

Emilio flipped a set of keys in the air and walked to a motorcycle parked on the curb, Annabelle practically skipping after him. She slid onto the seat behind him, pulling herself salaciously close. "Don't flirt with me, Drake," he said, kicking the bike awake. "You don't like it nearly as rough as you'd like to think you do."

I turned to Nicco. "He's not going to kill her, right?"

"No, not when she's so critical for the mission."

I hoped Emilio thought she was mission-critical. A part of me worried he'd kick her to the curb, open the gates himself, and go after Giovanna. I'd asked Dee to write the seven of us specifically into the incantation, just in case.

As they took off, I looked around. "So, how are we . . . ?"

Nicco slid his bag off his back down to his chest. "Like this." He grabbed me, and in a whirl, I was on his back, trying not to lose hold of the flowers.

"What are you doing?" I shrieked.

"Well, we won't arrive before sunrise if we have to walk at your pace."

"What do you mea-aah!" I let out another shriek as he took off. "*Niccoooo!*" I squeezed his neck, scarcely avoiding whiplash as we blew past Touchdown Jesus.

The remaining blocks of the French Quarter went by before my brain could reconcile the speed. The heightening elixir on Halloween night hadn't come close to this, and for the moment, I shut out the world and let myself be with him, breathing in his leather and soap scent as the breeze blew over our faces.

We zipped into the CBD, down the streetcar tracks at ten times its pace, and in no time, we were beneath the oaks of the Garden District, whipping past Sacred Heart, which was hardly recognizable in the blur. I hugged him tighter, already anticipating my stop. When we turned down Washington and slowed, my grip became aching.

I don't know if it was the post-superrun high or being outside of the protection bubble of the French Quarter, or just being pressed up against Nicco, but I felt more alive. *Everything* felt more alive. As the city slept, the gargantuan oak trees seemed to stretch further toward the moon, and the river roiled as if waking up from a long slumber.

The fog was thick and sticky as Nicco stopped in front of the iron gate.

I slid off and set my bag down, gazing up at the scrolling arc that spelled out **LAYAFETTE CEMETERY NO. 1.** His arms wrapped around me, and I twisted back to him. "I don't want to separate."

"I know. I'll find you as soon as I get to the other side, I promise."

"*D'accord.*"

But he didn't let go. Darkness shifted behind his eyes.

"What's wrong?"

"Nothing."

"It's not nothing. I can feel your heart racing."

"Adele, I just . . . I need you to know that it's okay if, after this trip . . ." His stare hardened. "It's okay if you feel differently about me."

"Why would I—?" I remembered the conversation with Gabriel. "Nicco, I don't care about your past. It has nothing to do with me. It has nothing to do with you, now."

He half-heartedly smiled as if he wanted to believe me. "You will care."

My hand slipped up his face, forcing him to look at me. "There is no one in this world or *any* world that will make me feel differently about you." He leaned into my touch. "I promise. *Je promets. Lo prometto.*" I kissed his cheek.

He returned the innocent kiss, but when I felt another just below my jaw, I softly gasped in surprise. He went for another, but then his muscles locked with familiar restraint. "I'm sorry." His tone turned serious again. "However you feel, I will still help save your father, and I will still kill Callisto so you and your friends can live in peace again, I swear on my soul."

"Please have more faith in me, Niccolò."

"I have faith in you; I just don't have faith in me. Or me from some other time."

"It's a good thing I have enough faith for both of us."

"*Ciao, bella.*" He pinched my chin and pecked my lips.

Thump-thump.

It wasn't a *kiss*-kiss, but I was pretty sure part of my brain melted. "Get to your gate and set up," I said—I think I said—and I traded the poppies for the axe.

He glanced up at the cemetery gate, seeming as reluctant to leave me as I was to leave him. "Valence isn't too far, and the streets are silent. If you scream, I'll be able to hear you."

"I'll be fine." But when I turned to the gate, a beautiful old tree just beyond the iron bars made an avalanche of anxiety crash down on me. *The bark rough against my face.* A statue of the Virgin Mary glimmered dewy in the moonlight, just like the one I'd almost been smashed by. A hundred mausoleums were perfect spots for Ghost Drinkers to lurk.

I stepped back, knocking into him.

"You've got this, *bella.*" He brought my left hand beneath my shirt and curled my fingers around the hilt of the dagger. "No hesitating."

I nodded, picked up my bag, and strode toward the gate.

At the archway, I switched the axe to my left hand so my right was free for magic, like it was the most natural thing in the world. Just as I willed the gate to open, I realized it already was. *Thump-thump.*

Is someone here?

When I passed through the arch, the wrought-iron gate closed behind me. I knew inexplicably that something magical had closed the gate . . . and that it hadn't been me.

My lungs pinched, and I looked back.

I could scarcely see Nicco through the fog, and then his pale face disappeared completely. In his place, the dagger brought a little comfort, but only when I caught the glint of the hexenspiegel above the ironwork could I release my breaths with ease.

I activated the light on my phone and walked down the path, stepping through damp leaves and fallen magnolia blossoms, through rows of algae-covered statuary. I had no idea where to set up Nibo's altar, but the deeper I went into the city of dead, the more I sensed a thread pulling me, just as when I'd found Adeline's necklace beneath Brooke's feculent clothes.

I moved faster, scared I would lose the hint of magic in the thick fog.

Three rows later, the trace vanished, and I took a heavy breath. A hint of white glimmered in the moonlight. The tombs weren't as condensed here, and the plot before me was bigger than most. The fog dispersed as I stepped forward to a mausoleum unlike any I'd ever seen.

An ornate iron fence surrounded the stark white structure. Its walls were perfectly square and the roof perfectly triangular. The plaster hadn't chipped away to reveal the brick beneath like its neighbors, nor was it sprouting bright green ferns. Florid tracery decorated the tops of its arched windows and twisted into spikes bordering the perimeter of the roof. Suddenly, out of the darkness, a prick of light glowed from within the jewelry-box tomb.

I flattened against a tree. Was it a soul? *Are Ghost Drinkers here?* I squelched the impulse to scream for Nicco. *It's too small to be a soul, Adele.* Not much bigger than a firefly.

I looked back. The glow grew. It wasn't the eerie cool tone of a lost soul. It shone brighter, illuminating the stained glass, filling the windows with mosaics of birds and snakes and angels. It was warm and bright, and every magical part of me knew it was a flame.

I stepped through the gate in awe, feeling like I'd discovered a hidden treasure. Close up, the stains of rust on the edges of the walls became visible, and I realized why this tomb was so different. Beneath the white paint, the entire structure was cast-iron.

A diamond amongst all of the death. The tomb was so perfectly delectable, I half expected a wind-up mechanism to turn and for music to play.

This is it. This is where I need to be.

With a swish of my hand, the door unlocked, and I savored the fleeting feeling of my magic working before hurrying in.

I slid the rusty metal bar in place behind me.

A long marble crypt stood in the middle of the otherwise empty tomb. There was no candle. No flame. No orb. Just the moon's beams peeking through wet foliage smeared across two skylights above.

Am I losing my mind?

The dampness brought me back to hiding in the alcove behind the statue of Mary. I trembled as I set my phone down, angling the light. *I'm safe. I have a weapon. I'm under my coven's protection spell. I can scream for Nicco.* My phone lit up with messages. *Shit.* The others were already in place. *Hurry up, Adele. You can't be the one to screw this all up.*

I texted back that I was almost set up and then swung my bag onto the marble slab. Hurrying, I pulled out the supplies and set the sanctuary candles around the crypt, mentally reciting everything Désirée had told me about Ghede-Nibo to calm my nerves.

He was beautiful, effeminate, and young. Died brutally. He's the patron of those who've died by disasters. If that's true, I thought, then he must be the patron of this city. As soon as I set the last one on the ground, they lit ablaze in a wave. I thanked whoever was guiding me along.

There was nowhere to set up the altar but atop the crypt. I fluffed the silver and black scarf over the marble. And then a sparkly purple piece of fabric. I set out the pot of eye glitter. *He carries a staff and a pouch of poisonous leaves.* I plated the offerings. A thermos cap of fresh coffee. An abalone shell of pistachio nuts. A Zulu coconut. A pack of cigarettes and a cigar. Matches. I opened the jar of piman, wafting away the smell of the spicy rum, and hoisted myself on top of the crypt. *He's a healer, and a raucous dandy, and the Baron's number one son, and the leader of the spirits of the dead. He has a nasal voice. And he's very . . . promiscuous.*

I looked up into the skylight—nothing.

My hands shook as I struck a match, cursing Callisto and all of the Animarum Praedators for stealing my Fire. I lit the small, thin candles on the altar, half black, half purple, and checked my watch. Two minutes to spare.

I unfolded Dee's paper with the incantation: Nibo's vèvè was above it. *Shit!* I dipped into an Altoids tin full of cornmeal and carefully sprinkled it on the altar, trying to use both hands in unison like Dee had taught me. The gesture mimicked the fact that the vèvè operated in both worlds. The design mostly consisted of a large heart, two moons, and a few spears, which I couldn't help seeing as phallic.

That's it. Done. I crossed my legs, laid the spell down in front of me, and used the axe to keep the paper secure. I took a deep breath, and then another, starting the near-impossible task of emptying my mind as Papa Olsin had taught me.

Papa Olsin.

A boom sounded in the distance. Through the skylight, nestled among the stars, an outline of two skulls, one with a top hat, the other with a veil, twinkled purple. *Baron and Maman. It's Dee's sign.*

The first words of the chant slipped out, and a breeze whipped around the room.

> *"O Baron, O Baron Samedi, master of the*
> *cemeteries, we call you!*
> *O Baron, O Baron, au nom de La-Croix,*
> *transporter of the dead!*
> *O Baron, O Baron, au nom de Cimetière,*
> *guardian of the dead!*
> *We ask your permission, and that of*
> *Maman Brijit,*

To serve your family, at your Gates,
To enter your world, we ask be our fate,
To leave the living, to dance among the
        dead.
O Baron, O Baron!"

The paper fluttered away, and I tried to grab it but missed.
It doesn't matter, Adele; you know it. Listen to your heart.
The words flowed out to the rhythm of the drums circling the room, echoing in the tiny chamber. The stained-glass birds chirped, and the snakes hissed, slithering out of the window-panes, but I was too enthralled to panic. The level of magic was like nothing I'd ever felt. Wolves howled in the distance, owls shrieked, hens clucked. Birds chirped and fluttered, circling high above the seven gates as we sang our song. Warmth crackled through my limbs, and I realized I wasn't on the cold marble anymore; I was hovering just above it. *Oh my Goddess. God. Ghede, whatever.*

        "O Baron, wow!
        O Baron, wow!
        I seek Ghede-Nibo."

My voice rose louder, the songs of my fellow witches soaring in my ears. I let the energy flow through me. *The Ghede, the Baron, Maman Brigit.* "Nibo!" I yelled. "Nibo!"
        "Nibo!"
        "Nibo!"
        "Nibo!"
A blast of magic exploded from the vèvè, sending the contents of the altar scattering. I clutched the sides of the crypt, my eyes smashed shut as everything shook.
The breeze died, and the chanting silenced, and in the dark quake of my mind, a little *tink* hit the floor. I waited, a

bit terrified to see what—or rather, who—was causing the noise.

Tink.

Tink.

Something slurped, and the comforting scent of coffee wafted toward me. I opened my eyes.

Just before me, a man was crouched on the altar, which was somehow now perfectly intact despite the explosion moments ago. He gazed at me, waiting. A pistachio shell rolled onto the floor. *Tink.*

In the warm candlelight, he was . . . *stunning.*

Skin as black as the midnight sky, eyes as alluring as the setting sun. He didn't look much older than me beneath the dramatic ensemble: his black Victorian riding jacket had a double collar studded with silver spikes. The long jacket hung open, revealing a shiny purple body suit that dipped low, showing off his thin chest adorned with rosary beads. It was all framed with a zebra-hide cape that hung down his back and was accented with two huge neon-pink feather puffs, one at each shoulder.

"You're-you're Ghede-Nibo," I stuttered. It wasn't exactly a question.

"Were you expecting someone else, *ma chère?*" he asked in nasal French. Two unlit cigarettes dangled from the corner of his magenta-painted lips, which matched the chrome polish on his stiletto nails.

"*Non!*"

"You're kin to Adeline Saint-Germain."

"*Oui! Vous connaissez Adeline?*"

"Everyone knows Adeline."

I hoped that was a good thing.

"Tick-tock. Tick-tock," he said, bobbing the triangle earring dangling from his left lobe. An assortment of rings looped up his right ear, and two pairs of rhinestone cat-eye sunglasses were stacked on top of his closely shaved head. Out of thin air, an hourglass appeared in his hand. He set it on the altar and flipped it upside down, letting the sand pour. "*Alors, tu veux aller à Guinée?*"

"*Oui*. I want to go to Guinée. I *have* to get to Guinée."

"You *haaaaave to?*" He put another pistachio in his mouth, somehow still able to hold the cigarettes between his lips. There was a sharp crunch as his teeth broke the shell and a *tink* when he spat it to the ground. A second later, he spat the nut out too.

I guess he saw my confusion. "Ghede can't eat. Can't drink, can't fuck. Not without a cheval."

"Right." I glanced nervously at the chili pepper rum.

He laughed. "Want to take a drink?"

"As thrilling as I'm sure that would be—"

"Why do you want to go to Guinée, white girl?"

It suddenly occurred to me that the answer was incredibly incriminating, supernaturally, anyway. But Désirée had said that the Ghede's purpose wasn't to serve judgement. "*They hate lies more than anything. Hypocrisy.*"

"I need to see the spirit of Jakome Salazar." *It wasn't a lie.*

"You need to *see* him?" he asked, eying the ghoststick poking out of my bag. "Try again."

"I need passage to Guinée"—my throat went dry—"so I can find the spirit of Jakome Salazar . . ."

"*Annnnnd?*"

"Kill him."

"Better." He took a sip of the coffee and then spat it on the floor. "You think you can kill Jakée Zee?"

"If that's Jakome Salazar, then *oui*." I picked up a pistachio. "I know I can."

As I brought it to my mouth, he slapped it out of my hand. "Mine."

"Oh, right, sorry." *Jesus, Adele, you can't eat the offering.* I eyed the hourglass: it was at least halfway poured. "What's your second question?"

"Simple," he said, peering at me through those enormous feather lashes. "Tell me your greatest desire, and I will take you to Guinée."

"Easy. To save my father from the Salazars."

His head shook back and forth with the wag of his finger. "*Quelle*?"

He grabbed my throat, eyes lighting up like glowing amethysts. "Tell me zha truth, or I won't take you to zha Afterworld."

"It is the truth!"

He let me go with a sigh of disgust. "If you can't tell Nibo zha truth, you'll never survive Guinée."

"It is the truth! It is my deepest desire!"

"*Non*. It's for your own protection, Addie."

"*Oui, ça l'est*! I don't want anything more than to save my dad!"

"There is no doubt you want your father back and that you would do anything to secure his safe return, but there is something you desire even more." He stood the axe up on the blade, and it grew until it touched the ceiling like a long pole. He hooked a lanky fishnet-covered leg around it and took a spin. "Locked away in the darkest part of your heart." He spun and spun and spun until he was upside down. "You desire something you've never told anyone because it scares you." He stopped right in front of me, face to upside-down face. "Tell me the one thing you want even more than saving your dear old papa?"

Sweat broke out across my hairline. The sand was running out. *There's no time for this! I have to save Mac!*

"Show me what's in your heart," he demanded.

"I am!"

Nibo disappeared, and the metal bar on the door slid aside.

As the door creaked open, I scurried backward, but the voice was familiar. "Adele?"

"Nicco?"

"Tell me your darkest desire, Adele." Nibo said inside my head.

"What are you doing here?" I rushed down from the crypt. "Why aren't you at your gate?"

His arms wrapped around my waist. "You were yelling for me."

"No, I wasn't. I was yelling for Nibo! The chant. Nicco, you have to get back!"

"Is zhis what you desire, mon petit chou?"

"No, you were yelling for me to come." His lips brushed my cheek, and I shuddered. "That I had to come now."

"Nicco, there's no time."

"We have to succeed in loving each other so greatly, we live outside of time." He lifted me onto the crypt. "Like a work of art, in a state of enchantment." His mouth came to mine, but I slid back, the marble cool against my skin.

"Nicco, the gates!"

"Bella, look!" The grains in the hourglass had stopped pouring, frozen in time.

He was right. I pulled him onto the crypt. Onto me. "We have time."

His hand raked up my thigh as he kissed my neck, and my naked limbs wrapped around his bare body like a closing fern. "We have forever," he said, and his lips finally pressed against mine. The breathless kiss I'd always wanted. My grip became desperate, and the crypt beneath was no longer cold against my skin but plush, the scent of dead flowers replaced with fresh night blossoms all around us. He was all I wanted. He was all I desired.

He is all I would ever desire.

"We have forever," I whispered and kissed him so hard I forgot who I was.

"Was zhat so hard?" Nibo asked. "Scratch zhat, from the looks of your face, it's very hard."

Nicco rippled over me like a crashing wave, and I held him tighter, moving faster. The Ghede lwa danced around the crypt over us, hooting, piman sloshing from his cup. Drums circled and darkness enveloped, and the pressure built, and built, until a spark exploded and my mind free-fell into the abyss. This wasn't what I was supposed to be doing. I was here for something else.

A hearty laugh echoed around me, a cane tapped, and boots slid across the floor. I somehow knew it was the Baron.

The first to pass through my gates was the young Aether witch, whose fiery spirit rivaled the piman she poured all over her sumptuous curves as she danced the banda with my daughter Plumaj. She wanted the Medici book of shadows because above all else, she desired power. To be worshiped. Idolized. In her heart, she saw a future where temples were constructed in her honor, and all of the land worshipped at her golden feet like those of Demeter and Circe and Hekate combined.

The Great French witch was the next to enter, her buxom beauty tormenting Zaranye's soft disposition. Zaranye spun them into a web so tight, they could have stayed forever, but the Aether opened her bleeding heart and dissolved the sticky threads. Beneath the vampiress's carnal blood-lust, her undeniable love for her Maker, and her new blood-pull to the Air witch, her darkest desire rose to the surface: final death. She desired nothing more than to be with her dead triplet sisters.

The Water witch passed with just one failed attempt: to see his grandfather one last time. Oussou knew that his greatest desire lay in bringing the souls to their final resting place. Not because the boy cared so much about their eternity, although he did. He lived in constant fear that what the puritanical witches said was true: that his mixed-magic family wasn't as powerful. That they were charlatans whose magic wasn't strong enough to contain the souls. And that one day he'd come home, and they'd all be Possessed.

The Earth witch, my bébé, breezed past Masaka in a cloud of dark perfume. It didn't take her long to realize she wasn't simply trying to prove to Ritha that her modern coven was just as good as the traditional path. The real reason she wished to go to Guinée was to fix a tear in her heart that had formed before it had pumped its first blood. She needed to know if Marassa ever found Makandal. Whether her family had been healed in the Afterlife on the mythological African coast.

The Air witch struggled, but not nearly as much as the final two. A boy truly with a heart of gold. The Hero. The loneliest of the bunch. All he wanted was to love and be loved in return. Or so he thought. Doubye forced him to look deeper into her mirror, lest he not pass her gates. Even to his own surprise, there was one thing he desired deeper than seeing his mother one last time, deeper than the Fire witch's love, which he insisted was the truth. In the darkest spot in his heart, what he wanted more than her was the youngest Medici dead. And for the admission of truth, his gate opened.

Now that just left the Kitten and the Tiger. With Nibo and L'Oraille.

As the Kitten confessed to Nibo the only thing she wanted more than saving her father, L'Oraille had the Tiger in a corner . . .

"Da truth, Niccolò!" L'Oraille towered over me as I angrily pushed my hands through my hair, her presence even more formidable from the floor of the tight, cramped mausoleum. Her curls were larger than several people were wide and bounced with her every movement, as did her considerable breasts, covered by only two triangles of mesh chain that sparkled like a disco in the moonlight.

The metal hoops of her cage crinoline underskirt knocked into me as she stomped her demands. I hadn't seen one worn in at least a hundred and fifty years, and it was quite a fashion statement as an outer garment. "Tell me what ya *really* wanna do to her, or you're not gettin' by me." She crouched down. The purple patent-leather stripper platform stilettos, however, were squarely of this era.

"Tell me," she whispered in my ear. "Tell me what your heart really wants."

"I *already told you* that I want her."

Her orchid-colored eyes glowed bright. "Beddin' dat girl isn't all you wanna do to her." She made a thrusting motion with her pelvis, slow and sure, arms reaching behind her head. "No, you want more than a long, luxurious lay." She laughed.

My fangs snapped out, and I sprang up, knocking her to the floor. "I want her!"

"You wanna fill her up, but you wanna drain her too!"

"*I want her forever.*" The whine in my voice didn't match the grinding of my hips.

She gazed up at me with a wicked smile. "Say it, Niccolò. Say it or ya never gettin' to Guinée, and ya can tell everyone it's because you're no longer a witch. Dat would be betta than telling them what ya heart truly desires."

The compulsion built as I rocked harder. "I want her." I yelled it again, the blood-lust rising.

"Are you a witch or a monsta, Niccolò? *A witch or a monsta? A witch or a monsta?*"

"Both!" I growled. "I want to *kill her.*"

I fell over on my back next to her, clutching my chest.

"I want to kill her."

She crawled over me and kissed my cheek. "*Bienvenue en Guinée, mon amour.*"

PART II
THE AFTERWORLD

Those who sow the seeds of wickedness plant them upon the heads of their children.

—*Yoruba proverb, Baba Ifa Karade*

CHAPTER 19
STREETS OF THE DEAD

A moan echoed in the black abyss, and it took me a full second to realize it was my own.

"Told you so," Nibo's voice taunted in my head.

I ripped my hand out of my pants in panic and sat up, covering my face. "Oh my God," I huffed, damp with sweat, blazing with impropriety.

"Vous désirez donc Niccolò more zhan even your father's return." He appeared next to me, lying on his elbow, head in his hand, but I was so stunned by my own immodesty, it took several more breaths before I could even turn to look at him.

A lone candle burned in front of him, the shadows deepening the caverns of his hollow cheeks; I nearly snuffed it out with my fingers so he couldn't see the embarrassment on mine.

"You can be my cheval anytime in the Natural World if we get to take a ride on him." He wagged his double sunglasses over his eyes. "I bet he's an agile lover, vampire and all."

"We would not—!" Nonsensical syllables sputtered from my lips. I was unable to comprehend that I'd just had a sex dream in front of a Ghede. *With a Ghede?* "Nicco and I are just friends!"

"D'accord. I'll be his friend with you."

"*Ugh.*" I scrambled to my feet. "We're not that kind of friends."

"But you wanna be."

Heat seared my cheeks as I shuffled away, the ground crunching beneath my feet—it was covered in white shell fragments.

"She'll be back," he said to no one as I walked further into the darkness, waving my illuminated phone.

Nothing broke the flood of light. No candles, no flowers, no pistachio shells. The stained glass windows were gone—there was nothing beyond but blackness. I spun back around, sending up a puff of gray dust from the ground. "We're— Where are—? Where's the tomb?"

"In the mausoleum, *je suppose.*"

"And the mausoleum is?" I peered out into the void. "We're . . . not in the mausoleum."

"She's not a very quick one, *est-elle?*"

"Are we in Guinée?"

"Isn't zhat where you wanted to go, Mademoiselle?"

"*Oui. Oui. Oui,*" I replied, but my brain was still unable to reconcile the reality of the granted request. "We're really in the Afterworld?" I lifted my boot, realizing it wasn't shell fragments I was stepping on—it was bone. I reflexively hopped away, but they were everywhere. There was nothing else, no one else. Just me and the skeletal, purple-spandex-clad figure and thousands— millions—of pieces of bone.

He laughed, his fishnet-clad knee flapping open, and I was unable to avoid a glimpse at his very prominent lower region. The bodysuit left little to the imagination.

I quickly refocused on his face.

"You can look."

"Wha—? I wasn't."

He shrugged nonchalantly. "*C'est très* impressive," he said, thrusting his pelvis forward the way a debutant thrusts out her hand to show off her engagement ring.

"Yep, *c'est impressionnant.*"

In a blink, he was twirling around me, our shoulders knocking. "Where are the others?" Why had I assumed that when we crossed over, we'd all just miraculously be back together?

"We're in le Vieux Carré. They're in le Vieux Carré."

"*Ce* n'est pas *le Vieux Carré.*" Remembering the ghoststick, I possessively scooped up my bag from the ground as we began to walk. "I know every inch of the Quarter."

He draped his skeletal arm around me like a dapper older brother. "Maybe if you'd come out of your shame-spiral and open your eyes, you'd see, *ma chère.*"

Great, one more person telling me to relax.

I let out a heavy exhale, and the bells of the cathedral rang above us; the ground below turned to slate. I raised my arm out to my side, like I used to do when I was a child when walking past St. Anthony's garden, past Touchdown Jesus. Sure enough, my fingers *bump-bump-bumped* against the wrought-iron fence. We were in Pirate's Alley. It was still nighttime, but it was as if everything was muted with a dusty, midnight-blue filter. I should have been more nervous, being separated from my friends in the land of the dead, but walking side by side with Ghede-Nibo had me oddly at peace. Gabriel's voice echoed in my head, telling me to be en garde. I reminded myself of the mission.

Nibo swung the axe as we walked beneath the lamplight. "You answered my two questions. I'll answer two of yours."

I nearly blurted out the same question on the whereabouts of my friends, but then realized I might get the same vague answer back. *Be smart, Adele. You have to find Jakome.* The question became obvious. "Where can I find—?" *Wait, no. Think. Strategize. What would Nicco ask?* There was something even more important than killing the spirit of Jakome Salazar: getting everyone out of here unscathed.

"Tick-tock. Tick-tock."

The Ghede won't lie to you.

"Okay. First question. What's so dangerous about the Afterworld?"

"*Pfft. Guinée n'est pas dangereux.*"

"*Right.* Ritha went through hell and high water trying to keep us away from here."

"Some mortals think zha Ghede are . . . overly hospitable."

"*Hmm.*" I crossed my arms and tapped my foot, waiting for him to elaborate.

He jumped up onto the fence and pranced across the spiked posts, raising his staff to the moon, ribbons blowing like a St. Anne reveler on Mardi Gras day. "We like spirits. Especially magical spirits." With a twirl, he hopped down at the corner of Royal, landing with impossible finesse considering his silver-glittered platform stilettos. "When spirits enter the Afterworld, they're supposed to *stay.*"

"That's ominous." The millinery shop was on the corner just like in the Natural World, although in this version, the dramatic hats were missing from the lavish window displays and had been replaced with ball-worthy gowns. "What do you mean by 'stay'?" I peered through the window at the beautiful dresses.

When still no answer came, I turned to Nibo, but he was gone.

The serene feeling I'd had with him by my side dwindled, and cold flooded my veins. "Nibo?"

I ran back the way we came and peered around the corner at the Old Absinthe bar, yelling for the Ghede. Fog rolled in from the river, tunneling down the short alley streets in ghostly waves as I hurried up to the square. "Nibo! I still have one . . . question." My voice faded into the fog.

The thick air rolled past, and the square emerged into view, bustling and lively with people. They were pale and ashy but not skeletal like Nibo. Street performers juggled butcher knives high into the air, tarot card readers sat hunched over candle-lit tables with their cards, while others nearby shot dice. A man standing behind a cart topped with an elaborate set of potion jars filled with water played a tune with a spoon. The calliope whistled in the distance.

It was Jackson Square, and it wasn't. It was the square I knew, and the one my grandparents would have known, and Adeline too. Ladies in hoop skirts with tight ringlets walked with women in beaded Mardi Gras gowns. Men in beaded Mardi Gras gowns. Gents in Revolutionary War uniforms and baseball uniforms chatted with androgynous folks rocking pink glitter beards and matching tiaras. And teen queens in disco dresses twirled preppy boys in bell bottoms, chatting animatedly in different languages as if this night was no different than the one before.

They were African and Caribbean, French and Spanish, Vietnamese and German in traditional dress—all the ancestors of the witches of La Nouvelle-Orléans. And while their clothes and hairstyles might have been from different decades, they all had one thing in common: marks on their left arms. And they all turned to me as they passed, glancing to the spot on my arm covered by the leather jacket, then back to my face, with looks of confusion.

They knew I was a witch, but also that I was something different. A beating heart in the streets of the dead.

I gazed around, but there was no sign of Nibo.

I pulled Nicco's jacket tighter. The chill was unsettling. Like a cold, spectral hand traveling up my spine, clutching the back of my head. Was this how Isaac felt all the time around the dead? I wondered where he was now—whether this whole trip would be worse for him because of his Spektral. *You didn't make him come, Adele.* But I couldn't convince myself it was true. Just yesterday I was hell-bent on protecting him from this place; tonight, I'd pressured him in front of everyone. *Yesterday Callisto Salazar wasn't holding Mac prisoner.*

He'll be fine, I told myself. But much to my surprise, I found myself wishing he was here . . . so I could protect him.

"Opening night's upon us!" yelled a man in a loose-fitting tunic and leather pants, a glow of neon pink highlighting his dark skin. He stood in front of a booth in the middle of the square; the sign above the booth read: "**TICKETS.**" Next to him, a skeletal girl with a headful of long brown braids, wearing a gown comprised entirely of wispy white threads, stood on an apple crate. Her eyes twinkled amethyst, and something told me she wasn't a street performer about to hold still like a statue for tips. Her back had a slight hunch and her arms waved out in front as she spoke.

"Zhere are only a few tickets left!" she said, as the crowd drew around as if caught in her web. "*Akelarrenlezea Spectacular!* It's bound to be a performance like none zhat's ever been seen in the Afterworld. To be remembered for eternity!" The whimsical dress, the softness of her French-accented voice, and her enchantment with the show gave her a lovely delicateness despite her sharp, skeletal appearance.

"If you're in it, Zaranye," yelled a woman in a polka-dot suit, "it's bound to be one for the ages."

Zaranye? The Ghede? I twisted around, looking for Lisette in the crowd.

"Here you go, miss." A dainty, white-lace ruffled wrist thrust a flier in front of me. "You'd better get tickets before the show sells out."

"Oh, thanks, but I . . ." My voice faded as my eyes met hers, and an eerie familiarity washed over me. She was a little younger than me and wearing a centuries-old black dress. Her long, curly hair was so dark it shined blue beneath the stars, and it wasn't tied up to match the period of her dress but left long and free, draping over a long black cape.

"You must come. Any witch who's any witch will be there."

"Um," I said, staring into her porcelain face.

"You are Adele, correct?"

"*Oui.* How did—?"

"Nibo said to make sure I told you about the show."

"Nibo?"

"Yes. He said to find the uptight girl with purple boots."

I took the flier, remembering what he'd said about the Ghede wanting spirits who entered the Afterworld *to stay.*

TOULOUSE STREET THEATRE
Opening Night
AKELARRENLEZEA SPECTACULAR!
STARING GHEDE-NIBO & FAMILY

Nice try, Nibo.

"Thanks, but I won't be here tonight." I tried to hand it back. "No need to waste a flier."

She looked at me, confused. "Of course you'll be here tonight. We'll all be here tonight. Every night."

Shit. "Of course," I stuttered. *Jesus, Adele, why don't you just stand on the crate and announce to everyone that you've crossed over to hunt down Jakome?* "*Merci beaucoup,*" I said, pretending to take another look at the flier. "As soon as I find my friends, we'll all get tickets."

She smiled. "You must be new here."

"First day— night."

"Welcome to eternity." She smiled. "Hope to see you there." She turned back to the crowd, passing out more fliers.

I released a breath, folded up the paper, and stuffed it into my pocket.

If Nibo wasn't going to help me find Jakome, I could think of only one other person who might, but I didn't know where she was either.

I headed back down to Pirate's Alley. *Where would you be in Guinée, Adeline?* Maybe the better question was: *Where would you be in the Vieux Carré?*

When I got back to Royal, a man with a pointed beard, slim pinstripe trousers, and a pocket watch popped out of the dress shop. "You're just in time for your appointment, *ma chère*." He had dark skin and kind brown eyes, one under a gold-rimmed monocle. They twinkled purple. Was he one of the other Ghede? He didn't look skeletal like Nibo or Zaranye, nor was he adorned in elaborate decoration.

"Oh, I don't have an appointment," I said when I realized he was staring at me.

"Of course you do." He grabbed my elbow and pulled me into the shop, a hop in his step.

"No, no I don't. I was just looking for someone. Do you know her—Adeline St. Germain?"

"Madame Saint-Germain was here yesterday. Today is your appointment."

"I *don't have* an appointment. I have to find Adeline."

He ushered me deeper inside the shop, despite my protests. "But of course you do! Miss LeMoyne, you must be fitted for your dress. We've been excited to receive you for days!"

"Days?" My eye couldn't help but catch each of the garments as we walked past them. "How do you know my name?"

"We all know your name, Miss LeMoyne."

"Who is we?" *Surely not Jakome?* "Have you seen any of my friends?"

The mannequins in the dress shop beckoned as we passed, and I gaped as each of them turned, trying to hold my attention for just a moment longer with their shiny satins and intricate laces, beadwork twinkling like distant galaxies. What material could twinkle in such gloomy lighting?

"Are those beads glass?" I asked the tailor, but he didn't stop until we were in a lush back showroom for fitting private clients.

The walls were lined with bolts of specialty fabrics, and a dress form my size, with a measuring tape around its neck, stood next to racks of gowns that seemed to be pulled to my taste. The desire to investigate them embellishment by embellishment grew with each passing moment. I couldn't help but inch closer.

Two chirping ladies sat at a round tufted settee in the middle of the room, nibbling treats from a serving cart, where tea steamed from a kettle beside a tower of lilac-colored macaroons. It all glimmered just like the garments. Another girl gazed out the window into the foggy night, sipping from her cup as if in deep contemplation.

The tailor pulled me along to the first rack, but my attention froze on the white-blonde hair of one of the sitting girls. "Lisette!" I leapt toward her. She'd changed clothes since we'd left and was now in a Rococo-style robe à la français, dotted with mint-green bows. "Did the tailor make you this dress?"

She looked up at me with a pouty smile. "It's been nearly three centuries since someone's mixed me up with my youngest sister."

I gasped.

"*Je m'appelle* Cosette."

"You're— you're . . . Cosette Monvoisin."

The girl next to her giggled. Her long black hair was separated into two bundles framing her face, silver ribbons binding each in the middle— another face from our casquette girls painting came to life.

"Morning Star?"

"Yes, little one."

I dropped down in front of her. "Oh, Codi is going to be so excited to see you! Did you know I grew up worshiping your ceremonial dress? And that was even before I knew it was magical. It made me want to learn to sew. We *have* to find Codi."

"In time," said the blonde woman in the window, and I stood. "But first, you need a dress." The heavy velvet of her gown swished as she strode toward me. Her sleeves bunched with black ribbons all the way up her arms, distinctly different from the French attire of the two ancestors. She stopped right in front of me. "You're just as beautiful as I imagined." Her accent too was different from theirs, yet familiar. She picked up a scrap of delicate fabric and draped it over my shoulder. "I think *mio fratello* would love the lace on you." The light reflected on her golden hair, and I saw Gabriel's nose on her face.

"Giovanna Medici!"

The glint in her peridot eyes gave me my answer.

CHAPTER 20
DATE NIGHT

I couldn't open my eyes. I wasn't ready. I shivered, lying in the dark stillness, a breeze rolling over my face.

Did I pass out? The last thing I remembered was Ghede-Doubye dancing across the roofs of the mausoleums in St. Roch, waving Adele's hand mirror in the air. My mind would hold onto that image for the rest of my life: her sheer black dress billowing in the foggy night air, the crown of keys forming a halo around her head, her eyes glowing the same purple as the protection net above us as she promised to take me to Guinée.

I patted the ground around me. It was rough and damp just like the tomb she'd made me lie on at the end of the ritual. *Thank God.* There was no way some purple-haired Ghede lwa transported me from the Natural World.

"If you're so sure, why are you scared to open your eyes, Isaac?" A chill rippled up my spine. A hand touched my leg, and I flinched. Another poked my shoulder. *"Who is he?"* I jerked away as their cold touches seeped through my jeans, my hoodie, and my hair, flooding my skin with goosebumps. *"He's not even dead!"* They were all so cold, just like the spirits always were in the cemetery.

I'm still in St. Roch, I told myself.

"Is that you, Corpse Whisperer?"

I stiffened. Only my crew knew that stupid nickname— I finally opened my eyes, and found an older Latino man with a friendly smile hovered over me. "It *is* you, Corpse Whisperer!"

Dozens of others were gathered around us. Their clothes spanned centuries, and they all had an ashen hue to their skin and marks on their arms. I scurried backward, only to hit the knees of those behind me, who leaned closer with curiosity, sniffing, prodding. I wasn't on the tomb. I wasn't in the cemetery. *Fuck.*

"You don't recognize me, do you?" the man asked.

I shook my head.

He snapped his fingers, and his eyes disappeared, leaving two gaping holes—a dense swarm of flies poured out of them. I swatted them away, spitting and writhing as they touched my lips, my nose. His face turned blue and began to bloat; the skin sloughed off, little white worms pushing out of his cheeks. A maggot fell onto my leg, and I yelled, shoving back even further. "You're number seventy-six!"

He snapped his fingers again, and the grotesque façade dissolved. But my pulse raced as the putrid smell of the house came back to me, the little closet room submerged by the Storm. I now saw the black circle on his arm. Had it been there when we'd found his body? It must have been, but that was before I got my mark, before I even knew about the witch's Maleficium.

"Jorge Sánchez," he said, extending his hand.

I grasped it, and he helped me up. "Isaac Thompson."

Damn. I couldn't help but wonder why he stayed behind when the Storm hit. Being an Aether meant he could've used his magic to get out if he didn't have the means. He could've forced anyone to give him a ride out of town, but instead he drowned in a closet with his candles and prayer cards and family pics. I guess not every Aether is Annabelle Lee Drake. I guess everyone has their reasons.

A steam whistle blew.

Calliope music played in the distance, and I could hear waves breaking on the rocky shore—*Am I on the Moonwalk?*—I looked out for the river, but the fog was too thick to see anything.

I turned back to Jorge, but he was gone. They were all gone.

In the misty air, it was just me, the pipe organ music, and the pulses of hundreds of other spirits not making themselves known, but whom I could feel. I pulled a gentle breeze to stir the fog, and a shape came into view just ahead. *A carousel?* It was more Central Park than Coney Island, with pastel-colored unicorns wearing silver saddles, shiny swans with golden bow ties, and regal white rabbits with glowing pink eyes, all of them moving up and down as it went round and round.

A figure appeared on the platform.

I walked toward her, mesmerized by the motion of the ride. Spirits popped up by the dozen on either side of me, a sea of ghostly witches, but none got in the way as I made my way to the Ghede.

Even with her shiny thigh-high boots, Doubye was barely five feet tall. Her wavy, stringy, pale lavender hair hung down to her knees over the sheer black dress, and her skin was so pale, so completely devoid of melanin, it seemed almost lavender too. Her petite stature, long hair, and large violet eyes gave her a doll-like appearance, like some kind of weird Victorian death doll, which seemed par for the course around here.

I wanted to take my sketchbook out of my bag, open it to a fresh page, and capture her against the dancing animals.

I was sure Adele would be obsessed with her dress. It had long sleeves and a high neck. A black corset bound her slight bust, and a dingy white ruff, like the Edwardian paintings at the Met, framed her face. A dozen strands of what looked like pearls draped her neck, but they'd hung in my face when she'd climbed on top of me in the cemetery, and they were most definitely not pearls. They were teeth. Human teeth.

A single key hung from beads down the center of her forehead like a crown jewel.

I stepped onto the carousel and wove between the gilded cotton-candy-colored animals to her at the center of the ride. The hand mirror in her hand had been replaced with an ornate opera glass, but instead of a pair of lenses attached to the silver handle, there was a single *blinking eye,* glowing violet with long pale-white lashes like her own.

What had Désirée said about Doubye? That she could give her chevals the gift of clairvoyance? Maybe she could tell me when we were going to get the hell out of here.

She was there, and then she and her third eye were gone. She reappeared on the back of a pony that went right past me.

"Doubye!"

I waited for it to loop. This time I was ready and swung onto the animal next to her: a swan with a pink bow tie.

"Welcome to Guinée," she said. Words I could have gone the rest of my life never hearing.

"Where's everyone else?"

"Am I not enough?" All three of her eyes dipped to the floor, like I really had hurt her feelings.

"I just meant . . ."

"They are where they're supposed to be."

"Uh, then why am I here?"

"Because it's where you want to be."

"Oh, this is not even remotely where I want to be."

She gave me a sharp look, and I decided it might not be best to express my disdain for this supernatural road trip to my hostess. She'd done nothing but what I asked, and for only the small price of ripping apart my psyche with her two simple questions for entry.

"I mean, I totally want to be here. That's why I begged you to take me."

She snapped her fingers and disappeared.

"Doubye!"

She reappeared inches from my face, straddling my lap on the swan, her wraithy being emanating an icy aura. Her gaze rested on my chest, and she cupped the wolf's tooth hanging on the leather cord, as if entranced with it. It was impossible not to stare at her gaunt, ghostly face. "You don't need to be afraid of the spirits, Isaac." She tugged the necklace. I couldn't tell if she coveted it or just wanted me to be rid of it, but the more I felt her desire for the tooth, and the more it felt like ice was freezing in my veins.

"I'm not afraid of them." My teeth chattered.

Her eyes narrowed and I remembered what Dee said about lying to the Guinée.

"I mean, I might be a *little* afraid of them. Not all of them. Not Julie."

"You need to embrace zhe dead if you're ever going to fully realize your power." Her French accent grew stronger. "You're going to be a great witch one day. People need you."

"I'm trying . . ."

"Are you?"

"I'm here, aren't I?"

Her eyes lit up, and she yanked the cord from around my head.

Cold pummeled me like a frigid wave, lifting me from the swan, threatening to spin me into a roiling torrent. "I'm sorry, I need it!"

"You don't need it!"

"Yes, I do!" I barked, gripping her boney wrist, taking it back.

She leaned away with a pout, her third eye drooping, but I

slipped it back over my head. *Moron, Isaac, why don't you go and eat some food of the dead while you're at it?*

"Mr. Thompson!" a man called.

I turned toward the river, but the fog was still too thick to see anyone. I just *knew* that when I turned back, she would be gone. And she was.

The man called my name again.

I hopped off the swan.

Maybe I could ask him where to find Ghede-Houson, aka the Soul Keeper. That's where Dee and Codi would be heading.

I headed deeper into the fog, and a gigantic riverboat came into view, docked at the pier—I *was* on the Moonwalk, or some version of it. The calliope pipes whistled, and the great red paddle churned the water. Glitzy people in formal clothes hurried aboard. I followed them.

"Ticket, please?" a man asked.

"Oh, I don't—"

He plucked a piece of paper from my hand.

"How did that get—?" It glittered purple for a blink.

"Move along."

"Mr. Thompson, there you are!" A dark-haired white guy in gloves and tails rushed to my side and took my arm.

"She's waiting for you."

"Doubye?" Couples whisked past us in fur stoles and top hats. "I'm not sure I'm dressed for this . . ." The lights on the boat spelled out *Natchez*. "Whatever this is."

"What are you talking about? You look smashing. Debonair as ever, Mr. Thompson. You'll have all the ladies' stolen glances tonight."

"Uh, I don't know about that."

He straightened my tie.

Wait, tie? I looked down to find a full tuxedo. *What the fuck?* I didn't own a tux. I hadn't even bothered to rent one for prom last year.

"Miss LeMoyne is on the upper deck."

"Adele's here?" Did that mean Jakome was here too? Was this really about to happen?

"She's waiting for you."

"Me?" I pushed my hair behind my ears.

He dusted off my shoulders like I was a statue. "Now, don't be nervous, Mr. Thompson. We're all rooting for you. Never have two souls been so perfectly fitted together."

I didn't know who this guy was, but I liked him. I followed him through two decks of dining rooms, libraries, and cocktail rooms, each livelier than the next with blissful spirits enjoying the night. I kept an eye out for anyone who looked even remotely like they shared DNA with Callis; why would Adele be here if she didn't think Jakome was?

"And here we are, Mr. Thompson." He held open the door.

I stepped out onto the upper deck, and he dematerialized like Julie sometimes did.

Adele was standing at the rail, gazing out over the water. She wasn't wearing Nicco's clothes anymore. She was in a little black dress that covered her arms but dipped low at the back and sparkled like the moon on the water beyond. My heart thumped. Was she really waiting for me? She'd nearly ripped my head off before we left.

I broke a sweat as she turned around. But then she smiled. At *me*. The ache inside my chest grew.

She looked relieved as I approached. "I was worried about you."

"You were?"

She stepped right up to me and slid her arms around my neck. "I shouldn't have made you come here."

I froze, hardly able to contain my shock. Why the change of heart? But her face brushed mine, melting away my fear.

"You didn't make me come here. I want to save Mac, and Ren, and everyone."

She pressed up against me. "I know."

"Adele, I'm so sorry. I'm so, so sorry." I wrapped my arms around her, and tears filled my eyes as she pulled me closer. I had thought she'd never let me touch her again. "I should never have used magic on you. I was scared—it's not an excuse. I swear, I will *never* do anything like that again. *I swear.*"

"You better not."

"I won't. I promise."

"I didn't mean to scare you." Her voice cracked. "I just want to save my dad."

"We're gonna get him back. We're gonna get through this."

She nodded. Our lips touched, and I felt almost faint. I praised every Ghede who had brought us back together.

"Thank you," I whispered.

"I love you, Isaac."

"I love you." My magic reeled through me, her warmth melting the cold of Guinée. Doubye was right: I didn't need the tooth; I just needed her. "I love you more than anything, Adele."

She kissed me again, and I could have stayed in the Afterworld forever, as long as she was with me. But we had important things to do. I stroked her cheek. "We can do anything if we stick together. Let's go find Salazar and get your dad back."

She nodded and slipped her hand into mine. As we stepped away from the rail, the boat jolted, and she bumped into me.

"Oh, shit," I said. The *Natchez* was leaving the dock.

We watched as the boat paddled away from the Moonwalk, a glimmer of violet on the water.

She looked back at me with the hint of a wicked smile. "I guess we'll just have to find something to do until we dock again." Her arms looped back over my shoulders, and she pulled herself closer for another kiss. She tasted like strawberries. And mint leaves. And everything that was good in the world.

A man cleared his throat. "Mr. Thompson, your table is ready!"

"Our table?" Adele asked. "What did you do?"

"Um, got us a table, apparently."

She pulled me along, hurrying to the penthouse deck.

A jazz quartet was playing cheerily for the dining room full of lavishly dressed people. Waiters whizzed by with trays of champagne flutes as others opened lids of silver platters revealing roasted quails and shiny asparagus. The elegant diners, all with frilly clothes and pomade-slicked hairdos, turned as we passed, admiring Adele with stolen glances. Not that she would have believed me if I told her.

"Everything's so beautiful here," she said as we sat at the table by the window with a view of the moon.

"*Mm-hmm*," I said, staring at her.

She blushed.

As the waiter jotted down our order, we hardly took our eyes off one another. I couldn't believe this was happening. The trip to Guinée was already worth it a hundred times over.

She leaned in as we spoke about magic and fashion and places that we wanted to travel one day. I found it peculiar that she didn't want to talk about the mission, but I wasn't upset by it. I was hoping she'd say she had changed her mind and wanted to go back home, but that didn't happen either. Instead, she excitedly talked about what life would be like when it was all over. *"Surely we won't have to keep our magic a secret from Mac after all of this, right?"* Her love for her family and her magic, and the way she played with my fingers while she spoke, made me fall even deeper in love with her.

All around us, glasses clinked as people merrily chatted. I hadn't felt so at ease since before Nicco was released from the attic. "I'll be right back." I leaned over and kissed her cheek.

As I headed over to the bar, I did my best to control the ridiculous beam on my face. "Two glasses of champagne, please," I asked the bartender. Surely no one would card me in Guinée, right?

"Make that four," said a man with a *very* familiar voice.

"Pop?" I turned toward him in a swirl of confusion. "What are you doing here? How did—?"

"Son, I know it's been a rough year for us, but I wouldn't miss your big night. Not for anything in the world. Congratulations." He shook my hand.

"Here, here!" came another voice I recognized.

I spun around. "Mac?"

"Welcome to the family, son." He pulled me in for a hug.

"Mac . . . how did you? Does Adele know?" *Is that why she wasn't talking about the mission?* "Now we can all go home— No ghost killing!" Hisses came from all around.

He laughed. "Well, I'm not a fan of fancy parties either, but you don't want to disappoint your guests on a night like this."

"A night like what?"

My pop put a glass of champagne in each of our hands and raised his. "To Adele and Isaac."

"To my new son-in-law," Mac said.

I choked, spitting the champagne back into the glass. "What?"

"Oh, sorry. Is it bad luck to say that before it's official?"

My attention turned back to Adele. She'd moved to a bigger table in the center of the room and was holding out her hand to a bunch of girls, including Désirée. Oh thank God, she found us.

As they fawned over her, I wondered if the rest of the crew was here, if someone knew what the hell was going on, but then Adele looked up at me with a smile, and my heart swelled.

"Come on, let's join them," my pop said. "It is your engagement party after all."

"Huh?"

They escorted me to the table, drinks in hand. I'd never seen my pop drink champagne. It seemed too happy of a drink for him. He and Mac sat beside each other, chatting like they'd known each other for years—but they'd only ever met once, as far as I knew, and my pop had been such a dick.

"There you are," said a girl with long, curly red hair, getting up from the table. She had on a long white dress with little blue flowers in a style that pushed up her cleavage. She looked like someone from a storybook. She pulled out a chair for me at Adele's side like she knew me.

"Thanks." I quickly turned to Adele, meaning to ask her a question, but I kissed her instead. I held her hand, feeling for the ring on her finger; it had *a diamond.* "This is real," I whispered, looking at it.

"It's perfect," she said, and then brushed my face with her hand. "You seem nervous."

"What? No. I'm just . . . in disbelief that this is happening. That you want to marry me."

"Don't be silly." She kissed me again, and the girls next to me cooed.

They seemed familiar. The redhead had pale skin with a light dusting of freckles and a mischievous expression. Next to her, the brunette was all smiles, teeming with excitement. Her dark, wavy hair was loosely twisted up, but the way the tendrils hung in front of her face reminded me of someone . . . She held on to the redhead's elbow like they were BFFs. "Will this make us sisters, Susannah?" she asked with a French accent.

The redhead turned to her. "We're already sisters, darling. In magic."

"Susannah Bowen!" I yelped, and everyone turned to me.

"Did you think I'd miss your engagement party?" she asked. "You did come all the way to the Afterworld to celebrate with us all."

"Holy shit! I-I have so many questions . . . ." But in that moment, I couldn't think of a single one of them.

"Later, Isaac," she giggled. "Tonight's about you and Adele!"

"And your utterly brilliant love," said a blonde French girl, draping over their shoulders.

I blinked for a second, swearing it was Lisette, but her eyes were bright with joy. "Cosette?"

"Minette," she corrected, sitting at the brunette's other side.

"Whoa. Lisette's going to be *stoked* to see you."

"That's lovely, dear, but let's talk about the wedding. We're all so excited!"

Well, that was kind of cold. Did she blame Lisette for her death?

The brunette sighed dramatically and rested her head on Susannah's. "Thank heavens you proposed, Isaac."

I what? Why couldn't I remember this? Had I been in some kind of accident?

But then I recalled a beautiful moment: the two of us, on the Brooklyn Bridge under the stars. Me on one knee. The surprise in her eyes.

"I was beginning to worry she was actually going to fall for that youngest Medici boy," she added.

Adele's gaze dropped to the table as they giggled again.

I pulled her closer. "I wasn't worried." The warmth from her smile gave me life. "I never thought for a second you could love that monster."

She kissed me softly, her nose brushing mine, and I wanted to remain in that moment forever. The kiss deepened like we were the only two people in the world, but then hoots came from around the table, and it became impossible not to laugh.

"Isaac," said the brunette, who, *duh*, I now realized was Adeline-freaking-Saint-Germain—*Wait, there's something I wanted to ask Adeline. What was it?* "Tell us all about the moment you knew you were in love with my little Addie?"

The table fell silent in anticipation.

"This better not be anything dirty," Mac said.

Adele groaned. I pulled her beneath my arm and looked

deeply into her eyes as I thought about it. "It's hard." I felt the weight of everyone's stares, waiting for my response.

"You don't have to say anything," she whispered.

"It's hard to even remember a time when I didn't love you." Sighs went around the table. "But if I had to pinpoint it, I think it was at the café. When you told me that if I didn't like my coffee, I could go back to New York." My dad laughed. "Before that, I just thought you were the prettiest girl I'd ever seen." She blushed and coiled away, but I pulled her back. "But after that, I knew I'd do anything to get you to talk to me."

"And he did," she said to the table, and she told them the story about how I'd weaseled into her art lessons.

"Now it's all making sense," Mac said, lovingly shaking his head.

"And, Adele, when did you know?" Susannah asked. "That you were unequivocally in love with Isaac?"

"Easy," she said, blooming. She turned to me. "It was . . ." Everyone waited for her to continue, but she seemed to lose her train of thought. "It was the time . . ." She fell silent again, blushing.

Nervousness fluttered in my stomach, and I held her hand, trying to make her more comfortable.

"When we . . ." Her forehead pinched like she was trying to remember something specific.

As much as I wanted to hear her answer, I didn't want her to be stressed. The night was already perfect. "Don't worry abo—"

Dee leaned in from her other side. "Didn't you tell me once . . . Wasn't it the time you were in the amphitheater, and he was juggling your Fireballs with his Air? You said it was the most romantic thing *ever*."

My nerves began to settle.

"I loved that," Adele swooned. "Wait, no . . . that was right after I got into a big fight with Nicco. It was another time."

"What other time?" Susannah leaned into the table with a

stern brow, seemingly annoyed that she'd brought up Nicco. *Welcome to my life.*

"Just . . . give me a second." Adele guzzled the champagne.

"When he let you read his grimoire?" Minette asked with a slight blush. "That would have done it for me."

"When he stayed with you in the attic while you *dream-twinned* with another man?" asked Adeline. "Now, that is trust."

"When he punched that photographer!" Désirée said.

"The garden for Brigitte!" Susannah yelped. "He ripped out every weed and twirled you into the Air in a tangle of flowers and kisses and magic."

"No." She shook her head to each of them.

I stared into the bowl of soup, and an eyeball popped up to the surface. I blinked hard, and grabbed my spoon, moving the chunks of crabmeat through the swirl of dark roux and rice.

"I'm sorry," Adele said. "I can't remember."

"It's okay." I cupped her cheek. "All that matters is right now."

She nuzzled her face against mine. "I love you."

I kissed her again. "I love you too."

"*Isaac,*" Susannah said sharply. "You have to leave here."

"What?"

Adele curled around my arm.

"*Now,*" Susannah said, getting up.

"Don't leave me," Adele said. "I'm sorry I couldn't remember. Please don't leave me!"

"I'm not gonna leave you, babe," I said softly.

"Isaac, you have to get out of here, right now!"

Adele looked like she was about to cry.

"We're on a boat. We can't leave."

"You're a bird; you can fly!"

"Susannah, chill," I said under my breath.

"*Isaac, you don't have much time!*" Susannah's voice billowed from up above, rather than from the girl sitting at the table next to Adeline. *What the fuck?*

"They really are the perfect couple," my pop said to Mac, who nodded in agreement.

"*Isaac Norwood Thompson, come with me, this instant!*" The air above the table tore apart, and a hand ripped through, extending out to me from a black void. "Isaac, take my hand! You can't marry her!"

"Isaac, don't leave me!"

I looked around the room, my pulse racing. The four musicians were no longer in their dapper suits. They were rotting corpses, blowing wretched notes through banged-up trumpets.

"*Now*, Isaac, I can't hold this open for much longer!"

Adele clung on to me. Eyeballs floated up from the soup again. Worms crawled through my now putrid green steak. The calliope blasted eardrum-blowing chords.

"Will it be a fall wedding?" Minette asked.

"Oh, a summer wedding!" Susannah said. "On the beach!"

"In Bermuda!" The girls all squeed.

"Isaac Norwood Thompson, *now!*" A pointy boot stomped down onto the table from the tear above, and two sturdy, feminine hands grabbed my collar and lifted me from the seat onto the table. Everyone around us screamed and laughed with glee as the room descended into chaos.

Adele clung to my leg. "Isaac, please!"

"I'm not leaving her!" I yelled.

"That's not Adele!"

I looked down. Adele's face was replaced with a decaying skull. Her arms were bone. "*Agh!*" I screamed, jerking my leg. "*What the fuck?*"

"That's *not* Adele!"

I stopped resisting and let the arms pull me through, back into the dark.

CHAPTER 21
MARTA

"Masaka?" I called out from the floor, a metal pole jutting against my back.

I sat up, pushing clothing from my shoulders and head, and then fumbled for my phone in the dark. The songs of the owls and cicadas and frogs were gone, as were the stars overhead. *It worked. The ritual worked!* But where the hell was I?

I activated the light, buzzing with anticipation, and flashed my phone around. I'd crash-landed into . . . a dress rack? If you could even call them dresses. Sequin bras and rhinestone panties. Harnesses. A lime-green leather whip. *Okaaay. Why do I feel like I'm in some dominatrix's closet?*

The Ghede's proclivities came to mind, and I refused to acknowledge the budding nervousness. *Whatever, I'm not a prude,* I told myself; at least, I tried to.

"Masaka?" I called again, pulling my bag from the pile of scanty stripperwear, ready to find the others. "Isaac?"

As I stepped through the dark, the floorboards reverberated with the bass of a nearby speaker. The flood of light from my phone hit a thick salmon-pink velvet curtain. Noises came from the other side: the clinks of glasses and the deep beats of a slow jam.

I edged along the curtain, trying to find the end before saying *screw it* and slipping beneath it. A pink spotlight hit my eyes. A whip of violet feathers brushed my face and a lanky leg swung over my head. *Shit.* I leapt out of the way and slid down the stage floor, narrowly avoiding smashing the dim round bulbs lining the front edge. Shielding my eyes, I gazed out into the crowd of silhouettes in the audience as the dancer twirled around the pole in a blur of patent leather, upside down, lace-covered legs spread.

You have got to be kidding me.

I hopped down into a sea of mostly empty cabaret tables. Lone figures sat at a few of them, hunched over drinks, crunching ice from the bottoms of tumblers, swirling lemon rinds in martini glasses. Old green velvet couches lined the walls along with paisley chairs that looked straight from my great-aunt's 1970s time capsule of a house. A neon-blue sign behind the bar blinked: "**HURRICANES.**"

No. No, no, no. My heart sank, realizing the ritual hadn't worked after all. *But why did I wake up on the seedy end of the Quarter instead of Holt Cemetery? What did I do wrong? Shit!*

I mentally retraced my steps as I meandered through the tables, trying not to think about arriving home or the looks on Manon and Remi's faces when they learned that I'd blown the ritual and sent us to Big Daddy's instead of Guinée. Did I not perform the ritual correctly?

The music pumped louder. I *know* I did it right. "Shit!"

Heads turned my way.

"What?" I grumbled.

The scent of night blossoms still drenched the air amongst the meld of cigarette smoke and bleach—you knew those flowers came from a witch's garden if their scent could cut through a

French Quarter strip club. My hand brushed a table, and I ripped it away. *Gross. Don't touch anything, Désirée.*

"You'd think for a child who grew up in da Vieux Carré, you'd be a little more open-minded 'bout da clubs."

I whipped back around to the stage as the dancer swung around the pole. I squinted. Beneath the three pounds of face glitter and four sets of false lashes—and wearing not much more than a leather chest harness, matching thong, lacy lavender thigh-highs and spiked boots that I kinda wanted—it was *Masaka.*

"Hey!" I yelled. I didn't even want to think about why a Ghede lwa brought me to a strip club. "There weren't supposed to be any pole-dancing pit stops! We need to go!"

"This ain't a pole-dancing pit stop."

"Not that I have anything against pole dancing," I said, realizing I'd reached into my bag and was spritzing sanitizer all over my hands.

"Right," said a blonde woman behind the bar, and the patrons in the room snickered.

Whatever. "I'm not anti-sex work." I spritzed the air around me for good measure. "I'm just anti-germs." I dropped the bottle back into my bag, giving the bartender another look. Her gauzy peach-colored dress didn't really fit the typical Bourbon-vibe. It was dainty and frilly, like she should be walking through the garden of a Jane Austen novel with a parasol. To each their own.

Masaka twirled around the pole again, and I tried to temper my annoyance. "I answered your questions. You said you were taking me to Guinée!" *Did my friends also get dropped off up and down Bourbon? Oh, Goddess.*

A smile spread across the Ghede's face, and the bartender laughed again. Her honeycomb-colored hair was swept up in a bunch of tiny braids, but not in that white-girl-tryna-be-fly kinda way. The hairstyle was regal, almost, like her dress. "What is it you seek in the Guinée, baby?" she asked, lighting up a cigarette.

Ugh. I held my breath. "What do *you* know about Guinée?" I muttered, turning back to Masaka. "Let's boun—"

"Everything there is to know," the bartender answered, "and nothing at all, I suppose. Even after four hundred years, I learn something new every day, it seems."

"Four hundred years?" My attention flipped back to her. "What do you mean *four hundred years*?"

A couple sitting at the bar eyed me as I approached. A woman who looked more Dickensian than Austen and a guy with teardrop face tats. "She seems different," she said quietly to the man.

"I don't think she's dead," he whispered back in disbelief. In a ghostly blink, he was standing right behind me.

I twisted around. "Okay, you can back the hell out of my bubble, buddy."

"I didn't mean no disrespect lady, you're just so . . . warm."

I was pretty sure it was the first time anyone had ever called me warm. Flames were tattooed up both of his arms, but they weren't what caught my eye. It was his Maleficium; it was just like Adele's.

Dickens lady had a Water mark.

That can't be a coincidence. I strode to the nearest table where a blue-haired hipster with safety pins in his earlobes who looked like he'd had a little too much fun in the eighties sat sucking down a drink. *Another Water.*

Masaka howled with laughter as I wove through the other tables, not so casually investigating the patrons' arms. "Now bébé's getting it."

Three Airs, an Earth, and another Fire, I counted, coming back to the bar. *The bartender's an Aether.*

"Welcome to the Afterworld, love," she said. "Can I get ya somethin'?"

"Th-this is not the Afterworld. Not Guinée."

"Of course it is," Masaka said, sliding down the stage floor into a split.

"No, *no,* it is not."

"What were you expectin'?" he asked.

"I don't know?"

"Yes, you do."

"I don't know, a beautiful African coastline? Beaches, water, nature, something? Not a strip club!" I turned back to the bartender. "You're telling me that you've had to spend eternity slinging drinks in a dank room with scratchy speakers? What kind of bullshit is this?"

She shrugged as she stacked glasses on top of one another.

A bony arm appeared around my shoulders. "Don't fret, *ma chère.* This may not be your fate. Da Afterworld presents itself to you however it sees fit."

"What does that mean?" I wondered if Ritha got her esoteric tone from talking to the lwa.

"You aren't dead. Guinée shows itself to you familiarly."

"What about me says 'petri dish'?"

"Stop focusing on the minutiae." Masaka's shiny black fingernails strummed my arm.

How was I supposed to not focus on bacteria when we were in a nightclub?

A woman's scream made me bolt upright. All the spirits jumped up.

"*¡Qué demonios!*" the Fire witch yelped. He ran out of the room, the rest of us following close behind down a dark hall lit up with neon glow-painted graffiti and then twisting into the club's crowded dance hall. The music pounded and strobe lights flashed. I barely kept up with the Fire witch as we pushed through the droves of people dancing. There were daisy chain-wearing Woodstock girls, men with *Soul Train*-level afros, and a throng of nineties ravers with holographic halter tops sucking fluorescent pacifiers. A Sid Vicious wannabe slammed into me, doing a move that might be considered dancing in some white-people world, and I fell back into the crowd. When he came at me again, I rammed him with my shoulder.

"*Mosh!*" he yelled.

"No!" I bulldozed through them, shoulders high, cringing at the idea of coming into contact with strangers' sweat. *Did dead people sweat?*

The next hallway was dark and the crowd thinner, mostly couples making out against the walls. I saw Masaka up ahead, going out the front door. "Wait!"

With a final sprint, I spilled onto the street, catching my breath under the moon.

The heavy door slammed shut, and the streets were quiet. The silence was so absolute and eerie, it made me instantly want to be back in the harmonic chaos of the club.

Something here was not right. I could feel it in my bones.

We appeared to be on Toulouse, right off Bourbon. Or at least, some Afterworld version of it. The streets and buildings were the same, but something felt askew, as if someone had turned the kaleidoscope just a hair. Like the Quarter at night wasn't bad enough in the Natural World. The hairs on the back of my neck stood up. Maybe it was the overwhelming pulse of magic? No. I'd been around magic my whole life, and it never made me feel vulnerable—the opposite, in fact. A shiver went up my spine. As I wondered where Isaac was, I realized that I was . . . alone.

All of Ritha's warnings rushed back at once. "*The Afterworld is for the dead, Désirée.*"

"Masaka?" I yelled. My voice echoed down the street.

I pulled out my phone and attempted to send a message to the group. No signal. *Duh.*

A clank hit the pavement, and I peered down the street toward the river. Two spirits were changing the sign above Le Chat Noir, which looked more like it probably had in the olden days, like a proper opera house. But here the exterior had an otherworldly effect, sparkling like it was made of jewels, twinkling in the ashy sky.

The sign blinked on:

Opening Night!

"Masaka!" I whispered loudly.

And for the second time, a woman's curdling scream split the air. I looked around. She screamed again. *What if it's Adele?* I ran toward Rampart, toward the voice, blowing past shops for broomsticks and candles and potion bottles. Everything was the same, and nothing was the same.

"*Hilfe!*" the girl shrieked.

As I turned onto Bourbon, trash cans rolled out onto the street in a loud crash, and a hooded figure twisted out from amongst them and darted past me, his dark cloak trailing behind. He stopped dead in his tracks and turned back to me, his eyes narrowing as if confused by my presence. The cloak's hood cast a shadow over his white face, and a band of smoky makeup stretched from one temple to the other across his eyes.

I reached for my mini-mace in my back pocket. *What the hell is mace going to do to a spirit, Désirée?* He stepped closer, and I nearly bolted into the nearest club, but then . . . he took off running.

I almost collapsed in relief, leaning into the hitching post next to me, not even caring—momentarily—how many people had probably pissed on it. *Oh, Goddess, yes I do.*

As I reached for my hand sanitizer, the woman's voice murmured from the dark, desolate street, panting heavily between rushing words. Swedish? German?

"Hello?" I called out. "Are you okay?"

When she didn't answer, I stepped cautiously through the weaves of neon lights and shadows looking for her. I'd never seen Bourbon so devoid of people, even after the Storm, but she was nowhere to be found. In the pink glow of a blinking "**DANCE, DANCE, DANCE,**" sign, an ivy vine had grown into the middle of the street, thick and lush. *On Bourbon?*

The vine trailed down the street. I kept close to the buildings, following the plump leaves. It spread out into a patch, which then coalesced to a peculiar mound about six feet tall and at least that wide. A nest? No, more like a cocoon of twisting vines and wildflowers, at least a dozen varieties in unnatural shapes and colors. Winding stalks grew out of it like tentacles, extending out to either side of the street, crawling up the wrought iron gallery posts to the rooftops of buildings. Flowers were still sprouting up along their paths.

It was extraordinary. A floral pod that could have displayed Gran Bwa himself.

As I walked through them, I could sense it move ever so slightly, up and down with the breath of the girl I swore I could now hear crying. Was she *inside it*? I wanted to help, but the Quarter rat in me was wary it was some kind of *Alien vs Predator* trap and the murmurings were a lure.

"Hello?"

"*Er hat mich angegriffen!*"

I didn't need to know German to hear the distress in her voice. "Hello!" I called out, pulling at the structure. Did that man do this to her? Was he some kind of Earth witch? For shame.

I waved my hand, but I felt a mental pinch. Were the vines fighting my magic? *Oh hell, no.* I mentally yanked them harder, but they wouldn't budge. I panicked at the thought of my magic not working in the Afterworld. But why would that be? *It's the eternal land of the witches!*

The flora was tightly woven together, and it was difficult even to get my fingers between the vines. I tugged one of them out, ripping out wildflowers in the process. The girl became more hysterical; I pulled harder, but without much luck—until I found a place that was damp, the vines blackened with rot. I focused my magic and yanked the rotted vines with all of my might and all of my magic until one snapped. My Elemental sparkled green before fading out. *It still works!*

Footsteps pattered behind me, and voices whispered throughout the street. As I thrashed through the remaining foliage, people crowded around, helping, tearing apart the cocoon, until the sides came crashing down.

Inside the pod, a young blonde woman cradled her legs tightly into her chest, rocking back and forth. Her red face was damp with tears, her ringlets disheveled, and her kerchief hiked around her neck, exposing her bust. One of her skirt layers was ripped and burnt, and her stays had twisted halfway around her chest, like she'd put up a struggle.

I knelt next to her, seething. *Even in the Afterworld, women still have to worry about being attacked? Even in Guinée? What the ever-loving fuck?*

"Are you okay?" I asked, despite it clearly being a ridiculous question.

Her face was round like a cherub, with sparkling blue eyes like one of those old Hollywood starlets. I didn't know what else to do. "*Ça va?*"

Her eyes lit up, and she continued in hysterical French, but I couldn't keep up. Where was Adele when you needed her? It was something about a man. A Black man. No, a man in the night? In the dark? The shadows! Madame Cecilia would be *très* unimpressed considering my eight years of French at the Academy.

"*Meine Magie!*" she yelled out to the crowd.

"Marta!" A blonde woman, in similar dress, pushed through

the spirits. "Marta!" She fell at my side, and they spoke in rapid German.

The crowd around us whispered in disbelief. I hoped that meant women being attacked in the streets wasn't a regular occurrence. People were pointing. Not just at Marta. At the vines and the wildflowers, which had been bigger and brighter than even those that filled Ritha's courtyard. Now the petals were falling away, littering the breeze. The vines around us blackening. I'd never seen anything like it. Whenever my family's Earth magic faded, it just sort of dispelled. The plants didn't rot, and they certainly didn't die.

Marta clutched her friend as we tried to reassure her that she was safe now.

Another white spirit-girl, one with wavy brown curls, emerged from the gathered crowd. "What happened?" she yelled in French-accented English.

"She was attacked," I said. "I think."

"Attacked? This is the Afterworld. There aren't any . . ." When she caught sight of me, she did a double take, pausing before asking the question directly to me. "Who did this?"

"I-I don't know. I saw a man running away."

"*Er hat versucht, mir meine Magie wegzunehmen!*" yelled Marta.

"What man? Who?" the French girl asked.

"White. Twenties. Thirties, maybe. Dark hair, I think. Black cloak with a hood. Kohl across his eyes."

"We need to go after him! Where is Adele?"

"Adele? Adele LeMoyne? Have you seen her?"

Marta screamed as if in grave pain—and *disappeared*. The crowd jumped back. But then she reappeared.

I blinked hard. *What just—?*

Marta grasped onto the vines in a panic, like someone was trying to pull her away.

"Adeline?" another French-accented voice called. A young Black woman in a gold tignon was pushing her way through the crowd.

I reached out for the brunette's arm. "You're Adeline Saint-Germain?"

"Where is Adele?" she asked me again.

I hardly heard the question because at that moment I realized who the newcomer was. "Marassa!" I yelled, turning back to the crowd.

"Marassa's not here."

"Yes, she is!" I jumped up, but I could no longer see her. "Marassa!" *Where did she go?*

Marta was in better hands, and there didn't seem to be much I could do to help.

"Désirée, don't!" Adeline cried, but I darted into the crowd.

My eyes stayed locked on the gold headdress as I wove in and out of spirits who all seemed shocked and enthralled by the evening's events. Each step I grew more aggressive, fearful I'd lose her in the sea of people. I saw her turn onto Orleans, and I made a run for it. Without the neon lights from the clubs, the street was completely dark, and the crowd had thinned. By the time I passed Royal, the streets were quiet again, and I began to think I'd conjured her up—maybe Adeline had been right. But just as I was about to give up, I saw her shadowy figure turn onto Chartres. I swore she even glanced back at me, as if to make sure I was still following.

"Marassa!" I charged ahead.

I rounded the corner, but the foggy street was completely still other than a shop sign up ahead, gently creaking. In the Natural World, it was a store that sold brightly colored wool for knitters, but now the sign read:

MAKANDAL LIBRARY OF THE DEAD

Makandal? As in my ancestors? Was this their shop? Ever more curious, I hurried up to the door and tried the handle. It clicked open, and excitement grew in my belly.

As I stepped inside, I was so anxious, I didn't even announce myself, just continued looking around in awe. Dark green curtains were drawn over the large storefront windows, as if protecting the precious artifacts within. An oil lamp burned on the counter, illuminating the stacks. Rows and rows of books. Some new, some old. Some like pre-colonialism old. Every language of the Natural World graced the gold-leafed spines. My mother would fall in insta-love with this place. She was obsessed with books.

"Marassa?" I called.

As I moved into the next room, the tomes transitioned to scrolls, stacked in shelves all the way to the ceiling. There were stone tablets with hieroglyphics on display without glass coverings or protection of any kind. Pedestals held ancient-looking runes and antique talking boards. *I bet these stacks would blow Sébastien Michel's mind.*

A voice came from beyond an aubergine-colored silk curtain. "My mama makes the best *vani krèm.*"

"Marassa?"

I lifted the curtain to find a witch's kitchen. Marassa stood behind a boiling cauldron in a billowy white shirt tucked into layers of long red and orange skirts, steam coiling up around her. No one else here. Had she been speaking to me?

She looked up with a warm smile. "Do you want me to teach you how to make it, Désirée Nanette?" I had *much* more important things to do than learn how to make a crème brûlée, like finding Codi and getting the kishi to the Soul Keeper. "It's a secret Makandal family recipe." She stirred the contents of the pot, and for a blink, the mixture glimmered lilac. The urgency to find Codi seeped from my mind like a soft lullaby. *He's probably already delivered the kishi by now, anyway. And how long could it really take to make a dessert?* She handed me the wooden spoon.

"*Oui*, that would be amazing," I said, despite having revolted against taking home economics at school. This was different. I wanted to know anything Marassa was willing to teach me. I wanted to know everything about our family.

CHAPTER 22
MACABRE COUTURE

I couldn't believe I was standing face to face with Giovanna Medici. "Have you seen Nicco?" I asked. "Is he here?"

"Of course he's here. And you need a dress." Her smile turned devilish, and I wondered if she and Adeline still had any beef; and, more importantly, what that would mean for me. Could I trust her? Adeline had killed her . . . But that was almost three hundred years ago.

Giovanna held the dark lace up to my neck.

"I don't need a dress," I whispered. "We need to avenge your family, and I don't need to be tripping over a gown while doing so."

"*Bella,* you'll never even get through the door wearing"—her gaze raked the length of my body— "that."

"This jacket's made from the finest Italian leather. It's your brother's!"

"I've brought down many a powerful man in a dress. The more powerful the man, the more delectable your gown must be." She pushed the jacket off my shoulders, and another set of chilly hands untied the flannel from my waist: Morning Star's. Cosette tugged the elastic from my hair.

A breeze touched my legs, and when I glanced down, my pants were missing. "Hey! My jeans!" I frantically looked around.

"Do not fret, *ma fifille*, we'll make sure you can reach your dagger through your stays," Cosette said slyly, and they all smiled to each other.

"Stays?" I asked with a crushing gasp as she pulled the cords. "I can't wear these. I can barely breathe, much less move!"

Cosette twisted the laces into a bow, and Giovanna lowered the first skirt over my head—some kind of fine netting with tens of thousands of beads that glistened like a celestial wave of midnight blue. "Are you sure?" Giovanna asked, turning me toward a dressing mirror.

I couldn't help but make the skirt swish with a rock of my hips. I'd never seen anything so beautiful. "How is it so light? Beadwork this heavy should weigh twenty pounds!"

"It's spider's silk," Morning Star whispered at one of my shoulders.

"Strung with thirty-thousand droplets of morning dew," Cosette added, tickling my shoulder.

I raised my arms, mesmerized, as Giovanna slipped the bodice over my head. It was dark as coal, with a rainbow shimmer.

"It's made from the most exquisite moondust," she said, as her hands plunged below the neckline.

"Moondust!" I yelped as she lifted my breasts.

Cosette shook my hips, and everything settled into place. Morning Star tied the gossamer sleeves in place with black velvet ribbons: "They are threaded with moonbeams. Brings out the nighttime sky in your eyes."

"That's not even possible." They all backed away so I could see myself in the mirror, and the argument slipped off my tongue. I swished the dewdrop skirt, just to see it glisten like the ocean, and I moved my shoulders to see the threads sparkle. What else other than *moonbeams* could be so entrancing?

"You look just like a lunar goddess," Giovanna said.

I wished Nicco was here so I could show it off. I let the dress drop. What was I doing trying on pretty dresses like we were all out at the mall on a Saturday afternoon? My father was currently a hostage, and I was the only one who could help him.

I turned to Giovanna. "I need to find Jakome Salazar. Do you know where he is?"

The girls showered me with compliments, and she kissed my cheeks. "Now you're ready."

When I moved, the stays cut into my ribs. I fought to suck in a breath, but someone pulled the laces tighter. "Don't do that!" I jerked away. "It's already too tight!"

But the girls were gone.

"Giovanna?"

The laces pulled tighter again, and I gasped, whirling around. "Cosette?" *They were just here.* I clutched for the cords at my back, but I couldn't feel them. "Morning Star!" My breaths stuttered. "Get . . . it . . . off." I stumbled to the tailor's station, which seemed to flicker and shift in the light of the fat candle burning on the wall sconce above. Dizziness made the world tilt around me. I grasped at the objects on the table, knocking over reels of thread and brightly colored pincushions, looking for scissors or a knife, anything sharp. *Where is my dagger?* It wasn't here. Neither was my bag. *Did they take it? The ghoststick!* I pulled open the drawer and spotted a pair of tailor's shears through the black dots clouding my vision. Hands shaking, I forced the blades down the side of the bodice and squeezed them together.

The scissors crunched. *What the hell?* The bodice dug deeper against my ribs, hard and cold—the charcoal moondust had been replaced with . . . *bones.*

I screamed, but no sound came from my throat. Clutching

at the bones, I tried to rip them off, but the more I panicked, the tighter they squeezed, like the hands of the dead. The black dots filled my entire vision. *I'm sorry, Dad. I never should have come here.* I tumbled, grasping at the curtain on the way down.

I hit the floor and heard the curtain rod smash into the wall sconce before it cracked my head. The candle fell with it, lighting the drapes ablaze.

I tried to push myself up. My hand felt slick and warm—*Is that my blood?* And then I was out of air.

My cheek hit the wooden floor. I pulled down to the bottom of my soul for my Elemental—to stop the flames from growing. But no magic came.

In the darkness, I felt the heat whoosh over me.

CHAPTER 23
SWAMP WITCH

I gasped, breaking the surface through a tangle of vines, choking out the putrid black water. "*Dannazione!*"

Paddling through the water, I pulled a throng of lily roots from my shoulders and wiped my sopping hair from my face. *Where the hell?* I floated, trying to get my bearings. Bulbous cypress trees grew out of the water like knobby bones, stretching up to the stars. I might still have been under the Flower Moon, but I was no longer in Valence Cemetery; I was in the middle of a goddamn swamp. A woman's laughter echoed down from the sky above. *Thanks, L'Oraille.*

My eyes easily adjusted to the darkness as I swam, searching for the shoreline. How far was I from the others? "Adele?" I yelled.

The swishes of tree branches and groans of frogs responded. More girlish giggles, ghostly through the rippling water, echoed as I glided amongst the flora.

My fingers twisted into tufts of something too silky to be swamp grass, and I yanked my hand back. Pale arms floated beneath the surface. *No.*

I dove under, feeling around the murky water.

"Adele?" I yelled, swashing through the floating green algae, searching. It was her. I saw her face. "Adele!"

Wet arms slinked around my shoulders from behind. A whisper in my ear: "You'll never save her." The ring of her Venetian accent sent a chill down my spine. I'd forgotten the song of her voice. "You'll only destroy her, the way you destroyed me."

I twisted around to her, and her legs wrapped around me, just like they had when we'd snuck into her father's pools, the delicate chemise and her golden hair floating around us like Botticelli's Aphrodite. Droplets of water shook from her brow as I clutched her face close to mine; all I could do was stare into her eyes in disbelief. "Maddalena."

"She'll still love you, *amore mio.*"

"What?" I asked, the ache in my chest splitting.

Her nose brushed mine. "She'll still love you after you kill her, just like I do."

"I—I'm not going to hurt her."

She smiled, her lips so close to mine. My gums throbbed, keeping my teeth at bay. I didn't want her to see them. I wanted her to remember me like I was. *How could she ever remember you as anything but the monster who killed her, Niccolò?*

"*Sì, lo farai.* You're going to kill her just like you killed me."

"No." I blocked the image from my mind.

"She'll still love you, *lo prometto,* Niccolò."

"You don't still love me. Not after what I did."

"*Sì, che te ne voglio, amore mio.*"

All I'd wanted throughout my first century as a vampire was to hear her voice again, but now her words filled me with dread.

"*You're going to kill her. And you're going to live happily ever after, for eternity.*"

"I can control it now. *Ti prego perdonami.* I'm so sorry for what I did to you, my dove."

A voice came from above. "Even you don't have that kind of

control, *Niccolò*." The voice I'd tried to forget for the last three centuries.

My fangs snapped out, and I pushed Maddalena behind my back.

Séraphine was moonbathing above us. Her supple nude figure draped over a tree branch, her long silvery hair hanging down to the water. "*Ciao, amore mio,*" she said and dove into the water. Séraphine always spoke Italian when she wanted to be seductive, and French to be demanding.

I commanded myself to swim away, but I didn't move, just watched the ghostly curve of her back, mesmerized, as she glided toward us. Her pale face broke the surface of the sable water just inches from mine. She was somehow even more beautiful than I remembered, like she truly had been touched by the moon. I pulled her closer, the gaze of her smokey-quartz eyes unlocking a minefield of memories of our bodies twisted together. There was nothing like the love of your Maker, and now I yearned for it like I was just turned yesterday.

Her hand slid up my chest. I didn't remember getting undressed, but I was.

"What kind of magic is this?" I asked, the words catching in my throat.

"You're going to kill her," she whispered, her lips remembering the most sensitive part of my neck, just below my ear. "And you're going to enjoy sucking every last drop of her blood. Just like I taught you. Lapping it up like a little puppy."

"I will not." Her breaths on my skin made me stutter. I ordered myself to push her away.

My attempts were futile, just like I'd failed hundreds—thousands—of times in the past.

Maddalena's lips too found the crook of my neck, and all thoughts bled from my mind. My head knocked back as her hands circled my chest, as Séraphine teased lower. "*You're going to kill her, Niccolò,*" they both whispered. "*La ucciderai.*"

I no longer argued. I could no longer think about anything but my need. They whispered it again and again, their voices blending together into a single siren's song. Just as I began to lose my mind to desire, the words echoed in French. Through my heavy eyelids, the blurry figure of another girl swung on the twisted vines of a willow.

"*Bonjour, Monsieur Cartier.*"

My spine stiffened. The girls looked up with curiosity just as the newcomer arched her back and let herself fly into the river. Her dark curls blended with the water as she swam toward us. Maddalena's arms clung onto me tightly.

Thump-thump.

Thump-thump.

With the sound of her heartbeat, I knew exactly who it was. The one person I'd been hoping to avoid in this voyage.

Her face reemerged. "So you're going to kill my descendant, Niccolò Medici?" The swamp water glistened on her plump lips.

I shook my head.

"*Sì, la ucciderai.*" Maddalena shifted to my right shoulder, making room.

"It's the only way he'll ever find happiness—if he has her forever," Séraphine said, floating up beside her on my left. "He'll never find happiness until he accepts who he truly is."

"I have accepted who I truly am," I snapped.

They all laughed. Adeline swam close, circled my neck with both arms, and jerked my face close to hers. "You're going to turn Adele into a monster? Would that be your ultimate revenge on my father? Destroying our magicline for good?"

I vehemently shook my head. "I would never do that to Adele. I would never hurt her."

"You killed me, and you'll kill her, Niccolò," Maddalena cooed.

"You lied to me for forty years," Séraphine whispered. "How

long will you lie to yourself about her?" The three of them twisted around me.

"I never lied to you."

Around and around.

"You told me you loved me."

"I *did* love you. You made me love you!"

"It's positively ambrosial," Séraphine taunted, "that beneath the decades of your hardened heart, you think Adele will be the one to escape your clutches. Your undying hope is why I loved you more than the others. Your naïveté."

"You were the naïve one," I snarled.

"You're going to kill her the way you killed me."

"You're going to drink from her plentifully, and when you do, the true monster will emerge. The one you've kept locked in a cage for four hundred years."

"She loves your darkness, *amore mio.*"

"How much harder is it to be around her now that you've drunk her blood in the bell tower?"

"*Harder,*" I pined. "*So much harder.*"

They all laughed.

"*We know you want to taste her. To drink her. To drain her.*"

"*She's going to end up just like us.*"

"*You'll be too much of a weakling to turn her.*"

"*You'll lose her forever.*"

"*We already have a spot picked out for her.*"

"*A grave to lie in.*"

"*A gown to die in.*"

"*A crown of bones to wear forever.*"

"*Killing her is your destiny,*" Adeline said. "*C'est la vie.*"

I thrust my hand forward and grabbed her neck with a growl. "This isn't real."

The two other girls hissed.

"Adeline Saint-Germain knows I wouldn't kill Adele. She saw to it! This is some kind of trial!" I shoved her away with a splash.

As her head reemerged from the water, she flashed a pouty smile. "Trial? You're paranoid, Niccolò."

"He was always paranoid," Séraphine said.

I slapped the water. "This isn't real because *you* wouldn't be in Guinée." I spun back to Maddalena. "You weren't a witch, either," I hissed at her, fracturing a part of my heart.

"You're still going to kill her," she hissed back, eyes suddenly black as onyx.

"You're still going to kill her," they all hissed, over and over like slithering snakes gliding over my skin, until I . . . just . . . let go.

I let myself sink beneath the water.

Drifting down and down, until they were nothing but ghostly figures through the brackish swamp.

Until there was nothing but blackness.

But still their voices sang in my head. Louder than they did in my dreams. My fantasies. My nightmares.

I'm not going to hurt her. I'm not going to kill her, I repeated faster and faster as the water filled my nose and ears and rushed into my mouth.

"I will never hurt her!" my voiced gargled as I gave myself over to the swamps of Guinée.

CHAPTER 24
MISSING GIRL

I stormed out of the kitchen, back into the library, breaking the illusion. *Freakin' Ghede.* Adeline Saint-Germain had been right —Marassa hadn't been in the crowd—this was all just one big Ghede mind-trip. It all made sense now—my Elemental magic not being able to untwist that crazy vine, the girl being attacked on the street. "Guinée being a strip club, my ass!" I glanced around at the ancient runes and stone tables. I should have known this library was too cool to be real. I grabbed a leather-bound tome from the counter and started to hurl it at the window, but then I heard Ritha's voice in my head. "*Please, think before you act.*"

I set the book down *just in case* I was wrong and this place had some validity. I didn't want to be the fool smashing up my ancestral rite. I can't believe I let the Ghede dupe me.

I'd even fed him the damn info. He knew he could distract me with my ancestors because I freaking told him it was my true desire for coming here. "Well played, Masaka, well played." I charged to the door, sure that when I opened it, I'd see crystal blue water and dense vegetation and all of my magical ancestors welcoming me home with drums and chanting and tongue clicks and dancing with half the Òrìshà in attendance.

The magic in my veins pulsed stronger, ready for the grand reunion. Ready to leap into the real Marassa and Makandal's arms. I burst through the door.

But there was no sunshine and no ancestors and no lesser African gods.

I was still on Chartres. Everything was the same as it had been before I'd followed Marassa inside. I glanced back up at the gently swaying sign. It still said: **MAKANDAL LIBRARY OF THE DEAD.** My head spun. When exactly had the illusion started? In the kitchen? I groaned.

Whatever. No more distractions. I needed to find the boys. Adele and the vamps would be looking for Jakome, but Codi and Isaac would be looking for the Soul Keeper. Where would I find Ghede-Houson? "Masaka!" I shouted as I walked down the street, back to the Square.

I loathed being this unprepared. I wanted a map of this place. Hell, I wanted a full-blown guidebook.

Leaves of paper now littered the street. As I turned onto St. Peter, fliers were taped to gallery polls and alley gates, papering the façades of the buildings. It was one of those missing girl ads —a photo of a pretty blonde girl with both ringlets and breasts that looked like they bounced jovially when she walked. She looked like . . . A breeze swirled a few of them into the air, and I grabbed one.

MISSING GIRL
Marta Guldenmann

Isn't that . . . Codi's German ancestral line? Marta's a Guldenmann? How could she have gone missing? I'd left her in a crowd of people.

Last seen one week ago.
If you have any information, please stop by
732 Royal Street

"One week ago?" I blurted. Should I stop by and tell them what had happened on Bourbon? *It's Codi's family.* 732 Royal was the tearoom. Would his ancestors be there? Would he? I slid the paper into my back pocket, popped my hood over my head, and took off.

The bell above the door dinged as I entered the shop, just like it did in the Natural World, but no one greeted me. "Hello?" The light was off, which seemed odd considering the door was unlocked, but then again, what did I know about the Afterworld? "Hello? Is anyone here?"

Nothing appeared wildly different from how it looked back home, pre-soul sanctuary, but there was a lot more greenery. Enormous philodendrons took up all the space in the front windows. Pothos vines crawled down from the topmost shelves, weaving between crystal balls. *Are the dead still concerned with the future?* Fishtail palms and birds of paradise flanked the fireplace, along with several more species exotic to my eye with variegations and leaf patterns I'd never seen. *Cool.*

But as I made my way around the room, I noticed that at least half of the plants were wilting, browning, or curling into crisps. A few even looked dead. I hoped Codi wouldn't see this place; it'd be a depressing site for a botany major, not to mention a witch with half-Earth family. Being surrounded by so many dying plants creeped me out. I held out my open palm and blew magic toward a withering calathea on the fireplace mantel whose purple and green leaves had coiled back up like they were trying to protect themselves. With the touch of Earth magic, the plant sparkled a bright shade of green and instantly perked up, the dying leaves unwinding as the magic crept into the vines, crawling all the way back to the soil, strengthening the roots. The velvety leaves seemed to exhale a sigh of relief.

Seeing the transformation was so satisfying, I couldn't help myself: I waved my hands around the room, bringing all the flora back to peak health.

The shop looked like an oasis by the time I was finished. *Much better.*

But what had caused the state of decay to begin with? I raised the hinged counter and let myself through to the back. "Hello?" I called again, peeking behind the curtains of the psychic booths.

No Daures to be found.

I hustled up the stairs, stopping on each floor to look for signs of life, er, spirits. But the place was dead. Empty, that was.

On the third floor, I tried to open the door of the Daure family room, but the protection spell zapped my hand. "*Ouch!*"

"Hello?" a voice echoed up from downstairs. "Papa?"

"Codi?" I ran down both flights of stairs and burst back into the shop.

"Désirée!" He was standing in the middle of the room, arms wrapped around the kishi. "Stay back!"

I froze in place.

He looked around the room. "Is my grandpa here?"

"I don't think so. The place was empty when I got here. Why?"

"Nothing."

"*Codi.*"

He clutched the kishi. "We might have a little problem."

I stepped forward.

"Stay back!" He yelled, and again I froze. "It's more like a thousand little problems." He slowly relaxed his arms, and the kishi's swamp grass stretched apart, a glow bursting through the seams.

"Oh shit!"

He quickly squeezed it tight again.

"Codi, we're in Guinée! If the souls get loose— we could destroy the entire magical world!"

"I know!" His voice shook. "That's why I came here. To see if my grandpa could help!"

"No one's here but plants."

He went pale. His arms wrapped around the basket were slick with sweat. It didn't seem like the greatest time to tell him about the Missing Girl flier.

"Okay," I said, starting to pace. "Okay. We've got this."

"I've been doing this spell since I was a kid! I don't know what I did wrong . . ."

I could almost hear Poppy chastising him in his head, like she'd done earlier with the tobacco spell. "I'm sure you did the spell right. But the kishi at Choctaw summer camp weren't holding the souls of thousands of New Orleanians. Did we use mundane swamp grass or something?"

"No, my Aunt Fiona enchants the materials right after she harvests them."

Well, if the plants here were any indication of his family's Earth magic, there was room for improvement. I hated that I even had the thought, but I was glad he went Water.

"They're pushing harder," he said, adjusting his grip. "We need a spell to subdue them or something."

That would be great, but I had no idea how to subdue a bunch of souls, and if there was a spell in either of our grimoires, I was sure our parents would have used it by now. I glanced around the shop—the flora seemed to be doing fine with my magical boost. I raised my arms.

"What are you doing?"

"I'm just going to give the kishi a little support." And by a little, I meant *a lot*.

I shut my eyes, calling for all the plants in the room, but this time, instead of just pushing my magic on them, I listened to their hum. They were abuzz with the danger in the air. I waved my hands, feeling for their vibration. It was a strange sensation, my magic entwining with someone's other than my family's or my coven's. I could sense the underlying power in the plants' roots, but something was very, very wrong. It was thin and weak, unable to make it through the stems to the leaves. Like a disease had infiltrated the cells, leaving them vapid. I let my Spektral magic pour through the empty cells, orchestrating them to not just recover, but strengthen, trying not to just heal the plant, but the magic within.

"Whoa," Codi said, and I opened my eyes.

The plants were growing thicker and longer, reaching down to the floorboards and up to the ceilings, crawling to the windows and spreading over the counters, vines strong as ropes and petals tough as leather. They slithered up Codi's legs and spiraled around the basket all the way up to the lid. I twirled my finger, and the tip of a vine looped through the hatch and tied itself off into a cute, organic bow.

As the vines stilled on the counters and the leaves stopped rustling, Codi's breaths became loud in the silence. He relaxed his muscles, slowly loosening his grip on the kishi. "That was dope."

"No big thing," I said, trying to be chill. Should I tell him that his family's magic had felt like Swiss cheese when he was carrying a basket of souls? Even if I had reinforced the kishi? What had caused the effect on the magic in the first place? I shuddered. My magic was so woven into my being, it would be like someone had punched holes into my soul. I moved my shoulders, letting the tension release from my back like my therapist had taught me when I was in seventh grade. "Let's go," I said. "We need to find Ghede-Houson. Who knows how long that Earth magic will last."

He nodded. "Um. Do you think, you could . . . let me go?"

"What do you—?" I realized honeysuckle had twisted all the

way up his legs, around his hips, and over his perfectly round butt. "Oh!" I snapped my fingers and the vine unwound itself.

"Not too fast," he yelped, going up on his toes as it slipped through his legs.

Oops.

The vine softly flicked up from the floor like a tail wanting to be stroked. Codi obliged.

I strapped my bag back on. "Did Oussou give you any leads on where Ghede-Houson is?"

"No, he was more interested in the piman than our mission." He set down the kishi, as if something had just occurred to him, then hurried behind the counter. I followed. "Okay, this might be a long shot but . . . in the Natural World, we have this directory, it's generations old and— Yes!" He pulled out a black leather-bound journal and showed me the cover. The silver leaf had mostly worn away, but it still sparkled in patches, enough to make out the words: VIEUX CARRÉ DIRECTORY.

"Do you think it's the Afterworld version?" I asked, approaching.

"We're about to find out." He flipped through it and dragged his finger down the G page. "Ghede, Ghede, Ghede. Jesus, you weren't kidding when you said there were hundreds of them. Here. *Houson.* Soul Keeper. Looks like he has a stall in the French Market."

Is that really a directory of the dead?

He closed the book.

"Wait—" I reached out for the book, but then a wave of anxiety roiled through me. What if Marassa hated me for not joining the family coven? "Never mind." I pushed the book away, and he slid it back under the counter.

"You okay?" he asked.

Just tell him that you want to look, Désirée. Marassa didn't join the family coven either. She didn't have a choice. She was forcibly separated from her family and sold off like a horse. You *had a choice.*

"I'm fine." I strapped on my backpack. "French Market, let's go."

I held open the door for him as he fitted his backpack on his chest and then carefully placed the new souped-up kishi on his back.

As we stepped onto the curb, I glanced back at the plants one more time. They still looked great. Better than great. Magical. Although nothing like that amazing freaking floral cocoon thing that had been holding Marta, or all of those wildflowers that had grown straight out of the street.

Weren't the Guldenmanns supposed to be badass Earth witches? Why had their magic weakened? When exactly had they merged with Water? Could it be true that mixing Elementals weakened the magical line? Would Codi's Water weaken one day?

I glanced at him, trying to figure out how to bring up the defective magic. As if the whole kishi thing wasn't already bad enough. "In your family . . . does the magic strengthen with each generation?"

He looked at me funny. "Uh, isn't that how magic works?"

"Yeah, as long as the new generation carries on the tradition."

"What's that supposed to mean?"

"Nothing."

"You don't think I'm carrying on our tradition as much as you are?"

"No! It's not that!"

"Then what is it?"

"I-I was just wondering if it worked the same in your family . . . because of . . ."

His eyes narrowed. "Because of what?"

Shame heated my neck, and I could barely mumble out the rest of the sentence. "Because of the mixed-magic."

"Our magic doesn't work any differently than yours," he said flatly and turned to walk away.

"Codi!" I leapt after him and grabbed his arm. "I didn't mean it like that." I pulled him so that he'd face me. "I-I think it's cool."

"Then why are you asking me this?"

Again, I thought about the flier. And again, decided to wait to bring it up. I hated seeing the pain in his eyes. I hated when the stupid white girls at school treated me differently even though my parents were just as rich as theirs. Even though my family had been in New Orleans longer. Even though my father was more powerful than all of theirs combined. "I'm sorry. I was just worried about you . . . where do you think your ancestors all are?" *I'll show him the flier after we deliver the souls.*

He shrugged. "Maybe they're at the house on the bayou, or on vacation, or something? Dude," he said, turning to me, "what if they were there, and we just couldn't see them? What if we just needed Isaac?"

"I could see the spirits at the strip club."

"Strip club?"

"Masaka."

"*Ah.* Did he teach you to dance on a pole?" He poked at my side, and the tension in the air released. I swerved, feeling a swell of relief.

"Guess you'll never know." I couldn't help a tiny, teasing smile.

"Or maybe . . . one day, I could?"

I looked straight ahead.

"I just meant— I've heard it takes serious core strength to do those moves. Some girls in my dorm used to go to this class at the gym."

"My core's pretty taut."

"Oh, I didn't mean—!"

"Keep an eye out for Isaac. Maybe he's on his way to Houson too."

"Your core is perfectly fine the way it is—not that I've seen it or anything."

I walked faster, my eyes on the sky. "Yours is too. And I've seen it." My lips pinched together, feeling him smiling at me. "Wanna find your family after we deliver the souls?"

"That would be dope."

Perfect. We'll find Olsin, and if something is up, he can tell Codi. Tell us.

CHAPTER 25
ASH AND BONE

The charring scent of smoke wafted, filling my lungs, and I stuttered awake with a cough. My head pounded. Dark plumes choked the room, and bright orange flames ripped around the walls as the rest of the curtains caught fire. Warnings exploded in my foggy brain. *Get up, Adele.*

Some witchy instinct within threw my hand toward the flames, compelling the fire to extinguish, but the flames just shone brighter and danced higher, and the smoke coiled around me, blackening my skin, the heat burning my hair. I pulled again for my magic, but it wasn't there. It was with Callisto and the rest of the Salazars back in the Natural World.

I twisted onto my elbows, gave a deathly hack, and began crawling across the room. The bolts of ethereal fabrics lit ablaze. *Where did everyone go?* "Nibo!" I tried to scream. The bones of the corset heated my torso, starting to roast my insides. With a final burst of energy, I pushed myself up, ducked low, and ran through the shop. The flames leapt from mannequin to mannequin, always one step ahead of me, melting their faces off like candles. Fire engulfed the room, swallowing the front door —there wasn't time to think, there wasn't time for magic. I charged toward the bay window display, shielded my face, and hurtled myself toward the street.

I crashed onto the slate sidewalk in an explosion of glass, rolled, and came to a stop near someone's boots. A storm of people stomped all around me, faces looking down in surprise, shouting, *"Fire! Fire!"* I scrambled to my feet as more people flooded from the buildings, crowding the already busy street.

I got swept up among them as they rushed through Pirate's Alley, the inferno racing aside us in marigold waves, plunging through each building. And as the throngs of people poured into Jackson Square, so did the fire, taking the Cabildo and the Pontalba. How could the Afterworld be burning? Was it not made of something more ethereal than organic matter?

"The bells!" yelled a man in an unfortunate Confederate soldier uniform. An elderly woman's voice echoed the cry.

I searched the crowds for my friends, lungs burning from smoke inhalation, but there was no one but the dead. I stepped up on the lamppost to get a better view over the sea of people. Tortured screams came from the distance. People burning. Crying for help. Could spirits die in Guinée? *What the hell is happening, right now?*

A pretty Black girl in an antebellum dress paused by the lamppost, gasping, and looked up at me. *"Les cloches, mademoiselle!"* And a young boy with tight golden ringlets tugged my fingers. "Miss, the bells. You have to ring the bells!"

"What? Me?"

He pointed up to the cathedral. The bell tower. *The bells. The warning bells!*

"Oh, I can't—"

You can't even move a chair; how would you fare out there?

The memory lit me ablaze, and I threw my hand toward the tower—to the very place where I first felt my Fire.

The crowd chanted, *"Ring the bells! Ring the bells! The city will burn! The people will burn! Ring the bells!"*

Sweat dripped down the curve of my spine. I pulled and pulled and pulled, feeling for the metal, visualizing the bells, trying to grasp onto a tingle, a spark, a wriggle of magic. *I know I can ring the bells.* The fire leapt onto the left tower of the cathedral. I screamed in frustration as the ice-cream-cone steeple disappeared behind a curtain of orange. "*No!*" I threw my arms out again. The shouts from the crowd became more aggressive.

"*She's a fraud!*"

"*You aren't even a witch!*"

"*You have no magic!*"

"*Tu n'es pas une sorcière!*"

"*Who let her in?*"

"*How'd she get into Guinée?*"

"*Throw her out!*"

A spirit yanked my dress, and I teetered, clutching onto the lamppost. More of them grabbed at me. "You put it out!" I yelled. "You're all witches!" Why did it have to be me? This suddenly felt like some kind of test.

"Look at him go!" the little boy yelled, pointing up, diverting everyone's attention back to the cathedral.

A shadowy figure was scaling the far right steeple. The crowd cheered as he leapt to the bell tower like a spider. The wind picked up, and the flames stretched closer as he punched through the shutters. *He'll never survive.* The fire was too strong. Could spirits be harmed? They could if they were Possessed with a soul. But then just as he slipped inside, the corset bones squeezed my heart. *Nicco. It's Nicco. No.*

"*Ring the bells, ring the bells!*" the crowd cheered with excitement.

I jumped down from the lamppost, craning my neck to keep my eyes on the growing inferno. "*No.*"

"*No.*"

No.

The flames licked the steeple. "*Nicco!*" I screamed. "Get out!"

My voice was swallowed up by the crowd. "I can't put out the fire, Nicco!"

The slate ground vibrated—the gong of the bells made my blood tremble. *Thank God.*

The people clapped and cheered, awaiting the shadowy figure's return, but the flames leapt to the middle tower, and a wave of heat rushed into the square, sending everyone running in a cacophonic fury.

"Nicco!" I screamed, pushing through them, toward the church. "*Nicco!*"

I leapt up the steps.

With a swing of my hand, the doors opened, and I tore down the center aisle of the empty cathedral. The faint smoke filling the space made the air taste burnt and tickled my lungs. I threw the dress sleeve over my face, forcing myself to take shallow breaths as the stained glass windows popped one by one and then in a long crescendo of shattering blows, raining mists of colored glass. I ran up the altar steps, but the air grew thicker and my movements heavier. I tripped, banging my knee, and crouched there for a moment, coughing. *Get up, Adele.*

The smoke thickened the deeper I went, burning my eyes. I coughed all the way up to the mezzanine, to the small wooden door that led up to the bell tower, screaming for Nicco until the smoke filled my lungs so completely, I couldn't get his name out.

"Adele?" His voice echoed down the spiral staircase as I bounced against the stone wall, no longer cool but hot to the touch.

"Nicco!"

"I'm trapped. Don't—!"

"I'm coming!" I coughed.

"*No!* Get out of here!" His voice became louder as I burst into the room. "This tower is a stone oven!"

From the smoke ahead emerged a grid of iron bars dividing the room—Nicco on the other side. I collapsed against them, only to spring away with a seared shoulder. My skin bubbled as I writhed in pain. *This is not a test.* But I hardly noticed it. "What are these bars?" I shrieked. They were bolted into the stone floor, up to the ceiling.

"Adele, look at me!" He was drenched like he'd just gone for a swim. His hair hung in his eyes, dripping. "Get out of here!" I'd never heard his voice so panicked.

The windows were barricaded too. Was he trapped because I couldn't ring the bells? Use my magic? "Let him go!" I screamed. Was it because only witches were allowed in Guinée, and I'd allowed my Fire to be taken? "I am a witch!" I screamed. Smoke filled my lungs. I hacked as I stepped back, focusing on the bars. I needed my inhaler.

"Adele, get out of here! I will be fine! I'm immortal!"

He wasn't going to be fine. He was just trying to get me to save myself. I should never have asked him to come here. Everyone said it was too dangerous. *He said it was too dangerous.*

Why couldn't I have just rung the bells? *How will you fare out there?*

Nicco grasped two of the bars and tried to bend them back, a vein in his forehead bulging with the effort. He ripped himself away, the skin burning off his palms, sticking to the metal, and he zoomed around the tower, launching himself at the barred windows, cursing in Italian, blood pouring down his arms. "Get out of here, Adele!"

I promised I'd protect him.

"Now!"

I let his words wash over me and concentrated on the metal.

He dropped to his knees. "*Bella, leave*, I beg you. You cannot die over me. I'm a pathetic magicless witch!" A flame sprung to his back, and I screamed as he slapped it out, but another caught his shirt.

I pinched my eyes closed. I couldn't breathe, seeing him in

pain. I couldn't breathe because of the smoke. *This is a test, I told myself. This is a test, and you have to save Nicco.*

I shut him out of my mind and concentrated on the iron. Metal. It's just as simple as twirling a dime and pirouetting a nickel in the tip jar. As unlocking a door. As pulling down a zipper. It's just positive space moving into negative space. I pulled and pulled, tuning out Nicco's cries, the inferno scratching my face, and I felt the center bar bend. "*Yes,*" I gasped, the strain tearing my mind in two. *Just a little more.* Just enough to let him through, and then we'll run. We'll run faster than he's ever run before. Sweat poured down my face. *I compel this metal to move. To release my twin flame.* Magic swirled around me, and I rose from the floor, weightless.

"*Bend!*" I cried. A burst of energy released, and the metal moaned.

My heart finally felt open, just like Papa Olsin had instructed all those months ago. But as my feet touched the ground, my terror filled the echo chamber, and my scream blew all the bars from the windows to the moon.

Nicco was engulfed in flames, on the floor.

Not moving.

I felt time stop as I rushed inside, the once wooden steeple now nothing but a scrap of burnt tinder. My knees banged to the ground as I threw myself over him, slapping out the flames, the smell of burnt flesh and fried organs making me gag. When the flames extinguished, he was completely charred. As black as the smoking tinder of the steeples.

"*No!*"

Black as black as black as nothingness. Smoldering. I reached for his leg, and it crumbled, powdery. Bile rose in my throat. *I crushed his leg. I* crushed *his leg.*

"No. No. No."

I waved away the smoke but found no peridot eyes. No not-so-innocent smile. Just a hollow, lifeless skull that better resembled Ghede-Nibo. When I touched it, it fell off his spine, and I screamed, grabbing for it, trying to place it back upright. "You can't die. *You can't die!* You said you'd never die!" I shrieked. "You're a vampire!"

My mother died.

Giovanna died.

They were vampires.

Not Nicco though. Nicco couldn't die. I needed him. "We have a mission!" I croaked, tears streaming. I needed him because I loved him.

"It's him!" I screamed over the clanging bells. But Nibo didn't respond like I hoped he might. "I want him more than anything! I already told you! I told you the truth." I clutched my chest as the moan threatened to take my life. "Bring him back."

I collapsed atop him, unfazed when the pile of ash puffed up around me, cutting off the air, his charred ribs cracking to pieces beneath my weight. *I love him.* The pain rushed in so hard and strong, like wild animals tearing me apart.

The remaining bars clanked down to the ground, and the bells danced as I screamed, my tears muddying the ash and bone. "What good is magic if it couldn't save him?"

What good was being a witch?

I'd killed him, just like I'd killed my mother.

Why couldn't I have just rung the bells?

CHAPTER 26
FAIR TRADE

We stumbled into the darkness, falling to the rocky ground. "What the hell was that?" I scrambled back, kicking up dust. Nothing but a black void surrounded us. I trembled, unable to get the sight of Adele's corpse face out of my mind. No matter how hard I tried to keep them in, tears shook from my eyes. "What . . . what the fuck was that? What happened to Adele?"

"Oh, sweet boy, that wasn't Adele. That was just the Ghede messing with your head." Her accent was British. I don't know why I hadn't expected that. "They're showing you your wildest dreams so you'll stay here with them forever." She looked at me tenderly, and I felt an overwhelming surge of embarrassment, like she'd just walked in on me jerking off. No, I think this was worse. I pulled my knees into my chest. All I'd ever wanted was to meet another witch in my family, and now I could hardly look at the girl whose grimoire I'd carried every day for the last year.

"Are you okay, darling?" she asked.

"My wildest dream is an engagement party?" I wiped my eyes. "Good thing my boys from back home aren't here. They'd never let me live this down."

"There's no shame in loving someone."

"It doesn't matter. She's never going to trust me again."

"Then it will be her loss."

She helped me up. She was nearly as tall as I was. Her curly red hair was windblown, like she'd just come from standing on the island cliff she'd drawn so often in her grimoire. She wasn't as frilly as the girls in the fantasy. She wore a long leather jacket over her long flowy white dress. I could easily imagine her at the helm of a ship. Part of the fantasy lingered in my mind. The original girl with fire from my dreams: Adeline Saint-Germain. Now, I remembered what I needed to ask her. "Susannah, do you know where I can find Adeline?"

"She's probably with Adele. Why?"

"Nothing." I nudged the ground with my shoe. "I need to ask her something."

"Isaac." She took my hand. "You don't need Adeline; I can help you with whatever it is. You are my blood. My magical heir."

"Unless you know why she dislikes Nicco Medici then I don't think you can help." Her forehead scrunched in confusion, and I relented. "Adele thinks Nicco is on her side—and maybe he is—but it's only because she has something he wants. Everyone's warned her to stay away from him, even Adeline, but she won't listen!"

Her voice was stern. "Isaac, she doesn't *have* to listen to Adeline."

"I know . . . but . . ."

"Darling." Her hand brushed my cheek, and she softened her tone. "If I told you to stay away from Adele, would you listen to me?"

"Of course not. I *love* her."

She stared at me, letting her point sink in.

"No." I shook my head. "Adele doesn't love Nicco."

She crossed her arms.

"They're friends. She's infatuated with him because of his connection to her family." The look in her eyes turned sympathetic, and it made me panic. "Adele could never love a monster like him. He's a *murderer*." My heart pounded so hard, I thought I was actually having a heart attack.

He was a murderer, but I'd killed her mother.

I twisted away as she reached for my shoulder. "Do you know where I can find the Soul Keeper?" Hopefully I could find Dee and Codi there.

"Ghede-Houson? At the French Market, usually. He's a scoundrel, but I can fly you—"

I stepped away and leapt into the air. I was acting like an asshole, and I hated myself for it, but I couldn't take one more second of the pity in her eyes. I knew where the French Market was and could get there myself.

Her voice grew more distant with each pump of my wings as I soared down the trolley tracks.

She didn't know Adele like I did.

She didn't know Adele at all.

The archway entrance came into view below, leading to the long, open-air shopping strip. According to my friends, it used to be a bustling art-slash-farmer's market, but it had been a ghost town ever since I'd been in New Orleans. This version was literally a ghost town. Spirits chirped in and out, carrying baskets, shopping bags, and aprons full of purchases. Lone pirates with ragged clothes, aristocratic young men with shiny riding jackets, and families with more children than they could keep up with. All with the mark of the witch.

If the Soul Keeper was here, I could ask him where his miracle worker Ghede brother was so I could get the miracle-gad for Ren, and then I could go find Adeline and find out the truth about Nicco once and for all. Maybe Doubye could tell me where she lived. Not that I knew how to find Doubye. Or if she'd even speak to me after I took back my tooth.

A finger pointed up to me. *Thank fucking God.* Désirée was standing at the entrance below. And next to her, Codi was setting the kishi on the ground. I swooped down to join them, landing at their feet.

"We were getting worried about you," Codi said, slapping my hand as I stood. It was strange being able to turn so openly on the street.

"I've never been so glad to see anyone in my life," I said, adjusting my duffel on my back.

"Is that you?" Désirée asked. "Like the real you?"

"Have either of you seen Adele?"

"It's him," Codi said.

"Or any of the others," I quickly added.

"*Nada.*"

"No one but Masaka," Dee answered, "unless you count the people in my head. Then you could include Marassa and Annabelle," she mumbled.

"I guess that means you guys got sucked into some warped, lucid Ghede dreams too?" I asked.

"Mine was a nightmare. The worst." Codi stretched out his back so long, he looked part feline. "You were both in it. We were all doing coven stuff."

Désirée adjusted the ponytail high atop her head. "What's so bad about that?"

"Because *you*"—he looked to me and then to Dee—"were together."

"So what?" she said. "We're always together."

"No, not like together. Like, wouldn't keep your hands off each other, sucking face *together.*"

"Ew!" Désirée said.

I squeezed my eyes shut as if that might get the visual out of my head. "Ughh."

"Tell me about it. You both kept going on and on about how it was destiny that the Storm brought you together, and how it meant the merging of two of the most powerful magical houses in the world. Ritha kept going on about giving her grand-children."

"What?" Désirée shrieked, and I couldn't help but laugh.

"I don't think Ritha likes me *that* much, bro."

"Ritha doesn't like anyone that much. How'd you break the illusion?"

"That was the only cool part. My grandma Philly came in, magic blazing, and pulled me out of it. I hadn't seen her in *so* long. But then . . . she just kind of disappeared, so I don't know if it was really her or what?"

I thought about how I'd just run away from Susannah and felt like a total loser.

"That's so cool." Désirée shifted her weight to her other leg. Something seemed off about her. "The part about your grand-mother, not the part about . . ." She looked at me. "No offense."

I held up my hands, and the entrance to the market caught my eye. From above, it had looked the same as in the Natural World, but now up close I could see that the enormous archway was made entirely of . . . skulls. "So, we really going in here?"

"Why wouldn't we be?" Désirée asked, turning. She disap-peared into the crowd inside.

Codi picked the kishi back up, which was now wrapped in vines, and we followed her under the bone-archway.

"Of course it's made of skulls," I said, both of us stretching our necks like selfie-stick-waving tourists, looking for her over a family of spirits in white-powdered wigs.

The walkway was lined with stalls. In each, a ghostly vendor stood behind a table, offering different wares. Crates of beeswax. Wooden bobbins of spun spiderweb. Bottles of dewdrops.

Bundles of ashwood. Drums. Pipes. Lutes. Buckets of mushrooms. Dandelions. Tablets with Sanskrit. At least I think it was. A fat white man with only a few good teeth hovered over a table with rows and rows of raven skulls.

"My trial was a nightmare too," Désirée said as we caught up with her. She eyed a table of poppets as we passed by. "I thought it was going to be amazing. Marassa was going to teach me this magical secret recipe passed down from her mother."

"What was so bad about that?" Codi asked.

"*Annabelle.* All of a sudden, Annabelle was there, and Marassa was teaching her too, which wouldn't have been that big of a deal, I guess, but her vani krèm came out better than mine! Then we made this entire traditional African feast, and everything she did was better. No matter how perfectly I followed Marassa's instructions, everything I made was burnt or soggy or raw."

"The overachiever's nightmare," I said, and she elbowed me in the ribs.

"Who pulled you out?" Codi asked.

"No one. I did a spell that turned Annabelle to stone so she'd shut the hell up. The illusion started to break, and I figured it out."

I internally groaned. Of course Désirée pulled herself out of the Ghede's clutches. It made me feel even more stupid for believing that Adele had actually forgiven me. That she wanted to be with me.

"What about you?" Codi asked.

"Uh . . ." I twirled Ritha's parting gift around my finger. "I wish. Susannah had to rescue me." He glanced at my chest with a questioning look. "It's a wolf's tooth. From Ritha."

"Ritha gave you a gift?"

"Dude, it's not like tha—" A flash of red hair wove through the crowd up ahead. I stood on my toes, trying to catch sight of her again.

"What?" he asked.

"Nothing. I thought I saw . . ."

"So what was your trial?" Désirée asked as we walked past a shrine for a Ghede who wore a belt of *severed heads*?

"Who's Baron Kriminel?" I asked, hoping to change the subject.

"A headhunter. The manifestation of pure malice and violence, the spirit of the first murderer. You're stalling. You don't have to tell us if it's, like, personal or something."

"I'm not— It's not— Mine wasn't a nightmare."

"Ohhh, Doubye tried to lure you here by fulfilling your greatest fantasy?" Désirée asked. "You must have left *quite* an impression on her."

"I didn't do anything to her!"

"*Pfft*," Codi said. "Everyone's always crushing on you."

"Don't let the Ghede get in your head." Dee turned to him. "*No one* has a crush on him except Adele."

"Do you have to be so emphatic about that?" I asked.

"What do you care? You have Adele."

"Had. *Had* Adele."

"Things will settle down after this."

"Lisette's always staring at him dreamily," Codi said.

"That's because Lisette wants to eat him."

"And Annabelle's always about to jump his bones."

This convo was definitely not doing anything for my ego, but I was glad for the diversion away from my "wildest dreams."

Désirée turned back to me. "Sooo, what was the fantasy?" She flashed a wicked smile.

"Oh . . ."

"Are you blushing?" Codi asked.

"What? No."

"Spill it," Dee said.

"I was on a riverboat." I cringed. "We were. Our ancestors. It was this fancy party . . ." My instinct was to make up something harmless. "Adele was there . . . because . . ." I couldn't lie to them. Ever again. About anything. I puked it out: "It was our engagement party." I gazed into a stall full of books so I didn't have to see their expressions.

Codi hooked his arm around my neck. "Dude, that's so sweet."

A familiar head of red hair bobbed through the stacks. "Hey!" I yelled.

"What—?" they both asked as I shifted up a few feet, weaving between shoppers. There she was, chatting to the vendor.

"Come on." I ran into the book stall.

Spirits darted out of our way, whispering about who we were. I paused in the middle aisle, searching. She'd disappeared. "*Annabelle*, I know you're here. Why are you hiding?"

A few seconds passed, but then a designer boot appeared at the end of the row, and she swung around. "Oh, hey guys. Didn't see you there. How cool is this market?"

"What are you doing"—Désirée looked up at the sign—"at a rare magical book shop?"

"Can't a girl browse while she's on vacay?"

Désirée looked at me. Something was definitely off.

"Come on," Codi said, adjusting the kishi on his back. "We have souls to save. We should stick together. You're with us now, Drake."

"Okay." She bounced up to him, so close their hips brushed.

I pretended not to notice Dee's jaw tighten, and we fell in behind them. "So, Annabelle," I asked, "did Plumaj drop you into a nightmare or a fantasy?"

She turned back as we walked, letting her arms fold over her head. "Well, I think it was a fantasy. But I guess it's open for interpretation."

I already regretted asking.

She looked at Dee. "You were in it. And so were you. And so

271

were you. And so was Adele. It was still Beltane night, and we all went camping to celebrate. It was all very magic-norm. Daisy crowns, honey cakes, elderflower wine. We did magic until we were dripping with sweat, skinny-dipped in the lake, and danced naked under the Flower Moon." She hooked her finger in Codi's belt-loop and pulled him closer. "And then we all went wild like little bunnies."

I thought Désirée's jaws were going to snap. Annabelle saw it too. She glanced at Codi and then back to Dee, like she'd unearthed a golden secret. "Isaac and Adele were so *obsessed* with each other, they rolled away together, but the three of us did our best to shatter the earth—"

"You're lying," Désirée said, deathstare in the locked position.

"Okay, they didn't really roll away. I was just trying to make Isaac more comfortable. You know how he gets over little Miss Perfect.

"You bat your eyelashes excessively when you lie."

Annabelle tickled her fingers up Codi's arm, who writhed away. "Dee, tell me. Are you bothered by the idea of sharing Codi with me? Or is it about sharing me with Codi?"

Désirée's nostrils flared, and we all paused in the middle of the stall. *What the hell was that supposed to mean?* Annabelle stepped up to her. "Coven rules. Perfect love and perfect trust, is it? You tell each other the truth about evvverything."

"Shut up, Annabelle."

"I wouldn't want to *lie*. So, surely they know how long we've been besties? How you'd never been kissed until my lips touched yours?"

"*Annabelle!*"

"How we spent half of freshmen year in my parents' hot tub together?"

Whoa. Was not expecting that.

"Am I batting my lashes now?" Her hand crept to Désirée's waist.

Désirée swatted it away. I thought she was going to pounce, but instead, she blasted through us, eyes welling.

"Désirée!" Codi took off after her.

"Have you even kissed anyone since?" Annabelle yelled. The smirk of satisfaction on her face made me seethe. She turned back to me. "What? You're telling me that you've honestly never thought about the coven that way?"

I stepped close to her. "I've thought about the coven in a lot of different ways. At HQ. In the park. Behind the curtain at the Voodoo shop . . ." I leaned in. "But not once did it ever involve you."

The smug expression dissolved from her face. "Désirée was right. I went overboard with the story. Who'd believe Adele would be that obsessed with *you*? A lame high-school dropout with no magical family."

I didn't give a fuck what Annabelle Lee Drake thought about me. Plus, you'd never met a mean girl until you'd been to a high school dance on the Upper East Side. "You know, Annabelle, you could have been part of something really amazing. What the five of us have together is indescribably magical. I wouldn't trade it for anything in the world."

She rolled her eyes. "You're such a sap."

"I can only imagine what horror the Ghede put you through —that you'd be so desperate to cover up—that you'd hurt Dee. But I do know that Callis is going to suck your magic dry, and when he's done with you, you're going to end up alone, desperately clinging to your glory days of prep school when everyone had to pretend to give a shit about every single thing you did or said."

She crossed her arms without breaking her hardened stare. "You're correct that I'm not going to end up with Callisto." She glanced back at the bookstore sign. "But I'm not going to end up alone." Then she tightened the straps of her bag and took off in the opposite direction.

Good luck on your own. I wasn't chasing after her. She could get left behind for all I cared.

I jumped into the Air and soared after my friends, whizzing through spirits and past shrines honoring Baron Samedi and Maman Brigitte, trying to comprehend Désirée and Annabelle being together. How could Dee—? Annabelle was such a raging bitch.

And I was most definitely trying not to imagine it.

Definitely not.

I caught up to Codi right outside the market, standing next to the basket.

"I don't know where she went!" He threw his hands up. "I was behind her, but then these spirits came out of nowhere, rolling giant crates of potion bottles, and we almost collided, and I almost dropped the kishi!"

"It's okay, man. We'll find her." I picked up the basket, and we kept going down the street.

As soon as we turned the corner, there she was, leaning against a lamppost. She wasn't crying, just taking a breath. I paused. I didn't want to embarrass her. Not that she had anything to be embarrassed about. "Dee?"

She straightened, turning away for a second to blot her makeup, then looked back at us like nothing had happened. She came straight toward us, a determined expression on her face.

"Désirée," Codi said, "are you o—?"

She grabbed his shirt and pulled him straight into a kiss. His arm flailed, and I was too stunned to turn away. Codi stepped back, looking equally stunned. "You-you don't have to kiss me just to, like, prove that you're straight or whatever."

"I didn't say I was straight!" she yelled.

"I didn't mean it like that— I-I'm not even straight! You know my ex—he's friends with Thurston!"

"Yeah, Stephen's an asshole!"

"Well, Annabelle's an asshole!"

I had no idea if they were actually fighting or if they were about to rip each other's clothes off, but I started to back away. "I'm gonna take the basket and go look for the Soul Keeper."

"I'm going with you!" Désirée jumped toward me.

"I'm going with you too!"

"Ooookay?" I picked up the kishi as they both stormed back down the street.

I caught up with them, and as we re-entered the market, they walked behind me through the stalls, silently, side by side. *Please for the love of God let the Soul Keeper be close.*

An older woman with dozens of colorful beaded necklaces around her neck passed by, carrying a box on her head. I turned to her. "Excuse me, do you know where we can find Ghede-Houson?"

"Houson? Whatchou want with Houson?"

Something about her tone made me wonder how we got here. "Um. Just a little business matter, that's all."

She shook her head like any good grandmother seeing kids getting into trouble and then nodded to the far corner of the market behind us.

"Thanks," Codi said as we all changed direction.

I wasn't exactly expecting to walk into Sotheby's, but nothing quite prepared me for Houson's corner of the market. Outside the stall, piles and piles of junk stacked up to the rafters. Scraps of wrought-iron fence. Wooden crosses. Metal lanterns. Shovels. Lots of shovels. Women's gloves. Baseball cards. Walking canes. A hundred of them. There must have been a thousand pairs of men's dress shoes, all in varying states of decay.

Random pieces of scrap wood sat at odd angles to form the walls of his back-corner stall. The wood looked familiar somehow. . . those odd angles. "Oh, shit."

"What?" Désirée asked.

"It's made out of coffins." I turned around, examining all the junk. The baseball cards and dress shoes. "I think it's all . . . stuff people were buried with."

Codi let out a loud breath, and we turned to each other with trepidation. But then Désirée shrugged and lifted the curtain. A curtain that had most definitely been the skirt of a wedding dress. *Who gets buried in a wedding dress?*

The booth was dark, despite hundreds of candles flickering from skulls that lined the crooked shelves in the stall. Skulls that varied in shape and size and species. A coffin was propped up on four crosses as a counter, and a man who better resembled one of the shelved skulls sat behind it on a bone-chair. His skin was so taut and leathery you could see every bone beneath, and covered in a chalky powder that I couldn't imagine was anything else but the ashes of the dead. His black eyes gleamed with the same purple sheen as Doubye's, making him undoubtedly Ghede. He picked his teeth with a carved bone between his deep-purple-stained lips.

Both Dee and Codi gave me a quick glance. I'd almost forgotten that I was the one carrying the kishi. *Great.*

"*Alo,*" he said without removing the bone. A sucking noise followed.

"Hi." I set the kishi on the floor. "Ghede-Houson?"

"*Wi.* Whatchou want, white boy?" The candles on the coffin-counter reflected in his silver-sequined shirt.

"Well." I cleared my throat, eyeing his insanely long hot-pink fingernails that had been sharpened to claw-like points. Whose hands exactly were we putting these souls in? Jamal was in that basket. "We were told by two of your brethren—"

"Ghede-Masaka and Ghede-Oussou," Dee added.

"—that you were in the market for souls."

He leaned back and crossed his arms.

"Souls severed from their spirits," I added.

"You're a spirit-splitter?"

"No!"

"We would never!" Codi said. "It was the Salazars."

Houson flicked the bone-pick onto the floor. "How many?"

"A lot."

"Whatchou want for 'em?"

"Nothing," Dee said. "They're yours. We can't keep them in the Natural World. It's too dangerous, for them and for us."

With one finger, he motioned to bring them forth.

I stepped up to the counter and slid the basket to him. He leapt up on the coffin, and we all waited in complete silence as he undid the vine bow and peeked beneath the lid. His eyes lit up.

"Thank Goddess," Désirée whispered under her breath.

He shut the lid, shoved the basket back to me, and jumped down to our side, black metallic parachute pants puffing up on the way down. "No, thanks."

"What?" I asked. "Why?"

"Not dealing in souls anymore. Dealing in demons. Got demons? Worth a lot. Not like these nasty souls." He shoved the basket into my chest.

"Demons?" Codi asked.

"You have to take them!" My voice raised, exasperated. "We've brought them all the way from the Natural World!"

He disappeared, all of a sudden, and the room started spinning. He was on my shoulders, rocking me around. "I have to do what, white boy?"

The basket teetered as I struggled not to fall.

"Isaac!" Dee yelled, arms out to catch the kishi.

"I didn't mean it! Of course you don't have to take them. We just thought you would want them—an offering!"

"*Pish!*" He stepped back to the coffin and jumped back down behind the counter.

Codi leapt up behind me as I regained my balance. "Is there anything we can do to sway you?"

Houson sat on his bone throne and kicked his white leather cowboy boots up on the coffin. "Demons. Bring me demons, and I'll take your trash souls. Final offer." The bone pick appeared back between his lips.

Behind the counter in the darkness, I swore two little sets of purple eyes peeked from around the curtain with a ghoulish giggle.

Désirée huffed, and we exited the booth.

Just outside of the market, I sat down on a tiny coffin to rest, then shot back up when my brain processed the reason a coffin would be tiny.

"Just in case it isn't clear, we are *not* going demon hunting for Houson," she said.

"Désirée, I've never been happier to hear words come out of your mouth."

"Well, what the hell are we going to do with them?" Codi asked. "We can't just leave them on the side of the road."

"Better than taking them back to the Natural World," I said.

"Yeah, until someone lets them loose, and they attack the occupants of the Spirit World, including all of our magical ancestors."

"That would be baaaaaaaad," Désirée said.

I looked at them both. "We can't be responsible for the complete destruction of Guinée."

A little boy covered in soot, carrying a pickaxe, stepped up to me alongside a little girl in a dirty dress. *Where did they come from?* "You have to take them to the End of the World," they said in unison.

"You have to give them to La Sirène," the girl said, a twinkle of purple in her eye.

Before I could ask anything, they ran off giggling.

"Were those little kid-Ghede?" Codi asked.

"Yup," Dee said.

"The End of the Earth?" I asked. "I guess they left the Natural World pre-Columbus."

Dee and Codi looked at each other. "No."

Codi picked up the basket. "The End of the World—"

"We have to go to the Lower Ninth," Dee finished, a smile spreading on her face. "We have to find La Sirène."

CHAPTER 27
RIPOSA IN PACE

"You tried to save him," the French-accented voice mocked from a dark corner. "Don't be so hard on yourself."

I looked up from the pile of ash and bone. Nibo was leaning on his staff, eyes glowing purple in the shadows.

"*What* did you do?"

"I thought you were lying before about just being friends, but if he was more, you'd have saved him."

"He was *not* just a friend." I lunged at him, but he disappeared, and my burned shoulder smashed into the stone wall. "He was everything!"

He reappeared on the other side. "Why did you lie to me zhen?"

"I didn't lie!" Tears gushed down my cheeks. "We were just friends! He didn't feel anything more for me . . ."

"*Pish.* Well, zhen, poo-poo him. Time to let him go."

"No." I fiercely shook my head. "I will never let him go."

"Why would you love someone who doesn't love you back?"

I screamed, whipping my hands through the air, ripping the bells from their ropes, hurling them toward him.

He laughed as they went straight through his ethereal form.

"You can't hurt a dead man. But look at you, bébé, with your Spektral magic!"

"Bring him back," I begged. "You're supposed to be a great healer!"

"You'll need your magic if you are ever going to take down your enemies. You should be thanking me."

"I don't care about my magic!" The remaining bells chimed. "I care about *him*." I hurled another bell at the Ghede, and it crashed against the wall, a deafening clang ricocheting.

"Zhen why are you here, talking to me?" He vanished into the powdery air.

My gaze fell back to Nicco, broken over the stone floor, still far less shattered than I was. And I fell to the floor in tears that burned as bright as my phantom Fire.

Nibo's last words echoed with the gongs of the bells.

He's right. Why am I still here? My hands trembled as I scooped Nicco's ash and bone into my spiderweb skirt. *If Nicco's dead, his spirit would be here in Guinée. The final resting place for the magical.*

I pictured the grand palazzo in Florence. The hall of Great witches who'd come before him. *The Great Medici witches. Nicco would be with his family.*

I stumbled up with his bones, covered in his ash.

I had to find the Medici palace.

I had to find Nicco's spirit.

I hurried down the spiral staircase, bits and pieces of his skeleton threatening to spill out of my skirt. "Nibo!" I yelled, bursting out into St. Anthony's Garden. "I have my second question!"

He appeared, standing on the shoulders of touchdown Jesus.

"Where's the Medici palace?"

He placed his staff on Jesus' head and looked down at me, almost as if to ask, *Really? This is what you're wasting your final question on?*

"Where is it?" I yelled.

"Are you sure?"

"*Oui*! I want to go there now! I need to find him. I need to see him!"

"Are you going to tell him how you feel?"

"Just tell me where he is!" My voice boomed, and the surrounding wrought-iron gate wilted like a flower in the August heat.

He smiled at me and pointed his staff down Orleans. A sparkle dropped out and bounced down the street, leaving a lilac glow in its wake.

I hurried after the magical breadcrumb, my skirt pulled up to my chest, keeping Nicco's bones secure.

As I crossed Bourbon, my eyes welled. What would I tell Gabriel?

I'd promised to protect Nicco.

Alley gates creaked open and slammed closed as I walked past. Bars on windows fell from houses and rolled to the street, trailing behind me like a wrought iron train on the bone and spiderweb dress.

I hadn't hesitated to use my question to find Nicco.

I hadn't hesitated to release him from the attic.

I hadn't hesitated to go to the swamp with him or show him my magic. I wasn't scared of his dreams, or his fantasies, or his past, because . . . I loved him.

I love him.

Unquestionably.

I always had.

And now he was gone.

The pain ripped an irreparable tear in my heart. I tripped on a crack in the road, and a femur fell out of my skirt. "Nicco!" I grabbed for the bone but lost another small piece. I grabbed for that one too, and more of his ash puffed from my gown. "No!" I yelled into the night. I couldn't lose any more of him. I tightened my skirt to my breast, needing to keep every piece of him secure, as if I was going to find some kind of Victor Frankenstein who could put him back together.

Tears streamed down my sooty cheeks.

Windows rattled. The lamp posts bent down to the ground with agonizing creaks as I passed. I didn't care. Through welling tears, I focused on the glow ahead. What good was magic if I couldn't save him?

The Ghede breadcrumbs stopped at Rampart, and I looked up expecting to see the archway entrance for Armstrong Park, but there was only a thicket of forest. In the moonlight, the spindles emerged against the stars.

Thump-thump. Thump-thump. Thump-thump.

"Nicco!" I yelled, picking up to a run.

I sped through the mossy branches, and rippling oak tree roots, and songs of the nightingales, to a castle whose dark towers were barely visible against the nighttime sky.

CHAPTER 28
END OF THE WORLD

I knew the name La Sirène. There was an altar for the mermaid lwa at the Borges' that displayed glass bottles with messages on scrolls inscribed to the deity, offerings of colored sand and glittering oyster shells decorated with turquoise sequins and Mardi Gras pearls. She had wealth and beauty and was the ashe of seduction and sea water—and she was the first lwa Ritha had ever been taken possession by Her Met Tet.

As we walked down the desolate railroad tracks along the river in the Ninth Ward, Désirée told us more, occasionally referencing the pages of Marassa's grimoire by the light of the moon.

"She's arguably one of the most dangerous lwa in the Voodoo pantheon."

"Of course she is," I said. "Why would we be looking for anyone less?"

Codi adjusted the kishi on his back. "I didn't know La Sirène was a Ghede."

"She's not."

"Then why does she live in Guinée?"

"She travels back and forth. Her waters sit somewhere

between the realms, and she has a mirror that opens the portal. Her husband, Agwé, is the ashe of safe passage—he commands the ship that transports new spirits to Guinée."

"What makes her so dangerous?" I wasn't sure I really wanted the answer.

"She's a siren. With both her beauty and her song, she can hypnotize anyone who offends her and drag them down to the depths of the sea." Désirée looked up from her grimoire. "Not to alarm anyone, but it's rumored she has a palace of dead children at the bottom of the ocean."

"*What?*" Codi pulled her grimoire closer. "A mermaid kid snatcher? That sounds like an urban legend."

"Don't they all." I pulled my arm over my head, stretching my triceps, my mind drifting to the moon and back to Adele. *Where is she?*

"In better news, La Sirène's also the lwa of mysticism and the great keeper of occult secrets. If she lets you into her palace, you can come out leveled-up, magically speaking. Kind of like an initiation—surviving the drowning."

Was she out there looking for Jakome Salazar on her own? *Is she okay?* I got anxious, thinking about it. "I'm going to scope ahead." I jumped into the air, not waiting for a response.

The wind rolled off the river and rippled through my feathers, bringing an immediate sense of calm. Maybe La Sirène could tell me where she was. My feathers bristled with embarrassment, thinking back to the meeting with Susannah. I'd finally had the chance to meet another magical member of my family, and I'd blown it. Had I offended her by asking about Adeline? *I have to see her again before we leave.*

As the train tracks came to an end, I scoured below. A small stretch of beach covered the jut of land created by the intersection of the Mississippi and the Industrial Canal. Now I got why they called it the End of the World: behind us, you could see the city skyline in the distance, but there was nothing here and not much ahead, and it had a creepy feeling like you might tip over the edge of the horizon if you kept going.

Most of the area had been overtaken by a naval station, which, in the Natural World, had been destroyed by the Storm. Here the gray-concrete buildings didn't look so different: windows blown out, walls covered in graffiti—mostly *fuck you*s from Storm victims to the government, a couple specifically to Désirée's pop. A couple to mine. I wasn't sure what I was looking for, but nothing looked fit for the rulers of the sea in this world or otherwise.

I circled the area a few times and swooped over the water but found nothing but a couple of gulls sailing through the air and some wharf rats scurrying along the rocks at the shore's edge.

Dee and Codi arrived, and I landed on the beach to meet them.

"So this is the End of the World?" I asked.

Codi set the kishi down in the sand, and they both nodded, looking around, catching their breath.

"There's nothing here." I dropped my pack.

"There has to be something," Dee said.

"Or those little Ghede kids were fucking with us."

Codi dug his sneaker into a pile of oyster shells and damp firecrackers, as if there might be buried treasure beneath. Given the level of weird the Afterworld presented, maybe there was.

We peered up at the dilapidated naval facility. The biggest tag I'd ever seen spanned three buildings:

OPEN YOUR EYES

"Ha." I let out a laugh. "They're wide open."

"Are they?" asked a female voice.

We turned to Dee, who shrugged.

Codi squinted out to the water. "Is that . . . ? Is that La Sirène?"

Again, we both turned to Dee, who again gave us a small shrug.

We kicked off our shoes and ran down to the water's edge. Further out, a woman bathed in the moonlight, floating on a nest of black and pink . . . feathers? I rolled up my pants as the waves splashed up past my ankles.

"La Sirène?" Codi called out.

The woman dipped a wooden hand-net into the water and used it as a paddle, rotating herself just enough to see us. She raised one brow of her skeletal face to us like we were crazy.

"Thaaat's not her," Dee said.

"How do you know?" Codi asked.

"For starters, she has legs."

The woman stood. Her silver one-piece shined like metal and dipped so low it exposed the bulk of her breasts, but the matching arm guards made her look more Wonder Woman than *Maxim*. A purple silk hood was pulled over her head, and a tuft of curls swept across her left eye.

"Do I look like a lullaby-singin', dream-twistin', coral-collectin' half-fish?" she asked, peering pointedly at Codi, a wooden cross dangling at her throat.

"Uh . . ."

She picked up the pile of feathers and dragged it behind her as she strode *atop* the river surface toward us, the spiked spurs at the heels of her purple thigh-high boots kicking up water behind her. Her suit was made entirely of silver buttons, and a single black feather poked from her cleavage. *My feather.* "You're Ghede-Plumaj!"

Her purple eyes pulsed, and with a wave of her arm, the feather pile swooped around her like a cape. One shake and the water rained off, and it puffed up in the river breeze. Enormous raven skulls pointed to the moon, framing her shoulders.

"The Soul Collector," Dee added.

Plumaj lifted the net to her shoulder, and we all took a step back. It was hard not to be in awe in the presence of a Ghede.

"Speaking of souls," Codi said, nodding back to the kishi on the beach.

"If I wanted ya trash souls, I would've met ya in da cemetery, 'stead of sendin' Oussou and Masaka."

Codi rocked back on his feet. "Gotcha."

"Well, we aren't here to see you anyway," Dee said, crossing her arms.

"Good luck." Plumaj gave us a sly smile that said *You'll need it,* and she turned away.

A cold wind rushed over us. "Wait!" Codi yelped, and she turned back around. "Where is La Sirène?"

"She rarely leaves her palace."

"Which is where?" I asked.

She nodded out to the water.

"*Underwater?*" My pulse stuttered as I gazed out at the rocking river.

"Ya think da sea lwa lives in da clouds?"

"Well, she's pleasant," Codi mumbled.

I laced my fingers at the top of my head. "You'd probably be in a bad mood too if you got stuck bringing Annabelle over."

"Dat girl was so enamored wit da wild dream I conjured up for her, you'd've thought she'd used her Aether magic on herself."

"She couldn't have been *that* enamored if she escaped so quickly," I said.

"*Pish.*" Plumaj brought the net to her shoulder. "She didn't escape. I would've had her soul if it weren't for dat blonde witch who snatched her out, legs kickin', screamin' like a baby goat. Dat lady looked like she was gonna whoop her ass good." Plumaj laughed. She stepped into a shadow of a cloud, and when the moonlight came back, she was gone.

I squinted out to the water. "It had to be Cosette who pulled her out."

"Or Minette," Codi said.

"Or Lisette," Dee echoed.

"True." It was still strange to think of Lisette as a witch, as anything but a vampire. We splashed back to the beach.

"No wonder Annabelle lied." Codi pulled off his shirt and dropped it next to the kishi. "I bet her own family disowned her."

"I hope we have something in the picnic that will suit La Sirène's tastes," Dee said, and the conversation about Annabelle was over.

Codi and I made camp on the beach as Désirée dug through the pages of her grimoire, but I couldn't take my eyes off the water. All I could think about was Jade and Rosalyn and the waves sweeping over us. The water stifling their screams.

"*Isaac,*" Désirée shouted.

"What?" I jumped.

"Do you have any cakes in your pack? Anything sugary?"

They'd already contributed items from their food supply. I dug through my bag and found some angel food cake drizzled with a raspberry glaze.

"I wish we had some gin," she said, "or better yet, some champagne."

"What about this?" I pulled out a corked bottle filled with a frothy pink drink.

"That's perfect. Why do I feel like Papa Olsin was looking out for us with this spread?"

I handed it to Codi, and he smiled in agreement, but as he poured some onto a cluster of oyster shells, his eyes glistened. I wondered if Olsin had crossed over yet.

Désirée used a bare foot to smooth out the sand to build the altar, then began drawing lines with a stick, cross-checking with the reference in her book.

I glanced at the vèvè she was copying: a diamond turned on its side, sitting on a stack of inverted triangles—I slid the stick from her hand. "Why don't you gather some shells for the decoration." The list of things Dee had perfected was long, but illustration wasn't one of them.

When I was finished, I placed our largest shell in the center of the diamond, like an eye, and dotted the triangles with the smaller ones. She shoved a few candles into the sand, and Codi made a circle out of kelp, which I was pretty sure wouldn't be found at a NOLA river beach in the Natural World. We added the sweets and the pink drink, and Désirée crossed her arms, looking down at the makeshift altar. "Not too shabby considering the circumstances."

"Do you think she'll come?" I asked.

"Come? What do you mean?"

"Isn't that why we built the altar? To call upon La Sirène so we can give her the souls?"

"No," she said, lifting her shirt over her head. I instinctually started to turn my head until I saw the sports bra underneath. "The altar is just an offering."

"You know, so she doesn't drag us into the palace of dead children when we go down to deliver the souls." Codi was already stripped down to his boxers. "You can swim, right?"

"Yeah, but . . . how far down do we need to go? We don't have any diving gear."

"Bro, we're magical." He hooked my neck with a squeeze. "You might want to lose the jeans though. They'll weigh you down."

Fuck.

I took off my watch and dropped it in one of my shoes. Codi lit the candles as Désirée sat on the sand and wrestled off her constricting pants. I unlatched my belt. *I can't believe we're doing this.*

I dumped the rest of my clothes in a pile with theirs and lifted the kishi to Codi's back.

The three of us waded out into the water, the waves crashing over our ankles.

"It's kind of ironic that this is where we'd have to take the souls," Désirée said.

"Why?" I asked.

"Because in the Natural World, practitioners travel to the World's End to ask the water to take away unwanted things—troublesome neighbors, unwanted lovers."

"They're not unwanted," I said.

"I know." She looked at me. "Which is why we aren't asking the water to take them away."

We joined hands and Désirée led us in a little devotion to La Sirène and Agwé, asking them for permission to enter their waters.

> "O, Maîtresse La Sirène, we're here to
>   find you.
> O, Maîtresse, La Sirène, we're listening for
>   your voice.
> O, La Sirène, fire your cannon, sing your
>   song, guide us to your glistening rock.
> O, La Sirène.
> O, La Sirène."

The waves began to churn.

Désirée leaned close to Codi and spoke so low I could barely hear her over the rolling river. "Are you ready for this?"

"Yeah, why?"

"I mean, magically speaking?"

"Why would you ask that? Because of the kishi?"

"No. Well, yes, and the smoke plant back at your house. And . . . never mind."

"Désirée, those are spells. This is my *Elemental* magic."

"Okay. I'm sorry for bringing it up." She walked deeper into the river. "Come on."

He turned to me. The insecurity was still on his face, despite his best efforts to hide it. "You ready?"

I nodded, even though I was anything but. We were mere blocks from where the levees had broken the morning after the Storm. Okay, technically we were a world away, but still, I never wanted to be in this water again.

He slapped my back. "Well, then, get in there."

Observe. Adapt. Dominate.

I waded out to Dee, who was standing tall, trying not to shiver. *Just focus on saving the souls. Hundreds. Thousands of souls.* Most of these souls were Storm victims; they'd already been failed so completely both in their natural lives, and then as spirits. They deserved peace. I pushed down my fear, telling myself it was just another rescue mission with Pop. Only this one involved magically getting to the underwater lair of a possible child-stealing mermaid Voodoo lwa. Totally the same thing.

Codi followed us halfway out, his fingertips dragging in the water, leaving behind an iridescent trace of blue on the surface of the murky river. "On the count of three, dive as deep as you can."

I took a full breath, feeling the magic in the air as the wind rolled over my chest and through my hair. Codi sounded us off, and I dove, side by side with Désirée. I had no idea how Codi was going to get us down there, or whether we'd end up in a giant soup of dead ghost children and broken souls, but I plunged down into the water, in his magical hands, in perfect love and perfect trust.

A shock of cold zapped through my bones, but I swam deeper, the water enveloping me like a dark curtain. The taste of the brackish water pulled the Storm memories from the depths of my mind, and Désirée's hand disappeared into the gloomy swirl, just like Jade's had. I kicked harder, keeping up, until I could feel her wake as she swam just ahead of me. I followed deeper, anxiety building as my breath began to deplete.

A soft rope tickled my foot; I kicked it away, but it came for me again.

As I looked back, a glowing blue ribbon caught my ankle and spun me into a vortex of water. It twisted me faster and faster. Deeper and deeper. How far were we from the surface? I didn't have enough air to get back up. Oxygen bubbles escaped as I panicked. The magic shot me down, and I gurgled a scream, careening deeper into the river. My lungs lit up as I inhaled the muddy water, and it was the morning after the Storm all over again. The twister came to a sudden halt, and I slammed forward, hitting something soft that flung me back. A cerulean glow lit up all around me, and I hacked as I bounced around inside the bubble.

Codi floated up in another magical orb. "Sorry!" he yelled. "Once it got going, it just took off!"

"This is so cool!" Dee yelled from the bubble next to us, her voice warbling through the water.

Codi flicked his hands, and the current carried us even deeper, until the water turned completely black. My magic lit the tips of my fingers like a call-and-response—*Do not panic, Isaac*—and I tempered the desire to send a rip of Air down to pull us all out.

The pressure deepened as we continued to sink.

My breathing shallowed, and my hands tingled. *Can I even reach the Air from down here?* Alarm seeped into my bones, but then the water became clearer, like we'd entered a new stratum of the ocean. Schools of tropical fish that sure as hell weren't swimming around the bottom of the Mississippi swirled around us. Seaweed tickled the bubble, moving us through jagged corals and neon anemones and bright purple jellyfish that pulsed with light.

The water ahead transitioned to a magical shade of

turquoise, and beyond the patch, a structure glowed a salmon-pink color. But the closer we got, the more the water began to blur. A rushing, pounding sound grew louder. *Is that a waterfall? Under*water? We were heading straight for it. I scrambled, pulling for my Air, trying to push the bubble back, but nothing came—we were too far down. The vortex pounded louder. "We can't go through!" I yelled, waving to Codi. "The bubbles will burst!"

He was in a trance, focusing on his magic.

"Codi!" I threw my arms over my head as torrents of water crashed onto the bubble. Sucking in a giant breath, I waited for the inevitable. The sound became deafening as the water slammed down. I unpinched my eyes—the pink glowed brighter as we inched along—and then just as I thought I might have a stroke, the water burped the bubble out on the other side of the cascade.

We were no longer underwater, but floating on the surface of a pool in a mammoth cavern, high above the sea-shell spindles of a glowing salmon-pink palace below.

The water churned, Désirée screamed, and she and her bubble disappeared.

"Désirée!" Codi yelled. Just as I realized she'd been dragged down another set of rapids, my bubble tipped over the edge too. My voice echoed all the way down as I flailed. His magic broke, and the vessel popped. I attempted to rip a gust of Air, but it was too late. Dee shrieked as she hurtled into the water below. My side slammed into the shimmering pool.

Air bubbles rushed all around me as Codi plunged in beside me.

I kicked hard, desperate to reach the surface once again, and I sucked in some water with the first eager breath. Dee's head emerged nearby. I coughed as she swam to me, gasping for air. Her long, lanky arms slipped around my shoulders as she rested for a second, trying to breathe. I paddled harder, keeping us both afloat.

Codi popped up next. "Sorry about that," he said, wiping the water from his face.

Désirée pulled herself higher on my back.

"You know, you aren't exactly child-size," I said, starting to sink with her weight. Neither of them said anything as I pushed us back up, and when I regained my balance, I realized why.

Codi floated with the kishi, looking up at the palace, his face shimmering pink in its reflection on the water.

I'd witnessed a lot of surreal things over the past year, but this palace took the fit-only-for-a-mermaid cake. It must have been a hundred feet tall, nearly reaching the top of the cavern, and was constructed of more kinds of coral than I'd ever imagined existed, all different shades of pink. Cascades poured through a system of tunnels all around the cavern, creating an ever-present ambient motion. It felt crass to interrupt the harmonious song of the sentient sacred space with the sounds of our voices. Désirée nodded to a path of seashells that jutted out of the water, leading up to a gate of black pearls.

We floated through beds of seaweed and starfish and schools of seahorses and pulled ourselves up onto the seashell path in silence. We gazed at each other as the gates opened. Who or what was controlling them was yet to be determined.

I wished Ritha was here to see this. Désirée looked like a goddess herself in the halo of the palace's pink pearl archway. And I was pretty sure I wasn't the only person who'd noticed. Codi's gaze met mine, and he blushed. "What?" he asked.

"Nothing." I smiled.

The archway opened into a circular room, which was simply an enormous pool of water. The reflection of the mirrored walls sparkled atop it like diamonds in a treasure chest, and in the center of the pool, a rocky white path grew out of the water, leading to a small island of obsidian rock. Upon it sat two ten-foot-tall abalone shells perched upright, each with a giant black pearl at its base, like matching thrones.

The glimmering palace made it almost feel like we'd left the Afterworld for some celestial place in the heavens. *Almost.* I stepped to the edge of the archway, examining the walls. They weren't covered in mirrors, but doubloons. Gold, silver. Spanish. Dutch. French. From all over the world. And along the water-line, the walls were lined with skulls. Human skulls. Whose? Devotees who'd gone astray? Innocent children who La Sirène had longed to make her own?

We waded into the pool and swam toward the raised white path. The water was cool and silky and had a seductive quality to it, putting me perfectly at ease despite being surrounded by human skulls with a basketful of souls. The path was a lot farther out than it had seemed from the entryway, but I didn't mind, gliding through the magical water, muscles stretching, my head emptying after the stressful plunge to get here.

A slap made us all spin around.

Water splashed, and as it settled, a shadowy figure emerged, slithering beneath the surface, coming straight toward us. A feeling of imminent danger chilled my core—they must have felt it too, because all three of us dove toward the rocky path. A few more strokes, and we were there, only up close, it felt more like a wall. *A wall of giant white . . .* Codi and I boosted Désirée up, then we helped Codi up next. As I passed him the kishi, the chill deepened, and I realized I wasn't clinging to a white rock or shell, but to a pelvis bone. I nearly slipped off as he grabbed the basket. The entire path was a pile of femurs, hip bones, fish bones, rib cages too large to be human. Fingernails scraped against my feet like barnacles, and I squealed. Codi grabbed my hand and hauled me up. I whipped around just in time to see the long tendrils of curly pink hair and the fins of a shadowy tail before she disappeared beneath the path.

The water stilled. "Where'd she go?"

"Did we scare her away?" Codi asked.

A song filled the cavern, delicate and airy, and an arc of water sprayed over us as she dove high above us, twisting in the air, the scales of her enormous tail glistening like iridescent rainbows. She dove back beneath the water, heading for the obsidian jut.

We hobbled up the path, bones jabbing into our feet. As we stepped onto the rock, she leapt again, soaking us with an enormous wave.

I wiped the water from my eyes and hardly noticed when I fell to my knees. She lay before us, her dark mahogany skin and rainbow tail glistening across the shiny black stone. Her naked chest was decorated in necklaces with sparkling gemstones, like she'd pillaged pirates' sunken treasure chests. Maybe she had. Pink coils of hair eight feet long draped over her hips and down her tail. She was the most beautiful woman—or spirit? Or whatever she was—I'd ever seen.

She smiled, and I knew I'd sketch her for the rest of my life.

Désirée tugged my shoulder, pulling me up, and we all stood before her dripping wet. Codi set the kishi down. His light-colored boxers were plastered to his thighs, and I was grateful to have worn dark-colored briefs. Still, I folded my hands over my crotch.

"Three witches from the Natural World." La Sirène's voice was both sweet and sultry. "Three beautiful witches, why do you stand before me?"

When no one responded, I looked to Désirée, who seemed completely mesmerized by the lwa.

Codi cleared his throat, but Dee still didn't blink. "Um . . ." he started.

La Sirène stretched her arms back, writhing with a yawn. We were boring her.

"We've come to ask for a favor," Codi said.

"A favor?" Whatever mild curiosity she had in us dwindled from her face. "No alms today." She began to roll away.

"No!" I yelped.

Her hair swung around as she whipped back, and her amber-colored eyes turned to black bottomless voids.

"I mean . . . that's not the only reason we're here."

Dee glanced at me severely.

Trust me, I mouthed. I was starting to get how these lwa worked. They were like New Yorkers, and I could appreciate their hustle. We needed a new approach: *we* didn't need a favor; we were doing *them* a favor. "We heard that you're a collector of rare and beautiful things."

In a blink, she was gone. She reappeared, sitting on the pearl in one of the abalone thrones. Her fingertips waved into each other like jellyfish tentacles. "*Kontinye.*"

Dee nudged me on.

"We brought these all the way from the Natural World. There are thousands in this magical basket."

Her black eyes grew. "Thousands of what?"

"Souls."

She twirled a strand of pearls around her finger.

"They've been magically separated from their spirits, making them incredibly rare. We know how much you like precious things."

"Some of them were children," Désirée added, and Codi's face scrunched.

I thanked all that was holy that Jade had crossed over before Callis's Ghost Drinking power had become supercharged.

La Sirène slithered forward to Codi.

He glanced at me. I nodded, and he opened the basket lid for her.

Her eyes lit up, changing back to amber.

I stepped over and snapped it shut. "But we can only give them to you if you have an adequate place for them to live out eternity. We assume you have somewhere beautiful for them to rest?" I was pretty sure she could pound me into the rock with her tail and take whatever she wanted, but she looked at me with a seductive smile and slithered off the rock into the water.

"She wants us to go with her," Dee said. "Grab the kishi."

We dove into the water after her, exiting the grand pool into one of the tunnels, tiny glowing fish lighting the way. I kicked faster, hurrying to the surface for a breath before diving back down, almost compulsively afraid to lose sight of her fin.

A few breaths later, we tumbled down a short waterfall into another cavernous room. An old wooden ship stuck partially out of the water, and I half expected to see the skeleton of One-Eyed Willy at the helm.

"They can live here," La Sirène said, and she vanished into a cloud of pink sparkles and reappeared sprawled on the ship's bow, singing in a language I didn't know yet could somehow understand.

The kishi floated from Codi's arms to the surface of the water.

"*Vin jwenn mwen, ou lakay*," she sang, and the basket shook, and the vines slithered away.

Codi's gaze darted to mine and then to Dee's. It shook harder. The magic was breaking.

We lunged away as the lid burst and the basket tipped.

Désirée sprung to me as the souls spilled out into the water, but there was no need to fear. They were all floating to La Sirène, to the rhythm of her song. Tens. Hundreds. Thousands of glowing, broken souls floated to her like entranced jellyfish. She leapt into the water among them, and they swirled around her in synchronicity. It took me a moment to see some were forming a diamond. The others in the triangle arrangement. They were creating her vèvè, with La Sirène's face as the eye. Their vibration filled the cavern with a hum of contentment. Even the souls who had grown dim now glowed bright in her magical waters. They would never blink out.

The government hadn't been able to protect their bodies, and the witches hadn't been able to protect their spirits, but we'd saved their souls. It was the greatest miracle I could ever imagine, and it was something *The New York Times* would never write a headline about.

The souls were finally home.

R.I.P. Jamal.

R.I.P. everyone.

In the swirl of their dance, I couldn't help but think about Ren. As beautiful as the swirling neon soul-vèvè was, I couldn't imagine him floating around a pool for eternity. Ren's spirit should haunt the streets of the French Quarter long after his natural-self expired: popping up in the photos of tourists, stealing sips of boozy drinks at Le Chat Noir, and singing his pirate songs down Pirate's Alley at four a.m. I had to find him a cure. *I have to find the miracle man.*

"How do we get out of here?" Désirée whispered as we gently paddled away. "We can't go *up* the rapids."

"Watch us," I said.

I glanced at Codi, who gave me a quick nod, and then I swam a few quick strokes ahead. On the upswing, I took crow-form, gliding into the air. When I looked back down, they were both in shiny new bubbles, heading for the waterfall. I raised my wings and called for the Air.

Dee bounced around in her bubble, yelling, pointing, but I couldn't hear her through the pounding falls and La Sirène's song. The force from the rapids pushed them away, but I whipped the Air and my magic lifted their bubbles.

Up, up, up. Over the cascades.

As I set them back down on the water, Désirée still flailed about, but now I could read her lips: "*Isaac, you're flying!*"

No shit.

I tipped my shoulder to loop and swoop back down, and my heart pounded, realizing what she was saying. I felt my own body weight. I felt my fingers. I felt the wind in my hair as I dove. *I was flying. I was FLYING. In human form.*

"Désirée, I'm flying!" I screamed, swooping down beside them, pushing them back into the tunnel with a gust of Air, following the trail of blue magic left in Codi's wake.

The water level rose in the tunnel, frothing as it rushed upward, lapping at the walls. As it touched my toes, I gave them one final shove and dropped down over the sparkling waves. The bubble formed around me, and Codi pushed us through the rapids until we spilled back out into the palatial pool. This time, he was ready, and his magic held.

The next cascade was way bigger. I hoped I could lift all three of us at once.

"*I got this!*" Désirée yelled, and with a wave of her arms, blades of seaweed rose from the seafloor and glided us along, growing taller and taller until we got to the top of the falls.

Codi cast a current, and we rode through. This time I was filled with excitement rather than fear as the heavy water beat down on the bubble. As always, when the three of us did magic together, an elation swirled inside my heart that even a black river in the depths of the Afterworld couldn't quell.

"On the count of three," he yelled, and before I realized what was going on, the bubble burst and the vortex of water shot me upward, twisting and twirling. Then, one by one, we popped out of the river and up to the moon. I did a flip as I sailed back down and, for a brief second, I let go of all the horrors awaiting us back in the Natural World.

We swam the last fifty yards back to shore, and I was panting by the time we crawled up the sandy bank at the End of the World.

CHAPTER 29
GUINÉE

Isaac collapsed onto his back on the sandy shore, sucking in the air.

"You," I gasped, crawling up behind him, "were . . . *flying*." I fell at his side, happy to be back on solid ground, and rested my head on his abs. "La Sirène. Supercharged. You."

Codi stumbled up to us and toppled next to me, resting his head on my very unpillow-like stomach. My lungs pouched up for breath as I repeated the words, hardly even noticing when my hand fell on his chest. "I choked when we were on the spot—I should have stepped up. I could have gotten supercharged by La Sirène!"

"That was awesome," Codi said to Isaac, who stretched his arm out for a dab.

"No way, man. That was all you. We never would have found La Sirène if it wasn't for your Water."

"Well, we never would have gotten to the Afterworld at all if it hadn't been for Dee's nagg—"

I raised an eyebrow to him.

". . . her unwavering confidence in the coven."

"I told you we're all better together." My voice softened as I gently twined a wet curl of his hair. "We did it. We actually did it."

"We saved the souls," Isaac said, and we all looked back up to the stars in awe.

"Ritha's gonna be mad impressed." Codi's voice lingered, like he still had something to say.

"What?" I asked him.

"It's nothing . . ."

Neither of us spoke.

"It's just that, I think tonight will be the first night I've really slept in weeks. Knowing that my family isn't resting in a houseful of parasitic souls."

"Oh, that ole maybe-my-dads-will-get-possessed-tonight insomnia," I said, and we all laughed with relief. Still, I couldn't help but think about the souls, or the tragedy that had caused all those deaths. *The Storm.* The broken levees that had ravaged all those Black neighborhoods. A city my family was supposed to protect. A city this *country* was supposed to protect. It let them drown. Let us drown. It didn't care about people like them.

People like me.

No matter how many law degrees my family acquired, no matter how many economics PhDs we matriculated, political positions we held, spells we cast and gris-gris we made, it hadn't been enough to protect all of them. It wasn't enough to change this fucked-up system.

No magic could change the hate in people's hearts.

The pervasive guilt stirred beneath my skin. We had so much compared to most people. We hadn't even evacuated, and we'd been fine. The guilt wasn't just over our privilege, magical or otherwise. All these weeks I'd been so insistent on coming to Guinée, I'd wanted to save the souls, but I had another reason. A reason that served only me.

My voice floated up, softer, weaker than I'd ever allowed people to hear. "I have a confession too."

"This oughta be—" Isaac cut himself off, realizing I was serious.

"Finding the Soul Keeper wasn't the only reason I wanted to come to Guinée . . ."

They both looked my way, but I stared straight up at the Flower Moon.

"I wanted to see if it was true." A tear dripped down my cheek. "The old Black legend that folks told their kids. That their families would be reunited in Guinée."

"Marassa and Makandal," Isaac said quietly.

I nodded. "I just want to know if she found him. Goddess only knows what happened to him for helping her escape."

Codi sat up straight. "Then let's go find them."

"We have more important priorities," I said, wiping my eyes.

"I can't think of anything more important than this."

"Me either," Isaac said, the words catching in the back of his throat.

"I-I don't know where they are."

Isaac gently pushed me up. "Dee, we're magical—"

And Codi pulled me to my feet. "Location Spell."

"But I don't have a map."

Isaac grabbed the stick and smoothed out the sand with his foot. "Guinée seems like an alternate version of the French Quarter, right?" He began drawing the streets.

"You have Marassa's grimoire," Codi said, handing me my bag. "That might work as a talisman."

"Actually." I pulled out the ribbon tucked into my sports bra. "I have this." A small bone was strung on the ribbon next to my gris-gris. One end was sharpened to a point and stained with black dye.

"No way," Codi said. "That is not the bone your ancestor brought over from Africa? The one the first spells in your grimoire were written with?"

"Someone was paying attention." I took it off and handed it to him.

"When is he not paying attention to you?"

We both looked at Isaac sharply, and he laughed, rolling his eyes as he drew a stroke for Canal Street. "Please."

I had to command my face not to smile.

Codi handed the bone back. "It's so cool."

"I know."

I can't believe I cried in front of them. I can't believe we're doing this. I couldn't remember a time when I'd been so nervous in my entire life.

But with the two of them at my side, I knew that no matter what I discovered, I'd be okay.

The oak tree branches swayed above us as we walked down the neutral ground on Esplanade Avenue. The location map had put their house right at Bourbon.

Esplanade had always been one of my favorite streets in the city—the Creole folks' St. Charles back in the day—it seemed fitting that Marassa Makandal resided here in the Afterlife. The old double-gallery mansions were peppered with sycamores, silverbells, and blossoming magnolia trees. Their wrought-iron gates were twisted up with jasmine and honeysuckle. Even with the cold, dark chill of the Afterworld and its dead inhabitants, the street still felt alive.

Excitement bloomed with my every step as we searched for the house.

"I was kind of a dick to Susannah after she pulled me out of the dream," Isaac sheepishly admitted out of nowhere.

"I can see it," Codi said.

Isaac scowled.

"What? She pulled you out of your greatest fantasy. Your *engagement party with Adele.*"

I bit the insides of my mouth so I wouldn't laugh.

The apples of Isaac's cheeks turned pink. "I have to see her again before we leave. I don't want her to have that impression of me."

"We'll find her," Codi said. "I def wanna see Morning Star before we leave. All of my relatives, hopefully."

My fingertips felt for the folded paper in my back pocket. Now that we were free of the souls, I had to show it to him. But we were so close to meeting Marassa, I didn't want to ruin the vibe. I knew it was selfish, but I wanted him to be there and be his usual annoyingly happy self. Once we were settled, I'd find a quiet moment to pull him aside. *Ugh.* Now it was going to be weird that I'd waited so long. I was tempted to shake a palm tree and make some nuts fall as a distraction, so I could drop the flier and then pretend to find it. *Brilliant.*

He caught me looking at him and smiled. The thought of lying to him, even innocently, made me queasy. *What is wrong with me?* You were trying to keep his stress level down. The entire Magical world had been at risk with the kishi malfunctioning.

But why had it malfunctioned? And why had his smoke spell expired? Why had Fiona's orchid wilted? She's so meticulous with her flowers; I'd never seen wilted petals among her award-winning orchid stock before. And the tearoom, all those half-dead plants . . . was something wrong with their magic? Ritha would never let us—if his magic—*Désirée, there's nothing wrong with Codi's magic, it just got us to the bottom of the ocean!* I could hear my therapist's voice in my head. "*Oh, so now that you found someone special, you're already trying to find reasons that it won't work? His family isn't magical enough? He's not Black enough? He's not Ivy League enough?*"

"His family's fine!"

The boys both turned to me. "Whose family?" Codi asked.

"Nothing," I squeaked. "No one's. Mine. My family is fine."

"Duh," he said, with that cute little smile. He bumped my shoulder. "You nervous?"

"No," I lied.

"Good. You shouldn't be."

I tried to smile back, but it felt fake and unnatural.

My fingers reached for the flier again. Olsin had told him in the note that his grandmother was going to need him. Philomena had pulled Codi out of his Ghede-dream and then . . . disappeared? Was she missing too? *Désirée, you sound like one of those wacko conspiracy theorists.*

"This whole Afterworld thing is weird," Isaac said, and I grappled for the distraction. "Why does Susannah have to ride out eternity in the Quarter? How long did she live here in her Natural life—a year? She's a Bermudian, a New Yorker. And for that matter, why would Jakome Salazar be in New Orleans in the Afterworld? Didn't he die before New Orleans was even on the map?"

"I don't think the Afterworld is that literal." I thought back to what Masaka had told me in the strip club. "I think everyone is here because the Quarter was our point of entry. New Orleans is easiest for *our* minds to process, so that's how it's presented to us."

"So, like, if we'd entered Guinée in Germany, the Afterworld might be the Black Forest?" Codi asked.

"That's the only sense I can make of this."

Mhm.

We stopped at one of the glorious old double-gallery houses. It was olive green with white square columns, framed by huge palms that stretched up to the stars. Lush vegetation burst through every crevice of the short wrought-iron fence.

"This is it," I said, sucking in a deep breath. I stroked a magically enhanced elephant ear. "Earth witches."

We went through the gate, toward the porch. A warm light glowed inside. I felt movement through the bones of the old house, heard music and laughter. I stopped on the stairs, but a swell of anxiety made me take a step back. "What if . . . ? What if they don't want to see me? What if they're mad I didn't join the family coven?"

"Dude, they're your *family*," Codi said.

"That sounds like something *your* family would say. Have you met Ritha?"

"Yeah, try telling my dad that," Isaac said.

"They're going to be stoked to see you." Codi hooked his finger with mine and swung my hand. "Who wouldn't be stoked to see you?" My eyes caught his, and I didn't move. He leaned closer, his hand touching my waist. I saw the stunned look on Isaac's face—he slid his hand through his hair and turned away. *Oh my Goddess.* The ground rocked like a wave as Codi leaned in. *Stop freaking out. It's perfect.* Under the moonlight at the proverbial African coastline. Our lips brushed.

"You're right, it will be fine!" I yelped and turned away fast, slightly faint. I hopped up to the door and looked back. He just stood there, a little shocked.

Isaac pinched his mouth closed, trying to suppress a laugh. "We'll be right here if you need us."

"What do you mean?"

"Well, we're not just gonna leave you."

"Of course you aren't. You're coming with me."

"We are?"

"*Duh.* You're my family too."

As I turned to the door, he hooked Codi's neck. "So close, bro. So close."

"Yet so far." He laughed.

My insides smiled as I knocked, but as soon as the door opened and I saw the woman standing before me, my eyes filled with tears. "You're so . . . beautiful," I said, possibly the dumbest thing that had ever come out of my mouth. I couldn't remember a single line from the speech I'd prepared for this moment. A speech I'd been working on for years.

"So are you." Marassa's smile grew as big as the Atlantic.

This was no Ghede mind-trip; our magic had brought us here. This was *the* Marassa Makandal. The first African witch in the French Quarter. Original Casquette Girl member. Founder of the reigning Haitian coven in La Nouvelle-Orléans. Former slave. Rebel. Maker of vani krèm. And whose DNA clearly gave me my impeccable cheekbones. She looked to be about twenty-five, and wore a long gold and purple sleeveless dress with a matching gold headwrap. Her curls burst out of it at every fold. For a second, I regretted straightening mine.

"She's here!" Marassa yelled. "*Elle est ici!*"

Footsteps pounded down the hallway, and a young man popped out from behind her. I leapt toward him, unable to hold back the tears any longer.

"*Ma petite sorcière,*" Makandal said, catching me with a spin, just like he was my own brother. "You came!"

"You're here!" I said, absorbing the warmth of his greeting, the chill of his spirit, and the magic emanating from this ethereal being. When he set me down, I motioned to the boys. "These are my friends, Isaac Norwood and Codi Daure."

"*Byenveni.*"

Marassa hugged them both and ushered them in.

Makandal threw his arm around me as we all walked down the hall. "There are dark times up ahead, *ma chère,* but do not fret; we will prevail. But first, protection. We have everything ready for you."

"Ready for what?" I asked, finally finding my voice.

"The whole family has gathered." Marassa whisked me deeper into the house, and the boys hurried behind.

Every room we passed was full of people. Young, old. Men in pinstriped zoot suits. Women in Victorian funeral garb, others in hoop skirts, tribal regalia. Some hardly wore any clothes at all. I wanted to talk to every single one of them.

"Dude," Isaac whispered to Codi, "the magic in Désirée's blood runs deep."

He was right. I could feel it pulsing through the house. Through generations of Earth witch spirits. Through the children, the elders, and the music vibrating through the ceiling, like the house itself was dancing the Banda.

We went straight out the back door to the courtyard, where more people were waiting, slapping drums, shaking shekeres and leaf rattles, and dancing with bottles of booze sloshing onto the bricked ground. The scene felt oddly familiar.

A wrinkly, gray-haired woman knelt over a scarf heaped with a mountain of herbs, her cheeks full as she chewed big wads. She spat the pulp into a bowl and molded it with her hands.

My eyes went wide, my magic pulsing through my toes, as I realized what they were setting up for.

"There's no need to fear," Marassa said. "You have a battle ahead. The ceremony will give you the protection of all of your ancestors."

"I'm not scared," I said firmly. This was some old-old-old-school magic, and I wanted to be a part of it. I wanted this connection to my ancestors. To our homeland, the roots of our magic.

The woman had a scar on her upper left arm, and a visual from Adeline's diary rolled through my mind: Adeline and Cosette spying outside the slave house. Marassa's Garde ceremony before she escaped to the New World.

Isaac must have remembered it too. He stepped forward, reaching out. "Désirée—"

"It's okay." I took off my hoodie and handed it to him. "I want to participate."

"It's for her own protection," Makandal said, sharpening a blade. "Her own power."

"What is happening?" Codi asked as I sat on a stool and they doused my arm with a pungent rum.

Isaac leaned close, whispering, and Codi's brow tightened, but he nodded. "Cool."

He got it. *Tribal magic.* He got me.

The boys came right by my side, and my back pinched with anticipation as Marassa draped a scarf over my face. *This is happening. This is really happening.* The drumming quickened, the chanting started, and the Borges witches danced round and round. Sending me their energy, their magic, their grace.

"Why do they keep saying we're going into battle?" Isaac whispered to Codi. "Didn't we come here to avoid that?"

"I don't know, but I can't really imagine Callis quietly going away after we destroy his family's magical line."

Isaac squeezed my hand nervously.

"Chill," Codi said. "She can heal herself."

"Right."

I felt no pain, but I couldn't contain the scream as the blade sliced my arm. The chanting grew louder, and the dancing quickened, and the Petwo spirits were called upon. I panted with terror, but as I pulled the cover from my face, I'd never felt more alive—ironic, given we were surrounded by the dead. The old lady packed the cut with herbs and tied it off with a red scarf, sealing the strength within me.

Everyone crowded around, beaming with pride. They began introducing themselves, buzzing about our family and the magic of Africa and Haiti and New Orleans.

Tears dripped from my eyes. I didn't even know why. I was raised to suppress my emotions, to be strong, but I loved it all so much, I wanted to feel every last beat, and the joy just flooded out as I hugged every one of them.

The only thing that could have made it better was my gran being here, and my mom. Even my dad. I wished Adele was here too.

I threw my arms around Isaac and Codi, forever grateful that they'd stood witness to it all. "In perfect love," I said, a rush of emotions coming on so strong, I felt high.

"And perfect trust," Codi finished.

A twinge of guilt panged through the joy, knowing the flier was still in my pocket. *I'll tell him now.* But just as I grabbed his hand, Marassa and Makandal swept us into a dining room where a spread of food covered every inch of the table and then some. Baskets had been stacked on dishes stacked on pots: groundnut stew and spicy chicken yassa. Fufu piled to the ceiling. Baskets of fried klouikloui rings. Goblets of palm wine. The African delights were scattered between mountains of mac 'n' cheese and collards, fried chicken, and gumbo, and the meld of savory scents was intoxicating.

Isaac reached for a porkchop, but Codi smacked his hand.

"No food of the dead," I said, taking the seat next to him. Marassa sat at my right side.

"Oh, this is torture," Isaac groaned, and an old man across from us chuckled.

"Luckily, we have these." Codi set our bags down, took the seat next to Isaac, and the three of us ate every remaining morsel of Edgar Daure's Hexennacht feast.

As I polished off some poppyseed cakes, all but licking my fingers, Marassa whispered in my ear. "I see how you keep stealing glances at Morning Star's boy."

"No, I'm not!" I whispered.

Isaac smiled, and I glanced at Codi. *Dammit, I just did it!*

"You're sweet on him."

I nearly spat out my dandelion-plum wine.

She stroked my cheek. Her tenderness reminded me of my mother. Ritha rarely had a gentle touch for anyone. My mom said it was because she grew up in a different time, when Black women had to fight tooth and nail for every little thing. Most days it still felt like that. We had to be beautiful, but not the prettiest girl in the room. Intelligent, articulate, but not too loud. Strong, but still delicate, otherwise scare away a man.

Fuck that.

Sometimes it felt like nothing had changed, but I knew the adversities I faced day to day didn't hold a candle to what my mother had fought through, much less Ritha, and it only got worse the further back I went through the generations of women in my line, magical or not. We'd had it better than most because of our magic, but what did it all mean, other than that society was pathetic? Was I supposed to feel lucky that I hadn't been born during Marassa's time, a slave to the white man? Or shoved to the back of the bus? Or hung from a tree? I thought about the hoodie I'd worn tonight. We weren't supposed to wear them out of the house after dark. I thought about one of the altars in our house. My great-grandmother had first built it for the spirit of Emmett Till. But over the years, each generation had added to it. Every month I made sure it had fresh Skittles for Trayvon.

I wiped my eyes.

"It's okay to let yourself be vulnerable, my little one. No one will think you weak for giving your heart to someone noble."

I smiled, and another tear dripped out. I wiped it away. "I-I'm not afraid to be vulnerable," I stuttered, and quickly peered over to Codi. To my relief, he was deep in conversation with Makandal about tribal dance magic.

Isaac pretended to blot grease from his mouth, but I knew he was hiding a smug smile under that napkin. Judging from her expression, so was Marassa. I yanked the napkin away, and the three of us laughed.

"Susannah's boy," she said. "I visited her in New York once, you know?"

"Really?" we both asked.

"*Oui. Moi et Adeline, et Cosette.* Addie and I did everything together." She gazed at the three of us. "Do you realize how special it is that you all found each other? *Un miracle.*"

Isaac strummed his fingers on his thigh, anxious. Probably stressing about where Adele was. To be fair, I was starting to worry myself. We needed to find her.

He gave Marassa a troubled frown. "Can I ask you a question about Adeline?"

"*Oui, bébé.*"

"Do you know why she so strongly disliked Niccolò Medici?"

Oh, Lawd.

"Was there something more than Nicco being after her father? She told Adele to stay away from him."

Marassa snickered but appeared a bit confused. "Well, of course Adeline wouldn't want Niccolò Medici around Adele. He was the monster who killed her."

I could almost see the blood freeze in his veins.

Codi dropped his fork against his plate and reached for Isaac's shoulder, but it was too late.

"Isaac!" I yelled, jumping up.

He was already soaring over the table and down the hall, both of us calling after him.

Marassa grabbed my elbow, and I sat back down, stunned, and a little afraid that Adele was with Nicco right now. Even more afraid that Isaac was going to find them, and we'd have a repeat of the dumpster night when he'd broken three ribs . . . or worse. He could never go head to head with Nicco.

I turned to Marassa. "Nicco *killed* Adeline Saint-Germain?"

"*Oui.*" She answered like it was the most common-knowledge thing in the world.

"This has been awesome." Codi stood up. "But we've got to find Adele."

"We've got to find Isaac." I reached for my bag, but Marassa stopped me again.

"Not now. We have much to discuss."

Makandal placed his hand on Codi's shoulder. "You should stay."

The vibe in the room went from celebratory to severe with a quickness I'd come to realize was a Borges specialty.

"Please stay. I was so glad you got my message," Marassa said to me. "I was beginning to worry when you didn't reply. Of course, seeing you is much better."

"What message?"

Her brow pinched. She looked to her brother, and the room fell silent.

CHAPTER 30
HOMECOMING

The flutters of nightingales swooped overhead as I hurried up to the palazzo, breathless, losing more of Nicco's ash with each step. I didn't even have to raise a hand to knock on the gargantuan palace doors. They heaved open as soon as I neared, and I sped inside with Nicco's bones pressed tight against my chest.

In the courtyard, I paused. I wasn't sure why. To catch my breath? To collect myself? I marveled at the grandiose architecture. The flora alone was magnificent. Thousands of blossoms, pink magnolias and red roses crawled up the arches of the double loggia, and purple wisteria hung down several feet. Crisp red banners draped across the balcony, extending from a large crest. A golden-crowned cherub framed the top of the shield, which displayed six orbs and two large keys crisscrossed behind it like swords. I'd seen the coat of arms so many times in Nicco's dreams. Wasn't it only tonight that he'd promised to show me the real thing in Florence? A part of me had really believed he would. The tears rose again, and I could do nothing but let them spill.

Every decision I'd ever made in my life felt wrong, because

they had led me here. My lungs tightened as I realized the chalky taste in my mouth was his ash.

Nicco had always pushed me away in the Natural World. Only now could I admit that I'd always hung on to the hope that one day things would be different.

That hope had burned up with the fire, and I no longer felt whole.

I strode deeper into the courtyard, anxious thoughts bubbling up, filling me with dread. His whole family was going to be here. What if they blamed me for his death?

I didn't care. I had to give them his bones. *I have to see Nicco.*

As I passed a fountain, I caught my fright of a reflection in the dark pool, and another horrifying thought came over me: What if Maddalena was here? What if Nicco had been waiting to be reunited with her? What if that's why he rejected me all those times? Hadn't his father wanted him to marry her? My muscles burned from clutching my skirt, his bones, so close.

What if Nicco didn't even want me here? What if none of them did? I was a Saint-Germain, the great enemy of their family.

"*Cara mia!* You've ruined your dress!"

I looked up to find Giovanna Medici calling down to me from the upper loggia. She appeared both daring and regal in a gown of black velvet, quilted with golden threads and teardrop crystals. A scalloped black lace veil framed her face. Beside her, an elegant woman wailed.

"The dress you gave me of *bones*? Did you enchant it?"

"Bones?" she asked. "What do you mean? It's made of Moondust, I told you."

I looked down, and she was right. The bodice was back to its charcoal texture, burnt around the edges. The only bones were the ones in my hands. "But . . ."

In a blink, they were both next to me, the woman kissing

my cheeks between her cries. When I opened my skirt, she wailed even louder.

"Oh, Mama!" Giovanna shouted. "Why are you crying? You've been waiting nearly four centuries to see your sons!"

"*Il mio piccolo!*"

A ghostly man appeared beside them, slowly solidifying to a more human form. I recognized Nicco's father from his dreams. His unnerving stare never wavered as his wife grasped each of Nicco's bones from my skirt like they were precious jewels.

The ash puffed up around us as she scooped him out, and relief rushed up my arms, finally able to release the layers of spiderweb. All of the beautiful dewdrops had burned up in the fire, and now I was standing half-naked in front of one of the most powerful witching families in European history. I didn't care. All I wanted was Nicco. I wanted to be back in my bed, hearing him promise to show me Florence one day, but each tear his mother shed, each person who moved past us in mourning clothes, all the Medici pomp and circumstance, just reaffirmed that Nicco was really coming to join the dead.

As people flooded in, filling the balconies and the courtyard, Giovanna turned to me. "Papà has planned the grandest home-coming Guinée has ever seen! Do you really want to be covered in Niccolò's ash when he arrives?"

She had a point, but I wasn't leaving the palace doors. I wanted to see Nicco the second he arrived. She yanked my hand, pulling me along.

"Giovanna, I don't want to miss him!"

"He'll be here for eternity; you are not going to miss him. You look a fright."

Brass horns rose into the air with a blast, and all heads turned to the doors as they cranked open. *Thump-thump.* I broke away, excusing myself as I pushed through generations of Medici cousins and hurried to the front.

Everyone quieted as a lone figure wallowed sorrowfully through the door.

Thump-thump.

He seemed confused, disoriented maybe. He was even paler than he'd been in the Natural World, but it made the green in his eyes brighter. He ran his hands through his hair, and his gaze caught the coat of arms above. Comprehension settled in his face as he glanced around, and tears welled in his eyes as his parents stepped forward. He rushed to his mother.

"*Mio figlio!*" she wailed, and he clung on to her like a child, despite dwarfing her in size.

"*Mama.*"

I wished my mother was here. There were so many things I wanted to tell her. So many things I never got a chance to say.

When he finally let go, Giovanna sprung onto him like a kitten.

He held her preciously. "I scoured the Earth searching for you, sister."

"You can thank Adeline Saint-Germain for the wild goose chase. We have so much to catch up on."

"Now we have eternity, *angelo mio.*" He kissed her cheeks, and she made way for their father, the crowd leaning in as if awaiting a spectacle.

Nicco's gaze remained strong despite becoming teary once again. He quickly wiped his eyes, but as soon as he spoke, he fell to his knees. I might not have understood the language, but I knew he was begging for his father's forgiveness. Gabriel had confirmed what I had long suspected: that Nicco blamed himself for his family's slaughter. For the demise of the entire Medici empire, in both the mundane world and the magical.

Ferdinando Medici looked down to his youngest son, his would-have-been magical heir. "Niccolò Giovanni Battista, you do not have my forgiveness, and you never will."

Nicco held his practiced straight face, but I could see his

world shattering behind his eyes as the fear he'd carried for four hundred years manifested. It was *ridiculous* that this was Nicco's fault. I nearly threw myself between them and helped him up.

"Because, my son, there is nothing to forgive."

Nicco looked back up, waves of emotion crossing his face, making him tremble as he tried to stilt any emotion.

"The travesty that took down this family was no more your fault than the mighty Diana's."

The tears finally spilled from Nicco's eyes.

"If there is anyone to blame, it is I, for opening our secrets up to a boy who didn't share our name."

My lungs pinched.

"While he didn't share our blood, I truly believed he shared our heart. Please forgive me, *mio bellissimo figlio.*"

I could feel his relief as the centuries of anguish washed off Nicco's shoulders along with his father's words.

"Rise, Niccolò," Ferdinando said, offering both of his hands. "You are my son. And no witch, no monster, will ever change that."

They grasped each other tightly, exchanging soft, heartfelt Italian words. It was impossible not to be swept away by the love between them, but Ferdinando's mention of León echoed in my mind. What would happen when they realized his heir was amidst them? I took a step back, suddenly feeling like a lamb who'd wandered into the wolves' den. What if Nicco had no more use for me now that he was dead? Was the feud over? Or would Gabriel and Emilio continue on until no one was left?

Thump-thump.

Nicco's eyes opened, alert, and my breath caught as he noticed me.

Without a blink, he let go of his father; a hunter with eyes locked on his prey. The crowd turned to me, puzzled. I took a step forward, unsure of what to say. He came toward me, and before I could say anything at all, he scooped me up. "*Sei davvero qui, mia bella.*"

"*Niccolò,*" I gasped, hugging him tightly despite the extraordinary chill emanating from his ethereal form. I'd never let go again.

Once more, his eyes glistened as his face brushed mine. "You're so warm. You're alive. But how? The fire was too great to survive."

"I don't know," I whispered, and I truly didn't remember how the fire extinguished. "It's all a blur of screams and ash and bells."

He pulled me closer, softly cradling me. "*Grazie a Dio.*" He kissed my head, and I sank into his chest, unable to handle the relief of hearing his voice again. "Don't cry, *bella,* come and meet *mia famiglia.*"

As soon as the words slipped off his tongue, people crowded around, kissing me, hugging me, speaking in dramatic, drawn-out Italian. But then they all parted as his father came toward us.

My heart walloped, and I had to fight the urge to step behind Nicco.

"*Bellissima.*" He opened his arms.

I held my breath and approached. If Nicco hadn't been so close, I wasn't sure if I would have.

The Medici patriarch kissed my left cheek first and then the other. "Even more beautiful on this side of the veil." His warm expression made my breath release.

"*Grazie.*" Maybe they didn't know who I was? By blood, anyway.

"Niccolò, I told you, you'd find someone you'd love more than magic."

The crowd cooed, and I blushed deeply as Nicco stepped back to my side.

"Only took four centuries," Giovanna added, hooking her arm into mine.

Our gazes stayed locked as the crowd lifted Nicco up with a song. We joined the procession into the palazzo, and my watchful eye never left him.

"Can I dress you properly now that he's safe and sound?" Giovanna asked.

I shook my head. I didn't care if I looked like a walking corpse. I was never letting him out of my sight again.

When spirits come to the Afterworld, they're supposed to stay. Something Ghede-Nibo had said fought for space in my head. But the cheerful singing grew louder, pushing the thought away, and I was once again swept up in the familial love.

My magic pulsed stronger as we entered the castle, surrounded by the generations of powerful witches. Why wouldn't anyone want to stay here?

Giovanna's arm hooked tighter into mine. Maybe I did need a new dress.

CHAPTER 31
HOUSE OF MIRRORS

Nicco killed her . . .
Nicco killed Adele's magical ancestor.

Nicco had been after León Saint-Germain for centuries. He had killed Adeline Saint-Germain, and now he had Adele under his spell.

I pumped my wings harder, eyes on the street, cawing out to all the spirits below, asking if anyone had seen a girl with long brown hair, a leather jacket, a mark of Fire, and a strong pulse. Dozens responded, floating out of their homes and onto the street, but none with the answer I needed.

Olsin had been right. But . . . I'd seen the way Nicco looked at Adele, how territorial he got around her. How could he kill her if he was in love with her? Only a monster could . . .

I nearly fell out of the sky as it hit me. This was no longer just about the feud. *Nicco's going to turn her into a monster too, so she'll be at his side forever.*

Fuck.

I'd driven her straight into that killer's arms. If he hurt her, I'd never be able to live with myself.

I needed help. Susannah. Doubye. Anyone. I couldn't do a

location spell because Dee had put something in our gris-gris so we couldn't be tracked. *Shit!* I needed to find Adele before he did.

A woman's scream split the night, and my heart spilled out of my chest. I cawed and dove toward the voice with a whoosh of Air. Another scream rang out, short and sharp, then something in French. *I know that voice.* I wove through ghostly figures on the street and soared into a restaurant courtyard where a skeleton quartet played jazz. In the far corner, a blonde girl was curled into a ball on the ground, rocking and clutching her head. "*Pardonnez-moi, mes soeurs!*"

I dropped down, taking human form. "Lisette?"

"*Pardonnez-moi, mes soeurs!*" she kept repeating, eyes clamped shut, mascara smeared with tears, shreds of her hair torn from her head. *Jesus.*

"Lisette!" I shook her shoulder. "Lisette, look at me!" But she wouldn't. I glanced around. "Did anyone see what happened to her?"

No one responded, but then a woman in a boxy red hat put down her cup of coffee and pointed to a balcony above the open courtyard where a white lacy hammock cradled a skeletal Black girl. Her arm hung down toward us in a cascade of tight braids, and her soft features and longing expression made her appear dainty and demure. A tarantula ten times bigger than Spinderella rested on her shoulder, legs thrumming as if it were watching, waiting, its beady eyes glowing purple just like the girl's. *Ghede-Zaranye.*

"*Mes soeurs,*" Lisette mumbled.

"Lisette, it's Isaac!" I tried to sit her up, but she pushed back with vampiric strength and sent me skidding across the bricks. Jesus Christ, I didn't need this right now.

I hurried back. What the hell kind of nightmare did Zaranye have her in? "Lisette, listen to me!" Her hands shot out and clutched my wrists, the world spun, and I fell through the ground into darkness.

I landed with a thud next to her. She was still sitting up, hugging her knees, shivering. Her hair was wild and her eyes bloodshot.

Where are we?

Tall mirrors encircled us like in the Fun House at Luna Park. In them, a reflection of Lisette whipped around, taunting, "*Meurtrière! Meurtrière! Meurtrière de sœure!*"

"Lisette, come on," I said as gently as I could. "We have to go."

"*Elles me détestent.*" She looked up at me with her big golden eyes, fangs fully engorged. "I wasn't always like this, you know?"

"Like what?"

"I used to sing for the king, and I had suitors, and magic, and I adored the sunshine and fresh baguettes. My sisters loved me."

"They still love you," I said, and a swirl of laughter came from around the room.

Tears flooded from her eyes. "They hate me." Her reflection split in two, and the taunting doubled. "*Elles me détestent.*" She cradled her head, screaming.

One version of her in the mirror was ultra-prim, with hair tightly done up, and the other was sexy as hell, although I couldn't explain why, 'cause they looked nearly identical. The way she stood, the way her eyes pierced directly into my soul, the way her smile turned up the tiniest bit. Kind of how I'd always imagined . . . *Cosette*.

They weren't her reflection. *They're her sisters.*

"*Lisette*, this isn't real. You have to trust me!"

The taunting suddenly stopped.

"My sister," Cosette said to us, "once the most beautiful girl on either side of the Atlantic. Sweet as honey, the innocence of a virgin, and the budding magic of a great sorceress."

Lisette smiled and blinked away some of the tears.

"Now you're just a *whore* lying with that vampire!"

Lisette choked, holding in a sob.

"I died for you!" Minette told her, lip quivering.

"She wanted Gabriel to bite her," Cosette snipped. "She was always jealous of Adeline. She wanted to taste his blood!"

"No, I didn't!" Lisette yelled, shaking. "I didn't want this. You abandoned me!"

"You were a witch," Minette said. "The youngest witch! You're supposed to be the strongest. Why didn't you escape? You were magical!"

Tears burst from Lisette's eyes. "I don't deserve magic. I'm a monster. I've always been a monster. I want to die." She grabbed my shirt, pulling me closer with a snarl, and her hand whipped up my pant leg to the stake strapped to my ankle. "Please, kill me. I know what you think of me." She thrust it into my palm.

"*Whoa.*"

"You killed Brigitte; I know you can do it!"

"*No*. Lisette, you have to listen to me. These aren't your sisters. It's the Ghede messing with your head!"

"I just want it to end!" She grabbed my hand and pulled it close to her chest, the tip of the stake digging into her skin. "I know you want to kill me!"

"No, I don't!" I yanked my hand back. "And your sisters don't want you to die either!"

The two blondes danced all around us in the mirrors, jeering at her. Tormenting her. Lisette cried harder. She grabbed for the stake again, but I snatched it away. "*You are not a monster!*" I yelled and hurled it straight into the mirror. It broke with a thunderous crack, and I threw myself over her as it shattered. I held my breath, waiting for the glass to rain down on us—but it didn't.

We both peeked out from under my arms. The shards were

dissipating into glimmering waves of purple smoke. We were back on Bourbon Street.

Jesus Christ. Did she really want to kill herself? I sucked in a deep breath, trying to wipe the fear I felt for her from my face. "Are you okay?"

She nodded, unable to look up at me, still violently shaking.

I rubbed her shoulder, unsure what else to do, and gave Zaranye my best Borges deathstare. I began to explain to her that the Ghede had tricked each of us upon arrival, but I wasn't sure she was even listening until her arms slowly unlocked from around her knees and her eyes met mine.

"Before . . ." she said. "Were you just saying that?"

"Saying what?"

"That I'm not a monster."

"Oh." *Had I said that?*

"I killed my sister. My own triplet. My own darling Minette." A few latent tears dripped from her eyes.

"You're not a monster." I pushed her hair away from her face. "Gabriel Medici is the monster for what he did to you and Minette." I didn't even know what I believed anymore.

She sniffled sharply, and her fangs retracted.

"Merci," she whispered. She pulled me up and then wiped her eyes on her arm.

The stake rolled to my foot, and I slipped it back in place.

"You don't need that, now, you know? Emilio isn't going to attack you again."

"I'm not worried about Emilio. We have to find Adele before Nicco hurts her."

She scoffed. "Niccolò would never hurt Adele. Don't you see the way he looks at her? He loves her . . ." Her voice pulled back as she realized what she said.

"Well, maybe *that's* the problem."

"A problem for her? Or a problem for you? Niccolò has more

control of himself than I could ever dream of. More than any vampire ever known, his brothers say."

"So then it was premeditated when he killed Adeline Saint-Germain?"

"What?" Her surprise seemed genuine. "He must have been trying to break the curse. To save Gabriel."

"He would've had to kill her entire coven to break the curse, and that would only have worked if none of them had children yet."

"I guess she never gave them up. Even in death, Adeline protected her coven."

"*Your* coven."

"I don't have magic. I'm not a witch anymore."

I lifted her arm. "You still have your Maleficium. If it was good enough to get you into Guinée, it's good enough for me, and it should be good enough for you."

She smiled bleakly and murmured to herself, almost in disbelief, "Adeline protected our coven. My surviving sister. Our magical bloodline."

I picked up my bag. "And now we have to find Adele before Nicco can hurt her, or it will all have been for nothing. She's the last in the Saint-Germain magical bloodline."

Her brow furrowed with conflict. "How do we find her?"

"I don't know." I pulled out my grimoire. It wasn't a magical dilemma—it was a more dire flesh and blood dilemma—but magic was the only place I could think to turn. "There has to be something in here."

Lisette craned her neck up at the arachnid Ghede in her spiderweb hammock. "*Savez-vous où trouver Adele?*"

"*Elle était avec le vampire.*"

My pulse skipped. I didn't need Lisette to translate that one.

CHAPTER 32
UNSCARRED

Nicco's fangless bite sank into a roasted turkey leg, and I'd never seen such joy. Grease dribbled onto his chin—it was the most unkempt I'd ever seen him. After the cheerful singing and tearful reunions had subsided, we'd been seated at a long table, and a feast fit for Olympus was served. I reached for my chalice, but he stopped me as I brought it to my lips. He blotted his face with a napkin. "No food of the dead for you." He raised his hand, and in a blink, the contents of my bag were presented before me on a silver platter. The cookies he'd baked for Floralia, fresh strawberries, Edgar Daure's meat pies. I guzzled the fizzy ginger-lemonade.

Nicco's grandparents—the man who Jakome Salazar had killed when the Ghost Drinkers raided their home, and the woman who'd later sentenced them all to be buried alive—sat on my other side. His grandmother leaned into me. "Your eyes," she said. "Dark and blue as the bottom of the sea . . . just like León's." My pulse sped. Was this it, the moment I was going to be outed and then cast aside? "But they twinkle like a Medici's."

Breathe, Adele.

Her soft, wrinkly hand grazed the scar along my cheek. "Who gave it to you?"

"Oh." I touched my face, covering it up. I hated naming Isaac. It gave the wrong impression of him. "It was nothing. A bird— an accident." One he'd never forgive himself for as long as he lived. It felt like a million years since I'd last seen him. Everything in the Natural World felt a million miles away. I wondered where he was. Whether he was okay.

But then Nicco's arm curled around my waist, and he pulled me closer. "*Ciao.*"

And I was lost once again in his gaze.

The music started, and he swept me up and into a ballroom with his dozens of cousins, all wearing medieval tunics and sumptuous Renaissance gowns made of luxurious velvets. And lace. So much beautiful Italian lace. Couples paired off, falling into a formation inherent to everyone but me. It didn't matter, though. Nicco twirled me around with all the charm of a Medici, the grace of his centuries as a vampire, and the weightlessness of a wraith. But he was still strong and solid in my arms, just like always.

When the dance ended and people dispersed, he held me close, gently swaying to the lingering plucks of a harp. His peaceful smile made my heart swell so huge it hurt. He took a deep breath. "I've dreamt of this for so long."

"Of what?"

"Of being so close to you . . ." His arms tightened around my waist as he spoke softly into my ear. "Of inhaling your scent so deeply, of desiring you so achingly, and not wanting to hurt you." His not-so-innocent smile brushed my neck. "Of only wanting to taste you in ways that wouldn't send me to Hell." His soft lips nipped against my skin, and I held onto him tighter, trying not to melt into a puddle of spiderweb threads.

"You don't . . ." I sucked in a sharp inhale. "Believe in Hell."

He kissed me again. "You have to make me stop, *bella.*"

"I don't want you to stop." *Ever. I love you.*

"Tell him how you feel, bébé," Nibo's voice echoed in my head.

His kisses strengthened, and I curled into him, every dream I'd ever had of his touch rushing me at once. "Nicco, I—"

"You have to go," he whispered into my ear. "Now." His expression turned serious.

"I'm not leaving you," I said, despite the realization settling in: *he doesn't love me the way I love him.*

He tried to lift my arms from his shoulders, but I locked them like a child.

"You have to find the Salazars," he said.

"No." I shook my head.

He turned stern. "Adele, you have to kill Jakome."

"No, I don't." The music picked up. Louder and louder. The room spun like I'd drunk all of the Afterworld's champagne. "I'm *not* leaving."

"Adele, look at me!" He clutched my face. Droplets of water dripped onto my cheeks from his hair. He was shivering, soaking wet. "Adele," his voice trembled, no longer commanding. "I'm never going to hurt you."

"*What?*"

His forehead pressed against mine.

"You're freezing, Nicco."

"You have to believe me," he begged. I saw the flash of his fangs. "I'm never going to hurt you, I swear."

"H-ho-how are your fangs back?"

"You don't have to be scared of me, Adele."

"I carried your bones. I'm covered in your ash!"

"You're not covered in ash. You're beautiful," he whined as if in unbearable pain.

I looked down. The spiderwebs were gone, replaced with his flannel and jacket and my pants. The people were gone from the palazzo. It was just the two of us.

I blinked, and the dress was back. The harp player too.

"Get away from me, *bella*. You have to push me away!"

"*Je ne comprends pas.*"

"*Adele.*" His voice boomed from the sky.

A hand wrapped around my arm. It was his hand, but it wasn't. For a split second, there were two of him. The ghost of his former self, and the vampire I knew.

"Don't leave me, bella," the ghost whispered.

"I'll never leave you," I whispered back.

The other Nicco pulled my arm hard, lifting me from the ballroom floor, and I screamed as we went through the ceiling. Through a blast of light.

We tumbled into the night, rolling across a grass lawn, limbs tangled together before coming to an abrupt stop. The lights of Armstrong Park shone in the distance.

"They're wrong," he said emphatically. He locked his leg around me, pulling me close, his drenched pants soaking through mine. "They're all wrong."

"Who's wrong?"

"You have to believe me." Pain oozed from his voice. "I'm not going to hurt you."

"*I know that.*" I cupped his face. He kissed mine. "Nicco, what's wrong?"

He squeezed me tighter. Almost painfully so. "I can control myself, I swear. I can prove it." His tone begged for permission. My latent magic bubbled up within, as if in warning.

"O-okay." I didn't know what else to do.

He tilted me back on the grass.

"Why are you so wet?" I asked, trying to bring him back from wherever he was.

He nudged my chin with his nose, exposing my neck. "Nicco—?"

"They're wrong."

I gasped as his tongue swept up my jaw.

"It will only hurt for a second, *bella,* I swear."

"*What?*" The words rang with eerie familiarity. *His fantasy of us.* "Nicco!" His nail sliced my cheek, and I bolted up with a scream, but he'd pinned me down.

"Nicco . . ." His nostrils flared as he inhaled, and I felt the blood rushing from the reopened scar. He tugged his lower lip with his fang, staring at the blood dripping down my neck.

Thump-thump.

"*Nicco!*" I clutched him, tears welling. "I am *not* scared of you."

His eyes started to glaze over.

Thump-thump. Thump-thump. Thump-thump.

He lowered himself closer, his body pressing harder onto mine, forcing me to absorb his aggression. "I'm not scared of you, Nicco," I croaked. But he didn't hear me.

His lips touched the crimson drops on my collarbone, and a shudder rippled down his spine.

Tears shook from my eyes as his mouth swept higher. My muscles locked in terror, feeling his arousal. "You're not a monster, Nicco."

He dragged his mouth up the curve of my jaw.

"You're not . . ." I gasped, his tongue slithering up my face. "A monster."

Our eyes met.

The pain instantly began to fade. His forehead knocked against mine. "I'm never going to hurt you, Adele."

I nodded, unable to speak.

He kissed my eye, my cheek, my jaw, and shifted his weight so he wasn't so crushing.

I touched my face—the scar was gone.

He didn't hurt me. He healed me.

The shock was the only thing that kept all of my feelings from spilling out. Our noses grazed as his hand slid up my cheek, tilting my jaw to his. I'd never ached so badly for a kiss.

For anything.

But then he tensed. I saw the pain in his eyes. *He's about to reject me. He wants me. I know it.* The anxious thoughts rushed back, and the question spilled from my lips in a hasty whisper. "Are you still in love with Maddalena?"

His brow creased.

"Is that why you're about to push me away?"

"*No.*"

"What then?"

Thump-thump.

"I can't . . . be with you . . . because I have to tell you something."

I relaxed my grip, the hesitation in his voice filling me with more terror than his fangs had just moments ago. He pulled me onto my side next to him.

In the aching silence, his heart pounded harder than I'd ever felt it.

"I wasn't trying to hide my memories of Maddalena, or my fantasies about you, although I wish you hadn't seen those. I was hiding . . . something else." His gaze dropped. "A memory from another time."

Thump-thump.

The sorrow grew in his eyes. "I understand if you never want to—"

"They're memories, Niccolò." I slid my hand beneath his shirt, to his back, and pulled myself closer. "I don't care about your past."

Our gazes locked. "I killed Adeline Saint-Germain."

My arm froze around him. My gaze froze. I swore the air around us froze, crackling like a pond in midwinter.

He said something, pleading, but all I heard was Adeline's voice in my head . . .

"*Reste loin de Niccolò Medici.*"

CHAPTER 33
DEATHBED CURSE

Adele didn't speak.

She didn't retreat, nor did she break my gaze. I swore she was even tempering the rhythm of her heartbeat, a trick she'd surely picked up from me. Was she trying to figure out if I was her enemy? If I always had been? The taste of her blood swelled on my tongue, and Séraphine's voice sang in the back of my head like a creeping adagio. Slow and steady, demanding the attention of the finale. *"You're going to kill her, Niccolò."* I focused on the scent of the dead in the air, *not her blood.*

Thump-thump.

"Adele—"

"I don't believe you." She pulled her hand from beneath my shirt. Did she think she'd need it to reach the dagger behind hers?

"I should have told you sooner." A rush of nervousness caught me off guard; it had been so long since I'd felt the sensation. I was unsure whether I feared her reaction or my own as the taste of her blood dwindled. I wanted more.

Maddalena's voice hummed in my ear. *"She'll still love you."* That wasn't Maddalena, Niccolò.

"I don't believe you," she said, the shine in her eyes sharp as diamonds. "This isn't real. The fire wasn't real. The bell tower. The palazzo. None of this is real." She stood, taking a step back.

Thump-thump. Thump-thump. Thump-thump.

She knew it was real—her fear tugged at me, but I didn't move. I didn't want her to feel threatened. The restraint made my gums throb.

"You're just trying to push me away!" The blood pumped harder from her ventricles into her neck, and my head spun. She backed away, and I nearly lunged.

"She'll still love you, Niccolò, just like I do."

I pinched my forehead. *I have to have her.*

I needed her.

"You're trying to cover something up so I won't get hurt, like when you told me you killed my moth—"

"I'm not," I spat, the monster within ready to take control, to grab her, to incapacitate her with my venom. *You told her we shouldn't come here. To never trust a vampire.* I shouldn't have healed her scar. Tasted her blood. Not here. Not now. Not ever.

"You're not a mon—"

"I killed Adeline Saint-Germain!" I sprang up. "I drank every last drop of her blood for locking up my family—for killing my sister!"

A breeze fluttered her hair. She couldn't hide the shock from her eyes. Silent streams poured down her cheeks. "Do you regret it?"

It would have been so easy to lie. To smooth this whole thing over with a simple story of invented remorse.

"No," I said coldly.

She didn't flinch.

"Or I didn't regret it." My voice softened. "Until now. Because of the stake it will drive between us."

She stared at me, her eyes hollow, giving me no indication of her true feelings. "How did you do it?"

"Adele, it doesn't matter. I took her life."

"I want to know. Was she in pain? Did you hold her prisoner like the witches from the swamp? Torture her? Tell me."

"*Bella—*"

"Tell me!"

"The details aren't going to help—"

She raised her hand. "Show me the memory!"

". . . but I'll tell you anything—"

A white bolt shot from her hand, throwing me to the ground. *"Che diavolvo?"*

She stepped closer, her eyes bright with color but void of comprehension. "Show me the night you killed Adeline Saint-Germain."

I fell back, my head knocking the ground, and the dream unfurled before my eyes, a glowing curl of white light pulling from my mind.

The bells of the cathedral ring in the Square. It's time. I drink back the final sip of the absinthe, savoring the last bitter drops.

"Another?" the barman asks in French.

"Non," I answer, picking up my hat. "Ça sera tout pour ce soir."

"Meeting someone special?" he asks.

"A peculiar question."

"The glint in your eyes is twinkling like you're about to be touched by an angel."

"She's no angel," I say, tossing a coin on the bar.

He huffs out a laugh.

"I'll take the bottle." I set a few more coins down.

He wraps three cubes of sugar into a small cloth and ties it off with string "Melt a little of this into her glass and the Green Faery will tame your devil."

"Keep your sweets. I'll tame her myself."

The absinthe is for my siblings. Gabriel always enjoyed chasing la Fée Verte.

Of course, I have something far more delectable waiting for their welcome home: two French cadets, a strapping Spaniard sailor, and three of the Madame's sweetest tarts from all over the Caribbean. I imagine the girls back at the house, clothing each other, surprised to find the formal dresses I left for them. The high necklines and lacy neckerchiefs. The cameos on strands of pearls for their throats instead of risqué robes and provocative petticoats. I want Giovanna to take delight in unwrapping each of the beautiful presents.

I tip my hat to the barman and put the bottle in my satchel, tempering my excitement before I fade into the night. He needs to remember me as just another louse on the way to the whorehouse. I don't want to be memorable, not when so many would soon go missing.

No matter how hard I might try tonight, I'll never be able to control my siblings, not after they've been locked up for so long. The best I can do to avoid a vampiric spree through these slate streets is to have a private cornucopia awaiting to welcome them home.

I pull my collar higher and tip my hat lower, careful to keep a reasonable mortal pace. I'm sure every person I pass under the gas lamps can sense my excitement, no matter how hard I try to suppress it.

A few blocks from her pied-à-terre, I disappear into a dark alleyway and wait. The breeze rolls off the river, carrying the voices of the crowd filtering out of the basilica after the evening mass. I hear her voice among them, and I can hardly keep my fangs at bay.

Tonight is the night. *Every predatory instinct tells me so, and my phantom magical intuition agrees.*

I know every beat of her routine: when she mails her letters, when she buys her spell-casting supplies from the Kreyòl witch (always under the guise of drinking café au lait), when she makes love to her husband, and when she leaves her children with the nursemaid to attend an extra mass . . . and then slips away to her secret cottage. She longs for the excitement of Paris, for the proximity of the other chic European capitals. Her torrid rendezvous with the blonde French Aether witch are all that she lives for in this provincial hellhole of a town.

Well, Adeline, maybe if your father hadn't been such a rat-bastard traitor, he wouldn't have had to ship you off here.

Every inch of the pied-à-terre is warded to hell and back, but on the way, she lets her guard down under a billow of excitement and a cloak of invisibility. A garment Cosette gifted her.

I close my eyes, tune out the rest of the Vieux Carré, and listen for her pitter-patter. Each human's gait is unique, and her footsteps are light and quick, with the sharp click of aristocratic footwear.

She turns onto Rue Burgundy. I listen for her breaths beneath the invisibility, the scent of her sweet Parisian parfum. The waft of her magic fills my senses. Just as I start to lunge . . .

She pauses.

Her breathing halts. Her pulse spikes. And her shoes make the slightest scrape on the slate as she turns. I can't see her face, but I sense her surprise. The scent of fire wafts my way, the invisibility cloak hiding the flames in her palms, and the longing for my Fire makes my fangs extend.

She darts forward, and in a blur, I have her in my arms and sweep her into the alleyway across the street—the attack perfectly hidden by the Monvoisin cloak.

The hood slips off, and she screams for Cosette, but I jam my arm across her lips, stifling her voice.

She flails like a wild hare, but my fangs sink into her neck, and my venom releases. On her exhale, the blood spills quicker, and for a brief euphoric moment, I imagine that she is her father. She bites savagely into my arm, kicks my groin, and jabs my ribs with her elbow as I drink, but it's only when she rips the iron gas lantern from the wall and smashes it down onto my head that I notice anything other than her familiar scent and the taste of her Saint-Germain blood. Warmth pools into my scalp, but I shake off the glass and throw her to the ground. All I see is the look of León in her livid eyes as she scurries backward through the piles of trash and puddles of sewage where her family belongs. She's smart enough not to scream; her magic is a hundred times more effective than any man who might come to her aid.

She rips another lantern from the brick wall and hurls it at my chest, but I bat it away, carelessly breaking my hand. "You will never have my father." She seethes with defiance as she speaks.

I step closer.

She pushes herself away, each of her movements slower than the one before; the paralysis is settling in, my poison coursing through her bloodstream. She has nothing more to fear. I'm not going to kill her; that would just make it harder to find León.

"I know it was you who cursed my family," I spit.

"You are talking nonsense," she says in French. "Monsieur Cartier.*"*

I grab her hair at the scalp. "Do not act like a stupide petite fille *with me, Adeline. You're going to release my family."*

I let go, and her head flops. She no longer has control over the muscles in her neck. The pale kerchief at her collar is red with blood. "I know you locked them in the convent attic."

She gazes at me with a wry smile. "I only locked one of them in the convent. Two, if you count Gabriel's progeny."

I clutch her throat. "I'm not playing games with you." She gasps for breath. "There is more than one way to break a curse."

"My daughter will inherit my magic. Including my curses. I can already see her mark!"

I can't help but let out a little laugh. "You think I won't hesitate to kill your daughter?"

"I will protect all of my progeny from you, devil, just like I protected my father. Now and for eternity!"

I plunge into her open vein and suck. I'm not leaving La Nouvelle-Orléans without my family, and I don't care if I have to kill every single member of hers in order to do so.

"Monster," she gasps, clawing at my face.

Her heartbeat slows as her blood slurps between my lips. The Saint-Germains took my parents from me along with everything I loved. She'd have to slay me before I'd let her take my brothers. Before I'd let her take Giovanna.

Her palms warm against my back, but she cannot produce her flames through the paralysis. Her fingernails dig into my flesh as she fights through the venom.

She raises her gaze to the sky. "To the Old goddesses, I call to you.

> *"Give me the strength, ignite my magic one last time.*
> *Take my life, take my spirit, but upon my death, bind this monster's blood to mine."*

I tear her artery open wider, and she chokes out the words: "For the fruit of my womb, and all those born hereafter, as long as blood flows through his veins, I curse you, Niccolò Medici! If anyone who shares your blood or bears your family's name brings harm to mine, you will suffer the same fate—I curse you!"

Thunder booms, and lightning cracks against the sky. Desperate to silence her, I glug her blood faster than I can swallow, but I cannot stop her last three words.

"I curse you."

A voice bellows from the moon: "Stop her, Niccolò! You can't let her see this!"

"Stop what? She deserves to die!"

"Stop Adele! You must wake up! Don't show her this horror!"

Adele? Panic floods in.

Adeline's dead eyes stare back at me, and I toss her across the alleyway, realizing what I've done. What I've shown Adele. "No." *I shrink against the brick wall, arms curled over my head.* "Get out, Adele. Get out!"

I popped my eyes open to a bright, blinding light. The bolt fizzled as I regained consciousness. It was me lying on the ground, not Adeline. Adele wobbled in front of me—no, it was just my vision, seeing double. I touched the back of my bloody head, disoriented. Had it been another trick? I looked around for a Ghede, but then I remembered the argument. *The bolt of magic.*

"Adele, what was that?"

She stared at me blankly. Was she even aware of the magic she'd produced? She just *pulled a memory from my mind.* I'd always thought the dream-twinning was some product of the curse. Of us being magically linked by Adeline all those years ago. But had it been her magic the entire time? Plucking out my memories? My fantasies? Was that why I never saw hers?

"Adele—"

"You started coming around after I broke the curse . . ." A steady stream of tears poured down her cheeks. "Is that all I ever was to you? Something you've been forced to protect from your family lest you suffer the same fate?"

The question hurt me more than I could have imagined.

"You're going to kill her, Nicco." Voices swirled in my head, and I saw her face floating in the swamp with Adeline's, with Maddalena's and Séraphine's. *"He'll never want you after this."* I saw the Ghost Drinker slamming her to the ground to defile her —to hurt her because of me. *"She dies with her blood on your lips."* I heard the old psychic's premonition.

"Trouble follows her because of you!"

"You're a monster, Niccolò. A monster. A monster. Monster. Monster!"

Thump-thump. Thump-thump. Thump-thump.

"Sì." I stifled the emotion in my voice, looking up at her. Cool and stoic. "That's all you ever were. There's nothing between us but the product of a curse."

As I stood, her gaze rose with mine.

"You were a way to free my family. And a way to find León. *L'elisir di vita.* I told you to never trust a vampire."

I waited for her to yell, to throw her bag at me, to wield her magic and blast me to Hell, but she calmly stepped closer. "I can hear the thumps of your heart. You're lying, Niccolò Medici, and I know you can control yourself better than this. You're *letting* me hear them. You want me to know the truth."

I blinked the tears away before they could form, and she came nearer, unafraid.

"You told me not to let you push me away." The ache in her tone was splitting.

But I steadied my breathing, and my pulse silenced completely. "Do you believe me now?"

She picked up her bag and turned to walk away. "I'm going to find Adeline," she said, a deadness in her voice. "I owe her an apology. It's probably best that you don't come."

CHAPTER 34
HOUSE OF SALAZAR

I kept my pace steady just in case Nicco was still watching me walk away, but as soon as I turned the corner, I ran to the nearest alleyway, a memory flooding from somewhere deep in my subconscious—from when my mother's venom had flowed through my veins.

Nicco scooped me off the convent floor and raced me through the streets.

I'd felt his strength weakening as he carried me up the bell tower stairs, and in my delusional state, I'd thought maybe he was weak from being starved, or that he'd been hurt in the battle. He'd seemed so concerned when he gently set me down. When he made me take his blood.

So caring. Loving.

His heartbeats had grown slower. Fainter. *"You have to survive this, Adele,"* he'd said softly before his hand circled my wrist, two fingers placed over my pulse. *"You have to survive this for us."*

Thump . . . thump.

Thump . . . . . . thump.

Thump.

I hadn't remembered his words until now, but they'd planted an invisible seed of hope in my heart. Now they had a different meaning. He'd needed me to survive because if I'd died at the hands of his family, he would have perished too.

I was barely out of the moonlight and into the shadows before I lurched forward, holding my stomach, bile spewing from my lips.

I felt like I was expelling part of my soul. My twin-flame.

Adeline had died in an alley just like this one. Was this what she had been trying to tell me when I broke off the connection at the séance?

Of course it was.

My chest lit up like the bell tower fire. It didn't make sense. I'd been able to use my magic when I'd revealed my love for him. Ghede dream or not, the love was real. I hadn't even known what love was until those bars were placed between us.

It has to be real.

The truth dawned on me, clear as the morning light: just because it was real for me, that didn't mean it was real for him.

I bet Séraphine thought their love was real.

Never trust a vampire.

Never trust a Medici.

Reste loin de Niccolò Medici.

I leaned against the damp brick wall and counted my breaths. *Focus on the mission, Adele, the reason you're here.* Jakome Salazar. I forced the tears back and gargled a minty peach drink from my pack. I commanded myself to forget about Nicco as I spit it out and took off.

But wandering down the street without him at my side, everything went back to feeling wrong.

Aimless.

Somehow, my feet knew exactly where they were going, and soon I was watching the vines slither away from the brothel gate. I hurried around to the back, past the fountain and the pigeonnier, barely breathing until I found her. I collapsed at my mother's feet and rested against her cool bronze legs, no longer able to keep the torrent of emotion in.

Adeline had *died* protecting her father. Her daughter. All of her descendants. She had died protecting our magical line. She'd died protecting . . . me.

And I'd allowed our Fire to be stolen by Callis.

Under my watch, he'd taken my father.

I'd spent more time in Nicco's head than trying to figure out what it meant to be a Saint-Germain. *That's why you went into his head in the first place, Adele. To discover more information about your family.*

Oui, but it wasn't the only reason, I finally admitted to myself.

I'd hurt Isaac in the process, and I'd lost my best friend. Tears streamed down my face. I hadn't meant to. I did love him. It just wasn't the same.

He was never going to forgive me for it.

I was back on the little boat in the black sea. Alone.

"Mom, I'm sorry," I cried. "I'm sorry I didn't talk to you for so long. I'm sorry I didn't figure out your secret sooner. I'm sorry I couldn't save you—I'm a witch. I had magic. I should have. Adeline would have. I swear, though, I'm going to save Dad. I swear. *I swear.* I don't care what I have to do."

Her knees slid down my back, her arms around my shoulders. "You're not alone, baby. We're always with you. The spirits of your ancestors, magical or not."

I twisted around. "Mom?" My throat burned. Her eyes flickered violet before settling into the familiar gray-blue I remembered. She was so pretty. "You're not a witch. How are you in Guinée?"

"Adele, I'm always with you—since the very first moment I felt you kick—and I always will be. I may not have had magic to give you, but you have my heart, and I will always be behind you."

"*Mom, I love you.*"

"I love you too." She kissed my cheek. "My darling, you have to stop blaming yourself for everything. I was not your responsibility. Isaac is not your responsibility. Even your father. He's a very strong man."

The tears came harder. "Mom, I can't lose him."

"Then *get up* and fight. You have remarkable friends, Adele. And family isn't just about blood or magic or surnames. You grew up with every character in the Vieux Carré watching over you."

"I know." I shook my head. "But still— I'm sorry that I couldn't save—"

"*Shh.* I'm free now. Isaac freed me from Emilio Medici. From the torment of being separated from you and Mac. You're going to grow into a strong, beautiful witch, and you'll be able to contact me whenever you want. And if you don't, that's okay too. I'll still be with you in here." She pressed her hand over my heart. "Forever."

I nodded, trying to smile. It looked like there was still something she wanted to say. "*Qu'est-ce que c'est?*"

She hesitated, her eyes watering. "Could you tell your father something for me?"

"Of course."

"Tell him . . . that every decision I ever made was for us. Because I loved him. Because I loved you."

I nodded. "He loves you so much, Mom."

"And I'll never stop loving him."

I nodded again, the lump in my throat so large I couldn't speak.

"*Au revoir pour le moment, mon amour.*" Her eyes flashed violet again, and this time Nibo's face flickered in hers, and I knew he was the one who'd brought her here.

"*Merci beaucoup,*" I choked.

347

Her legs turned back to metal, and Nibo appeared next to me on the grass.

I took a slow inhale, twisting the ring around my finger. *Jakome's ring. When had I taken it out of my bag?*

"So. Did you tell zha vampire you love him?"

"*No*," I sputtered. "Thank God."

"Why thank God?"

My lips blew out with a huff. "It's complicated."

"All good loves are."

"This wasn't love; it was a delusion."

"Bitch, please. Did you think it was gonna be easy? He's a four-hundred-year-old vampire who killed one of zha most powerful witches in your family and is on zha hunt for zha other."

"You knew?"

"You didn't?"

"No!"

He shrugged. "So what?"

"So what? He killed Adeline!"

He shrugged again. "It was three hundred years ago. Besides, she killed his sister and trapped his brother. Left him alone in this cruel, cruel world. Seems fair."

"Fair! He didn't tell me about it. He didn't want to come to Guinée because he didn't want me to find out."

"He didn't want to come to Guinée because he didn't want to lose you."

"Then why did he come?"

"To save your papa. Because he knows it's what you need. And he put your needs above his desires."

"Yeah, because he's desperate for the Elixir."

"And why does he want zha Elixir?"

I held the ring up closer, examining it. "I don't know what Nicco wants. I don't know anything anymore." I rubbed my thumb over the mark of Fire.

"I thought you didn't care about your magic?"

I did my best to suppress a smile. "I care. I need it to save my dad. To find León and learn the truth." But it was more than that. "I need it because I'm a witch, and I don't want to exist without it."

"So zhen, what are you waiting for? A parade?"

Violins strummed in the distance. I turned toward the house. From the street beyond, a chorus of voices sang in Spanish, and the familiar beat of bass drums pounded through the ground and into my bones.

"What is it?" I asked, turning back, but Nibo was gone, only a purple shimmer remaining where he had been.

I made my way to the front of the brothel, where spirits glided down the street spinning ribbons in the air, swirls of periwinkle, rose, and orchid under the star-swept sky. Folks in papier-mâché skull masks tossed flower petals as musicians leapt joyfully, drawing bows dramatically across their instruments, playing a lullaby with the undertones of a dirge. A Ghede I didn't recognize twirled a young man down the street. The lwa's dark skin was taut across his bones, and the dust of ash gave him that ghastly Ghede appearance, but never had death looked so whimsical, with his long hair twists adorned with fluttering moths and his silver silk dress billowing with the ethereal danse macabre. Crowds had gathered on both sides of the street, and the family handed out masks and ribbons and chains of snapdragons.

A young Latina woman placed a flower necklace around my head. "My Miguel Ángel is finally home." Her gaze lingered on me, and an uneasy chill swept up my spine—could she sense my pulse like Nicco could? I thanked her and joined the procession, keeping near the drummers and their resonant beats. I accepted a ribbon and more flower chains and whatever else I was offered from the family so I could better blend in.

The celebration wasn't unlike a jazz funeral, but rather than a send-off, it was a homecoming for Miguel Ángel. A beautiful circle of death. As I was swept up in the ceremony of it all, a young woman in a long black cape passed in front of me pulling a young man along behind her. My eyes locked with his as he passed by, all raven-black curls and piercing blue eyes, and my pulse stopped as dead as the spirits around me. A triangular Maleficium peeked out just below his rolled-up sleeve.

Callis.

He turned back at me with a squint, but only the slightest hint of recognition formed in his gaze, and then he casually turned back around, the girl pulling him through the crowd. Fear swirled through my head as the ribbons swooped around my face. *Had he followed us? Had we left the portal open?* I inhaled sharply. *He doesn't know why you're here, Adele.*

Unless . . . *shit.*

Had Annabelle somehow communicated with him? I should have taken my chances with Emilio and left her to rot.

In my pocket, the ring warmed in my hand. I pulled it out and almost immediately stumbled, losing it from my grip. I lurched forward to snatch it back up, but it rolled away. *Is it urging me on?* Did it want to be reunited with Callis? I chased after it through buckled boots and glittered heels, like it was a runaway treasure along the Endymion route.

As I scooped it up, a woman offered me a skull mask.

"*Muchas gracias,*" I said and slipped it on, trying to find the head of dark curls in the crowd once again. *What is Callis doing here?*

When I caught sight of him up ahead, the panic bubbled just under my skin. *Was he Callis?* The guy might have been a little older. He was around the same height but more squarely built. Beneath the ghostly hue, his skin was darker. His tunic and trousers looked straight from a European history book.

My panic started to subside.

He wasn't Callis, but he was definitely a Salazar. He wasn't old enough to be Callisto's father. Was he a brother? Cousin? Whoever he was, maybe he could lead me to Jakome? I pulled my bag closer, feeling the ghoststick through the leather as I rushed forward. Going after Jakome by myself wasn't wise, but it might be my only chance to find him. I peered through the crowd one last time, hoping that some of my friends might have been swept up in the parade, but I didn't see anyone familiar.

I can do this. I'd used my magic earlier. It was still inside me, whether it had been a Ghede-dream or not. The pair turned off the parade route onto Toulouse, and I bounded forward to catch up, determined not to lose sight of those black curls. I couldn't help but remember the ring pulling me through the Salazar fortress, straight to Callisto at the side of his brother's bed. The fear I'd felt as his stare pierced me.

Hidden beneath the skull mask and mountain of flowers draped around my shoulders, I grew more courageous. But as I lurked through the shadows, I began to worry the festive props would draw unwanted attention. A couple walked by, one in a pink panda suit and the other in a corset and panties, and a smile grew inside me. No one was going to blink an eye. This was the French Quarter, Afterworld or not.

The Salazar couple turned onto Bourbon, and I wove in and out of the neon lights flashing on the busy street. Music poured from the open-doored cafés where spirits ate and drank and danced, living their best afterlives. It felt more like how I'd imagined Bourbon Street a century ago, before the T-shirt shops, feather boas, and neon-green hand grenades being slurped by sloppy-drunk tourists. *Where was the couple going? Dinner? Jazz? A magical cabal behind a club curtain?*

We turned off Bourbon, and the streets became darker and more desolate. A thought bubbled up: Could this be just another Ghede trick, leading me down another rabbit hole? *Shit.*

I couldn't risk losing the opportunity to find Jakome.

As we crossed Rampart, it felt odd leaving the confines of

the French Quarter. I tried to tell myself it was just because Rampart was the boundary my dad had always given me growing up. Pain twinged. I'd never complain about one of his lectures again, as long as I lived.

We passed Basin, and another memory stirred, making me faint. We were so close to the cemetery. The exact spot the Ghost Drinkers had chased me to. The exact spot where I'd— The next thought nearly knocked me over: *The Brute would be here in Guinée.* Wasn't he a Salazar? What if I was running straight into his lair?

I buckled over my knees taking a breath, losing sight of the couple as they rounded a looming tenement-style brick building. *Keep going, Adele. Just think about Mac. And of what the rest of the Salazars might be doing to him right now.* Fear rippled through my muscles in hot waves, but I sucked it up and ran toward the building. I was too late. They were gone. The windows in some of the apartments were open, and an aria in a language I didn't recognize floated out.

A man in a ribbed tank and tweed jacket sat on a lawn chair nearby, smoking a pipe. I slowed down, tipping my mask to him. "Did you see which way—?"

He nodded to the right, blowing smoke in my face.

"*Merci,*" I said, trying not to cough, and hurried around the building just in time to see them disappear into a lonely little Creole cottage right outside the cemetery wall.

The supernatural sensation overwhelmed me, just like the first time Callis had entered the café. Was this where they lived? The paint was chipped, and the roof sagged, but the plants surrounding it were lush and blossoming, a stark contrast to the cottage itself. The property was grim compared to the Medici castle, but for Fire witches, they sure had a green thumb.

I'll just look around a little, scout the property, and then I'll find my friends and return with them. As I edged out of the shadows, a light popped on outside the house, flooding over me, and the door opened.

A woman stepped out and looked straight at me.

I froze, every instinct telling me to get the hell out of here. The ring burned warm in my palm.

"My goodness." She dusted her hands on her apron. "They didn't tell us anyone was arriving today." She brushed her dark hair from her face, and I recognized her from the Basque funeral in the flashback—the sadness in her eyes. *She's Callisto's mother.*

Before I could step away, she rushed over, arms extended in a motherly embrace. "We would have come and received you! We don't often get new additions, but we still know how to celebrate!"

The mask, ribbons, and flowers. *Oh my God, she thinks I'm a dead Salazar.*

"And on such a magnificent day. Jakome is going to be beside himself. A gift from Illagari herself."

My pulse thrummed at the mention of his name. I let the ring slip back into my jacket pocket.

"You don't have to be frightened anymore, little one." Her hands were cold. "I'm Arrosa. What's your name?"

"Adele," I whispered, scarcely able to breathe.

"Zorion, put on the kettle!" she called, turning back toward the house. "Beñat, crack open a barrel of cider! Wake Donato and Clara!"

Two heads popped up in the doorway: the Callis lookalike and the dark-haired girl. She'd removed her cape and now wore only the black dress. *She's . . . She's the flier girl.*

"Adele?" she asked, rushing out. "When Nibo told me to make sure you got a ticket, I didn't realize— Why didn't he say —? No wonder you looked so lost!"

"Zorion, you've already met Adele?" her mother asked with consternation. "And you didn't bring her home, silly girl?"

"I didn't know! I wouldn't have left her!" She turned back to me. "Please forgive me."

"Of course." As she took my arm, I realized why she'd looked familiar when we first met in the Square. With her porcelain face and doll-like eyes, she looked like an older version of Celestina. Although her cheeks were rosier and she was so much more full of life, despite being dead. Had Nibo sent me to her from the start? Had he been trying to get me to Jakome all along? *Damnit!*

They ushered me into the house. *What if the Brute is here?* My heart pounded wildly as we crossed the threshold. *So much for waiting for my friends.*

"I'll show you all around Guinée," Zorion said, guiding me through a modest living room. "You can stay with me until we make up a room for you."

The furnishings seemed to have been collected from different eras: Persian rugs, gothic Victorian chairs, and dark leather couches, all worn down to the threads in spots. Stacks of fliers and show posters lined a mid-century coffee table. An iron was turned on next to a garment rack of brightly colored clothes, emitting a cloud of steam, freeing them from wrinkles.

"We're going to be the best of friends." Zorion was so chipper, it was hard imagining her related to Callisto or Celestina. She whisked me through to a simple kitchen. The stone floor and woodburning oven took me back further in time; it reminded me of *Hansel and Gretel.* I couldn't help feeling like I was about to be baked into a pie.

A pile of potatoes was peeled on the table, the scraps in a small heap. Arrosa hurriedly moved it all away. "Sit," she said, offering a chair.

Savory aromas filled the room from the oven. *This is crazy.* I hadn't even had to sneak in. Maybe this was going to be easier than I thought?

Beñat entered the room, popping the cork from a jug, while

Zorion placed four metal chalices on the table. She seemed a little younger than me. With Callisto as a brother, I shuddered at how she might have died.

"I brought something better than cider," Beñat said to me with a smile. "To remind you of home."

They all seemed so genuinely delighted. Not at all like a coven of malicious witches plotting to take over Europe. *It was centuries ago, Adele.*

They each grabbed a cup, and Arrosa handed me the fourth. *Shit.*

My stomach roiled as they raised their glasses. Why exactly weren't we supposed to eat or drink the food of the dead? Wasn't Persephone forced to remain in the Underworld after she ate three freaking pomegranate seeds? *Persephone's not real, Adele. Yeah, what if real is worse?*

The conversation paused as they waited for me to pick up the drink.

"Um." I lifted the cup.

They all smiled, holding up their chalices. "To Adele."

"What a terribly French name," said Beñat.

"I think it's pretty," Zorion said. "Does that mean Callisto settled in France? Did he marry a French lady?"

They think I'm his descendant. I wanted to hurl at the idea of sharing blood with him. Sharing anything with him.

The matriarch stared at me as she swirled her cup. "There's something different about you, and it's not just your name." She inhaled deeply. "You smell different."

"Mama!" Zorion's cup splashed a little over the rim. "Don't be a goat!"

Arrosa looked at me so curiously a rush of heat washed through me. "It's just . . ." *My beating heart.* "Lavender."

She brought her hand to her chest. "I beg your pardon. It's been so long since anyone has joined us, I'm afraid I'd forgotten that the newly dead sometimes arrive with the lingering scent of the living."

"It's fine." I gave them a little smile. "I'm sure I'll smell dead soon." *Soon meaning at least another fifty-plus years.*

They once again raised their cups, and I had no choice but to follow suit unless I wanted to further raise suspicion. They made a toast in Basque. The language didn't remotely resemble Spanish, which I could barely understand anyway, but I smiled and nodded, my hand shaking as I brought the cup to my lips. It smelled bitter like licorice. I must have made a face because Zorion started laughing as she gulped hers back.

"What is it?" I asked as she wiped the dribble from her chin.

Beñat's forehead scrunched. "It's pili, of course."

"What's pili?"

They all gave me a questioning look. *Shit.*

"Mandrake liqueur," Arrosa answered, as if it was as common as Coca-Cola.

"Mama!" Zori said, pouring another. "Maybe they don't drink pili anymore in Basque Country. Look at her strange clothes. Clearly things are different now."

"I-I've never been to Spain. I was born in New Orleans. My mother was French, my father American."

"*America*," they gasped.

"Of course. I'm so sorry." Arrosa held her hand over her face. "How could I be so thoughtless?" She squeezed the hands of her children, looking at each of them with glistening eyes. "You were the last generation born on our ancient ancestral grounds. It's just so hard to imagine our family in any other place."

My heart tugged for them. "I'd like to go there someday," I said, dazedly, reminding myself of the reason they'd been excommunicated.

Beñat laughed politely. "I think you meant, you'd like to have gone there."

"Right!" I jolted up, splashing a little of the liqueur on my hand.

Arrosa tried her best to hide it, but I could see the growing suspicion in her eyes.

"Sorry, I'm still getting used to the idea that I'm not going back." I suddenly found myself wishing Isaac was here with his fast-talking New Yorker ways.

But then Arrosa kissed my face. "You'll need to go no further to get a taste of the homeland. We'll fill your heart with all of her tales!" She went to the oven.

I'd rather give up my witch status than be further indoctrinated into the cult of Salazar. I barely heard what they said next; all I could focus on was the pie she'd removed. An intoxicating aroma wafted over us. I'd barely gotten away with not drinking the pili. As Zorion went on about the theatre and tickets and reserved seating, Arrosa cut four slices and put the plates in front of us. She watched me watching her, and I got the feeling she still wasn't a hundred percent sold on the story I'd spun.

"Quince and cherry pie," she said. Something in her voice let me know that this was a test. "Surely you like cherries?"

"*Mm-hm.*"

Zorion and Beñat picked up their spoons, shoveling in bites.

What would happen if I ate the food of the dead? What would happen if they found out I wasn't one of them?

I pinched off the tip and scooped it onto my spoon, half expecting worms or something gross to wiggle out, but it was just a gush of plump, perfectly baked fruit. It smelled delightful: buttery and sweet with a perfect hint of sour.

"You can sit next to me at the show," Zorion said. "It's going to be a *very* special performance."

"Very," her mother repeated, taking another sip from her chalice.

Maybe coming here by myself wasn't the brightest idea. I should have heeded my father's advice and not crossed Rampart

Street. Their bright eyes and bright smiles burned into my soul. *Come up with something, Adele.* Arrosa's gaze followed me as I brought the fork to my lips. Too late now.

I'm the worst liar.

Bottoms up.

I tried not to cringe as I placed the spoon between my lips.

A smile spread across Arrosa's face, one that seemed so warm and should have set me at perfect ease . . . and yet somehow it filled me with terror.

CHAPTER 35
LES FILLES D'OR

I don't know how long I waited in the park after Adele walked away. In my mind, I'd yelled for her to wait, but the words never left my throat. I'd known it was a risk coming to the Afterworld. She'd reacted as I'd expected she might: horrified. Although she didn't seem entirely shocked by my horrific deed, and I still hadn't decided if that made it better or worse.

With no plan and suddenly no raison d'être, I walked out of the park and back into the Quarter. I'd killed Adeline Saint-Germain in cold blood. There was nothing that could make it right.

You didn't have to hurt Adele.

It was for her own good. If I hadn't led Callisto to New Orleans, he would never have taken Mac.

Granted, if Adeline hadn't locked my family in the attic, we would never have been in New Orleans. Of course, if we hadn't been after León— If León hadn't stolen my grimoire . . . Everything always went back to León.

Now he'd taken her from me too.

She was never yours, Niccolò.

Put her out of your mind. Just eliminate these bastard Salazars and rescue Mac. Then my promises would be fulfilled, and I could take my family back to Florence where we belong. We would hunt León ourselves.

Surely Ghede-L'Oraille could tell me where to find the Salazars. It was the least she could do after dumping me in the swamp.

A sharp scream from nearby ripped through me like a steel blade. I took off in a dust of panic. *Why did I let her walk off?* Why did I push her away, *again*?

I whipped onto Orleans, just behind the cathedral, and slipped into a dark alleyway.

A man stood in the middle of the street, a black hooded cape billowing behind him, one arm lifted to the sky. A beam of light in his palm rose high into the air, illuminating the surrounding buildings. The magic jerked around as if it were attached to an invisible kite, ripping in the wind out of his control. He yanked the bolt, and another scream tore from the sky.

A woman was in his clutches. *Invisible.*

Had Annabelle gotten herself into trouble? Did I care? She was a lost cause, a liability, and I had no intention of letting her live when this was all over. The screams turned into French curses, a tongue sharp as a whip. A voice that unlocked long-forgotten memories.

Not Annabelle.

The hooded witch blasted a second bolt, and another scream came. Was he choking her? The magic felt familiar. It was not unlike the ethereal ropes the Ghost Drinkers had used at D-MORT.

Salazar.

I *will not* allow him to drink her spirit. He turned my way, as if he could suddenly sense my presence. My fangs ripped out. I may have only been a child when I last saw him, but I'd never forget Jakome Salazar's face. In a blur, I charged, crushing him in my arms. He roared and threw his weight back at me, refusing to let go of his magic. It burned bright around me, lighting us up like neon tubing.

"Who are you?" he growled as we tumbled to the ground.

"You murdered my grandfather," I hissed. He twisted away from my slashing bite, and we hit the curb so hard I popped up to the slate sideways, nearly breaking my ankle. Neither fang nor vampiric strength would be enough to kill Jakome's spirit-self. I needed the ghoststick. I shouldn't have let Adele walk away.

In a puff of ephemeral silver dust, he vanished. The bolt of magic broke.

The girl screamed as she fell. I caught her invisible form and set her down before I whipped to the street corner, and then to the next, trying to pick up a sound, a pulse, a scent, but there was nothing. I gazed up at the bell tower, cursing.

"*Niccolò Medici,*" the woman said.

The statue of Jesus stared down at me as if I was in trouble.

I casually turned around. She had reappeared down Orleans in the rising fog. Her slip was tousled, and her gaze was wild through the white-blonde hair hanging in her face, but I'd recognize her figure anywhere, even without her stays and bustle. I'm sure every man from eighteenth-century La Nouvelle-Orléans would have. And most of the King's Court prior. The pale pink satin slip draped each curve of her body like a gentle kiss.

Cosette Monvoisin was as mesmerizing in death as she had been in life.

I whipped toward her and asked in French: "Are you okay?" It was only polite.

"Back *away*," she said.

Midway to her, I came to a halt. Nervousness pricked me for the second time tonight.

Her face tightened like a cougar ready to charge, and for a moment, I hoped this was another trick of L'Oraille's. I took a step back and then ripped back toward the cathedral. *Not worth the risk.*

"Stop!" she yelled. I'd barely made it into Pirate's Alley. "Turn around."

Before I could even consider her request, my feet twisted, and I was facing her.

She walked toward me with long, confident strides, and her eyes pierced my soul, dredging up shame I didn't know I still had. She stopped right in front of me and leaned so close her breath bathed my ear. "Do you know that at night," she whispered in French, "I still dream about you?"

I smiled coyly. "Four centuries of men would envy me."

Her hand slipped up my chest to my shoulder, where she perched her chin like a prowling siren. "When Adeline is asleep, peacefully in my arms, I lie awake, fantasizing about killing you . . ."

I met her gaze. "Well, I guess it all worked out in the end. You get to spend eternity together."

"Climb the fence," she said, unamused.

"What?" But my feet were already turning to the cathedral garden, and before I could say another word, I jumped up, reaching for the wrought-iron bar, her magic washing through me like a bold Petit Verdot as I hoisted myself up onto the top of the fence.

"Higher," she commanded.

My muscles bent to leap, and I stiffened, trying to retain autonomy of my own limbs, but my legs bent to her will.

"*Higher.*"

I jumped onto the wall of the church and began to scale the building.

"You ruined my life," she said from down below, her aggression growing.

Niccolò, fight through it.

"You took her from me."

I climbed faster, reaching the bell tower steeple, and pulled myself onto the stone window ledge.

"You took everything from me!"

I turned to face her. The wind whipped so that I had to cling on to the shutters behind me.

"You killed my sisters." The air carried up her sharpening voice.

"That was my brother," I yelled, knowing that in this moment we might as well have been one and the same.

"You turned Lisette into a monster! She was so innocent!"

"She couldn't have been *that* innocent if she was entangled with Gabriel." I tried to pull myself backward into the bell tower, fighting hard against her Aether magic, but my arms wouldn't obey my commands.

"You're a disgrace to the witching world, Niccolò Medici. That Mark should be burned from your arm for the witches you killed." Her anger pummeled through my bones. "And your spirit never allowed to walk these sacred streets of Guinée!"

"Cosette!" I yelled, pleading. "This isn't the time."

"You destroyed my family. You killed my love."

The whistling wind stirred the fog below, and I stared down at the spiked fence.

"I will not let you kill her father, and I will not let you kill her heir!" She threw out her hands, and her strength crashed through me, spilling over my mind like a frolicking lullaby. *Is this what my venom felt like to others?*

"Jump," she commanded.

My body thrust forward, but I clung onto the shutters. *No.* I had promised Adele I would save her father.

"*Jump.*"

My body thrust again, and the right shutter broke off, crashing down, splintering when it hit the fence.

Her beautiful face contorted into a deadly sneer. "You will not take the Saint-Germains as long as my soul lives."

A sardonic laugh escaped my lips. Was his name to be

among the last words I heard before I met final death? The sweet irony of it all.

"*Niccolò, allons-y.*"

I stared down at the iron stakes. How many times had I wanted to shed myself of this fate? To reunite with my family. I shut my eyes as my body tipped forward, consumed with the truth that I had let Adele down, and I released my grip on the second shutter, unsure if it had been me or her Aether magic.

"*Non.*" As control slipped from my being, I remembered what fear felt like. "*Non!*" I yelled.

But then . . . gravity took me in her arms, and I felt free for the first time in four hundred years.

CHAPTER 36
THE MONSTER FALLS

"But where is the vampire?" I called out as Ghede-Zaranye disappeared into a cloud of ethereal glitter.

Shit. She was gone. I turned to Lisette. "Don't you all have some kind of freak-blood connection? Can you find Nicco?"

"I'm bound to Gabriel, not Niccolò," she said with an eyeroll. "We need my girls. Adeline will be able to find Adele. They share magic. And blood."

As I slid my grimoire into my bag, the sign hanging from the balcony where Zaranye had lain creaked in the breeze:

Les Confiseries Magiques de Ghede-Linto
L'homme miracle original

Miracle? A scent wafted out of the shop, like hot brownies and butterscotch and funnel cakes all rolled up in one.

The courtyard bustled with spirits licking ice creams and eating cakes. They stared at Lisette over their coffee cups and martini glasses, and from behind fans and hats and newspapers, eyes widening as she loosely tied her hair back from her face. I wondered what it was like to have everyone be scared of you.

But then she smiled at one of them, and he blushed. *Ohhh.* They weren't scared—they were just . . . admiring her. Well, I guess she was pretty.

I nodded up to the sign. "What does it say?"

"The miracle man's sweet shop."

Shit. The gad for Ren.

I drifted toward the window. An old man was behind the counter, slapping fudge against the marble surface.

"You can't eat the food of the dead," she said, following. "That includes sweets."

"I know." *And I can't help Ren now; I have to warn Adele about Nicco. I'll come back later.* "Let's go."

As we hustled back out onto the street, the noise dwindled. The spirit-crows sat in a row on the balcony above watching us, but no one else was to be seen.

"Where do we find Adeline?" I asked.

"I don't know." She shrugged. "I haven't seen her in three centuries."

"Yes, you do. *Think.* She was your friend. Your coven member."

"Well, we all lived at the convent, but Marassa and Adeline lived with Martine on Royal Street."

"Let's start there."

She nodded. I dove into the air, and she took off.

I was fast in flight, especially with my magical boost, but Lisette's speed was *insane.* I whipped another gust behind me and soared faster than I ever had in the Natural World. *Thank you, La Sirène.*

But the wind, the magic, even the supercharge couldn't blow the bloody images of Nicco from my mind. They flipped back and forth like a broken slideshow: Adele and Adeline, in the bar, on the street, in the park, in her bedroom. They all ended the same, with Nicco kissing their dead lips.

Up ahead, Lisette stopped at the corner outside Lafitte's

Blacksmith Shop, which seemed to actually be a blacksmith's shop here in the Afterworld.

I dropped down to her side. "What's up?"

"*Shhhh!*"

"What?" I whispered, and she gripped me tight with a shake.

Her forehead scrunched, and then her big golden eyes opened wide. She released me and took off toward Royal in a blur of blonde hair and chiffon skirts.

I jumped back into the Air and zoomed after her.

She stopped just behind the church, staring up at the sky in terror. Her face turned ghostly as I landed beside her.

Someone was teetering on the edge of the far bell tower. I blinked, peering through the fog. "Is that . . . ?"

"Niccolò," she gasped, her gaze now piercing through the garden to a girl standing in Pirate's Alley. The girl, barefoot and wearing nothing but a slinky pink slip, was staring up at Nicco on the tower, and she looked *pissed*.

Had he hurt her? I reached for the stake at my ankle.

"*Allons-y!*" she yelled.

Nicco lurched forward, ripping one of the shutters from the tower, nearly losing his grip. It smashed to pieces over the wrought-iron fence with an ear-splitting crash.

What the fuck is he doing?

"Oh, *non*," Lisette said. "*Non, Cosette.*"

"Cosette?"

Lisette gave me a frantic look. "Isaac, do something!"

Nicco teetered, and I realized her sister was controlling him.

This can all end now. I didn't even have to stake him. Adele, León, and all of their future descendants would be safe from this monster forever. We crept to the garden, and I fluttered up to the top of Touchdown Jesus.

"*Non!*" he yelled. It was the first time I'd ever heard fear in Niccolò Medici's voice. One gust of wind could save him. *No.*

Cosette is doing the right thing. I ignored the twinge of guilt that struck me. *The world is better without him.*

"Isaac!" Lisette screamed as her sister yelled a final command.

He glanced toward her voice, and our eyes locked. *Fuck you, Nicco.* His hand released from the shutter, and he tipped forward into the night. My magic lit up as he fell, but I didn't move. I reveled in being the last thing he'd see before his final death.

"*Sœur, non!*" Lisette glanced at me with a savage hiss and vanished. A brush of white painted across the dark garden, and she launched herself over the spiked posts like some kind of angelic superhero and caught him.

Fuck.

Cosette flailed, screaming in protest, but as the blur of blonde hair landed next to her in Pirate's Alley, her voice dwindled.

Lisette set Nicco down, gentle as a kitten, and stood in front of him protectively. But he no longer seemed to matter to Cosette as the two sisters cast withering stares at each other. Lisette's hand covered her mouth, and so did Cosette's, like they really were mere reflections of each other. Cosette collapsed to the ground, and Lisette wilted into a puddle of tears and a barrage of joyful French.

Nicco turned to creep away into the adjacent alley.

No. I dropped down to the street and charged straight toward him, stake in my hand. *I will end this for good.*

He whipped around and received me with a shove. I went sailing back toward the iron fence, but unlike the dumpster-night, I swooped upward just before my bones crunched against it.

Lisette gasped, seeing me hovering above them without taking bird form. For a second, even Nicco couldn't hide his surprise.

"Who is your friend?" Cosette asked.

"Susannah's heir."

Nicco spat at the ground just below me. "Maybe you should use your new magic to find the witch who attacked her. Next time, there might not be a vampire around to save her afterlife." And with a final smirk, he was gone.

CHAPTER 37
HEL MISS SPI

"What message?" I asked again, generations of my ancestors awaiting my response with rapt attention.

The lines in Marassa's forehead deepened. "The message I sent you earlier this evening. Isn't that why you are here?"

Codi turned to me, a hint of suspicion in his voice. "What's she talking about?"

I shrugged, equally disliking having missed said message and him possibly thinking I was hiding something from him. *You are hiding something from him. Yeah, but not an I-had-an-ulterior-motive-for-dragging-you-to-the-Afterworld kind of something.* "Sorry, but I think I would remember getting a message from Marassa Makandal."

"Ritha's oracle bones!"

"Hel. Miss spi!" My back stiffened as the foggy memory came back. "That was from you? But what does it mean?"

"Not 'Hel. Miss spi'!" Makandal said. "*Help. Missing Spirits.*"

"What do you mean, missing?" Codi asked.

My back tweaked even tighter, the flier now burning a hole in my pants.

"I mean one day they're here, just like they had been for

centuries," Marassa said, "and one day gone. Like they never had been!"

Oh shit, shit, shit. I reached into my back pocket and pulled out the flier, still hesitant. *Désirée, if there's a problem in Guinée that affects Codi's family, we need to fix it, stat.* "Is this one of the missing witches?" I unfolded the paper and smoothed it out. Everyone's gazes fell to the portrait.

"Is that?" Codi's brow tensed. "Where did you get this?"

"I found it on the street. I didn't realize she was your ancestor! I wouldn't have left her!"

"Left her?" Marassa asked. "You were with Marta?"

"Briefly . . . right when we arrived. An Earth witch trapped her in this floral pod. But I got her out!" I turned to Codi again. "I didn't know who she was. I would have stayed."

"You left her?"

"She was with her friend, or sister. And Adeline. At least, I think it was Adeline. Everything gets hazy around then thanks to Masaka."

"How could an Earth witch have attacked Marta?" Makandal asked, and all the ancestors around the room looked to one another, murmuring in a mix of tribal languages and French. "She's one of the greatest Earth witches I've had the pleasure of knowing."

"Well then, where is she?" Codi blurted out. "What if she's in trouble?"

I took his hand. "We'll find her." But Makandal had a point. As an Earth witch, why hadn't she released herself from the pod? She seemed to not even want to come out. I thought again about the strength of the vines and the lush, plump flower petals. Ritha was more into foliage than flowers like . . . like Fiona was. "Oh my Goddess . . . ooooh my Goddess." The pod. The flowers, the beauty. The only thing I'd ever seen like it was at the Daures' Hexennacht party. Horror trickled through me. "The man didn't trap her in the pod. She . . . trapped herself. She was trying to protect herself from him."

"From who? Why didn't you tell me? Marta Guldenmann's my grandma's grandma!"

"I'm *so sorry*, Codi. I was worried about you and the kishi."

His cheeks reddened. "You were worried about my magic?" His expression deflated. The exact reaction I'd been trying to avoid.

"Kinda," I finally admitted. "Fiona's wilted orchid. The tobacco smoke enchantment. Do you think that's why all your Earth magic spells—?"

His eyes grew wider.

"Whoever this Earth witch was," Makandal said, "he must have kidnapped her. Maybe it's not too late. We must find her!"

"I don't understand. She was on the street surrounded by a crowd of people when I left."

"Neither Marta nor her daughter Greta made it home that night," Marassa said, calmly stirring her tea.

"Greta is my great-grandmother." Codi cradled his head.

Marta's daughter? Could the other blonde girl have been Greta? They did look exactly alike. They just looked so close to the same age, I assumed sister. But I guess age was kind of relative in Guinée. Marassa didn't look too much older than me despite having lived a long life in the Natural World.

I recalled the terror on Marta's face. The weird way she'd kind of disappeared and reappeared like there was a glitch in the matrix. She'd kept screaming, "*Meine Magie!*"

Meine Magie . . . Meine Magie.

My magic? More pieces unfolded in my mind, twisting, turning, and then the route through the labyrinth unlocked, and my mind ran with a theory. *No, no, no. This is bad. This is really bad.* I hovered over Marta's picture. "When did this all start happening?"

"Recently," Marassa said.

"As in, since the Flower Moon recently?"

She nodded, and I wished I could cover Codi's ears for the next question. "If a witch doesn't have magic, then they can't be in Guinée, right?"

"Of course, but all witches have magic."

Codi's expression suddenly mirrored the panic I was trying to suppress with therapeutic breathing. "The man didn't kidnap Marta—"

"He took her magic," I finished.

He stared down at her picture. "They stole my family's magic . . ."

Makandal pounded the table with his fist. "What devil—?"

Marassa crossed her arms. "Bet it was a white man."

The room began chirping: *"Never in all my years!" "Black magic!" "No witch could do such a thing!"*

"We know someone who could." Codi looked at me. "And he's not an Earth witch. At least he wasn't naturally."

Was that Callis I'd run into on the street? Beneath the hood and the heavy kohl makeup? "It's not possible," I muttered. "There's no way they followed us in. They wouldn't have had the keys. The Ghede wouldn't have just let them in without the proper ritual, right?"

"Calm down, darling," Marassa said soothingly.

But I couldn't.

Codi got up and started pacing. "Do you really think we let the Ghost Drinkers in? How did they get through the protection spell at the cemeteries?" I'd never seen him this upset. Then again, if it were my family, I'd be freaking the hell out. He sank back into his seat. "Fuck." His eyes looked everywhere but at mine. "The hexenspiegel was from the Guldenmann grimoire. Marta's grimoire."

I sat next to him, pulling the chair close. "Codi, we're going to figure this out." I still refused to believe we'd let Callis in. "We all did the protection spell. It's bound with all of our magic."

"Did we destroy my magicline? I wanted to *protect* my family by coming here."

"Did you say Ghost Drinkers?" Makandal asked, a look of confusion on his face. "I'm unfamiliar—"

"Animarum . . . Praedators," said the elder man across the table from us, a haunting rhythm in his voice. "There was always a rumor of a coven of European witches who'd been roaming the Earth for hundreds of years. Never met one of them, though."

"I wish we hadn't," I said, mentally sorting the timeline. "Marassa sent the message before we left, so the magic thieving had to have started before we opened the portal." I turned to Codi. "Follow me here . . . For all these years—centuries—the Ghost Drinkers didn't have any power because their grimoire was burned and they didn't have their Elemental to bind their coven, right?"

"Right. Until Annabelle gave them her grimoire and they sucked out Adele's Fire."

"After that, Callis got juiced, magically speaking, but they were still weak after the battle at the convent with the vampires. They had their magic back, but it would have been difficult to find ghosts to drink to make them stronger."

"Until tonight, with the Flower Moon—"

"When they pillaged D-MORT . . ." I slowly shook my head. "All those poor souls lost in the Storm." I wanted to kill that witch with my bare hands. I leaned over the table, gazing out at each of my ancestors. "The Ghost Drinkers didn't follow us in. They were already here among you."

"There has never been a magic thief in Guinée as long as I've been here!" Makandal said, looking around to our elders, who all nodded in agreement.

"They were here," I said, "just unable to use their succubus magic. In the Natural World, Callis was using what little magic he had to feed off ghosts and stay alive. If he was weak, doesn't that mean his ancestral magicline would have been weak too?

His deceased family probably had just enough magic to remain in Guinée."

Codi slowly stood. "Then when he got juiced, his ancestors got juiced too."

"So for the first time since Callis's father arrived here, the Salazars have their full magic." The thought was chilling.

Codi's eyebrows raised. "A coven of succubi in the Natural World."

"And a coven of succubi in the Afterworld. And not just any part of the Afterworld—Guinée."

"A cornucopia of magic for the taking," Marassa said.

We were chest deep in a thicket of rose briars. Of the magical, poisonous, witch-eating variety.

"My grandma!" Codi's tone flooded with horror. "When she pulled me out of Oussou's dream, she disappeared. I thought she just had things to do, but do you think she actually *disappeared*? Like, from Guinée?" He began digging through his bag.

"If a witch's magicline is broken, it would affect all of her descendants," Marassa said.

"Oh no," I whispered. "Is this why everyone was gone from the tearoom? Why the plants were dying?"

"There was nothing wrong with the plants," Codi said, and extracted a folded note.

I didn't feel the need to tell him I'd breathed life back into them all before he'd arrived.

"How is he still here, then?" Makandal asked me, nodding to Codi.

"He's a Water witch." Some people in the room seemed confused. "Mixed magic family." A mixed reaction followed, and for a moment, I was ashamed of my family.

Codi read the note again, the words catching in his throat. "He knew—my grandpa knew. He said that Philly would need me, and I didn't help her!"

I held onto his arm. "Codi, we're going to find them. If

Callis had drunk their spirits, their souls would be terrorizing Guinée, and I'm sure we'd have heard about it."

But he was inconsolable. "I ruined my family."

"Not all of your family," a woman said from the doorway as her flowing blue dress fell into place around her. Tiers of bone and shell necklaces covered her chest, and she had two of the longest braids I'd ever seen, both wrapped in silver ribbons. Despite her petite frame, she had the kind of imposing presence that could command ten thousand men. A woman who could only be *the* Morning Star of the Choctaw people, the magnificent Water witches of the Mississippi, whose beautiful russet skin gave Codi his I'm-not-a-total-white-boy appearance.

Codi slowly stood, as if in the presence of a goddess. I knew the feeling.

"I've taken the rest of the family somewhere safe to hide." She held out her arms, and he stumbled over Makandal getting to her. I wondered if she'd been the one who'd married a German witch, or if it had been one of her descendants.

As they embraced, I huddled with Marassa and Makandal. "When you sent the bone message earlier, who else had gone missing?"

Marassa's face drew long. "A French witch very dear to me. Her name is Minette Monvoisin."

"*Shit!*" I whispered, just as the room went silent. Everyone turned to me as a horrifying thought percolated. "Has anyone else been attacked?"

"*Oui,*" came another voice new to the room, a disheveled blonde.

"Lisette?" Codi asked.

Morning Star pulled her close. "My dear Cosette, what has happened to you?"

"I'm fine." Tears trickled from her eyes. "But Adeline wasn't home. I can't find her."

Minette, Marta, and now Cosette?

"This can't be a coincidence," I said. "They're coming for us. They're going after the original Casquette Girls Coven to destroy our magic so they can take New Orleans."

Marassa pounded the table. "We have to find Addie. We must alert Susannah."

"Adele," Codi said. "Has anyone seen Adele since we've been here?"

"We have to find Isaac too."

"He went after the vampire," Cosette said. "And my sister went after him."

"Vampire?" Marassa snapped. "There are no vampires on this side of the veil."

"Niccolò Medici," Cosette said.

Marassa removed a knife from a slab of ribs on the table. "Niccolò Medici in Guinée?" She turned to me.

"Did I . . . forget to mention that?"

"We'll split up," Makandal said, unrolling a map of the city.

CHAPTER 38
MA PETITE SORCIÈRE

The flaky crust melted onto my tongue, then the deliciously caramelized tart quince. I chewed slowly, trying not to swallow it, trying not to panic as I felt the pulp of fruit dribble down the back of my throat. *No, don't swallow it, Adele!* Warmth spread through my limbs. I pretended to cough, trying to discreetly spit it into my hand, but the three Salazars didn't take their eyes off me, and I just ended up with a spray of cherry in my palm.

My mouth tingled. I bit down hard on my bottom lip but didn't feel a thing. It was numb. I wanted more pie.

Zorion handed me a napkin.

She's so nice. "How am I going to do this?"

"Do what?" she asked. *Oh God, I said it out loud.*

"Do what?" she asked again.

"Kill your dad." *Oh my God!*

"Pardon?" She laughed.

"My dad, I miss my dad!"

"Was your father not magical, dearest, or is it that he hasn't passed, yet?" her mother asked, sipping from her chalice of pili. "A child passing on before the parent is a tragedy I know all too well."

I shook my head, trying to keep in the torrent of words that desperately wanted to flow out. The room spun. "Both."

"A mundane?" Beñat asked, aghast. "In the Salazar line? Well, that explains a few things about the recent state of our magic, or lack thereof."

"Several centuries hardly count as recent," Zori said. She turned to her mother. "Do you think Callisto really married a mundane?"

"*Pfft!* Who would marry that guy?" I asked, gasping at the rudeness of my own question.

Arrosa's hand went to her chest. 'Well, clearly someone, if you exist!"

"*Mmm* . . . I dunno about that."

Adele, shut up! What is wrong with you?

My gaze fell to the pie. My tongue swelled in my mouth, wanting more, the compulsion taking over my consciousness so strongly I didn't notice my own drool until it dripped down my chin.

I quickly wiped my face then grabbed the fork and shoveled another bite into my mouth. "It's so good!" I hardly even chewed it before gulping it down. I glugged a sip of the pili. "Who'd have known quinces were so delicious!" I jumped up from the table and twirled around the kitchen.

Oh God.

Arrosa followed me around the room, brow tightened with concern. "Are you telling me that my son had a child out of wedlock?"

"Who cares how he had a child, Mother?" Beñat asked. "If he hadn't, our magicline would have ended."

"Your magicline's gonna end," I said with another twirl.

"Excuse me?" Arrosa demanded.

"Do you mean because you didn't have any children?" Zorion asked.

"No." A laugh sputtered from my lips. I could feel the plan

on the tip of my tongue, like it was a sweet piece of fruit about to be coughed out of my mouth. Just like the tiny buds of chamomile, only instead of my magic forcing it out, it was the pili coursing through my system. I leaned to the table to grab my bag to show them the ghoststick. *What the hell is in that pie?*

Stop it, Adele! I flung myself so hard in the opposite direction, I fell. "Ouch!" I said, hitting the stone floor.

"She's . . . strange," Beñat said.

"Indeed." Arrosa folded her arms across her chest. "Who are you?"

"Adele Le Moyne, French Quarter rat!" I raised my finger high, like it was my shining achievement. Jeanne and Sébastien would not be impressed. Arrosa grabbed my arm and shoved my sleeve back. My heart pounded wildly, but her grip loosened at the sight of my Maleficium—luckily, it was the same as theirs. "I used to have fire balls," I said, an overwhelming sadness filling my chest.

"Used to?" Zorion asked.

"I was like a hot Super Mario. That's what Isaac said."

"Was Isaac your husband?" she asked, pulling me up.

I sputtered out a laugh. "I'm too young to be married!"

"Who's Mario? Another suitor? You must have been very popular!"

"He's an Italian. Like Nicco. But a plumber." I bounced across the room. "He smashes all the Goombas and kicks all the Koopa shells." I chopped the air with my leg. "*Boop! Boop! Boop!*"

"Who's Nicco?"

"Aaaaaaaa boy who I thought I liked."

Zori clapped her hands together. "Oh, tell me everything!"

The overwhelming melancholy filled me again. "I think I still like him. But he doesn't like my family. And it's possible that he just wants to kill me."

"If a man bemoans your family, how could you ever trust him?" Arrosa asked.

"But . . . it was three hundred years ago."

Was it? He still wants to kill León. But I don't even know León. "It's confusing." I picked up the chalice, guzzled back the pili, and then slammed it back down, letting out a belch. Zorion laughed.

"She's mad," Beñat said. "That's why they didn't tell us she was coming."

A colorful rack of clothing in the living room caught my eye. "What are these designs?" Zori followed closely behind me as I raked my hand over the hangers. "So many pretties!" *Get your shit together, Adele!*

"They're for the show tonight. I was just doing some last-minute touch-ups."

"You made these?" I asked, holding an enormous sunflower costume up to my chest. "I like to make costumes too!"

"You do? You can help me backstage! It's opening night!"

"Maybe we *are* related," I said.

"Maybe?" Arrosa asked, sharply. She grabbed my arm and jerked me close to her side. "Why didn't we know you were coming? Why wasn't Jakome alerted?"

"*Mmm.*" The pitch of my voice rose. "'Cause we didn't want him to know."

"But why?" Zori asked.

"It would ruin the surprise."

She smiled. "That's lovely."

"'Cause I need my dad back."

Zorion put her arm around me. "Parting from the mundane can be the hardest aspect of transitioning, but once he passes on, you can visit him in his Afterworld realm. You're a witch! And no need to be sad; you have us now!"

"I can't believe we have mundane Salazars," Beñat said. "If

grandfather wasn't already dead, he'd die of shock. How very weak our family has become."

"My dad's not weak!" I jumped in his face. "He's a very strong man!" A surge of anger made me turn again toward my bag. *No, Adele. Fight through it.*

As I strained, the tchotchkes on the fireplace mantel began to tremble.

The compulsion ripped through me, and I stormed toward the kitchen. But a bright light sprang out of the floor, and I jumped back. Flames lit up all around me, sprouting from the hardwood like sunflowers. Words slipped from Arrosa's lips that I couldn't understand.

"Mama!" Zorion yelled.

I turned to her. "Don't worry. It's not real; it's an illusion. I'm not stupid." I waved my hand through the flames, and a scream burst from my throat.

Arrosa strode toward me. "I've had enough of this! Who are you, girl? What Fire spirit-witch could be burned by a flame?"

"Um. It didn't burn me," I wailed, tears streaming down my face. I hid my hand behind my back. "I need Désirée!"

"Let me see!" Zori said. "Your spirit self can't be burned. It's just your mind playing a trick on you, because you haven't acclimated yet."

"Can you put the Fire out, please!" I begged.

"Mother, you're scaring her!"

"If it's so scary, Adele, you put it out! Unless . . . you're not who you say you are."

"*D'accord!*" Sweat trickled down my face and my cheeks heated as I pulled for my magic. I pulled and pulled, but all I felt was a black hole. A void of nothingness where something once was. Something that had been stolen by these people. All that was left was a swirl of anger and despair in its place. "I can't!" I yelled.

"You aren't a Salazar!" Arrosa roared, her anger growing.

Shit. Shit. Shit. I reached into my pocket. "If I'm not a Salazar, then how do I have this?" I yelled, thrusting my fist forward, showing off the ring through the flames. The insignia flickered orange, causing gasps around the room.

Beñat stomped up. "That is a precious heirloom. How did you come by it?"

I wiped my brow. "Callisto."

"Mama, stop this. She's Callisto's heir! What more do you want?"

"No heir of my son's would have trouble dispelling a flame." Her tone was biting.

"Do I have to remind you," Zorion asked, "that even you couldn't dispel a flame mere days ago? How quickly we've forgotten our own misfortunes. She's traumatized!"

"It's really hot," I cried, cradling my hand as the smell of burnt hair filled my nostrils. "Put it out, please!" I began to cough.

"You put it out!" she growled at me, unrelenting.

"I'll put it out!" A woman yelled in French, slamming the door open with such might it shook the entire house. "*Arrêtez le feu!*" Her arm flung toward me, and the Fire sucked into the palm of her hand.

I fell to my knees, hacking. A circle had been burned into the floor around me.

"And who are *you*?" Arrosa demanded.

"Adeline." I chirped. "*Elle est Adeline Saint-Germain, mon ancêtre!*"

"Another descendant," Zorion yelled. "I can feel her magic! Oh, blessed be this night, Illagari."

Adeline looked around the tawdry room. "I am most certainly *not* your descendant. And neither is Adele." She rushed to my aid and kissed my cheeks back and forth. "Please forgive me, *mon petit chou*, the time just got away from me." She turned back to the family. "I was supposed to pick her up in the Square.

I just got so caught up in arranging her procession, I completely lost track of time. I can be so flighty."

"What?" Zori said, heartbroken.

"I'm sorry," I said to her as Adeline pulled me up, keeping me close. "My bag," I whispered. "We can't forget my bag."

Beñat shoved it toward me. "I *knew* we didn't have any mundane in our bloodline."

Zorion's lip quivered. "Does this mean you're not my family?"

"If this is how you treat your family," Adeline said, "then I should hope you were barren!"

Arrosa gasped in horror, and Zorion started to sob as Adeline pulled me through the door.

"*Merci*," I whispered.

"Come with me, my love."

"How did you get that ring?" Arrosa demanded.

"I found it on the floor at a tearoom!"

"It belongs to the Salazars!" Arrosa yelled. Her voice faded as we ran past the tenement building, but Zori chased us all the way to Basin Street. A strange sense of guilt washed through me —she really had been so kind.

"One moment," I said to Adeline, and we paused on the edge of the Quarter. I turned back to Zori as she caught up to us. "I'm so sorry for the mix-up," I said in earnest.

"This can't be right," she insisted. "I can just feel that we're sisters in magic."

"I really would have liked to be your cousin. Or niece. Or whatever we would have been." My head spun, and my blistered hand throbbed. "I don't know about your mother, though."

"I'm the one who is sorry," she said, weeping. "My mother means well. She's very protective of our family. It's just that we've been burned by other witches in the past. Especially Fire witches."

"*Mmph*!" Adeline huffed, raising her nose in the air.

Zori slipped an envelope into my hand. "I hope that you'll still come. You'll see that my family isn't bad. That we're full of love and life and enchantment."

The magic flickered in her eyes, which were such a deep blue, they were almost black.

A wave of nausea washed over me, and I was sure I was going to hurl. "*Enchantée!*"

With one hand, Adeline held back my hair, and with the other, she jammed a finger down my throat, and I gagged violently. "One more time!" she insisted. "We must be sure it's all out of your system!" I'd daydreamed about meeting Adeline in the brothel many times, but not one version ever involved my head in a toilet.

"*Merci beaucoup,*" I choked. "I'm good."

I rested against the tile wall, swigging back some more of the minty-peach drink from my bag, and she sat on the edge of the clawfoot tub and bandaged my burnt hand.

She was exactly how I'd pictured her from the pages of her diary, except her hair was down in soft face-framing waves, and instead of the restricting garments fashionable in early eighteenth-century Paris, she wore an elegant *chemise à la reine* with a pink waist-sash, straight from a Marie Antoinette garden party. The delicate, gauzy fabric bunched at various lengths on her arms and draped low at her shoulders and bust.

"I can't believe it's you," I said, putting extra effort into my French accent.

"And I can't believe it's you, *ma petite sorcière!*" She brushed my hair out of my face. "But why were those witches trying to burn you? And more importantly, why would they *ever* think you were their relation?"

"I was trying to keep them from foiling our plan . . . They have my father."

She lowered herself next to me in concern. "Who has your father? The Medici?"

"No, the descendants of those witches. The *Salazars*. Back in the Natural World, their coven kidnapped him, and they're holding him hostage. I need your help to get him back." The guilt overwhelmed me, and my eyes welled.

"Darling, don't cry." She brushed my cheek with her delicate hand.

How could I ask for her help after I hadn't heeded her advice? My voice became raspy. "I didn't know."

"Que voulez-vous dire?"

"He just told me." It was hard to even say the words out loud. "Niccolò told me about his role in your death."

"His role?" She laughed. "As the shining star, you mean?"

"I-I don't even know that person who attacked you in the alley. That monster."

She tilted my chin up to her. "And why does that make you cry now? Because you thought you could trust him?"

A dark cloud of shame cast my mind into shadow. I shook my head, hardly able to look at her. "Because I still feel like I can trust him."

She crossed her arms. "Is that so?"

"Adeline, if you just tell me where León is, I can end this feud between our families for good!" This was the exact opposite of how I'd envisioned this conversation going, but the plea just came out. Maybe it was the lingering effects of the pili.

She looked at me sternly. "I've spent three centuries protecting my father and our magical line; I will not put him in danger now!"

"I won't put him in danger, I swear."

"Ma petite sorcière, let me ask you one question: if I tell you his location, what happens the first time your enemies—many of

whom you've amassed thanks to your fraternization with the Medici—want to trade your father's life for the location of mine? What would you do then? Can you tell me León wouldn't be in danger?"

"I'm going to save my father," I snapped. "That's why I'm here!"

"Good! Ma chérie, I'm protecting you by not telling you, just as the Count protected me by not telling me of his location when he first sent me to La Nouvelle-Orléans."

I couldn't argue with her point. If I didn't know, I couldn't give it away. Not that I would, willingly. "*D'accord.* We have a much bigger problem on our hands than the Medici."

"*Oui, récupérer notre magie.*"

"Yes, getting our magic back *and* saving New Orleans from the real monsters: the Salazars."

"*Adeline! Es-tu là, mon amour?*" a girl yelled from downstairs.

Adeline's face lit up with joy. "*Oui!* Upstairs! One minute! I have a surprise for you!" She grabbed my hands and pulled me up from the floor. As we made it into the bedroom, a blonde barged in. Her thin satin slip-dress was dirty, and so were her feet. Her hair was disheveled and her mascara running. She went straight to Adeline and pulled her into her arms.

"*Qu'est-ce qui t'es arrivé, mon amour?*" Adeline asked, stress shaking her voice.

The blonde clung to her a moment longer, then pulled back and cradled Adeline's face. "I couldn't find you!" Her eyes shone with tears. "I thought something terrible had happened."

Adeline stroked her hair. "I'm fine, my love." She kissed her lips and pulled her down to the settee at the foot of the bed. "What happened to you?"

The blonde . . . *is that?*

"*Ça va,*" she insisted, although she was clearly not fine. Her eyes finally met mine, and she blinked in astonishment. "Adele!"

"Cosette Monvoisin!" I dropped to my knees beside them.

"*Des sœurs d'or.*" She smiled at the mention of the triplets' old nickname. "What happened to you?" I already worried it had something to do with us being here.

She threw up her arms in exasperation. "A man attacked me in the street!" She seemed humiliated to admit it.

"Attacked!" Adeline's tone sharpened. "What in the Goddess's name? Do you think—? Did he try to kidnap you? Like Minette?"

"If he'd wanted to kidnap me, he could have. He had me restrained with his magic, but it felt more like . . . he was trying to kill me."

Adeline's brow bent in confusion. "Kill you? This is eternal life."

"I don't know how else to explain it."

"Who was it?" I asked.

"A witch with dark hair and dark eyes. He held me in the air with his magic, and it was like . . . lightning burning through my veins."

My pulse raced. "And like ice choking your breath?"

"*Oui!*"

I knew the precise feeling. It had happened to me. My fists balled. "He wasn't trying to kill you; he was trying to take your magic."

Adeline gasped. "The horror."

Cosette turned to her with tears in her eyes. "Do you think that's what happened to Minette? That they stole her magic and expelled her from Guinée?"

Adeline stood, her chest puffing up with indignant breaths. "That witch will experience eternal pain when I am through with him." She turned to Cosette. "We *will* get Minette back. Over my dead spirit will he take her from us, I guarantee it, my love."

"Don't say such things," Cosette said. She pulled Adeline back down to the settee, her tone becoming even more serious. "There's one more thing, *mon amour*."

"What is it?"

"Niccolò Medici is here."

Adeline's eyes widened. "In Guinée? He's met final death?"

Cosette shook her head.

"*Non*," I said, and they both turned. "He's with me . . . At least, he was."

CHAPTER 39
HOUSE OF MEDICI

I paused on the Moonwalk, taking an unnecessary breath. It had taken three miles to lose Isaac. Based on his rising anger, I assumed he'd found out about my little indiscretion. Had he heard it from Adeline's lips? Or perhaps Adele had run straight back to him. The thought made me want to rip out the nearest oak and hurl it into the river. *It's where she belongs, Niccolò.* With the witches—the real witches. I can't believe I'd let her fairy-tale hope creep in. I might still have my Mark, but a witch I was not. Witches had magic. Witches were not affected by Aether mind-tricks. As the wind blew through my hair, I felt the heat rise to my cheeks.

I listened to the river crashing up to the shore, trying to forget about the incident with Cosette, but humiliation seeped into my bones. Isaac having caught me in such a compromised position was the cherry on top. What would have happened if Lisette hadn't arrived? I couldn't recall the last time I'd been so close to final death.

I needed to get the hell out of here. I needed to find Jakome. I needed the Ghede.

I zipped back to the square, entering the Place d'Armes.

"Are you going to make me beg, L'Oraille?" I shouted, dropping to my knees on a damp patch of grass. In the Natural World, I could have gone door-to-door and forced someone to give me Salazar's location, but vampiric thrall didn't work on spirits. *I should have kept that damn ring.* Surely I could have persuaded someone to cast a location spell with it. *Come on, L'Oraille.*

Her glittering outline appeared on the back of Andrew Jackson. "Giddyap!" she yelled, lassoing the air, her diamond-netting bra shimmering like the constellations above.

I rose to my feet.

"Whatchou want, boo?" she asked, looking down at me.

"*Pouvez-vous me dire où trouver Jakome Salazar, s'il vous plaît.*"

"I could tell ya." She slid down the statue directly to my side, her jewelry clanking, and looped her arm over my shoulder. "Or I could tell ya zha answer to zha question ya really wanna ask."

"I asked the question I wanted to ask."

"*Pish.* Ya might be able to lie to ya little girlfriend, but zhat ain't gonna work with me, child."

Maybe the door-to-door option would be better, even without my thrall or the talisman.

She walked me toward the gate at the cathedral end of the park. "You don't wanna ask because ya scared to know zha answer."

"So what if I am?"

"It's been soooo long since ya've been in a situation ya can't control, ya can't stand it. Ya can't control her, so ya pushed her away."

"I don't want to control her," I snapped.

"Just ask, and I'll tell ya where zhey are."

Once again, nervousness prickled up my spine. Adele had

the Schattengeist; even if I found Jakome, it wasn't like I could do anything. Was there really any harm in a quick detour? If anyone knew where to find Jakome Salazar, it was my family.

If they weren't in Guinée, all of my greatest nightmares were true: I'd really destroyed our family's magical line when we were all murdered. If they were here . . . it would inspire unfathomable hope. It would mean that maybe Adele was right all along—maybe there was some sliver of my magic buried in the pit of my soul.

"*D'accord.*" I turned to face her, and my entire body went numb as I asked the question: "*Où est ma famille?*"

A satisfied smile lit up her face. She walked to the nearest tree and plucked an overripe pomegranate. The juice dripped down her arm as she handed it to me.

It stained my pale fingers, but I knew better than to eat the food of the dead, vampire or not. Cupped in my hand, the fruit began to change, its rotting red skin turning hard and transparent. Inside the glass sphere, the seeds withered away, morphing into filaments. A light bulb?

"Have fun," L'Oraille said.

Lightning cracked on the river, and the bulb lit up. When I looked back, she was gone.

"*Merci mille fois, L'Oraille!*" I yelled out in frustration. I wasn't in a mood to play games on a regular day, but especially not after the fight with Adele and a brush with final death.

The bulb was round, like the kind you would find on old Broadway. Or like the sign in— "*Armstrong Park.*"

I sped through the gate, past the cathedral and out of the Vieux Carré to the park entrance, but once there, I came to an abrupt halt. What if they weren't here? What if the Ghede lwa was just taking pity on me, letting me finally discover the truth so I could go on with my eternal life? I paced the block once or twice or ten times, running my hands through my hair. I wished Adele was with me. Why did I push her away?

It was for the best, I told myself, and then whipped beneath the archway of lights.

Through the low-hanging boughs of oak trees and curtains of Spanish moss, a gothic palazzo came into view. It was exactly as I'd fantasized it—so much so that I questioned its validity. But I supposed that all of Guinée must be an abstract construction of our consciousness.

Our three Borromean diamond rings graced the imposing palazzo doors. Seeing the symbol of our family carved eternally made nostalgia rush me so hard, I felt lightheaded. I wanted them to be here. I *needed* them to be here. As the doors opened, I nearly fled, but curiosity's chain gripped me tighter than the fear, and I crept inside.

The gardens were lush, and the purple banners hanging from the balcony of the double loggia were crisp and clean; surely the palace wasn't abandoned. "Ciao?" I called out.

In the silence, I pressed forward into the courtyard, my vestigial pulse beginning to race at the lack of life—afterlife.

My family wasn't here.

I paused, unsure if I could go any further. I envisioned myself zipping around, checking every room, every closet, beneath every bed in a tailspin of disappointment and regret.

I turned to leave, to sprint away, and I saw her standing at the fountain.

"Are you leaving so soon, Niccolò?"

"*Mio angelo,*" I gasped, and in a whirl, I had her in my arms.

"*Il mio fratellino.*"

I could scarcely recall the last time I'd been brought to tears, but the song of Giovanna's voice nearly made me collapse. "Even more beautiful than I remembered," I said, kissing her face. The hardened edge that vampirism had bestowed was gone from her eyes, and the joy had returned to her smile. It gave me hope for a time when I would live again, a witch with my magic, and simultaneously made me yearn for death. "I scoured the Earth for you."

"And you killed the girl who slayed me."

I swallowed her with my embrace. "I missed you so much, Sister."

"And I you, Niccolò. We all do."

I pulled her away, almost unable to ask. "Where is everyone? *Madre, padre?*"

"They're waiting for us. Pre-show dinner!"

"The theatre?" I laughed. "You can't be serious."

She handed me a colorful flier:

Toulouse Street Theatre

Opening Night

AKELARRENLEZEA SPECTACULAR!

STARING GHEDE-NIBO & FAMILY

Akelarrenlezea was Basque for the witches' cave. "What is this?"

"I'm not entirely sure, but I have my suspicions." Her hand slipped into mine. "We'll find out soon enough."

"But we can't go to the theatre—there are so many important things to discuss!"

"And we will, on the way. First, to the tailor to get you some more suitable attire."

I gazed down at her Barocco gown. "I hope you don't think I'm wearing stockings. I don't care if the Pope himself is performing."

"Trust me, Niccolò, this is *not* a show to be missed, and we cannot afford to have you stand out before we are ready to make a splash." Her smile was devious. She was certainly up to something.

"Tell me everything," I said.

"You first." She took the flier from my hand and tossed it behind us. "I want to hear everything about Signora Le Moyne on the way."

Thump-thump.

CHAPTER 40
HOUSE OF THE CASQUETTE GIRLS

The fire lit up in Adeline's eyes. "I warned you to stay away from Niccolò Medici!"

"I *know*." I could barely look up from the floor. "We needed seven witches to open the gates." That was a lie. Nicco had come because I wouldn't have had it any other way. He was not a means to an end.

"He's not a witch!" Cosette said.

"Yes, he is," I rebutted, a little too shortly, "as much as your sister is."

She sucked in a sharp breath.

"He was a great Fire witch before he died. They all were. Your father has their grimoire, Adeline. That's why they're after him."

She shook her head. "My father never had a grimoire."

"He took it the night they were all murdered by a cunning vampire named Séraphine Cartier—she's the other reason they're after León. The Medici think they conspired together. Maybe they did . . . I don't know."

"So that's where they got the name Cartier," Adeline mumbled. Her gaze turned inward, and she gave no indication of her feelings about her father's presumed guilt. Did she not think he was innocent? Did she know something she wasn't saying?

"The Medici murdered?" Cosette smirked. "Why am I not surprised? I like this Séraphine already."

"Are you sure?" I asked. "Séraphine ended up with the Medici after Emilio hunted her down for killing a powerful French witch: the sister of Étienne Deshayes."

She sat up straight. "Deshayes? Étienne Deshayes is my grandmother's—"

"Magical ancestor?" I replied. "Still like Séraphine now?"

She wrapped her arms around Adeline, resting her chin on her shoulder. "You never told me your father conspired to take down the Medici dynasty."

"That's because it's preposterous."

I couldn't tell if the heat in Adeline's voice was directed at me or the Medici or Séraphine, or even herself for somehow not having figured this all out on her own.

"It's hard enough imagining the Medici as witches," Cosette said, "much less as knowing my family."

"The Medici and the Monvoisins go back to long before Nicco was killed. They are two of the European witching families who excommunicated the Great Basque witches."

"There were no Great Basque witches," Adeline said.

"Exactly."

"I remember the tales when I was a child," Cosette said in soft French, "of the witches who resided in the caves of Spain— the Akelarrenlezea—but they were just old wives' tales to keep us children from exploring in the mountains on our own."

"Is there even such a thing as an old wives' tale in the witching world?" I asked.

They looked at me tenderly, and we all laughed. A noise came from downstairs. Footsteps, bustling.

"Was that the front door?" Adeline asked.

"*Adeline! Nous avons des problèmes! Cosette?*" a voice called.

"It's Marassa," Cosette said, helping us both up. "They must have found Susannah."

We hurried out of the room and down the stairs, although I was the only one running. They glided over the floor like the graceful, enigmatic witches they were. By the time we got to the blue room, people were pouring in, including two of my own.

"Dee!" I yelped, running toward her and Codi. I was relieved to see both of their faces.

Codi grabbed me before I reached Désirée. "You're okay," he said, squeezing me tight.

"Yes, but we've got a big problem."

"You can say that again," Dee said, setting her bag down on the coffee table. "Ghost Drinkers in Guinée— What happened to your hand? I just healed it!"

"Played with Fire and I got burned." I winced as she unwrapped the bandage.

The room was abuzz with magical energy, everyone talking about the trouble brewing. As Désirée healed the blister, I found myself gaping around at everyone in awe. They'd found Morning Star and Marassa, and two young men that I could only assume were their brothers. It was unbelievable seeing our covens together. I sucked in a sharp breath with Dee's sweep of magic and felt a little light-headed as it did its thing. Codi held my elbow. I was barely able to tell her "thanks" before he whisked me away to meet his Water witches.

Morning Star was just as beautiful as I always imagined her. "*Halito*," I said. "*Chim achukma?*"

She smiled at me with delight and began speaking in Choctaw. Codi laughed as my cheeks flushed.

"I'm sorry!" I said, unable to keep up. "That was pretty much all the Choctaw I know."

Both she and the man next to her joined Codi laughing. It was clear where his big smile came from. "Adeline finally has a magical heir," she said, glowing with delight like I was one of her own. "She's so proud of you."

Is she? I haven't done anything to make her proud. The opposite, in fact.

"Meet my brother Nashoba."

"That means 'wolf' in Choctaw," Codi said, leaning in. He was bursting with pride, but I couldn't help notice how he twiddled his thumbs—he always did that when something was bothering him.

"*Halito*," I said to Nashoba, wracking my seven-year-old self's memories for more Choctaw words Codi had taught me. Nashoba had guarded Adeline in wolf-form when he'd suspected vampires had infested La Nouvelle-Orléans, and he'd perished at their hands for it. One more person in the room who'd been sent to Guinée by the Medici.

The front door slammed shut again, another pair of boots clicked down the hallway toward us, and Susannah Bowen hustled into the room. Her long red curls looked permanently windblown, like she'd just been flying. The double-breasted, long-sleeved bodice of her dress—blue and white pinstripes with large buttons—was still intact. It sat low on her shoulders, which she hadn't bothered covering with the dainty neckerchief of the time; just a ribbon was tied at her throat. She had traded her layers of skirts for leather pants that accentuated her athletic figure. Isaac must have been as enamored with her as I was with Adeline.

No matter the pending danger, no one seemed able to contain their excitement that we were all together. It was truly magnificent.

My mother was right. I wasn't alone. I never would be.

I stood on my toes, peering over headwraps and puffed sleeves and walking sticks adorned with feathers. "Where's . . . ?"

"Where's young Isaac?" Susannah asked, weaving through the room.

I turned to Dee, who looked at Codi, and the small deflection filled me with panic. I suddenly saw an image of him in a cold, dark alley, huddled in a PTSD coma, triggered from seeing all the dead. *I shouldn't have made him come with us.* "Has anyone seen him since we got here?"

"He was with us." Désirée glanced at Adeline then stepped nearer to me, leaning in way too close for her norm. "So . . . Nicco wouldn't kill him, right? Even if he was provoked? Like, not hurt him more than I could heal him?"

"*What?*" Susannah and I both asked at the same time.

"Well, he kind of knows about . . ." She paused, as if unsure whether to say it in front of me. She nodded to Adeline, as if testing the water.

"*Oh!*" I said. "I have to go—!"

Adeline gripped my arm. "Not until we figure out what's going on. It's not safe."

"No, I need to find him before he does something he'll regret."

In a puff of curls, red feathers, and magic, Susannah was gone, and Marassa was whisking me to the velvet sofa. "Susannah will find him quick. She's faster than the north wind and has a hawk-eye. It's her pirate blood."

Pirate blood?

Everyone followed us and seated themselves around the coffee table. Codi planted himself on my other side, and Dee sat on the floor across from us. The fireplace crackled with flames, and every candle in the room flickered as the others began talking about Mama Philly's disappearance. Olsin's message. Marta Guldenmann. The more I learned, the more my pulse rose. Was it Jakome who had attacked Marta, Minette, and Cosette? Did he know we were here? *I cannot freaking believe I told his wife my name.* My head swirled as I tried to focus on the conversation, but I couldn't concentrate, knowing that Isaac and Nicco were out there.

Désirée banged her bag on the coffee table. "Jakome's going after the Casquette Girls Coven to break our magiclines. He's beating us at our own game!"

"*Pardon?*" Marassa asked.

"Oh," Dee shrank back in her seat. "Did I forget to mention that's why we actually came here? To kill the spirit of the Great Basque patriarch. It was Adele's idea."

I shot her a look as all of our ancestors began clucking at once, shaking their heads ruefully before they realized we were serious.

Makandal turned to Dee. "Does Ritha know about this?"

"Um, she knew we were coming here."

I peered at Codi. Our legs were touching, but he seemed a million miles away. He had Marta's missing girl flier in his hand. I couldn't fathom what he was going through right now. As if losing Olsin hadn't been horrific enough. Her picture stared back at me, and it felt like she was trying to tell me something. Dee had said the Salazars were going after the original Casquette Girls Coven. "Wait, the Guldenmanns weren't in the original Casquette Girls Coven," I said, going back to her theory, "so why didn't he go after Morning Star's side instead?"

She shrugged. "Either way, it hurts the Daures."

I squeezed Codi's hand.

"Either way, helps them take magical New Orleans," she added.

She had a point, but why would Jakome Salazar care about taking magical New Orleans? Was that even what Callisto wanted? Maybe. It seemed to me, though, that all Callis cared about was power—being the Greatest of the Great. Just like his father had all those centuries ago.

Something Martine had said before we left came back to me: *"Why do they worship him like a god?"* I looked around the room for Lisette, but she wasn't here. The shrine. The Blood magic. Callis's endgame wasn't New Orleans—it was restoring his family to Greatness. Maybe Jakome was simply trying to elimi-nate any powerful witches in the Natural World who would try to stop Callis from using necromancy to resurrect him . . . just like the other Great families had stopped him back in the day? That would explain why he went after the Daures.

But he'd gone after Monvoisins, and he hadn't touched the Borges, so that didn't make sense. I mean, you'd have to be seri-ously delusional to mess with Ritha, but if I'd ever met anyone who was delusional enough, it was Callis. I twisted the ring around in my pocket, absorbing its warmth.

Désirée was right about one thing: Jakome was targeting specific people. He could be going on a Guinée magic-drinking spree, but he wasn't. "He went after the Guldenmanns," I mumbled. "And the Monvoisins . . . but he didn't go after Morning Star or Marassa or Adeline . . . or anyone else in Guinée."

Désirée crossed her arms. "*Yet.*"

"No . . ." *He doesn't care about the New Orleans witches.* There was one thing all of these old school witches cared about. More than power. More than magic. More than immortality. It was what drove Nicco to hunt León all these years.

Revenge.

I sprang up. "We shouldn't have let Susannah go off on her own."

Everyone turned my way.

"Jakome isn't going after the original Casquette Girls Coven. He's going after the Great magical families of Old World Europe —the ones who burned his grimoire and excommunicated his family from their birth rites in Basque country, and who *buried his family alive.*" My pulse raced. "The Guldenmanns of the Black Forest, the Monvoisins of Paris, the Norwoods of the British Isles, and the Medici of the Kingdom of Tuscany."

Désirée stood. "So by that logic, he's going after the Norwoods next."

"Or . . . the Medici."

"We have to find Isaac *now*," she said, and suddenly everyone else was up on their feet.

Alarm rang in Adeline's voice. "It's been centuries since Susannah's warded off an enemy. She needs us!"

"Adele, what did you mean, they burned Jakome's grimoire?" Cosette asked. "Without their book of shadows, their coven could not be this strong."

Codi and Dee looked to me like, *Who's going to tell her?*

"She wasn't my friend," I mumbled.

"*Damn you.*" Désirée sucked it up and turned to Cosette. "So . . ." And she began filling her in on everything that had happened, including Annabelle's role.

Speaking of . . . where was she? Still stuck in her trial, I hoped. Whatever. I had more important people to find. After our fight, Nicco'd be going to only one of two places: to hunt Jakome on his own—but what could he do without the ghost-stick?—or to visit his family. There was no way he'd leave Guinée without seeing his sister. *He's heading straight into danger.* My pulse knocked so hard inside my chest I had to sit back down.

"Location spell," Marassa said, spreading out a map on the coffee table.

"Here, use this." My fingers reached for the silver feather, but only grasped air. I remembered I'd removed it from the chain. "*Shit.*"

"Isaac's not traceable anyway because of the blockers I put in our gris-gris," Dee said. "We have to go out and search ourselves."

"Okay," I said, tapping my foot nervously against the floor. "We'll split up."

"Why?" she asked sharply.

"Because . . ." I couldn't even look up, I was so scared to see the judgement in her eyes. In Adeline's eyes. "We have to find Nicco. We have to warn his family."

"Adele!" Désirée snapped. "It's *Isaac*."

"I know! And he has all of you. Nicco has no one."

"*Look*," Codi boomed over both of us. "We don't need a spell to know where Isaac's heading."

Dee turned to him with hope. "You're coming into your family's psychic abilities?"

"No, just my manly instincts." He half-smiled at his own joke. When no one laughed, he got serious. "Look, every over-protective, jealous bone in my body says that if he isn't going straight to Adele's, then he's going straight to—"

"Nicco's," I finished.

"We don't have to split up. They'll both be at casa de Medici."

"Nashoba and I will track Susannah, just to be sure," Morning Star said, and they both dropped down into wolf form, huge and sleek and quivering with a wild energy that stunned me into silence for a moment.

"Unnecessary," came a voice from across the room.

Susannah strode toward us, Lisette and Isaac on either side. *Oh thank God.* He stared straight at me, jaw tight. *Shit. How much of that had he heard?* From the hurt look on his face, defi-nitely the part about my concern for the Medici. I grabbed my backpack. I had to find Nicco even if I had to go by myself.

"There's no need to go to the Medici's," he said. "Nicco's not there. No one was."

The room quieted.

"What do you mean?" I barely choked out.

"I don't mean anything. Just that the place was empty. I scoped the entire property."

I couldn't keep the tears from welling. *There's no way Salazar got the Medici magic. No way the Medici had disappeared from Guinée.* It would mean . . . Nicco was no longer a witch. I strapped on the bag. "I'm going."

Everyone started arguing against it.

"Adele, there's no one there." Isaac stepped toward me, and I snapped.

"Kind of like how you told me last night that you didn't know where Nicco was?"

His eyes drooped shut. "I *swear.*"

"You're going to have to drug me again to stop me from going."

Everyone froze, and I realized what I had said. My cheeks flamed red, and I pushed past him on my way to the door.

"Did she say *drugged?*" Désirée asked Codi.

"I-I don't know. What the hell is she talking about, bro?"

I couldn't stand to hear any more and ran down the hall before Isaac responded, slamming the front door on my way out.

I'd only made it halfway across the lawn before the door opened again behind me. "Adele!" Désirée called.

I stopped but didn't turn. Was she going to tell me not to come back if I left to find Nicco? I didn't care if they kicked me out of the coven.

"What did you mean back there?" Her voice was softer than usual.

I shouldn't have said that in front of everyone. It's not anyone's business but mine and Isaac's. My throat swelled as I turned to face her.

"What happened to you last night?" Emotion choked her words, startling me. "Before we found you on the Moonwalk? Who broke your hand like that?"

Latent tears spilled from my eyes. "I don't want to talk about it. Please don't make me."

"Adele, I'm not going to *make* you do anything." Her eyes glistened. "I just want you to stop running away from us. Codi and I have your back. You just have to let us help."

I nodded, and she reached me with a few quick strides of her long legs and practically lifted me onto my toes with her hug.

"I'm sorry, I'm so terrible at this," I said. "I guess I didn't have many friends before the coven. Just one really, and I haven't seen her since before the Storm. Unless you count Emilio pretending to be my friend in Paris."

"That is sad."

I laughed out the remaining tears.

"I mean, I didn't exactly grow up with a lot of friends either. Just cousins. The girls at school were too jealous."

A sharp laugh slipped from my throat, but I just as quickly smothered it and gripped her hands. "Dee, I have to find Nicco. I don't care what happened three hundred years ago."

"Then we'll find him. *Together.*"

"Adeline's going to be mad."

"Well, then, fuck 'er."

"Really?" I half-heartedly huffed.

"I mean, I hope not, 'cause she seems pretty badass, but you are the youngest witch in your family. You carry the magicline. If she's not gonna support you, then yeah. That's what covens are for. That's what friends are for."

"Adeline *is* pretty badass."

"Come on." She put her arm around me, and we walked back toward the house. "So I was right all along? I knew you'd go for the dark, broody one."

"It's not like that. We're just friends."

"Adele, I might have to give you a lesson on what that word means."

"He's not into me."

"*Hmph.* Maybe he's the one who needs the lesson."

"Dee, you will do no such thing."

"*Ha.*" We hopped up to the porch. "You don't have to worry about me getting involved. Isaac's still my boy and all." She paused and turned to me. "But, Adele, whatever happens with you and him, the coven's going to be fine, okay? You're not going to lose us. He'll get through it. We'll be there for him. We'll all get through it."

I hugged her again, this time actually feeling relief. "I love you, Dee."

"Ditto. Can we stop hugging now?"

"*Oui.*" I took a deep inhale.

"Now, let's go find that vampire, put that fancy ghoststick to good use, and get the hell out of here. As much as I'd like for this to be an extended family reunion, we have serious shit to deal with back home."

Yeah. We're coming, Dad.

As we walked back into the parlor, I couldn't help but notice that Codi and Isaac were now on opposite sides of the room. Désirée lifted her chin, just as sure of herself as ever, and her confidence felt like a radiant shield, protecting me. I did my best to stand taller too. She went straight to Codi, Marassa, and the Monvoisins, and dove into planning mode.

However, as much as I appreciated it, I didn't need a shield.

I padded over to Isaac. He looked up with surprise and broke away from his conversation with Susannah and Adeline. "You're back."

"I'm sorry for what I said. I shouldn't have brought it up. Not here, not now."

He shook his head. "I shouldn't have done it. Everything is my fault. I can own it."

I nodded, blinking away the welling tears.

"I swear, though, Nicco wasn't at the house. I promise, I will never lie to you again." His eyes shone with fear, awaiting my reaction, and I hated it. I hated that I just wanted to pull him into my arms and tell him everything was going to be okay.

I didn't want to lose him. *I do love him.*

My breath shuddered.

"Adele," he said gently. "I have to ask you something. I'm not trying to upset you . . . I just have to make sure that you know . . . that Nicco . . ."

I swiftly nodded. I didn't need to hear him say it. I didn't need to hear him say that Nicco killed Adeline. I knew why he needed to tell me, and that was what I meant to say to him, but the words didn't come out. Nothing came out. All I could do was keep nodding.

"*Breathe*," he whispered.

And I did.

CHAPTER 41
A QUICK PEEK

I lingered in the moment with Adele for just a second longer.

I couldn't believe she still cared about whether Jakome Salazar took the Medici family magic.

She was Nicco's perfect victim: innocent, kind, and desperate to know about her magical lineage. But she was also smart and sharp, and she didn't trust anyone . . . so why had she let him in? What did he do to make her so blindly protect him?

Adeline had been enamored with Gabe, maybe even had a thing with him, but when he became too much of a threat, she still banished him to the attic.

Where was the line for Adele? *His enemies had taken her father.*

I took the damp flier I'd found at the Medici palace out of my shirt pocket. Thank God Nicco hadn't been there; it only would have ended badly for me, no matter what the outcome. Even if I'd managed to stake him, Adele would never have spoken to me again. "I found this floating in the fountain in the courtyard." I handed it to her. "Check out the date."

"*Akelarrenlezea Spectacular.*" Her brow scrunched as she looked it over. "It's for Zorion's show."

"Who's that? One of the Ghede?"

She glanced up at me. "Callis's sister. Tonight's opening night."

"Do you think that's where Nicco went?"

"It's . . . Jakome's show."

At the mention of Salazar's name, everyone turned our way.

"But . . . " Worry sprawled all over her face. "Nicco wouldn't know that."

"*Akelarrenlezea Spectacular?*" Susannah pulled a billfold from her jacket pocket, removed the same flier along with two tickets, and held them out for us to see. "Someone sent me these."

"Same." Cosette pulled two from her garter. "They're for tonight."

"Who sent them to you?" Adele asked.

Susannah shrugged. "The envelope just had my name on it. No sender. My father got them too. We were going to take my grandparents."

More of our magical family? I wanted to meet all of the Norwoods.

Adele walked to the center of the room, and everyone gravitated toward her orbit. She had one of those looks on her face—where her thoughts were charging faster than she could explain. "Did anyone else get tickets from a mystery sender?"

The other witches shook their heads, and she turned to Codi. "How much do you wanna bet that if we rummaged through Marta Guldenmann's stuff, we'd find front-row seats?"

I saw what she was getting at. "It's a trap."

"For the families who took Jakome down in the sixteenth century."

"That bastard," Cosette said. "He used *our* magic to take my sister's magic."

"I know the feeling," Adele said.

"I wonder if Minette started to figure it out and went sleuthing?" Lisette asked. "She's so brilliant."

"Or maybe Minette was his dress rehearsal?" Adeline said, a fire in her voice. She took Cosette's hand. "Thank heavens you didn't go to the show."

"Oh, she's going." Adele looked to Cosette and Susannah. "We're all going. We're going to break the Salazar magicline just like your Great families intended all those centuries ago. Only this time, the Saint-Germains will be with you."

"And the ancestors of Africa," said Désirée.

"And of the Mighty Mississippi," Codi echoed, cracking his knuckles, and I swore a breeze stirred the room and wolves howled in the distance. Their ancestors stood proudly behind them, and I nodded to Susannah. Her smile crooked feistily, like she was ready to steer the ship.

Adele removed the ghost-killing wand from her bag. "And we're going to do it with Marta's help."

Every person in the room scooted closer, as if her Spektral itself was pulling us to her. But it wasn't her magic—she was magnetizing without it. It was her passion. Her *com*passion. I slowly exhaled some of the night's pain.

Susannah leaned close to me. "I can see why you love her."

I bit my lip, swallowing the guilt and pain and regret. "I screwed it up, *really* bad."

She put her arm around me and pulled me close. Her curls matched the dust of freckles across her nose. "We Norwoods have hard heads. Sometimes we leap before we look. Sometimes there are sharks in the water. Sometimes there is sunken treasure. You're brave. And kind. And generous. Your family is so proud of you."

"They are?"

"Of course. Stop sounding so surprised."

I tried to smile, but I didn't feel like a witch they should be proud of. I couldn't believe I'd used magic against Adele. *I love her.*

"But Isaac, it doesn't matter how strong you are, or how fast, or how magical. You can't protect her from everything."

"I know. But I want to."

"You have to believe that she can protect herself. Otherwise, she'll always feel below you."

"I don't think she's below me," I whispered. "At all."

"You have a good heart. You'll find a way to show her."

I wanted to believe her, but I wasn't so sure Adele would ever forgive me. I wasn't even sure if I deserved it. Susannah squeezed my hand, and we turned back to the group.

"Do you think the ghoststick will still work?" Dee asked, giving Codi her most apologetic face.

"It will work," Morning Star said adamantly. "The branch and the stones act as sacred vessels containing the power. It's infused with our Tribal magic as well."

Adele balanced the smoky quartz end on the tip of her finger and then lightly tossed it into the air. "Dude!" Codi yelped. But it hovered before us, sparkling under the crystal chandelier, the mix of German and Choctaw words glowing around the branch.

"Oh my Goddess," Dee yelped. "You're using your magic, Adele!"

"*Oui.*" A smile spread across her face. I'd almost forgotten what it was like to see her smile. "Did I forget to mention I got it back?"

"*How?*" Dee asked.

"I remembered some advice Papa Olsin once gave me." She looked lovingly at Codi.

His arms stayed crossed tight, but his eyes watered. "We have to find my grandma."

"We will," I said. "All of them, I promise."

And Codi looked at me for the first time since I'd confessed to using the sedative magic on Adele. He gave me a quick nod that felt like it meant we could put it aside *for now*. I couldn't blame him. I'd have had the same reaction. No, let's be real; I'd have had a worse reaction. I turned to Lisette, who'd been almost dead silent since finding out about her sister's disappearance. "Minette too."

"We have to. My sister's never been alone a day in her life."

Adele nodded. "All right, we have the weapon. We have the target. Now all we need is a plan."

I pulled my grimoire out of my bag. "Who's been inside the theatre?" I sat down at the coffee table and opened it to a blank spread. Susannah sat at my side, and everyone leaned in.

"I've been there." Adeline sounded like she was ready to get into some trouble.

Marassa laughed. "In our time, she owned the building."

"It was originally meant to be Martine DuFrense's opera house. Her husband, Claude, built it. It only seemed right to honor her memory by continuing with the construction."

I uncapped a pen. "Okay. Tell me about entrances. Exits. Windows. Basement trap doors."

"Basements?" They all laughed. "In New Orleans?"

"*Ha.* My bad. Attics."

"The front entrance is here on Rue Toulouse," Adeline said, and I drew a line for the street. Cosette and Marassa began pointing out the courtyard and back alleyways, and my hand flew across the page keeping up. "The balcony wraps around the garçonniere and takes you to a back entrance." *Wait. I know this building.* I finished the staircase and turned it around to face Adele.

Her eyes met mine, and she scooted down from the sofa to the table across from me. "It's Le Chat Noir." My pulse skipped, feeling so in lockstep. "That should make things a little easier," she said.

"The doors might be in the same places, but I wouldn't expect too much else to be the same," Marassa said. "Don't get comfortable."

"And who knows what kind of dark power they'll be

harnessing tonight?" Makandal added. "They'll be sure to have the property strongly fortified, magically-speaking and otherwise."

"We'll stay in pairs." I heard my pop's voice creeping eerily into my own. "Watch each other's backs." We might have our differences, but the man knew how to create deeply thought-out plans, and I knew exactly what he would say: "The most important part—"

"Is getting Jakome—" Codi finished.

"Is the exit strategy."

Susannah nodded in agreement. "He's right. Jakome isn't planning to take down four Great magical families on his own. He'll have every Basque witch who shares even an ounce of his bloodline at the theatre. The Basque witches were one of the oldest magical families in Europe, which means they go many generations deep."

"You need to be ready to open the portal if chaos erupts," Marassa said. "To get back to the Natural World."

The thought of us all having to part ways already hung heavy in the air.

Dee nodded, opening her grimoire. "I'll be on portal duty."

"I'll help you," Marassa said.

"And we'll be your lookout," Morning Star said. "It's going to take a lot of focus to open a portal large enough for everyone."

Codi bounced up on his toes like he always did when he was pumping himself up.

"If Jakome is on stage," Adeline said, "he'll be using some kind of protection spell."

"*C'est un problème,*" Cosette said. "If we don't know what the spell is, we can't prepare a counterspell to break it."

"Or . . ."—Dee turned to me—"we don't need to break it. Remember the night we made the hexenspiegels? There was something in your grimoire to contain magic."

"A Witch Bottle," Susannah said with a sly smile. "Old Bermudian magic." And with a flick of her hand, the pages of our grimoire fanned. "It will be perfect. Although Salazar won't be using an infantile protection spell. It's going to take our collective power to contain it."

"The Makandals open the portal," Adeline said, "and while Adele locks her mark, the rest of us will pull the shield into the bottle."

As everyone agreed, she whispered something else to Cosette and then jumped up and left the room.

Adele took an excited inhale. "How many tickets do we have?"

Cosette confidently handed hers to Lisette. "For you and Adeline. No one will see me enter."

"*Merci,*" Lisette said, but passed her ticket to Makandal. "I don't need one either."

"But *ma fifille*, you don't have your magic!" Cosette said.

Lisette and I both let out a little laugh.

"What?" Cosette asked, unpleased to be left out of the gag.

"Lisette doesn't need magic," I said. "She's fast. Like, *really* fast."

Lisette blushed as our eyes met. I wondered how she was doing. Something told me that behind her perfectly timed smiles, she was full of pain being around everyone else with their descendants. Knowing what the Medici did to her made me hate them even more.

Susannah gave her tickets to Marassa. "For you and Désirée." She hooked her arm in mine. "I'm sure there's a chimney we can use."

"Or a *window*," I added with a little huff.

"There's one in the powder room," Marassa said. "We can open it for you."

"I can take you in my bag," Dee said to Codi.

"I'm not *that* small!" He disappeared, and then Onyx

415

jumped into her bag. He fit perfectly. She petted the top of his head, and he let out a purr.

"You will grow as your magic matures." Morning Star scratched his neck. "Nashoba and I will also find our way in."

"Just in case." Adele produced two more tickets for Morning Star.

Dee gave her a look of surprise. "Where did you get those?"

"It's a long story involving a chalice of mandrake liqueur, a slice of dead pie, and a run-in with three Salazars."

"Sounds like a Ghede-trial if I ever heard one," Dee said.

"I wish." Adele rolled her eyes.

"But how will you get in without a ticket?" Morning Star asked her.

"I grew up in that building. I know it like the back of my hand."

Cosette gave her a devilish smile. "Oh no, *ma fifille*, we have something special for you."

Adeline reappeared behind the sofa and waved her hands in the air. "Here you go, *ma petite sorcière*."

In a *swoosh*, Adele was gone. Everyone jumped back except for Cosette and Lisette, who let out girlish giggles, seeming to relax for the first time all night.

Adele swirled excitedly, and the cloak lifted up, revealing her body beneath it.

When she sat back down, Adeline hugged her from behind, pulling the hood from her head. "This should help you get in *and* stay hidden from the Salazars until you're ready to take your shot."

"*Merci beaucoup.*" She gushed more French to her ancestor before turning her attention back to the group.

"Your best vantage will be from the center of the lower mezzanine," I said, showing her on the map.

"We'll set up the portal on the upper mezzanine," Marassa

said to Dee. "Cosette can create an invisibility dome so no one will see us."

"*Cool*," Dee said.

Lisette examined the tickets. "I'll find Niccolò when we arrive so he can warn his family."

Adele looked relieved. "*Merci*."

Adeline stood, crossing her arms. "Are we really protecting the Medici family now?"

Lisette's fangs snapped out. "He's *my* family now."

Cosette's eyes widened with sorrow.

"I'm so sorry, Lise," Adeline choked.

"It's . . . It's not as bad as it was in the beginning," she said, but I was pretty sure she was just trying to make them feel better. My hand impulsively went to hers, just to let her know that she wasn't alone.

Désirée marked everyone's spots on my sketch. "Isaac, you're in charge of the Witch Bottle."

"Actually, could Codi be?" I glanced at Adele. "I don't want to leave your side this time." It seemed like just seconds ago I was closing the cemetery gates between us—a decision I'd regret for the rest of my life. "If that's okay with you?" I held my breath until she nodded.

Thank you, I mouthed.

She nodded again, and a glimmer of hope sparked inside me. Maybe all wasn't lost.

"Showtime is in an hour," Adeline said. "We've got a lot to do. Witches, make sure Désirée has everything she needs to open the portal, and make sure Codi has supplies for the Bermudian spell. We'll split up so we don't all arrive at once and raise suspicion. And theatre clothes, people! We need to blend in with the crowd. I want to see your Afterworld finest!"

Everyone began fluttering around.

Lisette raised a finger. "We have just one little problem."

"What is it?" Adele asked.

"Aren't we forgetting someone?"

"Nicco will be at the theatre. I know it."

"Not Niccolò. Annabelle."

Oh shit.

"Has anyone seen her since we arrived?" Lisette asked.

"Can't we just leave her here?" Dee mumbled under her breath.

"No argument from me," Adele said.

A mix of sadness and embarrassment filled Cosette's eyes.

"Let's go find her, sister," Lisette said. "Maybe the two of us can set her straight."

"I'll go with you," I said.

Dee gave me an *Excuse me, we've got a lot of shit to do* look.

"I can fly; it will go faster. Plus, I don't trust Annabelle as far as I can throw her, and the future of our magiclines depends on us not fucking this up. I'd rather know exactly where she is before we start executing such a critical plan." *Plus, I need to make a quick run to the Miracle-Ghede's shop.*

Susannah nodded. "I'll go too."

"Fine. But *no one* can tell Annabelle the plan," Adele insisted. "She might try to sabotage the Witch Bottle or something to save Jakome. After all, she did join the Salazars' coven."

"She won't be leaving my side, even if I have to magically chain her," Cosette said, walking to the door with Lisette. "If she tries anything, she'll be learning why my grandmother was called the great La Voisin."

Adele leaned close to Dee and whispered, "Did she really just threaten to poison Annabelle?"

"Talk about femme fatale," Dee whispered back.

Without thinking, I touched Adele's arm, and my pulse stopped. I expected her to flinch, but she turned toward me. "I'll meet you at the theatre bar fifteen minutes before showtime?"

"Okay. Good luck finding Annabelle."

Relief flooded through me. It's not like she was overjoyed or anything when she looked at me, but the fear was gone from her eyes. The anger. The nervousness. I relaxed for the first time all night.

"*Allons-y,*" Cosette said, and I followed the two blondes out the front door.

We split into pairs. Cosette and Susannah went lakebound, Lisette and I riverbound.

I soared high above the rooftops, scouring the courtyards, while Lisette zipped from one side of the street to the other, peering into the windows of cafes and shop galleries at the speed of light—it was pretty cool, even if she was a vampire.

When I spotted the bakery, I swooped down to the street.

"Did you see her?" She walked beside me through the gate.

"No, but I have to make a pitstop." I nodded up to Ghede-Linto's French bakery sign.

Her brow pressed in confusion. "But you can't eat—"

"I'm not looking for a cupcake. There's supposed to be a Ghede who's a medicine man. A miracle worker. And nothing other than a miracle is going to save Ren."

"Hurry," she said. "Maybe he can tell us where Annabelle is."

The bakery looked like an old soda pop shop. My mouth watered, taking in the scents of cinnamon rolls, churros, and pumpkin pie. The old Ghede was still behind the counter, surrounded by little ghost children whose cupped hands he was pouring candy, cookies, and marshmallows into. He couldn't have been more than five feet tall with a silver beard, a purple apron with long suede fringe, and a black straw Panama hat. A song that made the kids laugh scatted from his lips, and they ran out with pocketfuls of sweets.

"Fresh pralines 'bout to come out da oven!" he said to us with that Ghede-purple twinkle in his eye.

I leaned on the counter in front of him. "We're looking for something a little more, er, special."

"Ain't nuthin' more special than Linto's pralines."

"Oh, it's just that we're looking for something more *miraculous.*"

"Oh, you lookin' for a gad."

"Yes!" *Isn't that what Oussou called it?* "My friend Ren, he's really bad off. Witches attacked this ghost, Alessandro, and now his soul is trapped inside of Ren. If we don't get Alessandro out, he's gonna kill him."

"Ya wanna stop a murderer, you should see Kriminel."

"To be fair to Alessandro, he's not exactly a murderer. More like a parasite. It's not his fault his spirit was eaten for dinner by a feckless Ghost Drinker."

"Maybe it's his time to go?"

"It can't be." I pounded the counter.

Lisette flashed me a look.

"Not like this!" I insisted. "Ren's soul isn't meant to end up in a mermaid pool for eternity. He has too many songs left to sing, tales left to tell, chains left to rattle, or whatever his Bourbon Street-haunting ass would do after death!"

"I admire yo' passion young man." Linto paused. "But how far you willin' to go to help him?"

"As far as I need to—I came to the Afterworld, for Christ's sake."

The old Ghede turned to the oven and, without using so much as a towel, reached in for the sheet pan. He took a deep inhale of the pralines before setting them on the counter in front of us. "All miracles come with a cost." He spun around the room like a dreidel and returned with his arms full of jars. He flicked each one open and sprinkled pink crystals and orange spices over the confections. "Are you sure you're willing to accept the responsibility?"

"I'm sure."

"Accept the consequences?"

"Yes. We're talking about my friend's *soul*."

"Isaac . . ." Lisette touched my shoulder.

"What? It's *Ren*."

Linto plucked one of the pralines, dropped it into a wax bag, and tied it up with a string. "Then it's done."

"Thank you, thank you, thank you!" I reached for the bag.

He slapped my wrist and brushed his fingers together.

"Oh, my bad." I reached for my wallet chain. "How much?"

"*Pish*." He slid the bag further away.

Shit. This dude was totally cut from the same cloth as Oussou and Masaka. Think, Isaac, why would he want money? *What would a Ghede want?*

I opened up my bag and dug through what was left of the supplies from Dee, harking back to the ritual at St. Roch. Florida Water? I put the bottle on the counter, and his eyes lit up. I pushed it over to him.

Linto plucked off the cork and glugged back a swig. *Okaaay.* I didn't know people actually drank that stuff, although I guess he wasn't exactly a person. He spit it on the floor, but didn't seem unsatisfied with it.

I laid out a cigar, three matches, and half a pack of smokes. He put them all between his lips at once and lit them ablaze. "Are you sure you want— You know, those things will kill ya?"

Lisette leaned close. "He's already dead."

"*Touché.*"

With one long finger, he slid the gad toward me.

"*Merci.*" I wrapped the package up in an extra T-shirt, secured it safely in my bag, and thanked Ghede-Linto again.

"See you soon," he said, sprinkling green powder onto his pralines.

"Have you seen—?" Lisette started to ask.

"Stop looking for her," he said, "and start listening for her." In a blink he disappeared, along with the pralines.

"What did he mean by that?" she asked as I held open the door for her.

"Shit if I know. Does Annabelle sing?"

"Not that. The *see you soon.*"

"I dunno. I guess we'll all end up here one day."

A female voice made us both stop in our tracks: *"Is it true that the grimoire is in the Afterworld?"*

I gave Lisette a questioning look, and we both crept closer. Behind the folds of banana trees, a plum-colored curtain hung down from a sign that said: **FORTUNES.**

"Where is it?" the same voice asked excitedly. *"You have got to be kidding!"*

Lisette's face tensed, then she ripped backed the curtain. *"Voila!"*

Two girls were sitting opposite each other, leaning over a stack of apple crates doing some kind of reading—a head of crimpy lavender waves looked up. "Isaac!" Doubye yelped, leaping toward me, the key on her forehead bobbing. Her redheaded customer turned toward us holding the Ghede's wand up to her crown chakra. The large eye blinked at us.

"Annabelle."

Lisette yanked the wand from her hand and gave it back to Doubye, muttering something in French. I had no idea if Annabelle could understand French, but she rolled her eyes.

"Do you want to take a look through my glass?" Doubye held it out. "I know you want to see the future."

"No, thanks—"

"To see if she's zhere with you."

My pulse skipped. *To see if Adele . . . ?*

"Free of charge for you."

"Why does he get a look for free?" Annabelle exclaimed, her words a bit muffled. Beneath the wave of hair, her left cheek was puffed up, swollen. My eyes fell to a small dish on the apple crate. Inside it were a rusty pair of pliers and *a bloody tooth.*

"You traded a tooth? From your *mouth*? For a fortune?" I asked in disbelief.

Annabelle shrugged as if it was just her class ring she'd given up. "I'll get a new one when we get home."

Jesus Christ. Had Callis warped her brain?

Doubye inched the wand closer. Everything I wanted to know was *right there*: Whether Papa Olsin's premonition was true. Whether Adeline's warnings were warranted. All I had to do was look through the Ghede's third eye.

I touched the ornate metal. *I wanted to see* our *future*. Would we be in art school? Doing magic together. Taking over the bar from Mac. Or it could be a flash of fangs? A spray of blood. Tears at her funeral. Doubye could show me it all.

"Okay," I said.

The Ghede's face lit up as she pulled me down to the table.

I lifted the wand to my forehead, and her chill flooded my entire being, making my hands shake. Everything around me went black. But then . . . the Bowie record Adele always played faintly filled the void. I could smell her strawberry shampoo. A door cracked open, letting in light, and I heard her voice over the phonograph on the other side. I was in the little closet room in her attic.

I felt Doubye's magic pulsing through my muscles. *Just open the door, Isaac, and look.*

My pulse spiked. I reached out for the door . . . but I felt gross, like I was about to read her diary. *Only an asshole would do that.*

I stepped back. "I don't want to know."

But the door began to open, and her voice became louder. I leapt forward, shoving it closed. "I don't want to know! It's her future. I don't want to spy, or cheat, or try to change it."

The ambient sounds of the café filtered in around me as Doubye came back into view.

I pushed the wand away. "It's her life. Her choices."

I trust Adele. I believe in her. And I'll protect her from monsters with every shred of magic in my bones . . . as long as she wants me to. The Ghede's gaze was locked on my chest, fixated on the Wolf's Tooth. She snatched the cord from over my head and looped it around her neck. The cold rushed in so strongly it knocked me onto the floor. *Don't take it back Isaac.*

You don't need it.

I didn't need protection from the spirits; I needed to embrace them. To embrace my magic. I forced myself up, and the chill ran up and down my spine like an army folding in. For a blink, my left arm glowed beneath my hoodie sleeve. *My Mark.*

"Too much of a pussy to know the truth?" Annabelle asked, right next to me.

"I don't believe the future is that predetermined," I snapped. "I refuse to believe Olsin's premonition can't be stopped from coming true."

Annabelle's brow crooked. "What premonition?"

"That Niccolò kills Adele," Doubye answered.

Annabelle's eyes bulged. She turned to Lisette, who cut her off before she could say anything. "We need to go."

As we all started for the exit, Doubye stepped closer, peering into my eyes. "Your optimism is noble. Boring, but noble."

"You have no idea how boring he is," Annabelle said, and she walked through the curtain, letting it fall in my face. "*I got the grimoire,*" I heard her whisper to Lisette.

"*Que?*"

"Okay, I don't have it. *Yet.*"

On the other side of the velvet drape, I caught Lisette's look of confusion. What the hell were they talking about? What grimoire? Maybe Lisette had threatened to leave her here in Guinée if she didn't get their family heirloom back from those asshole Ghost Drinkers?

"*Merci mille fois* for the tooth," Doubye said, brushing against my shoulder.

"You were right. I need to fully embrace my magic."

Her eyes twinkled, matching her hair. "And I have something for you."

"Oh, you don't—"

She snapped her fingers, and the key disappeared from her forehead. One of the strands of her rosary beads appeared around my neck, the cross replaced with the key. I picked it up, inspecting it. Instead of metal, it was dingy white and light as air. I dropped it. "Is this made of—?"

"Bone? Of course, silly. It's a skeleton key. So you can return to the Afterworld whenever you please."

"I hate to disappoint, but this will be my one and only trip to the Afterworld until it's my time to go."

She held the wand up to the center of her forehead, and all three of her eyes slipped shut. "We'll see." Her tone sounded just like one of the psychics at the tearoom. Totally matter of fact.

"It's twenty minutes until showtime," Lisette said.

"Enjoy the performance." Doubye blew a puff of silver glitter our way.

As the cloud settled, my clothes tightened, and a hat appeared on my head.

Lisette and Annabelle's clothes from the Natural World disappeared, and they now wore dresses that seemed straight out of a Sherlock Holmes movie but also like they belonged to a New York club kid: long skirts puffed up over their butts, shiny black tops that might as well have been liquid latex cinched their waists, and there was so much glitter in their hair and makeup that they shimmered and sparkled when they breathed.

Annabelle looked at me with a laugh. "What's your look supposed to be? Undertaker chic?"

I felt my hair, slicked underneath a tall top hat, and peered down at the dark suit.

"I think you look handsome," Lisette said, and her pale cheeks turned bright pink.

"My tits look great in this top," Annabelle said, adjusting it to maximize her cleavage. "What's the occasion?"

"The theatre," Lisette answered, gathering up her skirt in her hands. "Cosette's saving you a seat."

"Will Adele be there?"

Why the hell does she care where Adele is?

"I'm not sure," Lisette answered.

"Groovy."

Lisette's gaze found mine. There was something more disconcerting about Annabelle being agreeable than when she was being a dick.

CHAPTER 42

AKELARRENLEZEA SPECTACULAR

The layers of beaded fringe hanging from my dress swooshed as I walked down the street. The noisy garment didn't seem wise for the mission, but at least I could move, and more importantly, breathe. I'd only narrowly escaped having to wear one of Adeline's tightly bound dresses with even further restricting underlayers because I'd spotted the delicate shift draped over one of the dressing screens at the brothel. *Thank you, flappers.*

I paused across the street from the theatre and brushed my hair out of my face, hardly able to see out of my right eye thanks to the flawless Marcel wave Cosette had glamoured my hair into. I dug to the bottom of my bag for a bobby pin—the coiffure, while perfect, didn't seem very practical for the markswoman. I didn't see why I had to dress up at all, given I'd be wearing the invisibility cloak to get inside, but Adeline had insisted we play the part.

The neon sign, *Akelarrenlezea Spectacular,* cast a glow of pink light over elegantly dressed spirits crowding the sidewalks, waiting to go inside. Others buzzed about the box office trying to score last-minute tickets. The words "**SOLD OUT**" blinked beneath the sign.

The bones of Le Chat Noir were the same, but it looked so much more like the opera house Adeline had built than the club I'd grown up in. More rock bands had graced the stages in the last three generations than *theatre* performers.

The building itself had a diamond-like sparkling effect.

I slipped past the lines and headed into the front bar, which was far more sophisticated than its counterpart back home.

Waitstaff in crisp white shirts served colorful cocktails in sparkling glassware to patrons. There was no sign of Isaac, so I took a window seat near the door to keep an eye out for him and pulled the remainder of my picnic from my bag, hoping it would prevent any waitstaff from coming over. The last thing I needed was more Southern hospitality.

I sipped the peach fizzy drink, staring out the window, and for a moment, everything felt so familiar. How many days had I spent in this seat as a child with my coloring books? As a second-grader with my library books? The stories in the pages never seemed as imaginative as the people who walked past the window: glittering dancers on their way to work, drag queens with orange wigs three feet high, tea-leaf readers with their jingling skirts, and street performers who could breathe fire.

My fingers absently rubbed the table where there was a carving in the Natural World. Once, when I was about nine and apparently thought I was a total badass, I'd carved my name into the wood with a pocketknife stolen from my dad's workshop. When I'd finished and looked up, he was staring straight at me. My heart had stopped, knowing that I was going to be in big trouble—which in hindsight seemed silly, because he almost never got mad at me or punished me. Nonetheless, I knew what I'd done was wrong, and I was *terrified*. He came over to inspect the damage, and every second he'd remained silent brought me closer to tears. First, he told me I wasn't allowed to play with his tools outside of his studio, and never without him, but then he picked up the knife and began carving something as well. He told me that the table was mine and it *should* have my name on it, and that one day the whole place would be mine.

I looked down and nearly choked seeing the message staring back at me.

MAC ♥ *ADELE*

"I love you too, Dad."

I pictured him back home trapped in that plantation. Tied up. His throat dry with thirst. Lashes across his back from when he'd tried to escape and got caught. I imagined that Irish witch whose hand I'd cut off getting his revenge by taking it out on my dad. My lungs pinched. *Please don't hurt my dad.*

Stop it, Adele. Stop thinking like this.

I took a deep breath and took the last sip of the peach drink, picturing Nicco and his family already in the theatre. What was Salazar's plan for them? Nicco had already lost so much of his witch identity; there was no way I was going to let that asshole take away the last bit I knew was buried deep inside.

Suddenly I worried—what if we'd been wrong and Nicco wasn't at the show? I wouldn't go through the portal without him, no way. Gabriel would think I'd planned it all along. I glanced at the clock above the bar. Twenty minutes until curtain up. *Come on, Isaac.*

Out on the street, the spirits seemed exuberant over the show. A man with long green hair and a woman with a buzz cut and fairy wings walked by. Another woman, who had matched a tuxedo jacket with baseball pants, tottered by on gold lamé stilettos. In Guinée, no one was afraid to live their inner truth. And why should they be? They were dead.

As unique as their styles were, they all had the same ashen hue. Otherworldliness exuded in their voices, in their optimistic auras, and in their graceful movements. They had a transparent, weightless feel, like they could float away to nap in the clouds or dance with the stars.

What would it be like to push the ghoststick into Jakome's heart? Did spirits have hearts?

I wondered if Chatham had ever used the weapon before.

The spirits seemed so delicate, like it wouldn't take much to penetrate their forms, but then again, their ethereal nature also had an indestructible quality to it, just like fire or water or air or earth.

Well . . . fire could be suffocated, water could be boiled away, air poisoned, and earth eroded. Was anything truly forever? Even magic could be broken. Eradicated.

My heart pounded, deep and resonant. Would I really be able to do this? Kill a man . . . a ghost. *A witch*? I checked the clock again, feeling like a spy in a James Bond movie, only instead of a gun strapped to my garter or a throwing star tucked in my hair, I had a magic wand made from a tree branch and smoky quartz. If Isaac was late, I was going in without him.

"Hey."

I sprang up. "Hi."

We both leaned in and almost kissed—and we both stopped ourselves, awkwardly pulling away. "Sorry," I mumbled.

He gazed at me, a little taken back. "You look, um . . ." He struggled to figure out what to say. "Like a movie star."

Harmless.

"Thanks." I didn't know what to say either. "You look . . ." He looked quite dashing, but it somehow felt inappropriate to mention after all of the fighting.

"Undertaker chic?" he offered, and I couldn't help but smile.

"Yeah, actually. In the most debonair of ways."

"Ghede-Doubye hooked it up." He offered me his elbow. I didn't see why it was necessary, but part of me was nervous, and that part of me was comforted by the solid muscle of his arm.

Besides, playing the role alongside this incredibly dapper version of him made me feel even more Femme Fatale.

As he held the door open, he leaned close and whispered, "They're everywhere." His breath hit my neck, sending a wave of tingles down my chest and confusion into my head.

I pinched my brow.

"They have the theatre surrounded. The entire block secured. Don't look now, but one's just back there, in the other window seat."

We stepped out onto the street, and I casually glanced back. Sure enough, a woman was sitting in the window opposite the door where I'd been, eyeing the street scene over the top of her book. She had a dark green velvet dress, thin gold-rimmed glasses, impeccable wing-tipped eyeliner, and a black cape just like Zorion's. I'd never have noticed her if Isaac hadn't pointed her out. I guess Adeline had been right to insist on our costumes.

And just like that, the mission became real. I allowed myself one more quick moment of nervousness. Of doubt. And then I was done. I looked up with a smile, just like Adeline or Cosette would have done. Or Giovanna. Just like Isaac was doing now. We were just a happy couple on our way to the theatre.

Peering through the fake smile and shiny eyes, I could examine the streets more naturally, turning my head as we pretended to talk or laugh. I spotted the succubus witches sometimes even before Isaac pointed them out. They were the spirits who seemed like they didn't belong, looking a little too serious, gazing a little too hard, and without the excited curiosity of opening night or the glamour of theatre attire. They wore silk, leather, and everything in between, but they all had pointy boots and black capes, hoods loosely hanging down their backs. Just like the Ghost Drinkers back home wore during their rituals.

I squeezed Isaac's arm, and he tightened his biceps.

Taking care not to look at them as we passed by, I wondered

what was going through their minds. What was it like to abruptly have your magic after centuries of being so weak? I thought back to the shrine we'd found in the cathedral. Did they think they'd soon be strong enough to break free from the Afterworld? Had Callis really amassed that much power? He'd shown no signs of effort when he'd flown across the water carrying my father.

"There's an alleyway up ahead near Royal."

I nodded, and we walked past the theatre as if we were just out on a stroll. My neck craned. "It's so strange and pretty. And sparkly."

"Trinkets of the dead," Isaac said as if he was now an expert on the Afterworld.

"What?" I twisted, my gaze on the building as we drew close. He was right. The building sparkled like diamonds because it *was made of them*—hundreds of thousands of them: diamond earrings, necklaces, and lockets; jewel-encrusted broaches, cufflinks, and pocket watches; and so many rings . . . the tokens of love and markers of relationship milestones, all buried with the dead. The sparkling building suddenly felt dark and morbid. I reached out, letting my fingers run across the precious metals and gems. Cold spilled into my veins, and a man in a suit flashed before my eyes. *He's nervous, his pulse racing as he lowers himself down on one knee, gazing up at a beautiful girl in a Victorian dress.*

I yanked my hand away, and the vision dispelled in an inky black cloud.

"You okay?" Isaac asked.

"Yeah. Just an overactive imagination."

"Adele!" squealed a girl loitering outside the stage door. She ran over to us, as delighted as anyone could be, her smile bouncing between me and Isaac.

Shit.

Isaac glanced at me with a look of confusion.

"Isaac, this is Zorion. *Salazar.* She was kind enough to give me the tickets. It's her family's show."

His eyes widened, and he nodded. "Hello."

"This is Isaac?" she yelped, leaning toward him. "I know that you weren't her husband, but I *know* that she likes you more than Mario. I have instincts about these things."

Isaac glanced at me.

Just go with it, I tried to say with my eyes. But there was no need; Zorion didn't leave a breath unspoken.

"I didn't realize Isaac had passed on too! Was it tragic?"

"Yes," I said. "Very much so. We died together. An accident. A Storm."

"Witches dying in a storm? How peculiar." Her brow pointed. "I got the impression you are an Air witch?"

"I am, and it was." Isaac coughed. "But you know . . . even magic can't outperform Mother Nature at her finest." He circled his arm around me. "But all that matters now is that we get to spend eternity together."

Zorion cooed dreamily at him. "That's so lovely." She took our hands. "There will be a *big* celebration after the show. You'll have to come! I *know* Mother will be excited to see you, despite her initial impression. I can't wait to tell her you're here!"

"No!" I yelped.

Her expression turned questioning.

"I just mean . . . let's surprise her, after the show."

Her smile lit back up. "Yes, let's. And Father too."

The mention of her father made my legs jellylike, and I might have collapsed to the ground if Isaac hadn't been holding me. We hastily said our goodbyes.

"I'll meet you here after curtain call!"

We waved as she went back through the stage door. "Good luck with the sunflowers," I yelled, and Isaac whisked me away.

"Jesus Christ, that was close," he said.

Our pace quickened as we hurried to the alley ahead. "Too close."

Under the cover of the shadows, I pulled out the cloak, threw it over my shoulders, and adjusted the hood, watching as Isaac leapt into the air, taking crow form, and soared deeper into the alley. No matter how many times I'd seen him do it, it was still majestic. He flew back and hovered in front of me, as if asking, *Ready to go?*

I was, but I didn't move.

"What if I can't do it?" I blurted, and the hood slipped off.

He reappeared, standing before me. "What do you mean?"

"I mean . . . I've never used a ghoststick before—"

"You've totally got this, Adele."

"I've never used any weapon before."

His hands rested on my shoulders. "Just wait until you have a clean shot, and sling it as hard as you can at that asshole. He's already hurt Codi's family and Lisette's. We can't let him hurt anyone else."

"It's not like I have a lot of athletic prowess."

"It doesn't matter. You're a witch. You have magic."

"But I only just got my Spektral back! What if it's not good enough without my Fire behind it?"

His hands slid up my face, and he pressed his forehead to mine. "You *are* strong enough. You're the strongest person I know."

A wave of energy rushed through me, pulling me up on my toes, and I crushed my arms around him. It might have been wrong of me to do it. "I'm still mad at you," I said, and I felt his shoulders tense. "But I can't fathom heading into such a dangerous situation and not being a completely unified force." For all of the mistakes Isaac had ever made, that we had both made, he had *never once* made me question his loyalty.

"That's not something you ever have to fathom," he said, hugging me tightly.

I felt his heart pounding against mine, and it was calming. I knew that he would have my back until the day we died.

And I would have his.

"You got this," he said, holding me, trying to hide the nervousness in his voice. I didn't think it was because of the mission but because we were standing so close. Because the natural next move was for us to kiss. Make up. I would be lying if I said a part of me didn't want to. "You got this," he said again, brushing my hair.

I nodded, letting him go, not quite able to look him in the eye.

He let out a gentle laugh.

"What?" I followed his gaze up—all the metal garbage cans in the alley were floating high in the air above us. As I slowly exhaled, they lowered back to the ground, and for the first time since the night at the convent, I felt like I was a witch again. And I was grateful for him. For us. For our coven, and for Adeline's. I still didn't have my Fire, and I was no closer to finding León, but I'd never felt more like a Saint-Germain. "Let's do this, so we can go home and—"

"Save your dad." He pulled the hood back over my hair, and just before he adjusted it down over my face, he kissed my cheek. I blushed, but before I could react, he dove into the air.

He circled the alley, gaining speed, and we were off.

With Isaac soaring above me, I wove through the spirits on the street, careful not to knock into anyone, especially as we passed the Ghost Drinkers at their inconspicuous stations. *What kind of magic did they have planned tonight?* At the box office, I didn't skip a beat, following a couple inside when they opened the door and holding it just long enough for Isaac to swoop in.

I passed Susannah in the lobby and saw Dee and Makandal heading up the opposite staircase as I ascended to the second floor. I moved quickly, worried someone would mow into me. But even in the rush, I scanned the room for any sign of Nicco.

The hood obstructed my view, and the dense crowd of people made it difficult to see. As I faced ahead, two girls engrossed in high-excitement gossip were coming down the steps straight at me—I leapt out of the way, gripping the rail, and they sailed past. *Be careful, Adele!* The last thing I needed was to cause a scene.

I ran up the rest of the stairs, eager to get to my seat where I'd have a good view of the whole theatre. *Nicco has to be here.*

Isaac reappeared next to me as I walked onto the mezzanine, his hand briefly brushing mine through the cloak. I followed him to a pair of front-row seats reserved with beaded Choctaw sashes, and my nervousness morphed into excitement as we sat. The Water witches were here.

I opened my bag beneath the cloak and stared at the ghost-stick resting between Adeline's diary and the remaining Hexennacht cakes. *I can do this.* I took a deep breath, pulled it out, and pushed the bag under my seat. Weapon in hand, I fluffed out the cloak, making sure both the wand and I were completely hidden.

Isaac nudged me with his elbow and nodded down to our right, at the opera box near the stage. Adeline, Susannah, and Cosette were in place. Annabelle was in the seat next to Cosette, looking around suspiciously. *Damn, she hadn't been eaten by some kind of Afterworld arachnid.* She whipped open a silver lamé fan like a dominatrix looking for her next subordinate. Did she suspect we were up to something, or did she think it was just some good old-fashioned ancestral bonding?

Isaac walked to the mezzanine balcony and turned to me, casually leaning back as if checking out the grandiose theatre, but I could tell he was scoping the upper mezzanine, checking on Dee. When he smiled, I knew they were ready to go.

When he smiled, I desperately wanted everything to be normal between us.

With the luxury of invisibility, I glanced back to the upper mezzanine too. The crowd eagerly awaited the start of the show, but when I squinted, the air had a faint sparkle—the Monvoisin invisibility dome. *Badass.* I hoped Dee didn't have any trouble with the portal ritual. As cool as it would be to stay with Adeline and learn everything about our family, I needed to get back if I wanted to have any family left in the Natural World.

The lights dimmed, and Isaac ducked back into his seat; everyone around us teemed with anticipation, but none more than us. Just as I wondered if I should do a lap around the theatre to search for the Medici, I caught the bright blonde head of hair entering the opera box, stage right.

Thump-thump.

Lisette took a seat . . . right behind Nicco.

"*He's here,*" I accidentally whispered out loud.

Isaac glanced my way. I was glad he couldn't see the relief on my face.

Even in death, the Medici appeared regal, both in fashion and in stature. I'd hardly recognized Nicco in the high-necked doublet. A short ruffle circled his jaw, framing his chiseled face. Giovanna sat at his right in a beautiful black gown. At his left, I recognized his father from his dreams; his puffed sleeves made him appear twice as wide as his wife on his other side, donned in black lace. In the row behind them, Lisette sat beside two elderly couples. I'd assumed his family would be beaming with joy at his presence, but they all had sly, practiced smiles. It must be a family trait.

Lisette leaned close, presumably telling him that we were all here, but Nicco didn't turn around. He seemed to have no reaction at all. As if she'd simply told him the valet would be waiting out front at curtain call. Lisette was just as stoic as she sat back again, eyes on the stage.

Giovanna said something to him. He put his arm around her and looked up to the mezzanine. Our eyes met, and it was like he could see right through the magic.

ALYS ARDEN

Thump-thump. Thump-thump. Thump-thump.

He of course couldn't, and he casually turned back to the stage, his eyes grazing Adeline's opera box as he retained his signature perfect level of control.

Did Adeline know he was here? A quick look their way gave me my answer. *Of course she did.*

It was not only Adeline staring at Nicco, but Susannah and Cosette were too—and all of them with the piercing intensity of a seventeenth-century witchy girl gang. I'd have bet my life that somewhere above, Marassa and Morning Star were too. They were so protective of each other, and I loved them all for it, even if their current point of interest was Nicco. I squeezed Isaac's arm beneath the magic of the cloak, and I said a quick prayer to the universe for all of us. We were stronger together.

Jakome Salazar had once led the Catholic church on one of the bloodiest witch hunts in history. He'd attacked the Medici palazzo. He'd expelled Codi's family from Guinée.

His son had taken my father prisoner.

And now I was going to break their magical line forever, removing them from both the Natural World and this sacred place.

The lights dimmed again, and I leaned close to Isaac with a whisper: "It's showtime."

CHAPTER 43
KATTALIN

The curtain pulled back, revealing a sparse stage. In the darkness, the crowd clapped with anticipation, and under the cover of applause, the sound of sliding metal emanated around the theatre in a wave, as if invisible walls were locking into place. No one in the audience seemed to have heard the trapping spell being cast; even my sister's attention stayed steadily fixed on the stage. Giovanna had always been enthralled by drama. Or maybe I'd just grown used to her vampire senses.

I nodded back to Lisette.

"No one's getting in," she said, faint as a wisp, and I knew she'd heard the spell too.

"No one is getting out," I finished, just low enough for her vampiric ears.

Or so I thought. Giovanna turned to me, a question in her eyes. I gave her a simple nod, and she understood that it had begun. The way her terse pout rose just a bit brought me a hundred years of joy. A *whoosh* of air hit my neck—Lisette was gone. In a moment, she reappeared in the box directly across the theatre and took her place with her sister. Her coven.

Les filles aux cassettes.

My eyes locked with Adeline's. And then it wasn't just her—they all fearlessly gazed upon me like I was a demon they were about to send back to Hell. I imagined Gabriel being enamored with them in 1728. We'd all have had quite a time if we'd met under different circumstances.

The thought dwindled as I became curious as to how they'd all managed to reunite and hatch this mystery plan, conveniently without me. *Sì*, Lisette had delivered the message that they were setting it into motion, but what exactly? It had been wise of her not to say who knew what kind of listening-magic the theatre was rigged with—but then again, Lisette was also one of the witches who had locked up my brother. What if they planned to kill two birds with one stone? Take out Jakome and trap me in Guinée, as Gabriel feared? Bring me final death, as I had brought it for Adeline? Perhaps the New Orleans witches were surrounding our estate back in the Natural World at this very moment . . .

Adele would never betray you like that.

Like Adeline had never betrayed Gabriel?

The seat next to the Air witch was still empty.

Thump-thump.

Or so they wanted it to appear. I supposed Adele had made up her mind about me now that she knew of my entanglement with Adeline. Wearing the invisibility cloak I'd killed her in was a nice touch. Sitting next to Isaac, no less. *Quite the fuck you.* Message received.

It was not the outcome I desired, but the one I'd known would be inevitable in journeying here. Perhaps I should have listened to Emilio—not a thought I'd had many times in my very long life.

At least she knew the whole truth now. Whatever came of it was her decision.

"You're getting tense, Brother," Giovanna said from beneath my arm.

"Who wouldn't be, anticipating such a marvel of dramatic arts?"

"I think you've spotted your lover."

"She's not my lover."

"*Hmm.* And Gabriel wasn't hers." Her eyes flicked to Adeline's box.

Luckily, the orchestra started up. The lone strings of a violin, long and sure and deep, clearing the path for the pending theatrics to unfold. An oboe joined, fog colored with the dim glow of the purple floor lights rose from the stage, and the silhouette of a backlit broad-shouldered figure appeared center stage. Two large tufts framed the top of his hide-skin cape.

At certain angles, I caught a glitch in the air, and I didn't think it was for dramatic effect—sparkles of magic filled the proscenium arch, only further confirming Giovanna's suspicions. "Whatever he's planning," I whispered to her, "it will be from the stage." From behind the invisible curtain of a protection shield.

But unless Jakome had morphed into an African man with a penchant for high heels, this was not him ready to take the spotlight. The fog thickened, and lights flickered around the audience as the violin built to an electrifying crescendo, but just as it peaked, the light choked, and the room went dark and silent. I sat up, alert, removing my arm from my sister, trying to remain casual.

The actor was gone.

A greenish spotlight faded in, illuminating a new thespian floating high above on an ethereal cloud. *Ghede-Oussou,* I presumed. He was lying on his side, alluring in his low-cut disco-dress, the fabric draping down from the open slit at the top of his thigh. His head rested on his hand, long, thick locs spilling from his headwrap as he peered into the crowd as if in deep thought. No hooks nor wires were needed to make the Ghede float, and the cloud was made of something only a witch could conjure up.

"In the beginning . . ." came a narrator's voice, deep and resonant, "before there were witches, and before there was magic, there was Ama Lurra." Hands rolled against a drum.

"Jakome," my father grunted under his breath.

The theatre's domed ceiling distributed the unseen voice, making it impossible to determine which direction it was coming from. "Ama Lurra was the hull of the world."

Mother Earth, I translated as a set of mountains rose in the background behind the Ghede. *Riveting.*

"All that was sacred lived within her caverns, beneath her grounds. The goddesses and gods. The clouds and storms and rainbows. The spirits of the dead." A flute whistled, and dancers twirled across the stage in billowing costumes, whipping their limbs through the air. "The caves in Basque country were the entrance to her womb, where all creatures were born." Oussou waved his arm, and flora sprouted from the stage floor. Pomegranate flowers, gazanias, and Spanish bluebells. "Ama Lurra made the plants, and she made the animals." With another wave, swallows soared out into the audience, making the crowd *ooh* with delight.

But not all of the audience was so impressed. Adeline's attention had discreetly turned to the crowd . . . I followed her gaze around the theatre. Hoods tight over their heads, Ghost Drinkers were stationed in the places where the ushers might have been. As she turned back toward the stage, our gazes met, and I nodded to let her know there was one in the box above theirs.

"Ama Lurra made woman and man, and together they lived in harmony."

We both turned back to the stage where two actors had appeared in humble, mortal costumes.

"But the Earth was immersed in darkness, and darkness was the Devil's playground." The lights dimmed to a ghoulish effect, and demon-looking spirits lurked over the mortals' shoulders.

"Ama Lurra, we beg you!" The woman fell to her knees, praying up to the Goddess. "Help us fight the Evil spirits. We have no rest!"

"And so, Ama Lurra gave birth to her first daughter, Illargui."

The very moon goddess Callisto had called upon tonight.

Another Ghede floated down from the rafters in a glowing sphere, her albino skin and lavender hair beaming with cool-toned light.

"*Eskerrik asko*, Ama Lurra, thank you!" the mortals cried, but the demon-spirits crept back onto the stage, tormenting them again under the moonlight. "Please, Ama Lurra, a light so bright and warm it can overcome the darkness!"

"And so, Ama Lurra gave birth to another daughter, Eguzkia."

A third Ghede lowered, this time in a bright bronze sphere. L'Oraille's curly hair and caged skirt gleamed gold, and she shimmered brightly in her role as the Basque sun goddess. "And so da dawn was born, and daylight banished da spirits from the shoulders of mortals."

The spirits in the audience cheered, and I struggled not to roll my eyes as a chorus of dancing sunflowers twirled across the stage with the rejoicing mortals. Sunflowers were a sacred symbol to the Basques to ward off evil at night while the Devil played.

And what will we need to protect ourselves from your evil, Salazar?

A puff of magic burst over the audience, and my family all

jumped to our feet before realizing it was just an explosion of flower petals, now floating out over the crowd.

As we sat, my eyes shot around the theatre. None of the Ghost Drinkers had moved from their positions. The actors whisked off stage, and the audience applauded giddily at the Basque creation myth, but my mother sighed, unimpressed, and for a heartbeat, I wished to remain here forever with them.

Jakome's voice continued: "While the Sun warded off Evil, and the Moon guided the spirits of the dead, it was Ama Lurra's third daughter, Mari, who became her true personification."

In the distraction of flower petals, magic, and orchestral windings, the stage had been cleared, and the original actor appeared back in the spotlights. He was now facing us, and judging by the double unlit cigarette dangling from his glittering lips, he was Ghede-Nibo. He wore an ivy crown on his flattop and a skirt made of flower chains over his spandex body suit.

"The goddess of the Hearth and the leader of all the deities."

The other Ghede lwa appeared in an arc behind him, representing more of the Basque pantheon. As Nibo walked among them, flowers and grasses and even trees sprouted from the stage.

"She was the queen of Nature and the ruler of all its Elements. She was the goddess of Justice and the defender of Honesty. All adored her, all praised her." The orchestra clashed percussively, and Nibo soared up into the rafters as the lights dimmed. "She lived in a golden palace underground in the Akelarrenlezea."

When the stage relit, everyone was gone but a lone girl, played by Ghede-Zaranye, now surrounded by a flock of sheep. Even standing upright, the way her arms stayed hunched and her fingers spread, she still had a spider-like appearance.

"One morning a young woman called Kattalin went to the mountains with her flock." Zaranye danced around the stage with the sheep. "Reading, and sunbathing, and picnicking as they grazed." When the sun started to set, she yawned.

"It's time to go home," she said to the sheep and started to count. "*Bat, bi, hiru.*"

"But when she was finished," came Jakome's voice, "Kattalin realized one was missing."

"Oh no!" Zaranye yelped, holding her hands to her cheeks. "What will the nobleman do to me when he finds out?"

"She searched the meadows and climbed the mountain to find the missing sheep. When she reached the cave, she saw the animal at the entrance, and along with it, the most beautiful lady she'd ever seen."

"What is your name?" Nibo asked her. "And who is your family?"

"My name is Kattalin, and I have no family. But I need that sheep. She belongs to a nobleman in my village. He will beat me if I do not return them. I have no money—I will be indebted to him for the rest of my life!"

"Mari made Kattalin an offer," Jakome explained.

"If you spend seven years living with me, helping me," she said, "I will make you rich, and you will answer to no man. Noble or otherwise."

"Kattalin accepted the proposition and remained in the mountain cave, helping the lady. The Goddess taught her everything a mother would have: how to spin a thread, how to bake a bread. But she also taught her things that Ama Lurra had bestowed only to her: the language of the animals and the magical properties of plants, and how to harness the rays of the sun, and the beams of the moon, and the waves of the sea." The two Ghede lwa danced around the palace together. "The years went by quickly, and at the end of the seventh, Mari kept her word."

"Kattalin," she said, "you have shown me your devotion these last seven years. I will keep my promise and make you rich!"

"Mari handed her a lump of coalstone. Kattalin was

surprised by the gift, but she hoped it would soon turn to gold-stone, for the Goddess was clever like that. And so she gathered her things and began the journey home. The coalstone didn't turn to gold or pearl or any precious jewel. In fact, when the sun's rays touched it, the coal burned up; but still Kattalin clung to the ashes—it was a gift from her beloved goddess-mother. By the time she reached her old village, the moon had risen, and when Illagari's beams kissed the ash, a flame sprouted in her palm." Zaranye gasped in awe at the Fire and twirled round and round with it.

Behind us, Nonna grumbled in foul Italian, and I dared not glance at Giovanna lest I risk bursting into a fit of laughter like children at mass as Jakome continued: "From the Fire came more magic, and with it, riches and power. Kattalin bought her first sheep. And then a flock, and then an old *gaztelu* on the tallest mountain in the Akelarrenlezea. It was an ancient stone fortress, but she loved it. From there, she could see Mari's mountain peak, and so she gave herself the name Salazar, for she knew she would never be without a home again thanks to the Goddess."

Zaranye leapt around the stage, lighting the sconces of the stone-walled set with her Fire magic.

"Kattalin built Mari a shrine in the forest and worshiped the goddess until the end of her days, and for her devotion, Mari imbued her Fire to Kattalin's blood so that her children and descendants furthermore could carry on her devotion. And so the first Fire witches were born of the Akelarrenlezea."

Zaranye rose from the stage in a whirl of flowers and flames.

My father's eye pointed my way as they cleared the set pieces, shifting into what was hopefully the final act. "So now Jakome claims the Salazar magic was handed directly to his ancestors from the goddesses?"

"And not just any goddess," Giovanna added, "*the* Goddess."

I crossed my legs. "I am most certain the myth is supposed to end with young Kattalin's coalstone turning to goldstone."

"If you'd ever met Jakome Salazar," my mother said, her gaze still firmly on the stage, "you'd know he truly believes that he descended from the Goddess."

The lights dimmed to black, and the music picked up once again, this time dreary and foreboding. A flame sprouted from a hearth now set center stage as the narration continued: "Kattalin's Fire passed down for generations, for hundreds of years, and the Salazars thrived high up on their forest mountain."

I didn't want to take my eyes off the hearth, but a mumble of voices tugged at my attention.

"Their magic grew stronger with each generation, and their devotion to the ancient Basque Goddess never faltered."

I opened up my senses and listened. Beneath the deep rumblings of the orchestra, beneath the wild orations of the narrator, a choir of chanting picked up.

"Over the years, witching families sprouted all over Europe, and along with them, magicians and charlatans and alchemists."

Still as stone, I glanced at the box across the way. Adeline's witches were hardly moving their lips, but they were speaking magical words.

"The Church stomped out the Old Goddesses one by one— the Etruscans, the Goths, the Celts, the Norse—and instead of rising up, using their power, these witches went into hiding like common *rats*."

My father snarled at the mention of our ancient ancestors. Up on the mezzanine, the seat next to Isaac was still empty, but he too was whispering under his breath. More voices of unseen witches bellowed from the upper balcony. Was it a protection spell? I strained to hear the verses over the orchestra.

"Pin, needles, rum, and ginger."

"They formed secret societies and councils. Called themselves *Greats*. They created rules and limitations, and little by little they choked themselves and smothered their own powers, living in the shadows of mortal men."

"Pin, needles, rum, and ginger."

The glitches of magic protecting the stage were moving like static, pulling toward the ceiling. *They aren't doing a protection spell. They're breaking one. They're clearing the way for the kill shot. For Adele.*

"They didn't respect their gifts. They didn't respect their goddesses," Jakome bellowed. "But not the Salazars. Not us!"

"Pin, needles, rum, and ginger, bottle his magic so we can enter!"

The witches chanted louder, and the magical curtain pulled straight into the chandelier above, into a bottle floating hidden among the crystals. *They're using a Witch Bottle.*

The orchestra pounded in misery. "They tried to control us! They tried to diminish us." Jakome appeared behind the hearth in a swirl of midnight-blue smoke, the black hood tight over his head and a strip of black makeup across his eyes. "They expelled us from our sacred mountaintop!" His hood slipped off as he threw out his hands, casting two bolts toward Adeline's box. Cosette and a curly-haired witch screamed as the magic pierced their chests, lifting them from their seats, and dangled them in mid-air over the crowd.

Adeline and Lisette leapt up at once, screaming the bottle spell, unfaltering. *They'd been just as prepared for this trap as we were.*

The crowd showered Jakome with gasps and applause, like it was just a part of the show. I turned back to the mezzanine—

Isaac's fists were balled as if he was trying to restrain himself from aiding the witches in peril. I nearly rose from my seat. *Don't do it, Isaac, Adele is next to you. Don't make her a target.* The redhead screamed, and Isaac jolted up, whipping a whirl of wind around the theatre, straight through the bolts of magic.

Giovanna held me back before I could dart away. "*No, Niccolò, sei con la tua famiglia stasera.*"

But Jakome didn't retaliate—the Air had barely made the bolts waver. *What the hell?* So much for Guinée doing wonders for Isaac's magic. Jakome tugged harder on the redheaded witch. "They burned our grimoire!" Isaac fell against the mezzanine, grasping the railing in pain, and a flicker of Adele's arm peeked through the cloak as she jumped up and reached out for him. The redhead screamed, and he winced harder. *The redhead is his ancestor.* Jakome was drinking her magic, and he was losing power. *Shit.* The hooded witches stepped forward, falling in line as Jakome grew more enraged. "The witches of the Mediterranean cursed my house and killed my children!" *What? No we—*

"Has he gone completely mad?" my mother muttered, rising from her seat, but my father held his arms out over all of us. "Not yet."

"But you cannot destroy our magic. You cannot destroy our spirit or our name. With your Fire we will rise!" He threw out his free arm, and this time a fiery orange bolt came our way.

"Now!" my father yelled.

My mother tossed a bottle into the air, timed perfectly with the bolt's strike, and we sprang up, as it shattered, hand in hand, chanting. My every vampiric instinct was to break the line and cover them from the explosion of glass, but my intuition knew my mother's magic would protect us. The bottle shattered. The enchantment activated its liquid contents, and a glistening silver shield formed around us—but the bolt of magic penetrated, hitting my father.

"*Padre!*"

Giovanna squeezed my hand tighter, her voice rising louder, chanting the spell as the Salazar magic lifted him into the air. The silver spell coating my father's form boomeranged the bolt back, and it shot straight into Jakome. My mother hadn't just cast a shield, but a reflective pool that mirrored Jakome's own magic back to him. *Enchanted quicksilver.* Jakome clutched his chest, and the bolt choked his words, but still he didn't let go of the three witches in his clutches. Our voices sang louder, the spell growing stronger. The surrounding Ghost Drinkers lifted their arms in our direction, and it suddenly dawned on me: the full extent of the horror the Salazars could inflict if Callisto was able to raise his family from the dead . . . a cold sweat broke out on my neck. I'd never felt so useless in all my four hundred years.

A witch with no magic. A vampire amongst the bloodless.

My father cried out in pain. *How much longer would the quicksilver hold?* Who would perish first and release the other, Salazar or Medici? The two Great Fire witches. *Fuck this.* I jumped onto the rail, ready to leap down to the stage, but a loud scream—*Adeline*—froze me. She fell against the opera box rail. Giovanna snarled and threw out her hands, releasing a blast of magic toward Jakome.

The bolt struck his ethereal form, lighting him up like a dying star. He fell to his knees, but he held onto the three bolts of magic, drinking from my father, Cosette, and the Norwood witch. In the pandemonium of witches' screams, magic dust, and smoky purple lights, everything became clear—*we thought the attack was meant for us, but he's going after the families on the Great Council of the late sixteenth century.* I blinked as he became more translucent; he faded in and out as the quicksilver spell used his Spektral magic against him—*drinking his own succubus magic.*

He picked himself up and jerked the bolt holding my father.

It blazed orange, feeding him our Fire. My mother shouted the spell louder than my father's cries. Sparks burst from his chest. I focused on the words. The magical intention. And as my family chanted the spell, our voices echoed back down from the domes and it felt like the entire theatre had joined in. "*Riflettere! Riflettere! Riflettere!*" The Animarum Praedator magic blasted harder, but the shield deflected it back. Jakome began wavering, blinking in and out. We just had to hold the line, and he'd soon expel himself from Guinée. We wouldn't even need the ghost-stick. If his magicline broke, Callisto's bullshit immortality would dissolve too, and this would all be over.

Adeline screamed again, writhing in pain. *What the hell?* His magic hadn't even touched her. My gaze flipped from her to Jakome. *Che diavolo?* It was almost like the Quicksilver was hitting her too.

But that would mean . . .

No.

Adeline was becoming translucent. One second she was here, the next she was gone, like a flickering light, exactly what I'd imagined was happening to Callisto in the Natural World. Lisette shrieked, cradling Adeline in her arms as she began to disappear.

It can't be.

If Adeline was a Salazar . . . that meant León . . . "*Bastardo!*"

Emilio had been right all along. León had been a spy, infiltrating our family, our coven. *That fucking bastard.* But . . . The memories crashed down on me: in the bell tower, Adele had ripped the cross off the steeple and bolted me to the wall. At the convent when she'd pulled the slumbering spell from me. In the park earlier this evening when she'd cast the bolt and pulled the memory from my mind. Her Spektral magic wasn't telekinesis. It never was.

She was a succubus.

"*Femare*," I shouted. "*Femare!*"

"We can't stop, Niccolò!" Giovanna cried. "He'll break our magicline!"

I twisted to the mezzanine. Adele was standing next to Isaac, no longer cloaked, wand in hand. "*No!*" If she breaks the line, she'll lose her magic.

Forever.

CHAPTER 44
FINALE

My perfect vantage became obscured as haze filled the theatre. Explosions of magic blasted from each faction of witches, clouding the air like theatrical fog. The wand was in my hand; I was ready.

"Wait, the bottle's almost full." Isaac gripped the balcony, pain in his voice. He started to appear ghostly.

"Are you okay?" Panic rushed me. "Isaac!"

"Don't look at me—look at the target!"

I could see *through* him. My body shook so hard, I nearly dropped the stick.

"Adele, look at the target!"

I quickly locked my gaze back on Jakome, trying to tune out the chaos. *I have one chance. I'm going to save my father.*

And my city.

Isaac glanced back up at the bottle. "Now!" he yelled over the enveloping chaos.

"It's just positive space moving through negative space." As I launched my arm, a blur whipped through the haze, tackling me to the ground. The wand slipped from my hand to the floor. "Isaac!" I screamed, and he charged toward us.

I scrambled, trying to snatch the ghoststick, but hands grabbed my shoulders, lifting me up. "Adele, you can't," Nicco yelled, squeezing me. "Your magic is tied to his."

"What? You're wasting time!"

"Adele, listen to me. *Fucking listen.*" He shook me hard, and the horror in his eyes frightened me. "Your bloodline . . . it's linked to Salazar's."

"Are you insane?" I jerked away. "I have to stop Callis!"

He twisted me around, grabbing me by the back of my neck. "Look. *Look* at Adeline."

In the box below, Lisette was screaming for her sister, who was still dangling above, but she was holding someone tightly to her chest, gripping them as if they might otherwise float away. Where was Adeline? I squinted. The girl in Lisette's arms was so pale and ghostly, I could hardly make her out. "That's not—"

"Adeline!" Nicco yelled. "It's her! She's being expelled from Guinée, just like Jakome is."

"He must be using his magic on her!"

"He's not!"

I shook him off. "I have to save Mac."

"Adele, we'll find another way. We have to stop Callis without eviscerating your magic!"

I bent back down to get the wand, but my hand swiped right through the stick.

Isaac dropped to the ground beside me. "What's happening to you?"

"Adele, you don't want this life!" Nicco pleaded. "A magicless witch!"

"Please help me," I begged Isaac, trying to grasp the stick.

"I don't know if my Air is strong enough."

Panic overwhelmed me— I could see straight through him. "We can do it together." I pulled him up. "We'll be strong enough together."

He nodded, and with a gust of Air, the wand lifted into my hand.

I looked back at Nicco with disgust. "I am *not* a Ghost Drinker."

His arms circled around me, and Nicco pulled me into his chest. I heard the boy that I loved in his desperate voice. "Adele, don't! It's *your* magicline. Their succubus Spektral magic is just advanced telekinesis. Metal, spirits, magic—they're just taking positive space into negative space when they steal it!"

My pulse stopped. They were no longer his arms around me, but Callis's as I recalled that day in the yard when he taught me how to use my magic on the root. He'd softly laughed. *"Is that what you think? That your telekinesis is limited to metal?"*

"I swear, I will get your father back." Nicco's voice warbled. The floor warbled. Everything warbled. "This will destroy your magic permanently. So many before you. All after you."

"You are clearly an extraordinary witch," Callis had said. *"No doubt descended from one of the Greats . . . I knew that your Fire was special from the very first time I saw you light a candle. It had hints of the Old World that I hadn't felt since . . . well, since my father was alive."*

The power tingled beneath my skin like electric currents. I am *not* a Ghost Drinker.

"Mentally excavate the positive space from the universe and place it in another point."

Had he been trying to teach me something else? Test me? Is this why he wanted me in his coven so badly?

"You're the same person with or without your magic," Isaac said.

"You're stronger than you think, Adele."

"I will never be one of them!" *And I will kill one man to save the rest.* With a shove, I pushed Nicco back, twisted around, and hurled the wand—straight toward Jakome Salazar's dead heart.

"*No!*" Nicco roared.

And as magic blasted, and witches chanted, and the orchestra pounded, the wand lit up, soaring through the hazy maelstrom, the descendants of the Great witching families flickering in and out.

The aim was perfect. I barely saw Nicco's figure as he whipped onto the stage.

Thump-thump. Thump-thump. Thump-thump.

In front of Jakome.

"*Niccoooooooooo!*" I nearly dove over the mezzanine rail as the ghoststick struck his chest. Isaac's arms wrapped around me, and the shrill of my voice filled my ears as Nicco fell to his knees. Crimson plumed through his pale doublet like a blooming rose.

He collapsed in the spotlight.

"Nicco!" I twisted out of Isaac's grip and tore away, pushing through spirits as they stampeded toward the exit. I hurtled down the stairs and burst onto the main floor just in time to see Jakome running through the back curtain, with the Medici witches storming after him. My friends yelled my name from every direction as I ran down the aisle. I glanced back. A glistening purple hole had filled the center of the upper mezzanine—the portal. Dee and Codi yelled, waving their arms at me. Morning Star and Nashoba, both in ethereal wolf form, snarled at Ghost Drinkers approaching them from either side.

I reached the wooden stage and slid down onto the floor, through his blood. "*Désirée!*" I screamed. "*Désirée!* We need you!"

Nicco was clutching the wand with one hand and trying to staunch the blood with the other, both hands slicked red. "The portal," he said. "Go." Fear shone behind his eyes. I'd never seen him scared. Blood coughed out of his mouth. "I'll be fine."

"Don't talk." I screamed again for Désirée. I wasn't leaving without him. I'd promised Gabe I'd protect him.

"Adele, get up here now!" Codi yelled. "We can't hold the portal for much longer!"

I'd promised we were in this together. I wasn't leaving without him because . . . I couldn't live without him.

Two Ghost Drinkers climbed up onto the stage, and I threw out my hands, ripping the lights above free with a squeal of metal, and smashed them into the spirits, showering us with broken glass. The air smelled of magic mixed with burning electrical wires as they tumbled into the orchestra pit. Somewhere out in the dim theatre, Codi screamed my name again.

"I'm sorry," Nicco choked, blood dripping from his lips. "For everything. For bringing this into your life."

You are my life. Before I could say it, the two Ghost Drinkers were back on their feet. They lunged toward us, and I threw myself over Nicco. A bolt of magic blasted over my shoulder, directly hitting one of the Ghost Drinkers. I looked back: it was Giovanna. With a wave of fluttering Italian, she blasted more magic, but there were too many of them.

Men's boots pounded next to me. "Adele, let's go."

"I'm not leaving." I tried to focus on Nicco's face, but tears blurred my vision.

"Adele, *let's go.*" Isaac tucked his arms under Nicco's back and knees. "I've got him."

"Both of you, go," said a sharp French voice. "*Je l'ai.*" Lisette scooped Nicco up, and in a flash, she was on the third floor, going through the portal.

A curtain of taffeta, leather, and lace whirled around us. "Get out of here, *ma petite sorcière!*" Adeline cried, forming a wall around us with Cosette, Susannah, Marassa, and Morning Star.

"Hold on tight," Isaac said, pulling me up. His arm circled my waist, and his magic lifted us into the Air. Bolts of magic shot toward us as *les filles aux cassettes* chanted.

We can't leave them here with the Ghost Drinkers. I launched my arm toward the ceiling and slammed the Witch Bottle into the chandelier. The glass shattered, and the Salazar protection spell poured over them, deflecting the bolts. Susannah swept one arm wide and lifted them all with her Air. As they floated up past the opera boxes, Cosette made a gesture, and the space around them glimmered. Then they all . . . disappeared. They may have been invisible, but I knew they were shouting a chorus of profanities and magic spells. I knew that Morning Star would take them to wherever she'd hidden her family, and that Marassa would help protect them until the end of time, just like I would protect Dee.

As we floated up toward the mezzanine, I wondered if we'd ever see them again.

Isaac suddenly shouted in a panic. "I have to get my bag!" He dropped us near our seats, and we grabbed our things.

"The cloak!" I yelped.

"Got it," he said and stuffed it into his duffle.

As I slipped my bag onto my back, someone screamed his name from below.

We both looked over the balcony in confusion. I didn't recognize anyone among the throng of spirits still fleeing their seats.

"Adele!" Annabelle made herself visible. She was hiding on the floor between the rows.

She shrieked as the Ghost Drinker in the green velvet dress from the bar charged toward her yelling "*Traitor!*" But Isaac hurled a gust of Air and shot her straight up. I caught her around the waist and pulled her over the balcony. "We have to hurry," I said.

Isaac flew up to the third level, and only then did it register that he wasn't even taking crow form. The portal glowed brightly behind him. Dee and Codi were already a few steps down the ethereal tunnel. "I've got them," Isaac yelled back. "Just go!" He threw out another gust, lifting us both.

As my hand touched his, a blast of light exploded around us and Annabelle slammed into me. She fell out of the gust with a scream. Isaac grabbed my arm, and Annabelle grabbed for me, but only got my bag; it ripped open beneath her weight, and she dropped. "Annabelle!" She clutched my legs as the contents spilled around her.

"Adele!" she yelled, flailing.

Isaac strained, holding us both. "I've got you!" His arm was slick with sweat, and mine with Nicco's blood. I glanced down, and my heart sank, seeing that Adeline's diary had tumbled down to the mezzanine ledge.

She saw where my gaze had fixated. "I can get it!"

"No, we have to go!" I yelled. "Give me your hand!"

But she stretched out, reaching for the diary.

"Annabelle, forget it!"

"Use your magic!" she yelled.

I started sliding away from Isaac. "Annabelle, we're slipping!"

"I can't hold on much longer," Isaac grunted.

"Use your magic, Adele!"

"The portal's closing!" Isaac ripped a gust of Air beneath us, twisting us higher, and with a flick of my mind, I bumped the book straight up. We swirled into the cyclone of Air, and I clung onto Isaac as the neon purple glow began to whirl.

"Got it!" Annabelle said, a thrill in her voice.

Isaac blasted us through the portal with his Elemental just as it closed behind us.

"*Got it.*"

The majestic Ghede-purple dissolved, and everything went dark.

PART III
THE GRIMOIRE

The greatest secrets are always hidden in the most unlikely places.

—*Roald Dahl*

CHAPTER 45
MERCY

Isaac pulled me tight, trying to shield me from gargantuan tree roots as we rolled through the grass together. When he finally stopped the torrent of Air, we were both breathing hard. He leapt up, covering me. "Where are we?"

"Where's Lisette?" I stood, my eyes readjusting to the inky night as I surveyed the landscape. We weren't in Lafayette Cemetery. Or St. Roch. Or any cemetery, for that matter. We were surrounded by sprawling oaks that dripped with Spanish moss. Wings fluttered in the leaves overhead and frogs groaned, but it was hard to see anything in the dark. "Are we back?"

"I can't feel the cold anymore."

"Something's off."

A twig snapped, and we both swung around just in time to see a fawn dart away. The moon reflected on a pond, and I recognized the stone bridge that crossed over it. My dad used to take me here to feed the ducks when I was a kid. Isaac and I had kissed on that bridge and taken a photo to match the one of Mac and Brigitte on the Seine. "We're in City Park. I think there's an exit this way that will lead back to Esplanade, and then it's a straight shot to the Quarter."

"Why are we in City Park?"

"I don't know. Maybe the portal spell broke and just dumped us out?"

He brushed back his hair. "Do you think the others are here?"

"*Annabelle?*" I whispered. A chorus of cicadas hummed back from the canopy of trees above. "Maybe they made it back to the cemetery?" I rummaged through my bag. Most of the contents had been lost in the spill, but my phone had been spared. "*Dead,*" I said, letting it drop back in.

"Mine's dead too."

I glanced around through the dark trees. *Are* we back? Or was this some kind of Ghede mind-trip? It might have just been the aftershock of the theatre, but I swore I could feel magic in the air. "You know what would be really great right about now? My *orbs.*" I imagined them whirling over my shoulders, lighting the way. Neither of us called out for the others, and I didn't protest when he took my hand. As we walked, the clouds parted from over the moon, and I noticed a smear of red on a tree root. Up ahead, there were another few droplets on a magnolia pod.

Thump-thump.

"Nicco!" I whispered and took off running. I didn't need the trail of blood; I followed the slowing beats of his heart to a thicket of hydrangeas, now wondering if all that stuff Olsin had said about twin-flames was bullshit, and if the only reason I could hear his heartbeat was because of Adeline's curse. Nicco had once told me that we were magical together, and it had admittedly made me swoon—now I wondered if what he'd meant was that we were cursed.

Thump-thump.

The park had been decimated by the Storm. *He's here. I know he's here.* The plants were so overgrown, I barely noticed the greenhouse gate. The once-glass structure had few remaining windows and was now mostly an iron skeleton of its former self.

The sound of voices quickened my step. I trampled through the foliage, unfazed by the thorny vines ripping at my hair. I pushed aside a curtain of wisteria, and there they were beneath a stream of moonlight: Lisette hunched over Nicco's body, her arms stained red, the wand in her hand. He lay still on a bed of flowers.

"*No.*" I ground my teeth together.

"Get her away," Nicco grunted, as she held his wound. In the moonlight his blood looked black, like something monstrous was spilling from his soul.

"Nicco, you need to heal," she said in French, as if forgetting I could understand.

"Get her away!" He scurried back like a wounded animal, holding his gut, blood spilling between the cracks of his fingers.

"You need to feed, or you will die, Niccolò!"

"Then go find me someone," he snarled. "And take her with you!"

"There's no time; we're in the middle of nowhere!"

I threw down my bag and rushed to his side. "You can drink from me."

"I will not!" he hissed, fangs bulging, crimson lining the cracks of his teeth. His face was grayish, sunken, and gaunt. He shoved himself away again, hitting a stone statue.

I crept closer, pushing aside my hair. Pushing aside Olsin's premonition. Focusing only on the time he'd let me drink from him to save my life. *To save his life.*

I pulled his hand to my waist. "It's okay, Nicco."

"*No.*" The fear deepened in his brow as I leaned in, stretching the collar of my shirt over my shoulder. *Thump-thump.* "Just drink."

His eyes began to gloss over, but he blinked hard, shaking it off. "*No.*"

With his heartbeat pounding in my ears, I thought back to

his fantasies of us—of me—to the things he wanted to hear. "Do it, Niccolò."

His bottom lip quivered. "I want you," he whimpered.

"I know." I stroked his face, and his nose brushed my jaw. "Take me." I trembled, his breath bathing my neck, his lips brushing my damp skin. "*Il mio cuore ti appartiene*," I whispered, letting my eyes slip shut. He gripped me tight.

Thump-thump. Thump-thump. Thump-thump.

"*Never*," he growled, and with a vampiric shove, he sent me flying across the greenhouse.

I crashed into a rotting trellis, smashing it to pieces, rose blossoms falling all around me. Lisette cursed and tried to calm him down, but he threw her too, so hard that she crashed through the remaining glass roof. "Lisette!" I screamed.

His gaze locked with mine as the glass rained down, and fear flooded my veins like a hundred thousand creeping spiders. I hated that it did. "*It doesn't matter what kind of man he was,*" Isaac had once told me. "*He's a monster now.*" *No, he's not.* But I found myself eyeing a rusty potting shovel. It was too far away for me to reach it.

Nicco saw me spot it and watched to see what I would do, tugging his bottom lip between his fangs with a taunting smile. He looked just like Emilio. He lunged for the shovel, but I whipped it into my palm. He leapt again, and I screamed, dropping into a ball, covering my head. In my heart, I knew I could never use it on him, just like I couldn't kill Brigitte.

The crack of bones split the air, but not mine.

I opened my eyes as Nicco slid down the side of the stone statue of a Greek Muse, crying out in pain, muttering in Italian. I expected to see Lisette restraining him, but no one else was there.

"*We already have a spot picked out for her,*" he mumbled as he stood back up, hunched over and teetering, and then violently threw himself against the statue again. "*A grave to lie in. A gown to die in.*"

"Nicco, *stop!*" I sprang up, dropping the shovel. He was breaking his back.

He threw himself again. "*A crown of bones to wear forever.*"

And he slumped down.

"*Nicco!*" I rushed forward.

"Forgive me, *bella.*" Tears dripped down his face. "I am weak."

"No, you're not. You're as strong as the gods and as loving as a lamb!"

He lunged straight for me, arms outstretched, fangs stained with his blood, and I fell back into the trellis crushed beneath him, Papa Olsin's warnings scrolling through my head. Isaac's warnings.

Adeline's warnings.

Callis's warnings.

The tips of his teeth pierced my skin, but even then, I told myself he wouldn't kill me. If I died, he'd die; but as I struggled to push him off, reality weighed upon me—he'd lost control.

"*The most dangerous vampire I ever knew.*"

He grunted at the first taste of blood, his fingers curling around me.

"Niccolò, don't do this." I choked out a sob.

"*Dea abbi pietà della mia anima.*" His fangs sank into me, and I screamed.

"Nicco, stop!"

Who would save my father now?

Thump-thump.

A breeze tickled my face, lifting my hair. It swirled around us, warm and magical.

With a hiss, Nicco's head jerked up, blood gushing from his lips, a monstrous invisible fist clutching his throat. His nails scraped my arms as the Air yanked him across the greenhouse and slammed him to the floor with a crunch.

Isaac pounced atop him with blind rage, the stake in his hand. "I can't protect her from everything, but I can protect her from *you.*"

"Isaac, no!" I shouted.

"Just do it fast," Isaac said, dropping the stake.

"*Isaac, don't!*"

Nicco's face lit up as I charged toward them.

Isaac ripped the collar of his shirt. "Do it before I change my—"

Nicco surged up like a copperhead, striking Isaac's neck, and smashed him to the ground in a twining of limbs. Isaac squealed in pain.

I slid down to my knees, grabbing at Nicco's shoulders. "That's enough!"

He swatted me away like a fly.

I flung a gardening spade into my hand and charged back, but before I could bring it down over his head, Lisette crashed into them, taking Nicco with her—him spitting Italian curses as they rolled away.

I dropped the spade with a clatter and fell to Isaac's side, cupping his neck to staunch the bleeding. "Are you okay?"

He nodded, but he was sweating profusely, and his entire body shook.

"Can you move?"

He nodded again, and tears rolled out of my eyes. "Don't cry," he managed to grunt out.

I nodded, trying to hold them back.

"La Sirène supercharged my Air." His voice was raspy. "I wish you'd been there."

I had no idea what he was talking about—he seemed delirious—but I pressed my forehead against his in thanks. "Me too."

"She was so beautiful. Her tail was like a rainbow."

"She sounds . . . l-lovely," I stuttered.

"But she wasn't as beautiful as you."

"*Merci beaucoup.*" My tears fell on his cheeks. "Thank you for everything."

"I love you."

My throat was so choked up, all I could do was nod and lean closer, cradling him. His arms wrapped tightly around me, and we clutched each other, both trembling.

"Breathe," he said, stroking my back, and I shook harder, this time with a gentle ripple of laughter.

I glanced up. Lisette and Nicco were both watching us, she with one arm still around his shoulders, restraining him. The life was returning to his face, and the gash in his gut was the pink color of newly formed skin.

The ghoststick lay on the floor between us, covered in blood.

As she released him, they exchanged words in such rapid French I couldn't keep up. Something about magic in the air? Then they turned to us. "Is he okay?" she asked me.

"I think so." I checked his neck beneath my hand. The wound was still bleeding a little.

"Let me see." She strode over, and I tensed, clutching the bite tighter.

"It's okay," Isaac said. "Let her check it."

I moved my hand a bit, reluctant to let anyone near him.

"I'm just going to heal the wound."

I shifted aside, and she crouched beside us. My pulse raced as she inhaled, straining to hide her arousal. I squeezed Isaac's hand. She bent closer, her hair covering them as she nuzzled his neck, her head bobbing like a kitten. He let out a little gasp, and she quickly sat up, rosy-cheeked. I pretended I didn't notice as she licked the blood from her lips. Her vamp-saliva made the gashes close up, but sweat dripped from Isaac's brow in a feverish wave. He was getting paler. Lisette opened her mouth wider, exposing her fangs.

"No!" I yelped.

But then she bit into her own wrist until it bled. "Drink." She lowered it to Isaac's mouth, but he glowered and turned his head aside, lips pressed together. "You need it to heal. Too much venom is in your system."

I stood and walked away in case he'd take it without me watching.

Nicco had peeled off his tattered shirt and was using it to wipe the blood from his newly taut stomach, though his deep gaze remained fixed on me. He let the blood-soaked shirt drop as I approached.

I took off his jacket, unbuttoned the flannel, and handed him the shirt.

"*Grazie.*"

"I'm keeping the jacket."

He tried not to smile as he clothed himself.

I popped the leather collar, covering his teeth marks. Best to not tempt fate. But then in a blink, my arms were around his neck, my forehead pressed to his. The rush of relief was dizzying. "Please don't ever do anything like that again."

"I told you to get out of here. I told you to never trust a vampire."

"Not that, *idiota*. Please don't ever jump in front of a lethal supernatural weapon again."

"Oh, that." He hugged me closer, taking in a deep breath. I listened for the sound of his heart, taking comfort in the steady beats. "I couldn't let Callisto take your power from you, *bella*."

"I know."

"I'm going to save your father, Adele. I swear."

"No, *we*'re going to save him."

"*Sì*," he said against my neck, and I felt the heat of his breath and then the swipe of his tongue. I clutched onto him with a gasp.

The bite began to tingle as the torn skin tightened, healing.

He pulled back, looking deep into my eyes. "What I said before, in Guinée . . ."

"I know."

His mouth turned up the tiniest bit.

But then his back stiffened as he focused on something over my shoulder. I glanced back and saw Lisette had locked eyes with him . . . some message passing between them.

"What is it?" I asked, just as a shriek shook the remaining glass panes above us.

"That's Désirée!" Isaac said. In a puff, he took crow form, but instead of soaring away, he flopped back to the ground, the venom too much for his avian body. I scooped him into my arms and pushed back through the vines and broken glass, emerging into the dark park, the two vampires at my side.

CHAPTER 46
EARTH TO EARTH

Smoke wafted from the dried moss Codi had bundled onto the end of a stick. He fanned it, and the flames grew.

"You learn that at summer camp?" I asked, sliding my phone into the charging case. The battery clicked into place.

"Yup."

I couldn't imagine what he was going through right now. It made me even more anxious to get home to Ritha. If anyone would know how to help the Guldenmanns, it would be her. A breeze rustled the leaves of the ancient oaks above us, and I looked up at the stars, waiting for the phone to power up. "Why the hell did we end up here?"

"I don't know. I don't even care as long as everyone else made it back too. Does your phone work?"

"Yeah. But no signal." I attempted to send a text to Isaac and Adele anyway. I knew it was futile, even if we were back in the Natural World; this part of town had been a black hole since the Storm. My car's GPS didn't even work over here.

Codi kicked some brush from the ground. "Look, it's the choo-choo tracks."

"Did you seriously just say choo-choo tracks?" There was a

munchkin-sized train for kids that went around the park. I wanted to laugh, but I was afraid that if I did, it might uncork the tight-lidded emotions already threatening to pop. *Keep it together, Borges.*

"Is there another name for them?" He smiled. "If we follow the tracks, it will take us close enough to the edge of the park that we can find our way out."

I pulled the drawstrings of my bag and slipped it on my back. "Let's go."

But he didn't move. His forehead crinkled as he looked at me. I felt it too. There was something in the air that felt suffocating. Something sinister was creeping up all around us—through the fog rising off the pond, the swaying branches of the oaks, the ground beneath our feet. We backed up against each other, as if the park itself was closing in around us. I thrust out my phone's light as he fanned out the torch.

Had the Ghost Drinkers slipped through the portal with us?

Something brushed my ankle, and I sprang forward.

"What's wrong?" Codi whipped around.

I flashed the light, searching the ground. There was nothing there but knobby tree roots and sprawling ferns. "Nothing. Sorry." But it wasn't nothing. He knew it. I knew it. Something was here.

"Adele?" I called, no longer caring who might hear us. "Isaac?"

An owl cooed, drawing my attention up into the trees. They shimmered for a brief second. *Magic?* I blinked, and it was gone. It had seemed . . . familiar.

"Dee, was that you?"

"Was what me?" I turned back around.

"Désirée!" Codi hit the ground with a loud *thwack* like the earth had been pulled out from beneath his feet.

"Codi?"

He ripped away, flying across the ground.

"Codi!" I tore after him, the torch's flame bobbing up and down against the ground as he was dragged. If it hadn't been for the fire, I'd have lost sight of him. "What the shit?"

"It's got me!"

"What's got you?" I screamed. *Fuck, was it a bear?* I'd heard there'd been sightings of them after the Storm.

He cried out as it pulled him over two-foot-high roots. I charged ahead, arms pumping, and I got ready to ignite my magic against whatever creature had him. "Codi!" I said, breathless, as I slid through the wet foliage. But he wasn't there—he'd dropped the torch. "Codi!" I shrieked, twisting around.

A distant voice called my name, and I took off again.

A swell of magic whooshed up behind me. The brush stroked at my ankles like the flicker of snakes' tongues. I glanced down. Green fronds fanned up from the forest floor in waves, and I picked up my pace, kicking them away. But the trees became thicker, forcing me to slow. I swatted moss from my face as I tried not to slide on the algae-coated ground. Magic spilled from my hands like sparkling green nets, clearing the path ahead. Roots and branches and slippery swaths of wet leaves parted for me as I hurtled through.

A branch snapped underfoot nearby, and just like that, I knew I was no longer chasing but being chased. Taking a cue from Marta's playbook, I pulled the flora up from the ground beside me as I sped up. Elephant ears and banana leaves grew twelve feet tall, covering me from behind, and ferns blanketed my tracks as I tried to find a way out. *I'll come back for Codi with reinforcements.* How far away would I have to get from the park before I could get a cell signal?

Something tall loomed ahead, something my magic could not budge. *Shit.* The moon became brighter as I edged out of the dense trees—it was a brick wall covered in ivy. *So we're near the Botanical Garden.* I knew my way out of the park from here.

"Up!" I yelled as I jumped for a bowing oak branch, and it grew taller, lifting me.

"Down," said a voice.

What the fuck? The branch started to lower me again. "Up!" I yelled, throwing out my arm, and the green sparkles of my magic shimmered through the branch. It jerked again, and a glowing wave of dark green pushed against the shimmer, engulfing it. *I don't think so.* This might be my only chance.

With a scream, I launched myself toward the wall. My fingers jammed as I barely grabbed the top. I grunted, straining to pull myself up, clinging to the bricks.

Something slithered up my leg, and I kicked wildly.

It wound around my calf, growing stronger and thicker, and I really hoped this wasn't some karmic retribution for turning that frat boy's finger into a snake. *He deserved it.* Whoever or whatever was controlling the vine was about to pull it back; I could feel their intention coursing through the magic. *Fuck no.* A burst of adrenaline kicked in, and I hoisted myself up. I threw my arm over, clawing the bricks, willing the ivy to boost me—I could see the street on the other side—but the vine slithered up around my thigh, gripping me. I screamed, clinging to the damp wall as the vine slunk around my hips and coiled around my stomach where my hoodie had lifted.

I pulled with every muscle in my body, with every ounce of magic, but it wasn't enough. The dread of what was coming filled me; my back stretched as the vine tightened. *No.* With a grunt, I pulled one more time, but then . . . *fuck.* The vine yanked me down—I clawed at the earth as it dragged me backward, feeling my nails break and skin tear. The twisting plants flipped me onto my back as we torpedoed through my labyrinth of foliage and, in the moonlight, I realized it was all wilting, blackening, and . . . dead.

No. No. What is happening?

The vine paused, and I jerked hard, trying to break free, to break the spell, but a second vine looped through my ankles, latching them together. "What kind of bullshit is this? I'm an Earth witch!" *Thank Goddess Ritha isn't here to see.*

A tree branch scooped down and lifted me to my feet. I fought the glowing-green vine, but it wrapped tighter around my legs, and another bound my shoulders and chest.

"Unwind!" I commanded as it slithered around my neck, tightly pressing against my throat. Green sparkles sprayed out from the vine as if my magic was being choked out of the plant. "*Stop!*" Fear poured into my soul. "*Stop it!*" *I can't die beneath a tree in a park.* I didn't want my family to find me here. I would rather have been trapped in Ghede madness forever. "Codi!" My voice shook in a way I'd never heard it. What had happened to him? I frantically jerked back and forth, trying to loosen the vines, but they twisted around my face, over my mouth, muffling my screams. Even as the vine became suffocating, the magic felt like a warm, gentle caress. And it was terrifying.

In a moment of silence between my ragged breaths, a twig snapped. *Footsteps.*

And as the weight of the vines sank down on me, I realized why the magic felt so familiar: it was the Daures' magic. Marta Guldenmann's Earth magic. Fear flooded through me so hard, I teetered, light-headed.

A male figure appeared before me. He bent to peer into the small slit between the vines over my eyes, and I saw his.

"Hello, Désirée."

CHAPTER 47
WITCHES' FOUNTAIN

"The scream came from this direction," Nicco said as we adjusted our route deeper into the park. I cuddled Isaac's bird form tighter against my chest, longing for the protection spells of the French Quarter.

"Someone's here." Lisette zipped around us. "Some*thing*."

"It's magic." Nicco pulled me closer as a flock of small songbirds flew directly over our heads in an oddly aggressive fashion. "I've never felt anything like it. It's permeating everything."

Lisette cursed in French as she hit the ground with a hard snap. *What the hell?*

Isaac fluttered out of my arms, cawing frantically as something dragged her away in a forceful twist of angelic hair and swamp brush. She dug her hands into the ground, trying to stop it, but the forest floor was damp and unstable. Nicco sped after her. His injuries were no longer grave, but he certainly wasn't at peak strength.

I felt the magic closing in around us, as if about to swallow us whole. Had we really made it back to the Natural World, or were we still inside some kind of Ghede mind-trip?

The oaks began bending and swaying in an unnatural

harmony, their bark cracking, smaller branches snapping as they bowed in the direction Lisette was being pulled. "It's the tree!" I shouted, chasing after them. "The root has her ankle!" *The root.* Suddenly, I felt like Callis was taunting me. I could almost hear his voice through the rustling leaves: *"Is that what you think? That your telekinesis is limited to metal?"*

That *asshole.*

As I ran through the dark, I visualized the root. I tugged at it, tried to loosen it, but it was moving too fast. I stopped short and mentally jerked it with all my might. It ripped out of the ground all the way up to the trunk, spraying up an arc of dirt, whipping into the air like a tentacle, squeezing Lisette. "She's there!" I yelled, pointing as it shoved her into a cluster of branches.

The oak cracked and split as the boughs lengthened, twisting themselves into the clutches of the next tree. Nicco darted up a trunk and dove across the branches, always just one behind Lisette.

I ran beneath the canopy, trying to keep up with Isaac as he flew ahead. He dropped down to the ground beside me and threw up his Air, trying to bend the branches back, but they were too fast, passing Lisette deeper into the forest. The sounds of the wild grew into a symphony of hooves and screeches and groans. A murder of crows swooped over my head and into the foliage, pecking at Nicco so severely he dropped to the ground, covering his head.

"Don't," Isaac said, holding me back as the birds dove toward Nicco—dozens of them—a curtain of black feathers, glimmering with silver, their beaks and talons unnaturally long. "Something's not right." He whipped a strong gust Nicco's way. The birds screeched and flapped but wouldn't be deterred by Nicco's aggressive swats nor Isaac's Air. Dots of blood appeared on Nicco's pale skin, and we charged forward.

But then . . . they *lifted Nicco into the air.*

"What the fuck?" Isaac muttered under his breath.

"*Nicco!*" With a running leap, I latched onto his legs, but my feet left the ground too. I shrieked as wings beat around my face from every direction. As beaks tapped my back, sharp and quick like little daggers against my stomach, my arms.

"Adele, drop down!" Nicco yelled. "We're getting too high!"

A magic-possessed bird got caught in my hair, twisting, screeching, and I smashed my eyes shut with a swell of déjà vu. "*Get away!*"

But then one crow was louder than the rest, cawing shrilly, driving the others away from my face. They dove at him like little demons, swiping at his belly, smashing into his chest.

"*Leave him alone!*"

Isaac tumbled through the night. I looked down, but it was too far to jump: a twenty-foot drop to unwelcoming branches and stumps and God knew what else to be impaled on.

A beak plunged into my collar, and I let go with a scream. "*Isaac!*"

My jacket puffed up. A gust of Air broke my fall, and I landed in a pile of sopping wet leaves. I sucked in huge breaths and crawled toward Isaac, wiping rank, rotting foliage from my face.

"What the fuck was that?" he asked as we pulled each other up, our gazes locked on the crows flying away with Nicco, just like Callis had flown away with my father.

I knew it was him. "Callis is here. We have to keep going." I tugged his hand, and we ran after them. But almost immediately, I sensed Isaac losing stamina. An ominous feeling formed in the pit of my stomach—I'd never once been able to outpace him.

He stopped and bent over his knees, panting.

"Come on, I've got you." I slipped my hand around his waist, wondering if I should have made a nest for him in the greenhouse to keep him hidden and safe. But there was no way he'd have stayed behind, and I didn't want to go anywhere without him. He launched into the air one more time. I ran on, and he landed on my shoulder. I tried not to panic, no longer able to see Lisette's hair through the trees or Nicco's silhouette against the moon. All I had to guide us was the distant cawing of the crows.

The deeper we went through overgrown thickets, fallen branches, and uprooted trees, the more I swore I heard voices too. Isaac's talons tightened on my shoulder.

He cawed loudly, but his voice was drowned out by galloping hooves. I glanced back and let out a short scream—a herd of deer was charging up from behind. They spilled around us but didn't attack, just stayed with us, as if making sure we didn't veer from the path.

Ahead, a faint blue-green glow appeared through the trees. I ran toward it, plunging through the tangle of moss and spider-webs and leaves, until we burst into a clearing at . . . *Popp Fountain?*

A long stone path cut through a labyrinth of hedges and short stone walls, leading up a set of stairs to the enormous open-air Greco-Roman structure that housed the fountain. The circular pavilion platform, nearly a century old, was framed by gigantic white columns connected on top by a crowning ring. Codi and I had played here as children, splashing through the pool with his brothers, the pod of patinaed dolphins in the center of the fountain spitting water up to the clouds. In the dead of night, with the entrance columns now lit with torches, it truly looked like a place where the ancients might have worshipped their goddesses, bathing in the fountain and dancing in togas and ivy crowns under the moonlight reflecting on the glassy water.

Of course Callis would try claiming it for his coven.

From this distance, I couldn't see anyone there, just the pool and the arcs of water from the fountain glowing in the dark, giving off the ethereal sheen of magic. As I strode down the path, Isaac leaned forward, as if ready to spring off my shoulder. "Don't scope ahead," I said. "Who knows how many of them are already surrounding us."

The sounds of the forest quieted, and the gurgling of water picked up. The park had been closed due to hazardous conditions since the Storm, both to the public and its keepers. Dark mold now covered the stone steps, and ivy had overtaken the short stone wall enclosing the outer structure. As far as I knew, the fountain hadn't been operational for months, and yet tonight, the dolphins sprayed glowing arcs up to the stars.

The rushing water pounded louder with each step as I ascended the stairs. I paused at the pavilion entrance—the shallow pool should have been a cesspool of sludge, but it was perfectly crystalline, like liquid aquamarine, perfectly *magical*. On the opposite side of the fountain, basking in the supernatural glow, a robed figure watched me, his hood draped down over his shoulders. Callis had never been one to hide his face. My orbs hummed around his frame, a bright, fiery orange like fallen specks from the sun.

Rage sprouted roots in the pit of my soul.

His gaze followed me as I stepped up to the pool, entering his makeshift temple. We weren't alone. Ghost Drinkers stood ten feet apart between each of the columns, almost pious-looking in their ritual robes, their heads bowed, lips rolling with a rumbling chant. Someone was noticeably missing: Callis's giant sidekick. *That's what happens when you kill someone, Adele.* I wondered if the Irish witch had died too. *Did I kill two witches in the cemetery?*

Isaac fluffed up his feathers aggressively as I turned, eyeing the arc behind Callis. Cocoon-like structures of vines were adhered to the bases of several columns. The cocoon to his left bent and jerked with desperate murmurs, and a hiss came through Isaac's beak. My pulse picked up as I saw Dee's sneakers sticking out at the bottom—she was bound beneath the honey-suckle, gagged by the vines. Nicco was similarly bound to the next column by the roots of live oaks. The earth titled beneath my feet. Did Callis know I was the one who killed the Brute? Was this his retaliation? My jaw clenched as my eyes darted around the circle. Codi was in the cocoon of flora flanking Callis's other side, with Lisette next to him. One more cocoon completed the set. In the flickers of torch fire, I made out tangles of auburn hair knotted in the wraps of wisteria. *Annabelle*—tied up like a sorority-girl-mummy. I guess Callis hadn't welcomed her back with open arms.

How in the hell had he been able to control the forest like that? If Jakome had stolen the Guldenmanns' Earth magic, did Callis now also possess it? Callis had my Fire, the Daures' Earth magic, the Monvoisin grimoire, and who knows what else. I needed a playbook to keep up with their succubus magic.

I turned back to Callis, cool and stoic, channeling my inner Medici even as the rage flamed. But then Codi grunted franti-cally, trying to speak through the vines tight between his jaws, triggering my memories from the convent when they'd crushed his leg.

"Is he hurt?" I yelled in a panic.

"I don't think so," Callis said, shadows flickering across his face from my orbs. "Although he did put up quite the fight."

Désirée screamed a single syllable from the back of her throat, and Nicco jerked beneath the shackles, pointing with his head and eyes. I slowly turned around to face the darkness, half expecting to see a Minotaur or Hydra entering the ring to devour me while my friends were made to watch. I had, after all, attempted to kill the Salazar patriarch and wipe away Callis's magical existence.

But there was no one out there, at least not that I could see: no glow of beady eyes or snarls of gnashing teeth. My friends' muffled shrieks grew louder, and Isaac became frantic, jumping on my shoulder, pointing up to the sky with one wing. I looked up to the stars—to the arcs of Water spraying three stories high from the dolphins' mouths—and I no longer heard the muffled cries of my friends. Or saw Callis's anticipative expression.

The Water felt like it was pounding through me.

High above the shallow pool, a man was sprawled on his back, bobbing atop the arcs of magical Water as if being offered to Mari herself, and the syllable they were all yelling became clear: *Mac.*

"*Dad!*" I shrieked, edging around the fountain with quickening steps.

Isaac hopped to the ground, stomping toward Callis, and threw up a twister. "Let him down!"

Callis smacked the surface of the pool with his fist, and a sparkling wave shot up around Mac, blocking the Air. "I advise you to act a little more wisely, Mr. Thompson." He lobbed a grapefruit-sized ball of Fire over his shoulder at Dee.

"No!" Isaac blasted toward her in a whip of Air, taking the Fireball direct to his shoulder. He cried out in agony, his shirt burned through, skin seared and blistering. Désirée twisted in the vines, screaming, her eyes widening at the sight of his wound, but Isaac kept his gaze fixed on Callis as he stepped closer to her, shielding her behind his back.

My fingernails dug into my palms as my rage became an inferno inside me.

Dee can heal him, I told myself, blinking away the tears, refocusing on my dad. Use your magic, Adele. *Get him down.* In my mind, I saw the water disappearing, Mac plummeting, his body impaled over the joyful dolphins, blood billowing into the aquamarine pool. My lungs tightened. I was too scared to use my magic, too scared to touch him. If I dropped him . . . the water was so shallow, his back would break, or his head would split. *Stop it, Adele.* This was just what Callis wanted, a rise out of me, otherwise there'd be no need for the theatrics. Like father, like son. I wouldn't give it to him.

"Please put my dad down." I turned my attention squarely to him—also what he wanted. "I'll join your coven. I'll do whatever you want."

Nicco thrashed beneath the roots.

Callis's eyes narrowed at me. "I'm simply fulfilling my promise." His gaze usually felt like it was burning into your soul, like he was about to rip your spirit straight from your body. Tonight, something was slightly off, and it was disconcerting. It was like he was looking just past me. "I told you that if you didn't bring me the Medici book of shadows, I'd kill your dear Daddy."

The rage erupted. "And I told you, I *don't* have it. I went all the way to Guinée to ask Adeline where the Count was, and she wouldn't tell me!"

"Oh, is that why you went to the Afterworld?" His thin lips pursed as he held back a chuckle, like a patronizing older brother.

"*Yes.* To save my father."

"To save your father or to kill mine?" He leaned over to swirl his fingers in the water, and my friends gasped in pain. *The pool is the source of magic for the spell*. And he was tightening the roots.

"*Both*," I said, teeth clenched. I needed to do something, but there were a dozen of them and one of me. I needed a minute to think. So I kept talking. "I was naïve. Stupid. Desperate. I let Nicco convince me that going to the Afterworld was the only way to save my dad." I turned to Nicco. His brow tightened beneath the roots. "I let him convince me that he was on my side. That he loved me."

Isaac winced.

I turned back. "I even recruited all of my friends. This is my fault, not theirs." *Do something, Adele. Use your goddamn magic!* Keeping my eyes squarely on Callis, I envisioned the oak

486

wrapped around Nicco. *It's just moving positive space into negative space.* I felt through the universe for the tree root. "He used me to open the Gates to get to Guinée so he could kill your father, destroy your coven." My magic bumped the rough texture of the root. *Okay, just like that day at the fundraiser, Adele. Just like Callis taught you.* "He's obsessed with bringing down the Animarum Praedators because they're everything he wants to be: both magical and immortal."

"That is *not* immortality," Nicco scoffed through the oppressive binding.

Don't look at him. I felt the damp edges of the root twisted around his chest. Around his elbows and knees. Jammed between his lips. I tugged it hard, but it didn't budge. *Just find the end. Find the end and unwind it.* "But I'm thankful for Nicco's obsession, because without it, I would never have discovered my magical origins."

"And where did your Fire come from, *bella*?" The way Callis taunted me made me think he already knew.

"The last person I'd ever have thought to get answers from was Jakome Salazar of the Akelarrenlezea, of the Great Basque Country." I mentally rummaged for the end of the constraint, searching down Nicco's chest and hips and legs. *Where is it?*

"And what answers did my father give you?" He stepped toward me, his cape fluttering behind him in a gust that could have only been Isaac's.

I fought the instinct to retreat. "He taught me how Ama Lurra birthed the sun and the moon to scare away Evil. How we came from nothing." The words lured him closer, despite me being the one trapped in his web. And as he focused on me, my mind slinked in between the layers of roots at Nicco's ankles. They were thinner, twined with multiple loops. I combed through the twists. I was running out of time. "No money. No farm. Not even a name. He taught me how young Kattalin served Mari, and how, in return, she bestowed her with our

Fire." My pulse accelerated, hearing the words come out of my mouth. "Nicco killed Adeline. And tonight, he tried to kill me too, just like you said he would. Tonight, he almost succeeded in finishing what his grandfather started all those centuries ago." I wrapped my magic around the vine like it was a thread to untangle and glided over it until I found the end. *Yes. Yes. Yes.* "Thanks to me, he got a trip to Guinée, an assassin to kill your father, and the chance to break the Salazar magical line for good." *Quickly, Adele.* I freed the vine and unwound it from his ankles. From his knees. Thighs. He stayed perfectly still, careful not to draw the attention of the two flanking Animarum Praedators. "But what he doesn't know is that while we were on the other side . . . your mother found me."

Callis sucked back a breath. "What?"

"Arrosa, Beñat, Zorion." I added every name I could remember from the ring's flashbacks. "Antton, Donato, Clara. It was like finding the magical family I'd been searching for my whole life. Going to Guinée was my destiny."

"You met my mother?"

"She made me a pie. Quince." I smiled. "She's waiting for you to bring her back. For us to bring all of them back." I drew my hand from my pocket, wearing the ring. "They forged this ring for me from Mari's Fire, to match yours, and told me why your necromancy wasn't working."

His eyes lit up, but I couldn't tell if it was with excitement or envy. *Don't make him feel threatened, Adele.*

"I felt my magic as soon as I entered your father's theatre, and I knew I was home."

He stepped toward me, and my pulse stuttered.

He wasn't like his father in every way. He was impossible to read, and it scared the shit out of me.

I lowered to my knees. "I would never betray my bloodline. My magicline." The fear flickered in my voice. I didn't have to pretend—it was real.

He ran a hand through my hair, his fingers running over my scalp slowly, as if deciding whether to pull me up into his arms or break my neck. His touch felt strange, almost electric. Static-like. My pulse raced. What other magic did he have?

I pushed the words out: "So I threw the wand at Nicco instead of Jakome. If I'd had the strength of my Fire, I'm sure he'd have met his final death." I looked directly at Nicco, and the cold way he peered back at me sent a shudder up my spine. I also knew, deep in my soul, that we were in this together. Just like the night in the attic. Just like always.

I turned back to Callis, locking eyes with the gusto of Adeline or Cosette or any of *les filles aux cassettes*. "I want you to teach me. I want to return with you to the Akelarrenlezea. I want to relight the Fire at Mari's cave and restore our family's legacy, together."

My orbs floated around his shoulders, warm and hypnotizing. "You never have to be scared of him again, my little dove." I wanted my Fire so badly that a part of me truly did want to go with him. He offered me his hand and lifted me up.

"*Liar!*" Annabelle screamed, spitting out the piece of wisteria she'd chewed through.

I nearly bounded back and knocked her out, but I somehow restrained myself. *Stay calm.*

"She didn't throw the wand at Nicco; she threw it at *your father,* and Nicco leapt it front of it! She's lying!"

You fucking bitch.

Callis turned her way, and I frantically went back to working on the vine. As I pulled it from Nicco's shoulders, Callis swirled his fingers, unwinding the wisteria from Annabelle. "Am I really to trust an Aether? Especially one who's already proven herself a traitor?"

"I'm not a traitor! I went with them for *you.*"

Lisette screamed at her through the restraints, but Annabelle leapt out of the vines and grabbed her bag off the stone floor.

"Nicco didn't go to Guinée to kill your father—that's just what he told Adele because she'll believe anything he says. Her coven planned the whole assassination without him. Nicco was going there to get his grimoire!"

"You don't know what the hell you're talking about, Annabelle," I spat, desperately unwinding the magical root from Nicco, my concentration wobbling with her every word.

"*You're* the traitor, Adele. You tried to kill your own bloodline, and you're lying now, just like you were lying that night at the convent. Just like you've been lying to Nicco this whole time. You've had the Medici grimoire all along!"

The Ghost Drinkers' chant became louder, heightened with shock.

I rolled my eyes, but the distraction was just what I'd needed. As she stormed over to Callis, I yanked the root from around Nicco's throat, and it quietly slithered away. There was no time to unwind anyone else. *It's just us.*

Annabelle was practically salivating at Callis's heel. She dropped her bag, revealing a leather book. "But I'm the one who rescued the grimoire from the Afterworld. *Adele* doesn't care about her magic—she was just going to leave it behind."

Nicco didn't move a muscle, just stared at the book in her hands and then at me.

I let out a laugh of relief when I saw what she'd found. "Why don't you delight us with a reading? I'm sure everyone here would be entertained by the musings of a sixteen-year-old girl on her transatlantic voyage to the New World."

"Maybe I will," she spat. "Hope you understand Italiano." She waved her hands over Adeline's diary. "She's not a Salazar. She's too stupid to have descended from one of the Greats." She murmured words beneath her breath.

What is she . . . ?

The lock slipped off the diary and clanked to the ground. *Shit.* She was disguising it with her Aether magic. "Callisto

Salazar isn't going to fall for some bullshit glamour spell, Annabelle!"

The book grew taller and wider and thicker, the pages more plentiful, the leather morphing from brown to black. My heart stopped when I saw the symbol appearing on the cover: the three intersecting diamond rings. How could Annabelle have known to do that? It was just like I'd seen in Nicco's dream.

Darkness cast over Callis's face. "She's not casting a glamour," he sneered. "She's *breaking* one!"

A tsunami of panic flooded my bones. I thought back to the letter León had written Adeline when he'd gifted her the book, how adamant he'd been that she fill each of the pages with her stories. Had she disguised it for him unknowingly?

My gaze flicked up to my father. Isaac had been right about the most important part of a plan being an exit strategy, and I didn't have one.

Nicco's eyes were no longer on me but—ablaze with fury—locked on the grimoire in Callis's hands.

"Now what was that about Aether witches?" Annabelle crossed her arms as if waiting for her crown.

But Callis's attention didn't divert from me. "You are a disgrace to this family." He strode toward me. "Give me that ring."

"No. You're the disgrace." I reached behind my back. Was I truly on my own now? "You murdered your siblings and let the blame fall on the Medici. I bet Jakome doesn't know that. Or your mother. Did you kill sweet Zorion too?"

"And you'll be next!" Fire lit up around the circle, and his hand crushed around my throat. A blur whipped between us as I thrust the dagger low and deep. Annabelle screamed, and Nicco's fangs plunged into Callis's neck with a rageful curse. I staggered back, pulling the knife from his gut, my hand trembling.

"*Che diavolo?*" Nicco muttered in confusion. No blood dripped from his teeth.

The Ghost Drinkers chanted louder, none of them coming to Callis's aid.

He began to disappear beneath Nicco's grip—not like the spirits blinking out of the Afterworld but into an ethereal sparkle fading into . . . *magic*? His outline dissipated into the darkness, and in a glimmering blink, the grimoire disappeared too. I whipped around. The rest of the Ghost Drinkers were gone, and the blade in my hand was clean, as if I'd just dreamt the whole thing.

"Adele!" Désirée shrieked as the magic released her.

The glow in the pool began to fade.

"*Dad!*" I charged toward the fountain as he fell.

Before I could throw up my hand, the Water lifted from the pool in a wave, and a gust of Air blew through me, rushing into the water, pushing it higher.

My breath choked as my dad plunged toward the stone pool.

Codi and Isaac appeared beside me, their arms thrust out, concentration chiseled on their faces.

Their magic held, and the Water slowly released back into the pool, leaving Mac standing by the dolphins, drenched, coughing, confused.

I hopped over the ledge of the pool and waded toward him. "Dad!"

"Adele, is that—?"

"Dad!" I jumped into his arms, the rush of relief crushing.

"*Baby.*" He squeezed me tight.

"Dad, I'm sorry." Tears escaped from my eyes no matter how hard I pinched them closed.

"Where are we? What happened?"

"Everything's going to be okay." I squeezed him back. He felt skinnier. "Are you hurt?"

He seemed disoriented and ragged, but he shook his head.

My friends splashed into the fountain as he released me.

"Mac!" Isaac staggered behind, wincing and holding the arm

with the charred and blistering shoulder stiffly. "Glad to see you, man." He too had tears in his eyes.

I deeply regretted ever erasing my father's memory of him. If I hadn't, I knew he'd be bear-hugging Isaac as if he were his own son.

"*Adele*," Désirée said emphatically, "you had the *Medici grimoire*."

Thump-thump.

"I-I—" I flipped back to Nicco, the words choking in my throat. "I didn't know."

He stared at me coolly, the glint missing from his eyes.

"Nicco—"

He turned away.

"Nicco!" I splashed back toward him, but in a blur, he was gone. "*Nicco!*" The screamed zapped my last bit of energy, and I fell into the water at the pool's edge, my heart aching. *There's no way he could really think. I would never . . .* "I didn't know."

Codi's hand slid around my shoulder. "Let's get out of here."

A splash hit the water behind us, and Désirée shrieked. We spun around. Isaac had fallen over. "His shoulder!" she yelped. "Help me get him out of the water."

"I got him," my dad said, but Codi rushed over to help carry him out of the pool.

"Where's Lisette?" Isaac asked as they laid him on the stone floor.

"I think she went after Annabelle," Désirée said. "Stay still."

"You're bleeding," my dad said to me, his face lit up with concern.

I glanced down at the dark stain on my shirt. It was hardly noticeable, but when I touched my collar, my fingers came back red. *The bird attack.* Both Désirée and Codi gave me a look. "It's not what you think. It's fine—just focus on Isaac." Dee turned her attention to Isaac's shoulder, and we held him down. As her magic connected, he howled like I'd never heard him.

My dad watched with intensity, but not with the shock and awe I expected, and it made me wonder what he'd seen while with the Ghost Drinkers, but I blinked away the tears because all I had room for was relief. Relief that they were all okay. That I had my father back. For a moment, relief even filled the aching hole forming in my chest.

Could Nicco really believe that I'd been lying to him this whole time? That I'd been pulling the long con? *Breathe, Adele.*

I walked away for a second to collect myself. I didn't want them to see me like this. Not with Isaac lying on the ground. Not when we'd just gotten my dad back.

I lifted my arms over my head, took in a steady breath, and counted as I slowly released it. How the hell had I had the Medici grimoire this whole time and not known it?

When Isaac was ready to move and Dee had recovered from the recoil, we quickly gathered our things. My dad's gaze fell to the dagger in my hand, and only then did I realize I was still holding it.

"How is that knife clean?" Isaac asked. "I saw you gut him."

"Which was insane, by the way," Codi said. 'Where did you get that thing?"

I could still feel the sensation of pushing the dagger into Callis's stomach, but . . . did Ghost Drinkers not bleed? "And what happened to all the other Animarum Praedators?" I asked. "How did they all just vanish into thin air?" I turned to Dee and Codi. "What just *happened*?"

"I don't know," he said. "Can Callis teleport now?"

Désirée strapped on her bag. "If he had, Adele's blade would still be bloody. I think it's worse. I think he and his coven *astral projected.* Do you know how next level that is?"

I slid the Medici dagger back into its sheath and stepped up to my dad to hug his arm. I *didn't* actually know how next level that was, because I grew up with this guy and not a magical family, and I wouldn't trade him for anyone in the world.

"I can fly ahead and find a route out of the park," Isaac offered.

"No," I said. "We're sticking together."

"I know the way out," my dad said. "We used to play ball not far from here when I was your age. Everyone stay close. God only knows what's in this park since the Storm."

I turned to my friends, and we all tried not to laugh. He had no idea.

With the others following us, he and I led the way out into the decaying park, me unable to let go of his hand.

I was exhausted when we finally made it to the road. Mentally, physically, and magically.

Everything in this part of town had been desolate since the Storm, so when bright headlights approached, we all took an apprehensive step back.

"Poppy?" Codi yelled, peering at the ancient F-150 that rolled to a stop, windows cranked down.

"What are you waiting for?" she yelled back.

He smiled brightly and opened the door, holding it so Désirée could slide in first. "Did my dads send you?"

"Hell no. We're not allowed outside the Quarter."

Codi motioned for me to go next. I glanced back at Isaac, who was hopping into the truck's bed. "I'll ride in the back so you can be with your cousin."

"You sure?"

"Yeah."

Isaac held his hand out to me, and I climbed into the back of the truck. My dad was already resting against the cabin.

"So then how did you know we were here?" Codi asked.

Poppy laughed. "Magic, cuz."

I couldn't help but let out an exhausted laugh as we settled in next to my dad. Codi slammed the heavy door shut, and Poppy threw the old beast into drive.

My father squeezed my leg and glanced at me. "I love you more than you could ever know."

"I do know," I whispered and hugged him tight. I wanted to curl up into his lap like I did when I was a kid. I wanted to tell him about all the insane things that had happened since we'd last parted ways. I wanted to ask him a million questions about what had happened to him with the Ghost Drinkers, but he looked like he'd aged a decade since I'd last seen him, so I let him rest. And as we hummed down Esplanade, he almost instantly fell asleep.

I moved closer to Isaac, and we stared up at the moon together. I felt like Illargui was watching from the perfect crescent. I curled my arm into his, and our fingers wrapped together like it was the most natural thing in the world.

As we bobbed over the bumpy road, I turned toward him a little, and we locked eyes. "Thank you," I whispered, my vision blurring with tears.

"I told you we'd get him back."

I smiled a little, and so did he. "I shouldn't have made you go to the Afterworld."

"You didn't make me. I would do anything for you. And for Mac."

I believed him. With every bone in my body.

Leaning close, I pressed my lips to his cheek. Maybe it was habit, or a desperate need for comfort and love, but when he looped his arm around my shoulders, I curled up close. We watched the nightscape sliding by, and I thanked Susannah Norwood Bowen for coming to La Nouvelle-Orléans all those years ago and bringing him into my life.

I loved him. I loved him so much.

CHAPTER 48

UNQUESTIONABLE

Vodou Pourvoyeur was quiet when we walked through the shop doors looking like a pack of wolves returning to the den, exhausted, wet, and beaten down, but prosperous in the hunt. In silence, we passed the tourist thrills and Voodoo dolls, but when we entered the back room, Ritha yelled so loudly, she woke everyone in the house. Maybe everyone in the Quarter.

Folks came stomping downstairs to welcome Désirée home, including her parents, cousins, and other witchy relatives I didn't know. All with joyful expressions and questions about Guinée, the Ghede, and of course about Marassa and Makandal and all of their ancestors. "*What did she look like?*" "*Is he revered?*" "*Was so-and-so there?*" "*Did you still have your magic?*"

Edgar, Chatham, and the rest of the Daures burst through the front door before Codi could even think about leaving, and I'd never been privy to so many tears and smiles and fist pumps and chest bumps. Codi picked up Fiona's youngest daughter, Lilly, who told him she'd been checking the plant every day. I leaned against my dad, and despite being exhausted, he didn't complain. I didn't think he would have had it any other way.

"So this is how you've been spending your time?" he asked.

"*Oui.* You can thank your ancestors." I pushed up his sleeve and examined his arm, as if maybe I'd just somehow missed a big black triangle over the past few months. No Maleficium, of course, but I still couldn't help wondering if he'd ever thrown a flame. For the hundredth time, I thought about all the torches in his workshop and all the metal. Magical or not, he was his own alchemist of sorts.

Ritha hugged on Isaac like he was one of her own, and she inspected his shoulder and slathered on one of her salves. She made the rounds inspecting everyone's wounds, including the beak gash that had bled onto my collar. I let my hair fall over my neck out of paranoia, although I'm sure the vampire mark must have completely healed by now. While Ritha fussed over my father's health, I went over to Chatham, tail between my legs.

"Baby," he said, pulling me into his soft chest. "Your mama would be so proud."

"*Merci,*" I said sheepishly, and retrieved the ghoststick from my bag. "I'm sorry. It's . . . dirty. I can clean it for you."

He raised an eyebrow at its bloody condition. "Maybe after that I can teach you how to make one?"

"Really? You're not mad?"

"Dawlin', right now, I've never been so *not mad* in my entire life."

I breathed a sigh of relief.

Ritha put on the chicory, and Edgar pulled out boxes of ginger cookies and marmalade cakes and a huge pot of red beans. But one person was noticeably quiet. While the party was going on around him, Codi stared out into a shelf of herbs, an underlying somberness behind his eyes. I softly moved in front of him, breaking his melancholic reverie. It hurt my heart not seeing him in his usual role as the life of the party. I put my arms around his neck. I didn't have to ask him what was wrong. I knew.

"I feel like a failure."

"You shouldn't."

"I didn't help my grandma. I don't even know where she is."

"We're going to find her, Codi. This is *not* your fault."

"Yes, it is. I should have stopped Callis long before any of this happened. I should have never—"

"*I,*" Chatham said, stepping up behind us, "should never have let him into our house. We knew he was trouble, but we thought we had it under control. Son, this is not your fault." He pulled Codi into his arms, and Codi hid his face as he cried. "Do you hear me?"

As Codi nodded, I had another moment of déjà vu. "*I should never have let him into our house.*" It was almost exactly what Ferdinando Medici had said to Nicco in the Ghede trial, only he had been talking about León—about my family.

They were both talking about my ancestors.

I am not *related to Callisto Salazar.* My knees weakened, and I caught myself on the shelf, but not before I knocked over a jar of lavender. It shattered on the floor, tiny buds exploding everywhere. All the witches in the room turned my way. "I'm sorry!"

"Are you okay?" everyone started asking, rushing over, and I hated all the fussing. Désirée strode to my side, shooing them away, and with a single swirl of her hand, had all the little flowers in a fresh jar and the glass in a dustpan.

My dad slipped his arm around me.

"I'm fine," I said, before he could ask.

He took a deep inhale, and I saw the recognition behind his eyes. I was thinking about her too. It was my mother's scent. He looked dehydrated. I handed him my bottle of water, wondering how they'd treated him, and I shuddered. Would it have been any different had they known he was one of their own? The thought made me want to retch.

I asked for the tenth time whether he was okay. He reassured me he was, but I could tell something was lingering on the tip of his tongue. "What?" I asked.

"When you were there. On the other side . . ."

Right then I knew what he wanted to know.

My eyes welled as I nodded. "She was beautiful."

He gasped a little bit and blinked back tears.

"She told me that you were the strongest man she ever knew. That . . . every decision she ever made was because she loved you. Us. And that she'll love you forever."

He hugged me so tight I couldn't breathe. "I thought I'd lost you."

"You're never going to lose me, Dad. I'm magical. I'm a witch. I'll always protect you."

"That's not your job. I'm your father. I'm supposed to protect *you*."

"We'll always protect each other."

"Yes, we will." He kissed my head. "Yes, we will."

Ana Marie came over with two stiff glasses of whisky and handed one to my dad, which he gladly accepted. And for me, a steaming cup of peppermint tea. As she started to chat with him, I looked back to Isaac, who was fully immersed telling Ritha a story about La Sirène. I sipped my tea, wondering if his father even realized he'd left town.

We'd survived the Afterworld, met our ancestors, escaped Callis's magical clutches, and saved my father. My friends were safe. I even had my magic back, partially, at least. But as I looked around the room at all the smiling faces, I felt empty.

And I knew why.

Nicco wasn't a part of the joy. I imagined him back in the shadows somewhere, by himself, contemplating where he went wrong. Figuring out his next move. Chastising himself for not having predicted Callis's magical Earth-juiced ambush. It wasn't fair.

"We've had a hawk eye on that monster," Ritha said. My heart pounded before realizing she was speaking of Callis. "He hasn't left that compound."

"Well, actually . . . he did. Kind of." Désirée did her best to explain what happened at Popp's Fountain.

"Astral projection!" Ritha shouted, and Chatham hurried over with equal concern.

I could see where the conversation was heading. I may have saved my dad, but the city was still under siege. We had to drive the Ghost Drinkers out of town; whether that was back to Spain or to Hell was still to be determined. We somehow had to save the spirits of Codi's ancestors. And I sure as hell had to take my Fire back from Callis. I was ready for the war, but I didn't want to do any of it without Nicco.

And suddenly, I knew exactly where he'd be.

"Dad, do you mind if I— I need to go and . . . find someone really quick."

Edgar's ears perked up, and I had a feeling he knew exactly where I was going. My defenses rose, but he put his arm around my father. "Why don't I make you a plate, Mac, and fill you in on a few magical basics. I'm sure you have a lot of questions." He gave me a wink.

Thank you, I mouthed. And before anyone else could notice, I slipped past the Voodoo dolls and out the door.

I ran all the way to St. Anthony's Garden; through the back of the cathedral to the spiral stairs. *What if he's not here?* What if he went straight across the river with his brothers? Or even worse, on his own? I started to panic. He wanted that grimoire more than anything in the world. He'd die trying to get it back.

I suddenly felt sick. I should have gone straight to his house. I paused on the steps, sucking in air. But then, just over the sound of my breaths . . .

Thump-thump.

Thump-thump.

I leapt up the remaining stairs and plowed through the bell tower door like a mangy cat.

He was there.

Leaning on the stone window ledge in deep contemplation, gazing out at Callis's compound, the darkness weighing upon him. The air had cooled with the dead of night, and the cloudless sky made room for the stars to shine through. I knew he'd sensed my approach, but I had no idea what he was thinking. It seemed like years ago when we'd first come up here together. I was a different person then, but one thing remained the same.

I still felt exhilarated being here with him, high above the city.

I felt exhilarated being anywhere with him.

Softly, I settled next to him, elbows on the ledge in the sliver of moonlight.

He didn't stir. His clothes were tattered and torn, but his coloring was back, and the fatigue was gone from his face. Maybe it was just his natural vampiric regeneration ability; maybe he'd fed on someone on the way home. Either way, I didn't care. I'd never forget that feeling of devastation when I thought I'd lost him. I never wanted to feel that again.

My voice edged into the silence. "Niccolò?"

"*Sì, bella?*" He didn't look at me, just kept gazing out at the house with the saffron glow.

"We're going to get your grimoire back, I promise."

"Are we? Or is that just what you want me to think?"

The question cut into me like a dagger.

He turned to me. "You seemed pretty convincing back there with that story for Callis. Who knew you were such a gifted orator?"

"I was trying to save my father," I stuttered. "And my friends, and you—"

"You sounded just like one of them!"

"What is that supposed to mean?"

"A *Salazar.*"

"I am *not* a Salazar. I am a *Saint-Germain.*"

He scoffed. "Yes, you are. You're just like him. You have his eyes. You have his magic. You even had his grimoire. *My* grimoire. You're just like *le comte Saint-Germain*. Not even real. I should never have trusted him, and I should never have—"

"I am just like him!" I snapped. "Because I love you!"

His eyes lit up.

Thump-thump-thump-thump thump-thump.

"I have always loved you." I felt like I was having an out-of-body experience as the words came out. "I've tried to forget about you. To lock you away, out of my mind." My eyes welled in preparation for the rejection. "I've spent every day since we've met trying *not* to love you, trying to not be *in love* with you."

"Stop."

My heart cracked. "I can't. I don't know how."

"Stop." His hands slid up my face. "Stop trying not to love me." I barely heard the words as his lips touched mine. As he pulled me close like he was never letting go.

The blood pumped through his heart so loudly, it felt like it was flowing into mine. I let his jacket drop to the floor, and he pulled me back, falling against the ledge and kissing me deeper. Unrelenting. The feel of his desire was more surreal than all the magic in the world, and I needed more. I would always need more of him. My hands slipped up his back, and the magic under his skin burned against my fingertips, crackling like fire, but electric like lightning reaching up to the heavens.

I paused to take a breath, and his lips trailed along my neck, kissing the healed spot, and in the flutter of my eyelids, light flashed across the stars. I wrapped my arms tighter around him and gazed out at the sky. It was his magic; I'd seen it in my dreams.

"What's wrong?" he whispered.

"Nothing," I whispered back. He wouldn't believe me if I told him, so I reveled in the moment myself. His hands slinked beneath my shirt, arms circling my waist, and we clung to each other as I watched a second flash, dreaming of a day when he would believe he was magical.

His fingers gently traced my spine, making the small of my back arch up to him. The glint had returned to his eyes, and it had a magnetic effect, drawing me in. I wasn't sure I'd ever be able to look at him again without kissing him.

The murmur that came from the back of his throat lured me even deeper into the kiss.

We may not have won the magical war yet, but I'd gotten nearly everything my heart desired. "This is only the beginning, Niccolò," I said between breaths. "We're going to take back your grimoire, and my Fire, and destroy the Salazars for everything they've done to your family. To my family." I felt the Fire light up inside him. He kissed me harder, my arms circling him tight. His hand unabashedly slid into my pants, my magic releasing the metal closures, and his fingers dipped beneath the silk of my panties. "And one day, you'll have your magic," I whispered, and he touched me deeper. I could no longer speak. Or think. I could barely kiss him as his fantasies drenched my mind. Or were they mine? I no longer knew the difference, but soon I was clutching him with a frenzied whimper.

As my mind came back down from the stars, I saw that not-so-innocent smile, and I felt more exposed and vulnerable than I had in all of Guinée. In all of my life.

"I told you so," he said.

"Told me what?"

"That we're magical together."

I'd never beamed so brightly. "You didn't tell me so. I always believed you." I pulled him closer, and his mouth came down to mine. Every kiss, every touch made me ache. He paused, leaving me momentarily desperate. His fangs protruded, but it was his stare that was piercing. "You and Callis might have the same blood running through your veins," he said, his voice low and vehement, "but you are with me."

I kissed him hard.

"You will never be one of them."

"And you'll never be a monster to me, Niccolò Medici."

It was the easiest truth I'd ever spoken out loud.

Because I loved him.

Unquestionably.

His touches grew stronger along with his kisses, and magic swelled inside me, begging to be released. And for the second time that night, I let my mind go and my magic wander. Down his chest, sliding deep into his pants. His mouth gaped against mine, and I saw something in his eyes that I'd never seen before. *Awe.* "How are you . . . doing that?" he asked with a pant. I stroked him again.

"Magic," I whispered against his lips, and his head knocked against mine. My Spektral had nothing to do with metal or any material. It was simply an extension of me. A third eye, showing me things with its touch.

I felt powerful as he kissed me. As his squeezes begged me not to stop.

I didn't stop. I never would. I didn't know how to not love him.

"Adele . . . your Mark." His voice shook. Beneath my thin sleeve, my Maleficium was aglow like bright orange embers. My mouth crashed onto his; I could feel the old traces of my Fire. Of his through his whimper.

He may have been a vampire, but as I brought him to peak with the edge of my mind, I'd never felt so much like a witch.

CHAPTER 49
REFLECTION

"So was it that bad?" Dee asked, leaning on the counter next to me. The room was still bustling, but people were starting to wind down. Drinks were being drained and plans for tomorrow being hatched.

"Was what that bad?"

"The Afterworld, duh," she answered with a yawn.

"*Ha*. I guess not."

"You guess not?" Codi leaned down next to her. "We just met our freaking ancestors, and you guess not?"

"You're right. It was pretty cool."

He leaned back. "Sheesh. New Yorkers. Can't please 'em even if you take them to an underwater mermaid palace."

"Okay, *that* was awesome." The truth was, I wouldn't have traded the trip for the world. Not just the mermaid part, all of it. Just being there with them.

"What's this?" Désirée asked, examining the carved bone that hung from my neck.

I'd forgotten all about the skeleton key.

"It looks familiar." She removed her grimoire from her bag and opened it up, but before she flipped through too many pages, Ritha waved her hand, and the book opened to a precise location. Désirée pulled the key, along with me, closer to the page, growing excited. "I knew I'd seen it somewhere before. Isaac, this is a key to the goddamn Afterworld!"

"Désirée, *mouth*," Ritha said.

"There are only a few of them in the entire Natural World!"

I sheepishly looked at Ritha. "I hope I didn't offend you, giving away the wolf tooth?"

"Offended? Honey, that's why I gave it to you."

"Offended?" Désirée echoed. "That's like the best up-gifting ever. Dang. What did you do for Doubye for it?"

"What? Nothing. We traded."

"A common wolf's tooth for a key to the Afterworld. Ghede don't trade; they take."

"I don't know—I guess she wanted me to come back?"

Codi nudged Dee with his elbow. "What did I say?"

"Dude, not like that!"

"Dee," Codi said, "did your Ghede give you a parting gift?"

She smirked, crossing her arms. "Nope, what about you?"

"Nada!"

"You must have left quite an impression on her, Isaac," Désirée said.

"You guys are the worst." I batted her ponytail. "And by the worst, I mean the best coven ever. Speaking of, where'd Adele go?"

"Probably to find Nicco," Codi said. Dee shot him a look. "And Lisette," he added. "All of the Medici."

"You know, filling them in," Désirée said.

I did my best to contain my eyeroll as I grabbed my bag. She tugged my arm, a weird look on her face. "Chill." I kissed her cheek. "I'm just going to check on Ren."

"Ren's here?" Mac asked with a yawn as he approached the counter.

"He's been here ever since that outburst at the Marigny Opera House," Ritha said.

Mac looked perplexed. "That was months ago."

"It's a long story. We'll go over everything tomorrow."

I wondered if Ritha meant it, or if she was planning on memory-powdering him in the middle of the night. I hoped she wasn't. It was so cool not having to hide things from Mac, and it wasn't like he was going to tell anyone. I know Adele hated keeping secrets from him.

Mac looked around the room. "Where's my daughter?"

"She just texted me," Désirée piped in. "She's with Nicco, so you don't have to worry. Like for her safety on the streets or whatever."

By the way, Nicco's a vampire who almost killed your daughter tonight, so maybe you should worry. I pinched my mouth closed. I wasn't going to start shit now that Adele was talking to me again.

"She'll be back soon," Dee quickly added.

My lip curled. "You're being weird."

"No, I'm not."

"Well, I don't want to leave without her," Mac said. "Text her for me, will you? I don't have my phone." He yawned again. "Tell her to hurry up. I'm not sure how much longer I can last before I pass out in that chair."

Ritha took his hand in a matronly way. "You will do no such thing. You're staying with us tonight. Both you and Adele."

"I couldn't. You've already got a full house."

"I insist. Tomorrow, I will personally ensure that your properties are heavily warded against the enemy witches."

"Enemy witches," he mumbled.

"And I'll go with her," Chatham added, guzzling the rest of his drink. "Until tomorrow."

Ritha turned to Désirée. "Show Macalister up to the corner room. Zara's girls can stay with me tonight. Adele can stay with you."

My mood deflated. I'd kinda hoped Adele would invite me to stay over. Not in a we're-getting-back-together-way, just so I didn't have to return to my room at the shuttered bar by myself.

"Get the sulk off your face," Dee said. "You're staying here too."

"Isaac, you take the downstairs altar room," Ritha said. "Hope you don't mind the floor. The ancestors will keep you company."

I tried not to smile too hard. The little room behind the curtain was my favorite place in the house. It was where Adele, Dee, and I used to hang before we had HQ.

"This way, Mr. Le Moyne," Désirée said, motioning for Mac to follow her through the curtain.

I trailed behind them on my way to the back door. "I hope you like a very firm mattress," she said.

"I think I could sleep on glass shards tonight if I had to."

"Well, we do have a mirror room, but it's currently occupied."

He paused, mid-stair. "On second thought, maybe I should wait up for Adele."

"You look exhausted." Désirée guided him up the stairs by his elbow. "I'll send Adele to your room the second she walks in."

I went through the back door and dove into the air. She was definitely being weird. Why was she being so adamant about Adele's whereabouts? What was Adele doing with Nicco? I swooped across the courtyard, over the enormous sunflowers; they reminded me of the stupid Salazar play and how he'd dove in front of the ghoststick to save her magic. My chest pounded. What if Adele and Nicco went across the river to take down Callis?

Dee wouldn't let her do that. Right? Codi definitely wouldn't.

As I soared down the hallway of the guesthouse, I couldn't

shake the feeling. It was classic Adele, going off on her own, not wanting us to be in harm's way. I'd give Ren the gad and then go looking for her. I ran the last few steps, surrounded by the moans of the Possessed, almost forgetting that Ren didn't know about my crow-side. He always seemed to know so much more than a regular mundane.

"Yankee!" he yelled.

I crossed into the room, taking it as a welcoming sign. He was sitting on the floor in his usual spot, lookin' like a washed-up rocker who'd had decades of late-night drug binges but was somehow still kickin'. Only instead of his leather pants, he had on . . . no pants. Beneath his white ruffled shirt, his legs stuck out in front of him like two white twigs. He was so pale he almost looked lavender, like Doubye, and his stringy black hair was patchy at his scalp. *Jesus*. It was how my mom's hair looked before she decided to shave it all. That's what these parasitic souls were like: a cancer.

"How you feeling, Ren?"

He didn't answer, and rightfully so. It was a stupid question to ask. I'd always felt ridiculous asking my mom how she felt when doctors were pumping chemicals through her veins.

"So you know how we took this little . . . trip?" Optimism overwhelmed me, knowing I had the cure for him. "I found this guy on the other side. A miracle man. He was this old Ghede with a praline shop. You would have liked him."

He turned to look at me. "Did you get that vampire outta here?"

"Vampire?"

"Don't play dumb with me, son."

"I wouldn't think of it."

"I know vampires are real." His voice rose as he became agitated. "There was one in here just a little while ago!"

"What? Who? Nicco?"

"Young fella. Pointy teeth."

Why would Nicco have his fangs out in front of Ren? I'd hardly ever seen them myself.

"Spiky hair, big ole spikes through his ears. Someone needs to put one of those spikes through his heart!"

"*Wait.* Are you talking about Theis?" Ren's boyfriend had surgical fangs permanently adhered to his teeth. Not that I really got the appeal, but I assumed Ren was into it.

"Might have bitten my neck if I hadn't socked it to him good!" he roared.

"Ren, Theis isn't a vampire. He's your . . . your man. Wait, you socked him? *Again?*"

"Oh, this was no man. Pure diabolical."

Jesus. Ren and Theis were like relationship goals; now he didn't remember who Theis was? I prayed to whoever was taking prayers that this miracle praline wasn't just going to save him but reverse some of the damage the soul was causing. I knew that he could physically recover—he could always gain more weight and get sun on his skin—but I couldn't imagine the two of them *not* together. I wasn't even sure if it was a life he would want.

He turned back to me. "So, kid. Did you get the goods?"

"You remembered!" I slid my bag off my shoulder and sat down next to him on the floor.

"Did my map work? Did ya get down with the Ghede?"

"It did. And I guess, yes, if you count a fake engagement party. We also caught the opening night of a show called *Akelarrenlezea Spectacular* and visited La Sirène's underwater palace."

"Sounds fabulous. I'll put them both on my itinerary."

"You should. Wait, *no*! I mean, unless you mean later in life —death. You aren't going to the Afterworld anytime soon."

"Iiiiiiii don't know about that, kid."

"Ren, don't you hear what I'm saying? I got you the gad! The miracle cure!" I eyed a sealed coffee can on his desk and scrambled up. "The gad will release Alessandro." I popped off the lid and dumped out the pencils that were inside. "This should hold him. I've got some water in my bag." I knelt back down next to him. "Ren, don't you realize what's about to happen? You'll be able to go home soon."

"Home?" he asked. "I wanna go home. I wanna Purple Drank, and I wanna sing for crowds in the amphitheater and see the riverboats on the Moonwalk. I wanna see my city restored to its former glory!"

I unscrewed the cap of my water bottle and filled the canister halfway. "You'll be able to do all of that! And there's this amazing mermaid pool waiting for Alessandro." I couldn't wait to tell Julie.

"Yankee . . ."

I looked up.

"You know I call you that 'cause I love ya, right?"

I laughed. "Yeah." I wasn't prepared for the swell of emotion that followed. I hadn't even known Ren that long, but I guess every day in post-Storm New Orleans felt like a week in normal life.

An uprise of voices came from the hallway—the moans and cries of the Possessed. *Why are they getting all riled up?* They pounded on the walls and stomped on the floor. But then a burst of shrieks cut through the chorus of wailing voices. My back stiffened.

Concern lit up Ren's face. "Was that the young Miss Borges?"

"I'll be right back."

I raced down the hall and across the bridge to the main house. When I burst into the upper floor hallway, Codi was pounding up the stairs. Dee shrieked again, and we both barged through her bedroom door.

An enormous amalgam of plants was growing up to the ceiling in the corner, roots overtaking the floor, stalks, branches and vines twisting up at least seven feet tall. It looked like some experiment gone haywire in Poison Ivy's greenhouse. There was usually a huge monstera in that corner. I knew this because Désirée had given me an in-depth tour of her plant collection. More than once.

Mac was hunched over the enormous mass of plants as if trying to look inside it. The monstera's large terracotta pot was turned over on the floor broken, soil spilled like the giant roots had come alive. Had her magic gone berserk?

"Get him away from me!" Dee shouted.

"Désirée?" Codi asked.

"Did I stutter?" she shrieked.

"Dee, are you trapped in . . . this plant-pod-thing?" I asked.

Mac started to rip it apart with both hands. "Get 'er out."

Codi laughed. "Maybe La Sirène did supercharge you!"

"Isaac!" she screamed. "Do something!"

"Mac's getting you out!"

"Mac's the reason I'm in here!"

Codi looked to me, and we both stepped forward. Mac turned around swinging. I wasn't ready, and his fist smashed straight into my face, cracking my nose.

Blood gushed out as I fell against the wall, seeing spots. "What the fuck?" I spat, stunned by both the punch and that Mac could throw that hard. I knew he had some upper body strength from his metalwork, but *fuck*. My ears rang so loudly I couldn't focus on what Dee was saying . . . She was behind the plant-pod-thing, as if it were a shield. A plant fortress. *Wait.* Had she made that thing for protection? *From Mac?*

"Mr. Le Moyne!" Codi yelled, his hands in the air defensively. "It's Codi Daure!" He glanced at me. "Fuck, is he a fucking vampire? Did Callis somehow . . . ? This is like with Brigitte at the convent all over again."

A vampire?

At the sound of Brigitte's name, Mac charged Codi full-on, linebacker-style.

"Mac!" Codi cried as he was lifted off the ground by the

tackle. They crashed down to the floor. Codi twisted beneath him, trying to get away, but Mac dug his elbow into his spine, jerking his arm.

I yelled for Ritha and jumped on his back. The stake was still strapped to my leg, but I could *never . . .*

"You're all heathens," he grunted.

I tried to pull him off. Something was wrong, *very, very* wrong. I couldn't budge him. Mac was not this strong. No man was. Codi cried out. I slipped my arm around Mac's chest and pulled a gust of Air to assist, blood still pouring into my mouth, down my chin.

"He's going to break my arm," Codi said, voice pinched.

"No, he's not." Désirée broke out of the plants and ran to her nightstand. She snatched up a fistful of something and blew it into Mac's face. His grip immediately released, and he went down like a ton of bricks, slumping against my legs. Enchanted chamomile.

And for the first time it really hit me, what I'd done to Adele. She was half his size. With no superhuman strength or rage or even magic.

I felt sick.

Ritha stormed into the room with Ana Marie. "What the devil is going on in here?"

"I think I know." Désirée grabbed a hand mirror from her dresser. She knelt down in front of Mac and held the glass up to his face. Her eyes pulsed wide, and she turned back to her gran with a nod.

"*Shit*," Ritha said.

Désirée looked at me. "He's not a vampire. He's Possessed."

"What?" I asked.

Ana Marie pulled a towel from the bathroom door, hurried over with it, and blotted my nose.

"That's why Callis let us have him back so easily," Désirée said. "He'd already sentenced him to death."

My knees weakened, and I half-sat, half-dropped to the floor. Mac toppled over on his side.

"The three of you go find Adele," Ritha said. "We'll take care of him."

Find Adele? I couldn't tell Adele this. "Sh-she's already lost her mom."

"You stay here," Désirée said. "We'll go find her."

I hardly even remembered turning, but the next thing I knew, I was flying out the window.

I headed straight to the Medici's. They didn't answer when I banged on the door. I circled the estate. It was completely dark.

Next, I went to Adele's house. I became frantic when she wasn't there. I could try the bar, or HQ? But I knew she wouldn't be there either. She was with Nicco. *They've gone to take down Callis.*

I soared through Pirate's Alley to the Square and glided through the park, wondering if I should go get Codi and Dee before heading across the river. Why couldn't they have waited? That fortress was impenetrable. *We're stronger together.*

The church bells rang. I glanced up at the tower, and for a second, I thought I was hallucinating. *Adele?* She was in the bell tower window. What the hell was she doing up there? I swerved, flying higher on the loop back. A cloud moved from over the moon, and I saw his arms around her.

She was laughing at something he said, leaning back into his chest, her neck craned up to him as she spoke.

He leaned down . . . and kissed her.

What the fuck?

She twisted around in his arms, and he drew her closer, kissing her again. And not just any kiss—one that made her coil around him. He lifted her up, and they entwined together, falling against the wall in the darkness. A bright light flashed in my eyes like I'd been hit in the head. *What is she doing?* Why

515

wasn't she pushing him away? What had he done to her? *She wouldn't be with a monster.* He tried to *kill* her.

I heard Susannah's voice.

No.

She couldn't *love* a monster.

I didn't notice when I started to fall. I barely even realized when I hit the slate ground.

I rolled over with a grunt, the pain radiating from my dislocated wing.

The pain radiating from my heart.

CHAPTER 50
MAC

"Your phone's buzzing," Nicco said, breaking the kiss. I pulled him back, and his lips quickly found mine again. As if I cared about answering my phone.

"It's the fourth time," he said, despite wrapping his arms tighter around me.

Fourth? I paused, my hands on his chest, holding him back.

He moved out of the way, and I hopped down from the window, going for my bag. My heart raced as I adjusted my twisted clothes. Despite there being several feet between us, I could still feel the maps of his hands along my body. I could barely think, feeling the lingering heat in my cheeks. Why did I stop kissing him? *Phone, Adele.* Right.

I glanced back. He leaned against the ledge with a taunting smile that said to hurry back.

My phone vibrated as I pulled it out of my bag, and the screen lit up with missed calls. Mostly from Désirée. My dad was probably looking for me, and she was giving me courtesy warnings. I owed her.

Just a couple more minutes, and I'll go back to the shop. Although I wasn't quite sure how I'd ever pull myself away from

Nicco. As if he could read my mind, his arms circled my waist, his mouth pressing deeply into the crook of my neck. The spot he'd healed still felt tender. My entire body felt tender as his hands slipped beneath my shirt. I pushed against him, enthralled by his wanton touch. By my own desire.

The phone buzzed again, and a new message caught my eye. *S.O.S.*

I stiffened.

"What's wrong?" Nicco asked, instantly pausing.

Thump-thump. Thump-thump. Thump-thump.

Something had happened. *Callis.* Before I could press *call back*, the phone lit up again, this time a call: Désirée.

"What's wrong?" I asked her.

"Where are you?"

"Um." I glanced back at Nicco. "Close by."

"Get back to the shop."

"Désirée, what's wrong?"

"It's your dad."

My pulse exploded. "What about him?"

"Just get back here!"

I hung up, hands shaking.

"What's wrong?" Nicco asked, but I was already storming toward the door.

"I don't know. Something with Mac. She wouldn't say." Both of my feet lifted from the ground as he carried me into the night. We whipped out of the church, through the garden, and back to the Voodoo shop.

Désirée and Codi were waiting for us on the street. "This way," she said, hurrying us through the alley gate.

"What happened to my dad?"

"Um."

"Codi!" I yelled. "Did he have a heart attack? Is he okay?"

"He didn't have a heart attack," he said, unable to look at me.

We spilled into the courtyard. "I'm not sure where they would have brought him," Dee said, looking to the guesthouse and back to the front.

"Brought him?"

"Probably the mirror room," she murmured.

"The mirror room? But isn't that where . . . ?"

"Where what?" Nicco asked.

I tore into the house and up the stairs.

Ritha intercepted me on the landing. "He's in here." She led me down the hall toward one of the family's bedrooms. From the hallway, I could see him sitting on the bed, his head in the palms of his hands.

"Dad!" I yelled, but when I tried to go through the doorway, I fell backward, as if pushed by some invisible force, and stumbled into Nicco. "What the hell?"

"The doorway is warded," Ritha said. "You can't go in right now. It's too dangerous."

"What are you talking about? It's my dad!" I threw out my arm and pulled the spell away with one quick rip.

"Adele Le Moyne—" she said, but I was already in the room, dropping to my knees in front of him.

"I'll make sure he doesn't harm her," I heard Nicco say to her.

"He's not going to hurt me," I snapped.

"Adele?" my father said.

"Dad!"

"Why are they doing this to me?" His hands were bound together with thick vines. He looked scared, not at all like when Callis had held him at the bar, full of anger and fight.

Rage pummeled through me, seeing the restraints. I looked back to Ritha, fire roiling through my veins. "Take them off! Take them off or I will!"

"You won't be able to get those off," Ritha said.

"Adele, why are they doing this to me?"

I tugged at the vines, both mentally and with my fingers. They wouldn't budge. I could feel Ritha holding them in place. "I don't know," I said, starting to cry. "It's a mistake. I'm going to fix it."

Dee and Codi poured into the room.

"Where's Isaac?" I asked. "What the hell is going on here?"

Désirée knelt beside me with a hand mirror, and the world around me froze.

"No," I said, pushing it away.

"Adele . . ." She set it down, reaching out for me.

"No." I jerked away from her. "We saved him," I gasped. My lungs pinched. I hunched down on the floor, my throat closing up. "I can't."

It hurt so bad, it felt like *I* was having a heart attack.

Someone lifted me up. "Adele." I knew from his voice, from his grip, from the way his shoulders closed in over me that it was Isaac.

I twisted around. His shirt was bloody, but I wrapped my arms tightly around his neck like a child.

"Adele, breathe," he said, hugging me tightly.

"I can't," I choked with an uncontrollable sob. "I can't live without him."

"We're going to get through this. You're the strongest witch I know."

The words just made me cry harder. I didn't want to be strong. I wanted my dad. "We saved him," I said, letting go. "We saved him!" My lungs locked, and that was it. I choked trying to inhale.

I knew the more I panicked the worse it would get, but I couldn't stop.

"Look at me," he said. It didn't help. "*Look at me*," he said again, pulling my forehead to his so I couldn't peer away.

I slapped at the air, my voice not much more than a rasp. "My bag." It had my inhaler. "It's in the . . . bell tower."

Isaac blinked away tears like I'd stung him, and Nicco disappeared through the door.

Black spots appeared before my eyes. Nicco was fast, but not that fast. I wheezed. My dad wasn't even trying to help me. He wasn't saying all the things he usually did. The tears poured harder. Codi was saying them, but I couldn't hear him. Ritha was behind me, rubbing my back.

"*Breathe, baby.*"

I tried, but I couldn't. It hurt too bad. I shook my head, and the tears flung out.

"Everyone, give her some space," Isaac yelled, his arm slipping firmly around me. His other hand pinched my jaw. The spots burst into rainbows of sparkles as his lips touched mine. A blast of icy Air spilled into me, and my lungs opened up. I released the breath and sucked in air, gasping as I fell onto him, arms draping around his shoulders.

He held me, and I sucked in another breath.

And another.

Slowly, the spots went away, but everything still felt frozen around me, like I was suddenly on a different vibration from everyone else. I sat up.

"Are you okay?" he asked, his hand brushing my jaw.

I nodded, despite feeling like I'd swallowed fire.

I took the mirror from Désirée's hand.

"Adele, you don't have to," she said.

I turned to my dad. Now it made sense why he looked so bad. It wasn't just exhaustion and dehydration and imprisonment during magical warfare. There was another soul inside of him, eating away his spirit.

He looked straight at me with a scowl. "What was that? You some kind of cripple?"

Codi's eyes widened, and Dee's hand went over her mouth, hiding her face.

I handed her back the mirror. I didn't need to see the thing inside him. That wasn't my father.

Nicco appeared in the room with my bag. I didn't need it anymore. I didn't think I would ever need my inhaler again. I stood and walked to him. "I'm going to kill him," I said. He gently put his arm around me as I went out the door. "I'm going to kill Callis."

CHAPTER 51
MIRACLE

I stood, in a daze, wiping a smear of dried blood from my jaw. I'd grown up around some of the world's best obscenity spitters, but hearing them come out of Mac's mouth felt like the twilight zone.

"Désirée, give Mac a sedative potion so he can get some sleep," Ritha said, hurrying after Adele.

I pulled the bloodstained tee over my head. There was a plain white undershirt beneath it.

"Isaac, are you okay?" Codi asked.

"Yeah." My face throbbed from the punch. My shoulder throbbed from the fall. But I felt like I'd been given a heavy dose of lidocaine. Like I was walking on air. *What the fuck was going on?* The last half-hour felt more unreal than all of Guinée.

I walked through the doorway, trying not to hear Ritha talking to Adele and Nicco in the adjoining room like they were some kind of unit. Some kind of couple.

I went straight down the hall, the words Adele had said rippling down my spine: "*I'm going to kill him. I'm going to kill Callis.*" It wasn't the words that rattled me—I think we all wanted to kill Callis— it was the way she'd said them. The cold edge in her tone.

Mac had once said to me how Adele had her mother's warmth, and he hoped that no one would ever change that.

No one would. I was going to fucking kill Callis myself.

I reached into my pocket for my phone, but it wasn't there. I must have left it in my . . . bag. *My bag.* It was in Ren's room, and it had everything in it. *Shit.* I hoped he hadn't already papered the walls with my grimoire. *Oh, fuck! The gad.* I sprinted across the bridge and into the house, tearing down the hallway, the moans of the Possessed raking my ears. That thing wasn't going to get Mac. He was not going to turn into one of these empty husks. I didn't care what I had to do. I couldn't let him die.

He was more of a father to me than the man who shared my blood.

I stomped into Ren's room, coming to a stop right in front of him. My bag was open, and all of my things rummaged through. He hadn't touched the food, but he'd guzzled anything to drink, looking for booze, no doubt. Thank God I'd given the Florida water to Linto. My grimoire was on the floor—I breathed a sigh of relief that it seemed to be in one piece.

I began searching through the clothes and candles and seashells, looking for the brown bag.

"You looking for this?"

The praline was in his hand, which was dangerously close to his mouth. My heart backflipped. I was scared to move, like if I came any closer, he'd chomp it down.

"Where'd you get off to? What's all the fuss about?"

A breeze stirred the Air in the room, rippling through the papers on the wall as I held my emotions in. I'd gotten it for Ren. I'd promised I'd save him. My throat went dry as I wrestled with what to do.

But it's *Mac.*

The Air swirled harder, rustling the papers, lifting the hair from the back of my neck. I thought about how Mac had given me a job at the bar, a place to sleep, how he'd offered to help me with my portfolio, how he'd cared whether I went to college. I could still feel Adele's arms around my shoulders. Smell the strawberry in her hair. Feel her tears dampening my shirt.

"Ren, I need that back."

His brow scrunched.

My voice cracked. "I know it's a dick move. But it's Mac."

"I see . . ."

"He's been . . . possessed."

"Oh, I see." A deflated look of understanding washed down his face.

Weight, or gravity, or whatever it was that was anchoring me to this world felt like it had dropped out of my soul. Tears streamed down my face. Could I really order his execution?

I didn't know what to do. I couldn't let Mac die. I'd killed Adele's mom. I couldn't let her father die as well. I loved her. I loved him.

Suck it up, Isaac. I suddenly heard my pop's voice in my head. I was trained to take action in traumatic situations. To talk to people in peril. *Dominate.*

I met Ren's gaze. "It's going to be okay." My voice shook. "I'll get you another one. I have this key," I said, holding it up. "I'll have to tell you all about Doubye. I'll have stories for days when you're all better. A few you can probably even add to your tour."

"Kid, has anyone ever told you you're a terrible liar?"

My chest burned. "No, actually."

"Well, you are." He held the sweet out to me.

"Thank you. *Thank you.*"

"You're a good kid, Isaac."

"*No, I'm not,*" I whispered. Mac would never have been

taken if it hadn't been for me. I peered down at the candy. Would it really work?

"Well, what are you waiting for?"

"*Merci beaucoup*," I choked out.

When I got back to Mac's room, it had emptied out. He was lying on the bed, staring at the ceiling, arms folded behind his head. The light was off, but the curtains were open, letting in just enough light to show that his eyes were still open. He looked completely at peace, but I knew it was because of Dee's potion.

I sat down on the bed and paused for a second, letting my nerves settle. *I should get Ritha before I do this.* But what if she didn't want me to do it? What if there was someone else who needed it more? What if she wanted to break it apart and make magical medicines out of it?

I thought about what these Possessed looked like after time passed. The vile things they said. The abominable way they acted. I couldn't let Adele live through that. I couldn't watch Mac slowly deteriorate like my mom had.

He sat up next to me. "Isaac, are you dating my daughter?"

I looked at him with mild panic. "Um. No."

His eyes remained questioning.

"We were, and then weren't, and then we were."

"And then?"

"And then, I don't know. I don't really know what Adele wants." Tears dripped out of my eyes. "I know that I hurt her."

"Just give her time. I can see in her heart that she loves you."

I laughed, brushing away the tears. "We'll see."

"Is that a black eye?" He touched my chin. "You haven't been getting into fights, have you?"

"It wasn't a fight. Just a misunderstanding."

"Spoken like a true New Yorker."

Again, strained laughter huffed from my throat. "So, you know how we went on this trip? Well, I got something for you." I handed him the paper bag, and he pulled out the praline.

"Well, that was thoughtful. I'm not really into sweets, if I'm honest."

"Oh, you'll be into this one."

He smirked. "I guess it couldn't hurt. It's not like I've been doing a lot of eating these last few weeks. I swear those freaks across the river could live off of air."

"Close," I said.

"What the hell." He popped it in his mouth.

I froze, waiting.

"Well damn, that was delicious. Thank you . . ." His eyes bugged a little. He pressed on his chest. "This is why I don't eat sweets. Heartburn." He gripped the edge of the bed.

"Mac?"

"Something is not right," he said, and buckled over. He clutched my arms as he fell down to his knees.

Shit. "I'm going to get Ritha."

But he didn't let go. His chest lit up like one of the bottles in the tearoom. Beneath his skin and muscle and through his bones, I could *see* the orb floating inside him, whoever this soul was. Someone's son or daughter or sister or brother.

"What is happening?" he said, terror making his voice tremble.

"It's okay," I said, watching it travel from his chest, through his shoulder, through his arm, coming closer to me, and closer. And closer. He squeezed me tighter, and then my arms lit up too.

"What the fuck?" Suddenly the old Ghede's words rang in my head. "*Are you willing to accept any consequence to save your friend?*"

"Oh, *fuck.*" My head told me to let go, but then I pictured Adele. I felt the tightness in her chest and heard the sound of her tears, the coldness in her voice. "*I'm going to kill Callis.*"

Let go, Isaac.

But I couldn't. I loved her.

Let go, now!

She needed her dad more than she needed me.

I stopped fighting it, and the glow released from Mac and traveled up my arms. A searing pain flashed through my entire being, and I cried out, gripping him. But then it faded along with the glow that inched up my arm, until it dispelled into my Mark, making it gleam.

Then even that settled into nothingness. The room went dark again. My pulse raced.

"Are you okay?" Mac asked.

I nodded.

"What the blazes just happened?"

"Nothing," I said. His memory of it seemed to fade with each passing second.

"Are you sure you're okay? You eat something bad? You look queasy."

"I'm fine." I stared out at the wall. I didn't feel any pain, but anxiety stormed through me. *Now you've really done it.* Not even Ritha had been able to help the Possessed. "I'm fine. I'm a witch. I have magic," I stuttered.

"Yeah, that's what people around here keep saying."

I picked up the hand-mirror from the dresser and held it in front of Mac.

"Boy, do I need a shave," he said.

I nearly choked when I saw his reflection staring back. I raised the mirror, trying to prepare myself for what I was going to see when I looked into it. A demon? A monster? I started to turn it around, but then I twisted it away. *I'm fine. I'm a witch. I have magic.*

Mac's eyelids drooped heavily, thanks to Dee's potion.

"I'm going to let you get some sleep," I said, and by the time I set the mirror back down on the dresser, he was out cold.

I told myself to go downstairs to the altar room, to light a candle to our ancestors, but my feet didn't move in that direction. I went back through the taxidermy studio and across the bridge to the guesthouse. A wave of cold washed through me as I padded down the hall. The moans of the Possessed no longer felt like ice picks in my ears, but a strange song as I walked past their doors, like they were crying out to the universe for help. For the pain to stop. For everything to stop.

Their agony flooded into my veins, my Spektral amplifying their aches and loneliness and despair, and I suddenly felt like I was going to break in half. Would anyone even care when that was me? Would anyone even know when I was gone? I picked up to a sprint, and I didn't stop until I was back in Ren's room.

He hadn't moved. I sat down next to him.

I'm fine. I'm a witch. I have magic.

A song came out of his mouth, a dreary Italian dirge, and I knew it wasn't Ren there with me, but Alessandro. I imagined Adele walking into Mac's room tomorrow morning, using the mirror, and discovering the miracle had worked. It made me feel warm inside.

I didn't want anyone to take away her warmth.

Nicco would swirl her around in celebration.

It wasn't fair. He was going to live forever.

And now . . .

I was going to die so young.

EPILOGUE
WAR TIME

I'd walked back to my house at night a thousand times before, knowing that my dad wasn't going to be home. That he was at the bar, working, but that he'd be here when I woke up. No matter how late he arrived home, he had always checked on me to make sure I was safe in bed. Sometimes it woke me up, but I'd never cared. The small gesture let me know that he was home safe too.

Some mornings, after I started the coffee, I'd sneak into his room just to make sure he'd come home and I hadn't dreamt it. Now, I wondered if I'd woken him up too, and if it made him feel loved. *I hope so.*

Nicco squeezed my hand. All I could do was keep walking. Keep going forward.

When we got to the house, the locks of the gate slid open without me even having to give it much thought. Nicco hung back in the gateway as I went up the steps.

I turned around, leaning against the front door in silence.

The moon shone down on his cheeks as he gazed up at me.

He didn't say anything. I didn't want him to.

There was nothing to say.

I'd gone to Guinée to save my dad, to stop Callisto, and all we'd done was lose his grimoire to the Ghost Drinkers.

He came up the steps. I peered at him as he brushed the hair from my face and cupped my cheek. His voice was gentle. "We will find a way—"

I nodded.

His lips brushed mine, and I'd never felt both so alive and so dead inside.

"You should come stay at my house tonight," he said.

I shook my head.

"You can have my room. I'll stay on the couch. You won't have anything to worry about . . ."

I almost smiled. "I'm not worried about you. I don't want to be around people."

He sighed. "I don't think you should be alone tonight, *bella*."

With a quick flick of magic, I twisted the door unlocked.

"*Adele.*"

I slipped my hand into his and pulled him inside behind me. "I didn't say I wanted to be alone."

The house was dark and quiet, but I knew with him at my side, I could fight the emptiness from filling me. Nicco wouldn't let the boat tip.

With him by my side, we could win this war.

The door locked behind us, I pulled him close, and a deep kiss locked us together.

"You will always have me," he whispered, and I kissed him again.

Being together was not the end of the feud, but the beginning of something much, much bigger.

BOOK 5, THE EPIC CONCLUSION
STAY TUNED!

To stay up to date on the latest news on the final book in
THE CASQUETTE GIRLS series and other writing by
Alys Arden, sign up for her mailing list at:
www.alysarden.com.

ACKNOWLEDGMENTS

Many stars shine brightly in the galaxy of *The Casquette Girls* series, and from the bottom of my heart, I thank each and every one of you who has continued on the journey with Adele through the streets of New Orleans and now to the Afterworld.

This novel became stronger along the way thanks to a great number of people. As always, merci beaucoup to my editor Marissa van Uden, who I believe loves Adele and company as much as I do. To Laura Perry, Monica S. Kuebler, and Charlotte Ashley for rounding out the editorial team with magic, horror, and grace.

To say that Voodoo is a complex subject to tackle is a massive understatement. From the spelling of its name, to its oral traditions, to its history of secrecy, you will get a different answer to any question you ask depending on whose house you've entered. New Orleans Voodoo, in particular, is a culture and lifestyle and religion as nuanced as the city it was birthed. It has a history with deep-rooted horror in colonization and slavery, threaded with generational trauma, only to be further bastardized by Hollywood for decades. It's a subject I studied for years before feeling equipped enough to write it into Adele's story in a big way. I make no attempt to spill religious or cultural secrets, just to carve its rightful place in the world of The Casquette Girls. After all, what would a series about magical New Orleans be without Voodoo and the representation of the spirits who built this city? Both the lwa and the Ghede have given me enormous inspiration throughout the course of writing this story, for which I am eternally grateful. My only aim is to serve them well. With that said, I could not have done it alone. A massive thank you to a number of librarians, academics, writers, and occultists who have answered my questions or helped me find answers or research to formulate my ideas. And a special thank you to Lilith Dorsey, for sharing her infinite wisdom with me, and for her guidance helping me navigate the amorphous, beautiful world of Voodoo. Buy her book *Orishas, Goddesses, and Voodoo Queens: The Divine Feminine in the African Religious Traditions* to learn more.

As always, I have eternal gratitude for Emilie Gagnet Leumas, archivist of the Archdiocese of New Orleans. Thank you to Dhonielle Clayton, Zoraida Córdova, and Kami Garcia for your never-ending advice, support, and friendship.

Thank you to my agents extraordinaire, Alexandra Machinist and Zoë Sandler, at ICM Partners.

And thank you to all of the amazing people who continue to support me on my publishing journey, especially the team at Skyscape for their continued love and support for this series. Galen Dara for another magical and macabre cover illustration. Marita Crandle and the entire staff at Boutique du Vampyre. Thank you to Francesca Testaguzza, Julie Hernandez, and Sarah Hackmann for helping me with translations.

Thank you to all of my beta readers! Lindsey, Melanie, Melissa L., David, Zeena, Erin, Fallon, Chris. And especially to Melissa Criswell for reading every draft. To Alex, Lucas, Jackie, and Amy for listening to my endless babble.

To all of my readers, merci beaucoup.

ABOUT THE AUTHOR

Alys Arden was raised by the street performers, tea-leaf readers, and glittering drag queens of the New Orleans French Quarter. She cut her teeth on the streets of New York and has worked all around the world since. She still dreams of running away with the circus one star-swept night. Follow her adventures on Twitter or Instagram at @alysarden.